C000292295

ACKNOWLEDGMENTS

Once more my most sincere thanks to Rebecca Frew, Emma Sanford and Hannah McGregor-Viney, for giving so much of their time, and to all at Next Chapter.

PROLOGUE

The noose was tightening around the city of Karpella. It had been many weeks since the Aramorians had begun their siege. Their lightning advance up northwards from the Uplands of Ara into the Kingdom of Dazscor had been barely checked by the few Dazscorian troops who had decided to stand in their way; it had only been the stout walls of the capital city that had stopped the relentless force. Everyone knew, however, that in reality, the Aramorians had not been stopped by the grandiose defences of Karpella; they had merely been stalled. Every day more and more of King Sarper's under-trained and barely paid troops had deserted, some slipping over the wall and taking their chances surrendering to the Aramorians, some trying to make the swim across the River Arlen; and some lying low in the dark corners of the city's slums, waiting for their chance to claim their share of the spoils when the enemy outside eventually overwhelmed the defences.

Few in the city, however, were aware of what Hrex knew. Reports had come in late the night before that the wall to the east of the city's main gate was unlikely to survive another day of bombardment, that it was close to crumbling. What was more, the reports that had come in on the movements of the Dazscorian relief force had been even less welcome. In short, the Dazs-corian army in the north of the country had defected en masse to the Duchy of Aramore. A curt note sent directly from the force's commanding officer gave no illusion to the fact that Sarper IV, his family, court and the people of Karpella were now on their own.

All those in the court of Sarper IV who had been told this directly, and the many who had subsequently managed to find out through one dishonest, nefarious source or another, knew that this was the end. As soon as the general population found out about the desertion of their only hope for salvation, the only trained body of troops outside the city close enough to offer any assistance, the people's fear and frustration would doubtless boil over, and they would try to take matters into their own hands. The opinion of the court was that it would be better if the weak-ened section of wall collapsed before the dire news became common knowledge. At least the Aramorians were likely to offer mercy...

Preparations for the evacuation of the royal family had been moving at a breakneck speed. As Hrex shuffled as quickly as she could through the halls of Karpella Castle, she could see people running in all directions over the teetering pile of books and scrolls that she cradled in her arms. Guards clattered through the echoing marble corridors, servants carrying trunks, bags, and even the odd piece of furniture weaved to and fro through the castle, weighed down by their charges, whilst fraught-looking courtiers shouted panicked orders into the tumult.

Despite all of this activity, all the people that Hrex came across parted to let her through, but this wasn't any form of deferential nod to her position, far from it. The looks of fear were plain to see as the diminutive Lupine made her way through the corridors, and the whispers that followed her rang louder than the shouts and commotion of evacuation through the castle's chambers. It had always been thus, ever since Hrex had been brought to Karpella in the first place, but now the whispering had taken on a more panicked edge than usual.

'She can kill you just by looking at you...'

'The king has her and her Master working on a trap for the Aramorians.'

'Rubbish, he's getting them to place a curse on every scrap of gold in the treasury...'

Hrex ignored the mutterings that followed in her wake. She had learned long ago that most people had no idea about magic, sorcery, witchcraft, whatever they chose to call it. For the majority of the population of the Kingdom of Dazscor, and for those that lived far beyond its borders, magic was something that was to be feared, with those able to wield it classed as outsiders, outsiders that should be treated with caution and respect, but outsiders, nonetheless. However, the looks of fear that Hrex received were nothing compared to the way that people viewed her master. Hrex had seen even the bravest, most aggressive of people turn to quivering bundles of nerves when they found themselves in the presence of the Royal Mage to the Court of Sarper IV. Her master oozed power, but only Hrex dared to think that she knew the extent to which he could wield the arcane forces.

If the people living in this pathetic city knew what my Master was capable of, they'd have all fled long before those Aramorian pretenders showed up at our door...

The chaotic hubbub of the castle began to recede as Hrex turned off the marbled artery of the main building and began to climb a tightly twisting spiral staircase that led up towards the rooms that acted as the quarters and laboratory of the Royal Mage. Though the staircase was completely windowless, Hrex had ascended and descended these stairs so many times that she didn't need to see what she was doing. She knew each and every one of the smooth stone steps that the soles of her bare leathery feet touched, could feel the familiar grooves worn into them by her claws. She paused at the small landing at the top of the stairs, unconcerned by the fact that the solid stone wall she stood opposite had no visible doorway or other way forward. Shuffling the books and scrolls so that they were balanced in one arm, she drew a quill from within the folds of her robe and traced a symbol in the air, whispering to herself as she did so. As the nib of the quill cut through the air, it left a glowing blue outline, hovering in space, and once the symbol was complete, it drifted silently forward and sank into the stonework opposite. A split second later, the landing was bathed in the light spilling from the room beyond, now visible through the arch that had materialised there.

Entering the Royal Mage's laboratory, Hrex blinked as her eyes adjusted to the light that poured into the room from the three floor-to-ceiling arched windows that lined one side of the space, windows that Hrex knew were disguised as solid masonry to an outside observer. Shelves stacked to bursting with books, jars and boxes of ingredients, potion bottles, crystals and an array of delicately crafted spindly metal equipment, most of whose uses Hrex was oblivious to, lined almost every inch of available wall space. The only openings, other than the way Hrex had entered the room, were two small wooden doors, one leading to her broom cupboard of a bedroom, the other to her master's more sumptuous living quarters. The centre of the cavernous room was dominated by an enormous table, over which were strewn all manner of tools, pieces of apparatus, bottles and scraps of parchment. Hunched over a large round metal disc that lay on the tabletop, his face illuminated by the faint green light emanating from the metal, was Hrex's Master. He straightened up as Hrex entered the room and surveyed the Lupine as she staggered towards him under the weight of her burden.

The Royal Mage to the Court of Sarper IV, Aristotles, was tall and willowy with pale grey skin, which along with his long, sharply pointed ears gave him away as being a Shadow Elf rather than a human. His piercing, ice-blue eyes stared at Hrex from over the bridge of his long nose as she approached. Even from the other side of the room, she felt as if he was looking into her very soul. As she deposited the books and scrolls messily on the table, he stalked over to the pile, a long-fingered hand smoothing back his white-blonde, shoulder-length hair.

'You got all the volumes, I presume?' he spoke in a refined drawl, the words oozing into Hrex's ears in an unpleasant way as if they had a will of their own.

'Yes, Master, every speck of parchment with any reference to Kulittu.'

'Good, then we should have everything that we need. I've sketched out a pattern for the summoning circle, begin drawing it out. You should know all of the minor sigils and spells that go into it.'

Aristotles dismissed her with a wave of his hand and began to shuffle through the pile of books and papers on the table, one hand rubbing his smooth, sharp jawline as he did so. Hrex moved beyond the work table and pulled back a large thick carpet that covered the floor at the other end of the room. The wooden floor beneath was faintly stained with a multitude of coloured lines that had been drawn in chalk and subsequently erased. In the spot where Aristotles had been working was a large piece of parchment with an intricate diagram of the summoning circle drawn upon it, complete with numerous annotations, testament to the care her master had given to ensure that they would be as safe as possible.

Creatures and entities that had to be summoned using such circles were almost always highly dangerous and devilishly cunning. In her experience, such a creature would begin searching as soon as it was summoned for a way to exploit the slightest crack in a circle's defence so that it might break free of its bonds and attack those who had dared to summon it. Taking the document, Hrex's gaze fell upon the metal disc nearby. She could feel the power of the magic that her master had imbued into the metal, magic designed to make the object as resistant to damage as possible, ready to receive whatever power Aristotles asked the summoned entity to imbue it with. Tearing her eyes away, she took a stubby piece of blue chalk from a pocket and began to painstakingly draw out the circle onto the floorboards.

After nearly an hour of intense concentration, Hrex's fingers ached from clutching the chalk, which had stained the fur of her hand blue around the fingers, and her head was beginning to throb from the effort of drawing on and manipulating so much arcane energy. As she straightened up to relieve the tightness in her back, she stepped back to admire her handiwork. The floor space before her was now almost completely covered by the summoning circle, whose broad, thick perimeter shone with the arcane symbols of strength and protection that Hrex had enchanted it with. The interior of the circle was crisscrossed with a myriad of other lines, whose linked arcane symbols did not shine as brightly as those in the perimeter but which were no less potent. She had chalked four large diamonds, one in each quarter of the circle, where Aristotles would place the more powerful and more dangerous magic that would summon whoever, or whatever the circle was intended for.

'Good, you've finished. Let's not waste any more time.'

Aristotles' voice sounded directly behind Hrex, making her jump. He had an uncanny knack of moving as silently as a shadow, and she had to stifle the curse that rose in her throat.

'Here, take this, keep it open on that page and hold it up so I can see it.'

As he moved noiselessly past her, Aristotles handed her one of the large, heavy tomes she had brought up from the library, its pages encrusted in dust, small patches of mildew encroaching at the corners. As she manoeuvred the book in her hands so that the required pages faced her master, she caught sight of the title of the volume embossed in faded gold lettering on the spine.

The Heresy of Kulittu

Aristotles stood with his back to the window and faced the circle on the floor, taking great care not to step within it or disturb the chalked lines. The light that still poured into the room framed the Shadow Elf, casting all of his features into shadow. As Hrex shuffled round the circle, the book clutched awkwardly and uncomfortably in her arms so that Aristotles could see it, she saw him close his eyes in concentration. She felt the fur on the back of her neck begin to prickle up as he began to call on far more powerful magic than she had ever dared to use.

Hrex was mesmerised by what her master was doing, by the ease with which he manipulated arcane forces that could so easily have torn apart a lesser mage. His frosty eyes darted periodically to the pages of the book she was holding, and slowly but surely, the four diamonds she had drawn within the circle began to audibly hum with magical energy. Aristotles paused for a moment, inspecting every last inch of the circle one more time.

'You may put the book down now, Hrex, but stay close. I may need your assistance to keep the binding magic of the circle in check. Bring the disc with you, I want it close at hand. Watch and learn as much as possible, it will likely be many years before you see something of this ilk again...'

Hrex scuttled back to place the book on the table, snatched up the metal disc and returned to the Elf's side as he deftly drew the final activating symbol in the air with one of his long index fingers and then flicked it through the air and down into the centre of the circle. As soon as the symbol entered the boundary of the circle, all of the other symbols that had been drawn on the floor began to glow with an intense blue-green light, which vanished instantly as the activating symbol settled into its place in the nexus of arcane energy.

For a moment, nothing happened, but then Hrex became aware of the unnatural stillness in the room. An oppressive silence, as if some unseen person had clamped their hands over her ears. Then the light began to fade from the room as the lines and runes of the circle began to glow brighter and brighter once more until they were the only things illuminating the room. She turned back to look at the windows, which should still have had daylight streaming through them, but they were now lifeless portals looking out on to a black abyss rather than the city beyond. Hrex's head whipped back to the circle as she became suddenly aware of an intensely powerful presence there, far beyond the power of the magic she and Aristotles had put into the summoning circle.

A humanoid figure now stood in the summoning circle, but it was definitely not Human, Elven, or any other race that Hrex could name. It was immensely tall, well over ten feet in height; its head, shrouded in a deep hood that obscured its face, brushed the ceiling. The long black robe that hung limply from the creature's shoulders revealed its torso, legs and the tight knot-work of muscle through the centre split. The only other clothing it wore was a black loincloth. Its bare feet did not stand on the floorboards, but instead, the creature hovered about an inch above the floor and the nexus of the summoning circle. What struck Hrex most, however, was the stench of death and decay that rolled in a horrific wave from it, and she flinched back from the sudden sensory onslaught, trying to stop herself from gagging. Summoning all of her willpower, she dragged her eyes back to the creature. Its very being was pockmarked with patches of decay, bone poking through here and there from midst rotting flesh, and in the very centre of its chest was an enormous gaping wound, still stained with fresh blood.

'Speak quickly, mortal, your defences will last mere minutes, and I shall claim your soul if you summoned me here for nought...' Its voice rattled like a dying breath from out of the darkness of its hood; a stronger whiff of decay trailed after the words from the unseen mouth.

'Divine Kulittu, master of death, I bid you welcome.' Aristotles' voice was as calm and collected as ever, but out of the corner of her eye, Hrex could see the slight tremor of his hands. 'I have summoned you here to make a bargain with you, one that I hope you will find favourable.'

Pulling a scroll of parchment from a pocket of his long, velvet jacket, Aristotles tossed it towards Kulittu, a small flurry of magical symbols guiding the scroll on its way. As it passed through the magical barrier, the parchment was briefly engulfed in turquoise flames before it was snatched up with surprising speed by Kulittu's gnarled, decaying hand. He unfurled the scorched scroll and studied it carefully with his unseen eyes.

A thick heavy silence settled over the room as Aristotles and Hrex waited for Kulittu to finish reading. Hrex found herself holding her breath, not wanting to disturb the oppressive still-ness with the sound of her breathing. She knew that her master could have communicated what he wanted from the Dead God verbally, but she too had read the dusty, forbidden tomes on arcane summoning that had been kept under lock and key in the castle library. All of them had stated that when summoning a powerful being from another realm of existence, it was always safest to commit any potential bargain that you wished to strike in writing in the most watertight way possible. Otherwise, a magic-user could find their words twisted by a being hell-bent on gaining the upper hand in the deal.

After several dreadfully silent minutes, Kulittu dipped a dirty, broken fingernail into the blood that stained the wound around his chest and dragged the nail like a quill across the scroll, leaving a crimson trail behind it. He then extended his hand, and the parchment began to float back towards Aristotles on the other side of the circle.

'I agree to your terms, Aristotles, son of Scortlates, exile and traitor to your people. Make your mark upon the contract, and we can begin.'

Wordlessly, Aristotles plucked the parchment out of the air, which still had turquoise flames clinging to its edges from the return trip through the circle, and pricked his finger with a small knife before adding his own blood to the page. As soon as he had finished leaving his mark, the whole scroll vanished in a burst of turquoise flame, which made the Shadow Elf jump as the fingers of his left hand were singed.

'Good...' the word crawled out of the place where Kulittu's mouth should be. 'Now give me the object in need of enchantment.'

Aristotles nodded curtly to Hrex, who sent the round silver disc magically floating towards the summoning circle. Unlike the parchment, the magical barrier seemed to be attacking the disc much more forcefully, and the magical flames clung to the surface of the metal and had to be brushed off by Kulittu's dead hand. He laid the disc in the middle of his enormous palm, his right hand raised in the air above it, and he began to intone a spell in a language that Hrex could not understand. Though she didn't know their meaning, she could feel the power in the words, which grew louder and louder until there was a continuous echoing wave of sound rolling around the chamber. She clapped her hands over her ears, trying to block out the noise that was beginning to make her feel physically sick.

Eventually, the incantation stopped, and looking up, Hrex could see that the disc was still in the palm of Kulittu's hand but that now it emitted its own faint blue light. Kulittu's right hand moved now from above the disc towards his face and was momentarily lost within the blackness of his hood. When it emerged, it was clutching what looked like a mask. He turned his hand to face Aristotles and Hrex, and she could see it was indeed a mask that resembled an emaciated face whose expression was twisted into a horrific visage of pain and suffering.

'With these two objects, I have upheld my end of the bargain, and you will have what you need to uphold yours.'

This time, instead of magically sending the two objects back to the other side of the summoning circle, Kulittu began to walk slowly towards them. The warding symbols of the barrier flared angrily with blue light as he strode forwards, but it was clear that the magic trying to contain him was no match for the power of the Dead God. As the magic of the summoning circle collapsed, it sent a shockwave through the room that made Hrex and her master stagger back. Before they could react, they were both in Kulittu's immense shadow. One of the God's horrid hands snapped out and grabbed Aristotles by the throat and lifted him off the ground so that he was level with the black void of his hood. Instinctively Hrex swiftly sketched two symbols in the air and threw them at Kulittu, but with the barest incline of his head, they were dispelled. Kulittu's head snapped round to stare down at Hrex. A moment later, she was tossed through the air and was smashed into one of the window arches. Her vision swam drunkenly as she reeled from the blow, but she could still hear Kulittu's voice speaking across the room.

'Do not be fooled into thinking that you can contain my power. Many greater than you have attempted to rule me, but none have succeeded. Not even another deity for all her treachery was able to truly kill me! Now, prove to me that you were worth my time and are worthy of my benefaction. Bring me a good harvest so that I may grow stronger and allow you to feast on the scraps. I will know if you fail, and be warned, I will reclaim my investment from you no matter which realm of existence you may be on...'

With that, Kulittu vanished, sending Aristotles crashing to the floor. Within seconds of him leaving, light began to flood back into the room from the windows and the sounds of distant chaos in the castle could faintly be heard again. Hrex clambered unsteadily to her feet and tottered over to where her master was gingerly rising from the floor.

'I must go and rest, we have much left to do, but I cannot do it in my current state. Wake me in an hour, and we will complete the first piece of the puzzle. Here, keep this safe.'

He pressed the disc into her hands and began to make his way gingerly towards the door leading to his personal chambers.

He was still clutching the mask in his hand, and Hrex noticed that it had shrunk in size so that it was now no larger than his palm. She looked down at the object in her own hands and marvelled at what had become of the plain silver disc since Kulittu had touched it. She could feel the enormity of the power pulsing through it and the surface of the metal now swam with images and symbols that she could not comprehend, all of which were encircled by a snake devouring its own tail.

1

Fingers of weak morning sunlight crept through the streets and across the rooftops of Karpella as across the city its inhabitants stirred from their nervous, restless night. As the sunlight grew in strength, thousands of people held their breath, hoping beyond hope that the threat to the city and to their lives had slipped away in the night. It did not take long for the Sharisian army, which lurked within the rapidly shortening shadows beyond the city's wall, to make their presence felt once again on the inhabitants of Karpella.

Just as it had been every day for the last two weeks, the morning barrage of the walls was preceded by an ominous swish and snap of catapult arms flicking their deadly cargo into the air, shortly followed by the resounding crash as the missiles slammed into the walls. Occasionally one of these shots would go awry, pinging off the top of the walls or flying over them all together to wreak havoc amongst the buildings of the mainland portion of the city beyond. The strength of Karpella's defences was beginning to wane, and more and more of the shots were beginning to leave tangible signs of damage. Though the catapult stones dissolved into a cloud of dust and flying rock chips on impact, they left the stonework scarred and cracked, with the ground beneath littered with chunks of masonry that had been nibbled from the walls. Even from behind the lines of the Sharisian siege camp, the weakened state of several parts of the curtain wall could be plainly seen. The Sharisians knew that it was only a matter of time before the defences of Karpella began to give way.

This morning, however, the men and women of Karpella's City Guard had another threat in store for them. As they hunkered down behind the parapets and within the towers, desperately seeking shelter from the storm of razor-sharp stone that engulfed the defences, they were blind to the signs of movement that erupted from all along the siege lines, the pounding of rock against rock deafening them to the barked orders of Sharisian officers as they rallied their troops. It was purely a matter of luck that the City Guard were not taken completely by surprise.

As the Sharisians swarmed across the open ground between the siege camp and the city walls, one of their catapult crews set the trajectory of their piece a notch too high as they aimed for a weak spot they could see opening up on the wall in front of them. The thwack of the catapult arm reverberated through the wooden structure as they let fly, sending the shot hurtling towards Karpella, but instead of impacting on the weak spot, the shot smashed through the battlements and continued to sail onwards into the city, where it crashed through the roof of a nearby house.

Seconds before on the parapet, Osvald Thegnson, a rank-and-file Guardsman, had been sharing a measly breakfast with one of his comrades, Felthan. He had just torn a chunk of bread in two and was about to pass one half across to Felthan, when his friend vanished in a shower of stone and blood. Desperately clawing the dust and gore from his eyes, Osvald looked at the place where Felthan had been, now a mangled, blood-spattered hole that had been punched through the crenellations, and he crawled forward, hardly believing what had happened.

All that was left of Felthan was a ragged loop of leather cord with a battered brass charm, a bundle of ears of corn bound together, the symbol of the Goddess Freyd. It was supposed to have kept Felthan safe, but the Goddess of hearth and home held little power in this living nightmare... Osvald scooped up the charm and froze as he became aware of the sea of death that was surging across the ground below. Thousands of Sharisian troops were sprinting towards the walls, bearing ladders and grappling hooks, clearly with only one aim in mind. Osvald ran, shouting as loud as he could to alert the rest of the guards manning the walls, and soon horns sounded the warning up and down Karpella's curtain wall.

There was a crash as the Sharisian artillery loosed one last shot at the walls before the ceasefire was called, but as the echoes of the impact of those last shots died away, the sound of the Sharisian battle cries swelled to the fore, followed shortly by the clattering of ladders being thrown up against the defences. Thanks to Osvald's warning, the Karpella City Guard had been given few crucial moments to prepare, and as the first troops began to climb the ladders, the conical helmeted heads of the City Guard began to pop up all along the walls accompanied by the shower of spears, rocks, arrows and crossbow bolts. Screams of pain competed with the shouts of defiance from soldiers on both sides, and both the stones of the parapet and the ground around the ladders became slick with blood. For the Sharisian troops trying to scale the wall and for the City Guard desperately trying to defend them, it was impossible to know who had the upper hand. For hours, they remained locked in the bitter struggle for survival.

Eventually, as the sun crept up towards midday over the city, trumpets began to sound the recall from within the siege lines. The Sharisians retreated back across the killing fields, dragging their wounded along with them, leaving their dead piled up around the walls. Across the defences, shouts began to ring out from the City Guards, though they were not shouts of victory but shouts of relief. They knew that the Sharisians would be back, that their holding out today may just be delaying the inevitable until tomorrow. From his position in one of the towers, Osvald Thegnson watched the retreat joylessly. His keen eyes could already see the renewed movement of the crews around the catapults, and he knew that within a couple of minutes, the bombardment would begin again. He propped his crossbow against the tower parapet and looked across to where he had lost Felthan. There were several bodies strewn around the hole in the crenellations, obscuring the smear of blood that was all that remained of his friend.

He closed his eyes to try and stop the tears from welling up, and for a moment, his legs felt weak and he shuddered. However, he quickly realised that it wasn't him that was shuddering, but the whole wall. His eyes snapped open, and he clutched at the wall as a violent shock wave rocked the surrounding landscape. All around him, the City Guard were trying to keep their balance. Before his eyes, Osvald watched as the weakened section of wall, where he had first been stationed that morning, crumbled away to leave a gaping hole, strewn with rubble in the city wall. The shockwave passed as quickly as it had arrived, and for a second, all eyes on both sides of the wall were fixed on the breach that had appeared there. Then, the shout went up from the siege lines, and Sharisian troops surged back towards the city. Osvald snatched up his crossbow once more and loaded as fast as he could, his morning was far from over.

It was not just the defenders on the walls or their attackers who had felt the shockwave. All across the city people were picking themselves up from floors and flagstones, having been thrown off balance. As knowledge of the breach in the wall began to percolate through the streets, it was accompanied by speculation that the Sharisians must have undermined the walls, and it was the collapse of the mine workings that had caused the shockwave and made part of the defences collapse. At least one person, however, knew that this could not be true.

Admittedly, undermining of the walls had been the first explanation that had popped into Eleusia's head as she had felt the shockwave from her hiding place within a disused tower room in Karpella castle. She scrambled to her feet after having been unceremoniously knocked to the floor by the tremor and tried to beat the thick dust off her clothes that had settled on every surface in the room. The clouds of dust that rose up from her made Eleusia cough and splutter. She rushed to the broken window at the other side of the room to gulp down mouthfuls of fresh air.

As the coughing subsided, she took in the view of the city her vantage point gave her. The window she looked from faced out from the castle towards the rest of the city of Karpella, where she could see the ant-like throngs of people still crowding around the base of the edifice, hoping to find shelter within the castle's walls. Beyond, her gaze was caught by a plume of dust that drifted into the air from the curtain wall. Squinting, she thought she could make out a jagged hole in the defences emerging from within the dust cloud. As she tracked her vision back from the distant walls, however, she also spotted cracks that had appeared in the surfaces of the roads she could see, which appeared to emanate from the area of the castle, rather than focusing and spreading out from the breach in the defences.

Eleusia twisted her hair nervously around one of her fingers as she pondered what was before her. Though at first glance it appeared that the wall had been undermined, the cracks in the roads, and the fact that the shockwave had been felt so strongly within the castle itself, made Eleusia suspect that the real cause might well have something to do with the opening of the vault, deep below the castle. Regardless, the situation was not looking the most promising; the last thing she and her companions below ground needed right now were hordes of Sharisian troops running amuck within the city. She needed to warn them, and they needed to get moving fast.

Shaking her green cloak out one last time to rid herself of the last of the dust, Eleusia picked up her crossbow and stalked over to the door. Opening it a crack, she peeked out into the corridor and, confident the coast was clear, stepped out and pulled the door to behind her. As she was still wearing the armour and uniform of the Imperial Guard beneath her cloak, she walked quickly and openly through the corridors and down staircases, confident that in such a time of crisis, a soldier of the Imperial Guard moving swiftly and purposefully through the castle would raise few suspicions.

Moving through a large atrium on one of the upper floors, she nodded a greeting to a group of Imperial Guards who had liberated a large collection of chairs and tables from the neighbouring rooms to rest. They all looked exhausted, and many of them had soot-blackened faces and wore charred clothing. Eleusia had to conceal the smirk that spread across her face as she strode past them. She knew exactly why the guards looked so dishevelled because she was the one who had set the blaze going in one of the castle storerooms. She had heard the chaos from her hiding place in the tower, where she had decided to lie low until the heat had died down, and she hoped that it had provided enough of a distraction for Torben, Gwilym, Antauros and Hrex to reach the feasting hall and the treasure vault far beneath.

Turning down another labyrinthine passageway, Eleusia's swift progress was halted by the fact that the way forward was almost completely blocked by chests, boxes and piles of books that had been unceremoniously dumped in the corridor. A large set of double doors at the epicentre of the massed detritus were wide open and led to a room beyond from which panicked, absent-minded muttering could be heard. Slowing her pace, she wove her way through what looked like the entire contents of the nearby room. Though it delayed her progress, Eleusia knew that this was the fastest way to reach her destination and that picking her way through the scattered junk would still be faster than retracing her steps and trying to find an alternative route. As she got closer and closer to the doorway, she began to hear snippets of the conversation that the room's occupant appeared to be having with themselves....

'They'll never take all of this. Make sure to pack only the most important things,' he said, 'but everything is important! Now... medicinal herbs, very important, but largely useless without Phintel's Guide to Vegetal Potions and Poultices. Where did I put that? I saw it just a moment ago. Mímir save me, but this is hopeless... And where are those damn porters? They should have been here over an hour ago.'

The voice was high pitched, though definitely masculine. As Eleusia drew level with the open doors, she saw that it belonged to a gnome, wearing a once elaborate, though now rather threadbare, set of blue ceremonial robes. A curtain of blond hair surrounded a prominent bald patch at the crown of his head and dangled down over his ears and onto his shoulders. The room he was standing in was a chaotic mess of discarded books, broken glass and overturned tables. Innumerable half-packed bags and crates were strewn around the floor, and they merged into the items that had been dumped in the hallway.

He turned abruptly towards her, worrying one of his thick blond sideburns with one hand and adjusting the small pair of spectacles that were perched on top of his long, angular nose with the other. He stopped dead in his tracks as he saw Eleusia, who had been standing stock-still in the doorway, barely breathing, hoping that the gnome wouldn't notice her. He took a step forwards and peered up at her, his brown eyes magnified by the lenses of his spectacles.

'Ah, you must be here to help porter this down to the ships?'

'Errm, no, I'm not.' Eleusia straightened up and tried to inject a sense of authority into her voice.

'Oh, well, what are you doing then?'

'I'm...' Eleusia's answer had barely formed on her lips before the gnome's high voice cut across her.

'Well, it can't be anything too important; otherwise, you'd remember it.' He continued before she was able to speak again. 'Regardless of what you're up to, I need you to round up a group of porters and bring them here post haste! All of these items belong to the Imperial Mage to the Court, and it is imperative that they survive and are available for the resistance effort should the capital fall. As a member of the Imperial Guard, I expect you to take this order as if it had come from the mouth of Hastel himself.'

Eleusia nodded curtly and wordlessly to the gnome and then turned on her heel and continued on her way down the corridor. The tone of the gnome's voice had left her thinking that he was neither used to throwing his weight around, nor to giving orders, so she judged that the best course of action was to simply appear as if she was carrying out his orders immediately, hoping that his naivety in the workings of the Imperial command structure would mean that she would be able to get away without him complicating matters further. As she finally made her way out of the barricade of detritus from the room, she could hear the gnome muttering to himself again.

Now that she was back on track, it did not take Eleusia long to make her way down to the ground floor of the castle and the large, elaborate hallways that led to the numerous state rooms and her destination, the Great Hall. As she approached the enormous, highly polished double doors, the main entrance to the Hall, she slowed her pace as she saw two figures in military garb, one wearing the uniform of the City Guard and the other the much more elaborate uniform of the Imperial Guard, moving swiftly towards her along the corridor. The Imperial Guardsman was clearly an officer, as they were grilling the weary-looking soldier walking alongside them, whose armour was scratched and stained with blood and dust, who looked as if she had come straight from the defences. She was clutching a battered leather messenger tube in one hand, which Eleusia guessed must contain a report from the frontline.

'And you're absolutely sure that the fighting is beginning to spread beyond the walls?'

'Yes, sir', the guardswoman spoke through gritted teeth; clearly this was not the first time that she had been grilled about the contents of her dispatch. 'The wall has been breached in the western section, and the Sharisian infantry offensive has concentrated on the breach and has pushed back our forces almost to Medallion Square.'

'And why can't your commander bring in reinforcements from the eastern section of the wall?'

'Because, sir, not only have the Sharisian's begun focusing their bombardment on the eastern wall, they have also left an obvious contingent of infantry opposite the focal point of the barrage, so even if we could move the troops pinned down on the walls, that section of the wall would be almost immediately assaulted. Hence why Colonel Grimwold sent me up here, sir, to request reinforcements from the Imperial Guard.'

The conversation continued as the pair went past, the still unconvinced Imperial officer wafting a dismissive hand towards his forehead in response to Eleusia's salute. As they disappeared around a corner, she slipped through the double doors into the Great Hall.

Though it was the first time that she had been in the gorgeously decorated edifice, her mind was focused on the task at hand, and she moved towards the back wall quickly and quietly, keeping within the shadows of the covered colonnade that surrounded three of the four walls. As she approached the high table, behind which was the ornately carved imperial throne, she slowed even more and began scouring the floor and the mosaic that covered the back wall, looking for the entrance to the vault below. When they had been planning their infiltration of the castle, Hrex had been incredibly coy about where the entrance to the vault was, and it had only been through a very careful studying of the few words that she had said on the topic that Eleusia had narrowed down its location to the back of the Hall.

She began to run her hands along the mosaic itself, starting at one end and working her way along, feeling the sharp edges of the minute tiles tug at her fingertips as she tried to pick up any irregularities in the pieces, anything that might give away the entrance. She shut her eyes, trying to focus her whole attention on the sensations running through her hands until her eyes snapped open as she felt an ever so slightly larger gap in between a line of mosaic tiles. There was a thicker line of bare wall, hardly noticeable unless one was as close as Eleusia was to it, that divided the rest of the mosaic from a panel depicting a kindly looking queen, her arms outstretched in welcome. Following the line, Eleusia could see that it framed and centred the figure, and she began to study the mosaic queen, looking for the mechanism to open the portal. She pressed down hard on first one, then the other of the queen's sapphire eyes to no avail, and it was only as she stepped back to get a better view that her eyes were drawn to the large ruby set in the centre of her belt. Carefully, she pressed a long finger onto the gem and held her breath as it slowly began to sink into the mosaic and stonework behind. As it disappeared, the whole mosaic panel began to move, groaning as a set of double doors opened there, splitting the queen in two. Without stopping to find a light source, she plunged down into the darkness that rose to swallow her as the doors to the vault shuddered to a close behind.

2

'You trample on the legacy of my father and my people. Give me one good reason why I shouldn't take your head, thief!'

The Princess stared down at the figure of the dwarf before her. The point of her sabre was hooked under his beard, the blade held against his throat, and she could see her hand shaking ever so slightly, making the tip of the sword wobble imperceptibly. She felt groggy, as if she had woken from a deep, over-long sleep, but despite how she felt, she couldn't afford to let her guard down. A second of lapsed concentration, and this intruder could land a killing blow if he so wished... She willed herself into focusing all of her attention on the dwarf.

He was wearing armour reminiscent of the protective gear that her own guards wore, who were rapidly making their way across the piles of gold, silver and gems towards them, but there were distinct differences that puzzled her as she tried to pin down who this dwarf served. Although the long coat of scale mail was almost identical to her guards, the tabard was shaped differently, and it not only had the red rose of Dazscor emblazoned on the cloth, but also the gold stag of Aramore. He held a strange weapon loosely in his hand as well, a shortsword of a type that was not common within the Kingdom of Dazscor but which she vaguely recalled being known as a seax to the dwarves of the Union of Mishtoon to the south. The dwarf was likewise staring up at her, though she noticed that his emerald eyes were stained with tears, which were running down his face into the mass of black beard that clung to his cheeks and jaw.

As the dwarf was thrown into shadow by the guards who were rallying to their Princess and encircling him, he slowly lifted the hand carrying the seax above his head, where it was swiftly plucked from his grasp by a mid-height, strongly built man, whose closely cropped ginger hair and beard reflected the light that flickered from the torches and braziers set around the vault. The man, Captain Almar, tucked the seax into his belt and then pushed the dwarf onto his knees.

'Keep your hands where I can see them,' he growled.

'What is your name, dwarf?' The Princess' voice was clear, calm and level, testament to the hours of tuition in elocution she had been forced to undertake by her father.

'Gwilym, my lady.'

Gwilym spoke softly, his voice catching slightly in his throat. He knew that the woman in front of him was high status, so he bowed his head as much as he was able with the sabre restricting the movement of his head and threatening to bite into his neck.

'Well, Gwilym, tell me, why do you bear the symbol of the treacherous Duchy of Aramore on your tabard alongside that of my house?'

The dwarf's eyes momentarily flashed up to the Princess' face, trying to gauge the seriousness of her question. His expression was one of confusion as he hesitatingly began to answer.

'But, my lady, I wear the symbols of this kingdom... as they have been for nearly the last 200 years.'

'Do you know who I am?'

'No, my lady.'

'I am Princess Theodora of the Royal House of Dazscor,

daughter of King Sarper IV, so I rather think that I am qualified to know the symbols and emblems of my family's lands!'

There was a moment of silence as Gwilym's head snapped up to intently inspect Theodora, all pretence of deference forgotten. As he had no idea of what Sarper IV had looked like, it was hard to assess how much of a familial resemblance there was between the long-dead king and the woman stood before him. However, now that he studied her clothing and armour, he could see that she didn't bear the symbol of the Kingdom of Dazscor & Aramore on her clothes, but only the rose of Dazscor. Indeed, the heraldic shield that had been inlaid on the centre of her breastplate bore the symbol of an armoured hand clutching the rose of Dazscor. It was a coat of arms that he had seen before, inlaid into a fine set of golden dinner plates that had been procured through rather dishonest means and had passed through Björn's operation. The aged and crotchety treasurer, who had toiled away over the accounts in the basement of Björn's headquarters for longer than anyone could remember, had told Gwilym that the coat of arms was that of the old kings and queens of Dazscor, from before the invasion of the Aramorians, and that it was rare to see it nowadays.

Then, Gwilym's mind began to turn to why Hrex had wanted to gain access to the vault in the first place: to rescue her master who had apparently been held, suspended in time under the power of the spell. Then he remembered that there had been other bodies in the vault when he had entered, and why could they not have been sent into a magically induced hibernation, just as Hrex's master had? He had been so fixated on tracking down Hrex to get revenge for Torben that he hadn't stopped to think about the presence of other people in the vault…

Torben! Gwilym's mind began to whir as he became aware again of the fact that he could no longer hear Torben's cries of pain coming from the antechamber. He needed to act quickly, to get him help, but how? His train of thought was broken as Princess Theodora addressed him again.

'I want to know why you are here, who you serve and why I shouldn't slit your throat now for being a common, grubby thief?'

For a moment, Gwilym's mind was completely blank. He had no idea what to say or how to explain to these people, who were either deluded and possibly dangerous or who could well be people who had been imprisoned in the vault for hundreds of years, who might be slow to believe how much time had passed, how many things had changed in the time they had been trapped. Feeling the blade of the sabre press ever so slightly more forcefully into his throat, Gwilym began to speak, letting the words roll from his tongue, hoping that they wouldn't get him killed.

'Your Highness, you must forgive me for not recognising you and for my trespass into your hallowed halls. If you will permit me a few moments to explain, I can shed some light on who I am and why I am here before you.'

For a moment, the Princess' eyes glowered down at Gwilym, scanning his face for any hint of treachery, and satisfied that he did not present an immediate threat to her person, she lowered her sabre to allow him to speak more freely. In reaction to Theodora's movement, however, Captain Almar moved closer, looming over the diminutive figure before him, reminding Gwilym through his presence that he was still being keenly watched.

Gwilym stretched his back and rolled his neck, trying to ease out the aches and stiffness there that had begun to take hold, cleared his throat and began to speak.

'Now, Your Highness will have to bear with me on some things, as there is a lot that I will say that might be hard for you to believe at first... This land has been ruled by the Royal House of Aramore as the Joint Kingdom of Dazscor & Aramore since 375, when this city of Karpella was captured by the forces of the Duke of Aramore. The current year is 553, and I am afraid to tell you that your father was killed attempting to escape the city, and it was thought that you perished in the fighting and that your body was never discovered. That is why I bear both the symbol of your house and that of your enemy.

'As to why I am here, I warrant that you will at least be familiar with the name Hrex?'

The guards surrounding Gwilym murmured to one another as Hrex's name was mentioned, and Princess Theodora nodded in recognition before motioning Gwilym to continue.

'Well, I and my three companions were coerced by Hrex into finding the means to access this vault and to come down here with her so that she could release the one that she calls her master from the enchantment that was placed on the vault to protect it. She did not mention the presence of anyone else down here, and let me stress that my companions and I did not come down here of our own volition. She cast a terrible curse on one of my friends, who is still lying out in the antechamber, bleeding out his last. That vile hag used his life's blood to gain entrance into this place.

'You may not believe what I have told you, but please accept me now as a humble petitioner who wants nothing more than to save his friend. I beg you to let me go to see if I can aid him, or find a way to bring him back from the brink! In exchange, I offer you my services as a guide to what the world above has now become.'

Finishing his appeal, Gwilym bowed his head once more, his eyes fixed on the tip of the Princess' fine leather boots, trying to make himself look as contrite as possible. He could feel more tears running down his face, and they flowed down the ridge of his bulbous nose and dripped onto the gold coins that littered the ground beneath. Trying to control his emotions, he held his breath and waited; whether for the sword blow or salvation, he did not know.

Out in the antechamber, Antauros was struggling to keep calm. Since the dispelling of the enchantment, the space has become oppressively dark as the arcane light that the spell had thrown out had been banished as well, leaving the only light source as the flickering torches that were scattered about the vault proper. He was struggling to see what he was doing as he rooted around in his pack for anything that he might have that could aid Torben, but he was beginning to run out of ideas and out of hope.

Torben lay on the altar, his eyes staring blankly at the ceiling from which Hrex had magically suspended him a few moments before. The smooth white marble all around him was slick with blood that pooled around the young man who was now so pale the hue of his skin had almost become indistinguishable from the stone he lay on. A huge wad of bandages had been strapped to his belly, trying to stem the deadly flow emanating from the wound. He was still breathing, though his breath was now slow and shallow.

As he straightened up, Antauros placed one of his massive hands onto the bandages, applying pressure, and stroked Torben's head with the other, doing his best to calm him. Both of his hands, as well as the fur of his arms, was matted with gore, and he left small smudges of blood on the young man's head as he soothed him. The minotaur scanned the railings and the gate that separated the antechamber from the vault beyond for any sign of Gwilym's return. Since the dwarf had run off in pursuit of Hrex, Antauros had heard nothing except for a distant curse, which added to the bleak outlook.

He turned back to look down at Torben, whose eyes were growing dimmer and dimmer, and sighed deeply. He had lost count of the number of times he's watched comrades die, but this felt much worse than anything he had ever experienced. It felt as if he was watching his own son slip away before him. He bowed his head and closed his eyes as he felt the salt-sting of tears gathering there.

'I'm sorry that it came to this, Torben. I'm sorry that we weren't able to do something, anything... Where is the justice in this that you should suffer so much in such a short time, whilst the people who built this accursed place lived and prospered long!'

He opened his eyes and wiped them, smearing Torben's blood across his muzzle. As his vision cleared, the young man came back sharply into focus, and Antauros could see light flickering on his face and being reflected off his pale skin as it grew brighter and brighter. His head snapped around to the vault's gate, and he saw a group of figures bearing torches and lanterns making their way over the golden floor of treasure towards him. Leading them was a smaller figure, Gwilym.

At first, Antauros' heart leaped when he saw the dwarf, but his feeling of elation was quickly dampened when he realised that Gwilym was walking with his hands on his head, and that all of the people following him were well armed and armoured and that there were several spear points hovering inches from Gwilym's back, encouraging him forward. Slowly, his right hand began to drift down to the head of his war-hammer, where it hung in its belt loop, the other still maintaining pressure on Torben's wound.

As the lights that Gwilym's escort bore fully illuminated the minotaur's bulk, a shout went up from the back, and a group of the soldiers surged forwards, forming a shield wall in front of the rest of the group, spears levelled towards Antauros, protecting the others. From inside the mass of bodies and shields, Gwilym's disembodied voice could be heard shouting over the din.

'Calm down, he's with me, there's no need for all of this palaver...Your Highness, I can assure you that he will bring you no harm...Antauros, for the love of all the gods, get your hands up and don't bloody well do anything stupid!'

29

'Easy now.' Antauros' voice calmly rumbled from deep within his chest as he slowly moved his bloodied hands where the troops before him could see them.

His compliance clearly eased the nerves of Gwilym's escort as another short, barked order sounded from the centre of the formation, and the soldiers in the front rank relaxed, breaking the shield wall and bringing their spears up. From within, Gwilym was frogmarched out by the barrel-chested bulk of what appeared to be the officer who had been issuing commands to the formation of troops, a young woman with fine armour and clothes, who held herself in a very self-assured manner following a few steps behind.

'Allow me to introduce you to our new *friends...*' Gwilym eyed Antauros grimly from under his bushy brows. 'This is Princess Theodora, first and only daughter of King Sarper IV, and before you ask, *yes* as far as I can fathom, it is true. When the vault was originally sealed, she and her guards were trapped here along with Hrex's master, and now that the enchantment has been lifted, they have been reanimated, so to speak.' Turning to Theodora, Gwilym continued. 'Your Highness, this is Antauros, one of my companions of which I spoke.'

'Where is the one who is injured?' Theodora spoke curtly.

Antauros gestured to the altar, where Torben was still lying, and several of the guards, who wore large, heavy-looking packs on their backs, trotted over and began to pull medical supplies from them as they assessed the young man's injuries.

'Secure the perimeter!' Captain Almar barked, taking his hand off Gwilym's shoulder and moving to converse quietly with the Princess.

Sensing his opportunity, Gwilym gingerly removed his hands from his head and surreptitiously moved over to Antauros, who was half-watching the guards move around the space and half-watching the medics tend to Torben.

'How's Torben doing?' Gwilym strained to get a good view of the altar.

'Not well.' Antauros slumped down the side of the stonework into a sitting position. 'I don't know how much they'll be able to do for him... But I guess he's hopefully in better hands than mine now. What happened in there?'

'I didn't get to her in time.' Gwilym sat down next to the minotaur and put his head in his hands. 'When I caught up with her, it was too late. She'd found her master, helped him to his feet, and then vanished into thin air as she heard me coming. Just thinking of the smarmy expression on her face as she saw me and realised that she was away scot-free makes my blood boil!'

'What was he like, her master?'

'Hard to say, didn't get a good look at him, but my guess would be an Elf of some description.'

'Hmm.' Antauros surveyed the activity in the antechamber, trying to take his mind off the grim reality of Torben's prognosis. 'This lot seem to know what they're doing.'

'Well, they're Royal Guards charged with protecting an ex-heir to the throne, so you'd hope that they'd give an impression of competence.' Gwilym responded bitterly. 'They certainly pulled themselves together sharpish when they awoke. Before I knew what was happening, I was completely surrounded. That one,' Gwilym jabbed one of his thick fingers in Captain Almar's direction, 'he's a fierce dog to have on a leash. I wouldn't want to get on his wrong side. Having said that, their charge isn't a pushover either, she nearly shaved my beard clean off with that sabre of hers.'

'So, what exactly is the arrangement here?' Antauros drew closer to Gwilym and lowered his voice. 'Are they friendly, or are we prisoners?'

'Frankly, I have no idea,' Gwilym muttered back. 'I don't think the Princess or the Captain believed what I told them about how times have changed, but they didn't not believe me enough to kill me there and then. I managed to be persuasive enough so that her men would help Torben, but I can't help but think that, for the time being, we are at Her Highness' pleasure...'

They sat in silence, half-watching the activity going on around them, half-listening to the work and conversation of the medics around the altar and Torben above them. By now Theodora's guards had searched every nook and cranny of the antechamber. Several of them stood on guard where the stairs from the great hall above entered the room, whilst another group had been attempting, without success, to move some of the rubble that blocked what had once been another passageway that led out into the city. At the entrance to the vault, another group of guards were packing handfuls of coins and precious stuffs into packs and bags, apparently readying a small fortune to move out with them, wherever the Princess decided to go.

A low whistle sounded from the foot of the steps, and all of the guards in the room stopped dead in their tracks. One of the soldiers at the stairs had turned to face the room and gestured that everyone should be as quiet as possible. Around them, guards started to douse torches and lanterns and began to drift quietly across the room towards Theodora, forming themselves into a protective circle around her. Captain Almar and several other guards came and crouched by Antauros and Gwilym.

'Keep quiet, both of you,' he growled. 'Any sign that you'll betray us and I'll slit your bellies open.'

At the stairs, the guards there had moved away from the opening into the room and had pressed themselves against the wall, waiting for whoever they were expecting to appear. Complete silence settled onto the antechamber, broken only by the faintest whisper of Torben's weak, ragged breathing. They all watched and waited in near pitch blackness.

Eventually, another noise began to sound from the stairs, the slightest padding of feet descending the rough stone steps. Soon a faint glow of light showed on the topmost steps that could be seen from the antechamber followed shortly by the silhouette of a slender figure, holding a candle aloft to light their way.

As soon as the figure stepped into the antechamber proper, the guards lurking in the shadows on either side pounced. The chamber was briefly plunged into total darkness as the candle was knocked from the figure's hand and snuffed out, but then other guards in the room uncovered lanterns they had hidden, allowing dim-flickering light back into the space. As the light levels went up, however, more guards started to rush towards ambush point, now aware that all was not in hand.

Where the individual coming down the stairs should have been restrained, there were instead two of the guards, one clutching his hands to his face, where blood could be seen flowing from his broken nose, the other doubled over cradling his groin. The other guards were rapidly closing in on the far left corner of the antechamber, where Eleusia was retreating calmly backwards, sword drawn and held at the ready as she assessed her options. Fortunately, Antauros recognised her just before the guards began to close in around her, and he leapt to his feet, shouting above the noise that had erupted in the room.

'Stop, she's with us!'

'Eleusia, stand down for heaven's sake!' Gwilym added his petition to Antauros.

Slowly Eleusia lowered her sword and very reluctantly handed it over to the guard who came to take it, along with her dagger and crossbow from her. She was then led into the centre of the room to join Gwilym and Antauros, and it was then that she got her first sight of Torben. She rushed over to him, evading the swiping hand of the guard who tried to restrain her and sprinted to the altar. As the guard broke into a run to give chase, Princess Theodora coughed loudly and gestured for him to stand down. Eleusia bent her head over Torben, tears freely flowing. Gwilym and Antauros joined her, the minotaur placing a hand on her shoulder.

Slowly, the Princess' guards began to avert their eyes from the grieving trio, and they began to go back about their business.

'How is he, Beorhtric?'

Princess Theodora had moved over to the altar as well, Captain Almar at her shoulder, and addressed one of the medics who was still tending to Torben.

'Not good, Your Highness, I'm afraid that he is beyond the bounds of our expertise now.'

Gwilym cursed loudly and foully and kicked the foot of the altar whilst Eleusia bowed her head even further and drew her hood over her black hair. Antauros turned to face the medic, Beorhtric, and spoke softly. 'Are you sure that there is nothing else you can do?'

'I'm afraid that nothing short of a miracle will save him. He has lost too much blood, and even if we did have somewhere that we could take him for better treatment, it is unlikely that he would survive the journey.'

'I think it's best that you say your last goodbyes now.' Princess Theodora spoke with a much more empathetic tone than she had addressed them with previously. 'We need to get moving. I'm sending some scouts up to the castle to reconnoitre the situation and see if we can match what is going on up there to the information you have given us, Gwilym. When they return, we will need to move, and that includes the three of you. We can't risk letting you go and potentially spreading round rumours of my existence. We have no idea how many enemies of my House still remain alive, and doubtless, the current ruler would be rather unhappy to learn that a rival for his throne had reappeared. Rest assured, however, that you will be treated well and that we will pay you handsomely for the time you spend with us. We need guides who know the current situation and political lay of the land, and given that one of my father's servants forced you to come here and took the life of your friend here to free us, it seems that I and my guards owe you a debt.'

As Antauros and Gwilym began to respond to Theodora to accept the terms that she had put before them, Eleusia's mind was fogged with grief, and it felt as if her brain was lagging behind, still processing what Beorhtric had said, *nothing short of a miracle...*

'A miracle,' she whispered, the utterance of the word planting the seed of an idea.

'Beg pardon, Eleusia?' Gwilym asked.

'A miracle,' she repeated and turned to Beorhtric, 'you said that it would take a miracle to save Torben's life?'

'Yes. I'm sorry we do not have the equipment or resources, let alone adequate light down here to be able to treat him...'

Eleusia ignored the explanation that Beorhtric had launched into and turned to Princess Theodora, throwing back her hood to fully reveal her tearstained face.

'I think I know of how we can save Torben. We need to get him back up into the castle, now!'

3

Torben groaned as Antauros cradled him in his arms and made his way gingerly up the stairs from the vault to the great hall of Karpella Castle above. In front of him, Eleusia walked holding a lantern high above her head to light the way, and the two were led and followed by a retinue of Princess Theodora's guards, four on each side.

'You'll be ok, Torben, just hang in there. I know you're strong, you'll get through this.'

Antauros spoke to Torben even though he had no idea if he could hear him or not. He guessed not given that the young man was no longer aware of his surroundings and that only signs of life that he was now exhibiting were the groans of pain that rattled from his throat.

'Eleusia, are you absolutely sure about this?' the minotaur asked, worry written across his face. 'I'd hate to think that we're only making his last moments more painful than they have to be...'

'I'm sure, Antauros. I saw all of the stuff that was in that room, there was bags of stuff that was linked to healing. If anyone in this place is going to be able to get Torben fit and well again, then it's that Imperial Mage.'

'If you're sure, then…'

Antauros went back to trying to soothe Torben, wincing every time one of his heavy footfalls made Torben cry out in agony.

If Antauros and Gwilym had been lucky enough never to have the pleasure of having known Hrex, or of having seen what supernatural, magical things she was able to do, then they would all probably still be standing around the altar in the antechamber, watching for Torben breath out his last. As it was, they had been more receptive of Eleusia's idea to take Torben up into the castle and hope that the Imperial Mage to the Court of Hastel I would be able to bring the young man back from the brink. However, deep in the back of his mind, Antauros remained sceptical. Hrex was a being from another age who had been taught, by all accounts, to use arcane arts from a powerful teacher, at a time when the use of magic was much more commonplace. How was someone from a broken tradition going to be able to summon enough power to heal what in Antauros' experience he knew was a mortal wound?

He shook his head to dispel the thoughts and focused his energy on climbing the stairs as swiftly as possible.

Gods, I wish Gwilym were with us, he thought to himself. The dwarf had a knack for lightening even the darkest of moods, and should the worst come to the worst, then he should be here to say his last goodbyes… As it was, Gwilym had been forced to remain in the vault, a hostage of Princess Theodora. Although the Princess had not overtly threatened them, the insistence that Gwilym remain with her and the majority of her force, along with the fact that Antauros and Eleusia were being escorted by her soldiers, made it clear where the balance of power lay at that moment.

At the top of the stairs, the guards stopped, and the leader carefully manipulated the release mechanism on the back of the door and eased it open an inch. After a long moment, he swung the portal fully open, satisfied that the coast was clear. As they entered the light, airy space that was the great hall, the guard, who had been brusquely introduced to them as Ranulf, beckoned Eleusia forwards.

'Right then, lead on, but if you do anything funny...' He finished his statement by patting the hilt of his sheathed sword.

Eleusia nodded curtly and then headed towards the main double-doored exit from the hall, the guards fanning out to surround Antauros, lest he too should try and escape. Several of the guards had arrows already knocked to the strings of their short-bows, whilst all of the others, bar Ranulf, had their swords drawn or spears at the ready.

As they entered the main corridor beyond, Eleusia turned and retraced her steps from earlier, trying to remember the most direct route to the rooms of the Imperial Mage. Distant shouts could be heard echoing from other corridors and rooms in the castle, and Antauros pricked up his ears, trying to read the tone of the voices. Almost all of them sounded like worried, hastily issued orders, but he took comfort in the fact that he could not hear the sounds of fighting anywhere nearby. Whatever was happening in the wider city, the Sharisians were not yet directly threatening Karpella Castle.

As they moved through the corridors, the guards that were escorting them took in their surroundings nervously.

'I don't like it,' one of them muttered, 'it's like I've never been to this place, and yet I recognise its shadow. That should be the Queen's receiving room...' He pointed down a corridor where a storeroom could be seen beyond its open door. 'And there was never a door there before, that should be solid stone!'

'Quiet back there!' Ranulf's piercing whisper sounded from the front of the group, and the guard in question lowered their voice to a barely audible rumble but continued to chunter discontentedly to himself.

As they stalked through the corridors, Eleusia was checking off every turning, staircase and room they passed in her mind. She was hoping against hope that they wouldn't encounter anyone else, as they would be hard-pressed to explain what they were doing there. That is, if they were given a chance to attempt to explain what they were doing there at all. The uniforms and armour of the Princess' guards were distinctive enough that they would arouse instant suspicion from any Imperial Guards they met along their way, and soldiers trying to defend a city under siege would often fall back on the age-old fail-safe of kill first, ask questions later.

When they were a couple of corridors away from their destination, or so Eleusia believed, she heard what she had been dreading the whole time, the sound of footsteps coming towards them. She looked up and down the corridor for a side passage they could bolt down, but there were only rooms branching off the passageway. Ranulf had clearly heard the sounds of footsteps, too, as he turned to Antauros and the guards behind and issued his orders quickly and quietly.

'Peel off into the adjoining rooms. Roswit, you take the minotaur and the lad with your group, Eleusia, you're with me. If you find anyone inside, you know what to do, but make it quick and quiet.'

With that, Ranulf swiftly approached the door closest on the left, briefly turned his head to make sure his party were with him and then quietly opened the door and slipped inside. As Eleusia was ushered into the room beyond by the guards behind, she saw Antauros being shepherded by the guardswoman that must have been Roswit into a room slightly further down the corridor. As she passed through the doorframe, she was guided to one side by a guard, who held a finger to his mouth and pointed further into the space.

The chamber was clearly the accommodation of some mid-ranking courtier or the like. It was large and furnished with reasonably expensive-looking furniture, though it lacked the opulent feel of other parts of the castle. The side of the room they had entered was clearly meant to be some form of lounge area, with a collection of plush looking armchairs and couches arranged around a low table near to a large fireplace, which still held the ashes of the last blaze. The table still bore the remains of the last night's entertainments; the contents of a pack of cards, a platter with the sad-looking remains of a canapé-like meal and an empty decanter with two red-stained wine glasses nearby. The far half of the room was dominated by a large four-poster bed, which had the curtains partly drawn around it. The curtains fluttered in the breeze that flowed through an open window and which carried through the distant sounds of battle from off in the city, which were almost entirely masked by the rumbling drone of snoring coming from inside the bed.

Ranulf was already approaching the bed, dagger drawn, and as Eleusia focused on his creeping figure, she also heard the sounds of stirring coming from it, aside from the snoring, which were clearly what Ranulf was concerned about. As the soldier approached, an arm emerged and parted the curtains slightly on the other side. A woman stepped lightly and quietly from the bed. She was completely naked, her clothes, along with those of the bed's slumbering male occupant, strewn across the floor. Sensing the presence of four pairs of eyes watching her, she turned slowly to face Eleusia and the three soldiers with her, her face swiftly contorting into one of horror. The corners of her mouth twitched as she readied her scream, but then Ranulf was on her, hand clamped over her mouth. In the split second that she saw his dagger whipping up towards the woman's neck, readying to slit her throat, recognition suddenly blazed in Eleusia's mind, and she whispered sharply:

'Ranulf, stop!'

The command made Ranulf pause for a moment, and his eyes snapped to Eleusia across the room.

'What?' he mouthed.

'I know her. Please, you don't need to do that. She won't talk, I swear it.'

'What makes you so sure of that?'

'She's a whore, Ranulf. She works in Ivy House, a brothel on

Rose Street, Mid-Isle. She has nothing to do with this, and she doesn't deserve to lose her life for being in the wrong place at the wrong time.'

As she spoke, Eleusia quickly and quietly made her way across the room, picking up a discarded blanket from one of the chairs, and continued over to Ranulf and the petrified woman. Ranulf eyed her hard for a second and then withdrew his knife from the woman's throat. As he stepped back and took his hand from her mouth, he whispered in her ear:

'Make one sound and it'll be your last…'

As Ranulf stepped back, Eleusia stepped forward, wrapping the blanket around the woman and helping to guide her to the floor as her legs gave way in fright.

'Don't worry, it's all right. It's Saeth isn't it?'

The woman nodded, and her hands and bottom lip trembled.

'Eleusia, what's going on? What are you doing here? What are they going to do?'

'Ssshh', Eleusia soothed. 'Don't worry, Saeth, nothing's going to happen to you, ok. We're going to leave, and when we do you must gather your things and head back to Ivy House as quickly as possible, understand?'

Saeth nodded and eyed Ranulf warily, whose attention was now focused on the bed's still sleeping occupant, lest he too awaken.

'Saeth, Saeth,' Eleusia regained her attention. 'It's best that you know as little as possible about what we're doing, ok? You never saw us here, alright? The only person you should tell about this is Madame Fleurese, and I want you to tell her that I am safe, ok, that my friends Antauros, Gwilym and Torben are all safe…' Eleusia paused as she stopped herself from adding *I hope* after she spoke Torben's name. 'Can you do that for me, Saeth?'

'Yes.'

'Good.'

41

Eleusia knelt by Saeth on the floor, her arm around her shoulders, until the guard who was listening at the door signalled the all-clear and they began to move out. Eleusia gave Saeth a last encouraging squeeze of her shoulders and followed them out, Ranulf closing the door softly behind them as they left.

The other group were already in the corridor, and Ranulf gathered them together to re-issue orders.

'Now, Eleusia', he scowled at her, clearly still uncertain as to what to make of what had just happened, 'you said it's just a few more corridors until we're at the Imperial Mage's chambers?'

'Yes, I'm certain of it.'

'In that case, Roswit, take Sigeric and Eanwin and reconnoitre the castle and any potential ways out. Look for the old secret passages; hopefully, at least one is still usable. Pick up anything that might give us an indication of what the situation is here and whether this lot,' he eyed Eleusia and Antauros suspiciously, 'are telling the truth.'

'Aye, sir,' Roswit replied, taking two other guards and hurrying off back the way they had come.

'Now then, Eleusia, lead on.'

Eleusia turned and led them on, as the group walked the last few corridors in silence. Finally the space outside the Imperial Mage's rooms swung into view, still cluttered by the mass of boxes haphazardly piled outside. As they drew near, the sounds of the gnome's panicked scuttling around the room could be plainly heard from within. Reaching the edge of the chaos, Eleusia straightened, readying herself to enter the room, and Ranulf's face appeared at her shoulder.

'So, what's the plan?'

'I'm not sure yet...' she responded slowly and quietly. 'We don't have time to formulate a proper strategy, so I'm afraid you'll just have to follow my lead, understand?'

Before Ranulf could react, she began to stride quickly and with as much dignity as possible through the mess of boxes and packing cases and strode purposefully through the door to the rooms beyond.

As she entered, Eleusia was struck by how much more dishevelled the room looked than when she had last stood in it. By now, all of the shelves that lined the walls had been completely denuded of their contents, which lay scattered on the floor, as if they had simply been swept off the shelves by a careless arm. There had clearly been some attempt to sort some of the odds and ends in the room into coherent piles, but it was impossible to tell where one collection of objects ended and the other began. Scanning the room, Eleusia tried to spot the gnome; she could hear him, his voice muffled by whatever pile he was rooting through, but she was struggling to spot him.

'Gather only the key things, he says; we don't want to be encumbered with too many unnecessary trinkets, he says; *but oh, that is too precious, and I can't bear to leave that behind!* Oh, Mímir, spare me! Why don't I just set fire to the whole damn lot of it and damn his pomposity… Ah, I found it!'

Eleusia jumped as the gnome emerged triumphantly from the chest that he had stepped completely inside, clutching a large tome in both his hands, which looked so heavy that he could barely lift it. He heaved it and himself over the side of the chest and landed rather unceremoniously on the floor, a small cloud of dust rising up from his clothes and hair. He staggered to his feet under the weight of the book and then dropped it to the floor with a resounding thud, startled by the sudden presence of Eleusia, Antauros and the guards in the room. He hopped around on one foot, the other which had broken the fall of the book clutched in his hand as he massaged the top of his shoe and the foot beneath.

'What the blazes do you think you're playing at, you could have scared me to death, barging in like that without so much as a by your leave!'

'Apologies, sir, but we were told to find you with the utmost urgency.' Eleusia had snapped to attention, emulating the onparade stance she had seen true members of the Imperial Guard adopt.

The gnome looked hard at her for a moment as he gingerly replaced his foot on the ground. Then recognition flashed across his face.

'Ah, I remember you! You came back with help to start moving this stuff down to the jetty. Excellent, well, if we can start with the boxes in the corridor that will clear some more space for us to move additional things out there. Thank Mímir, but I might actually be closer to getting out of here…'

'Beg pardon, sir,' Eleusia raised her voice to speak over the gnome, 'yes, I did speak to you about shifting this luggage before, but that's not why I am here now.'

'Oh, it's not?'

'No, I've been ordered to seek you out to provide emergency medical attention to this guardsman.'

Eleusia beckoned Antauros forward, and for the first time, the gnome was able to see Torben's bloodied, crumpled body clutched in his arms. He took a step back, nearly tripping over the book on the floor as the colour drained from his face.

'I'm afraid that's impossible,' he stammered. 'We are only supposed to conduct our craft under the strict instructions of the Emperor and no one else…' His voice faded away as a green hue began to spread up his face as he stared at Torben.

'This order does come from the Emperor,' Eleusia snapped, hoping against hope that her bluff would work. 'This guardsman has just returned from the front with vital information that needs relaying to the Imperial Commanders, but he is in no fit state to deliver the message in his current condition. We were ordered to come straight here so that extraordinary medical attention could be given to him.'

The gnome's mouth opened and closed several times before he finally spoke again, 'But this is a highly irregular case…'

'We were led to understand that the Imperial Mage to the Court was specifically trusted with the health of the Emperor and that they are able to use their skills and power to protect and sustain him from all ills.'

'Well, yes, that is true, but the Imperial Mage isn't here!'

'What?' Eleusia's voice cracked slightly as the wind was taken out of her sails.

'The Imperial Mage left with the Emperor on the first evacuation ship to leave from the castle dock.'

'Then who the hell are you?'

'Me? Well…I'm…err, his assistant.'

'Right…' Eleusia paused as she digested this information. 'Well, in that case, you'll have to do. Put him down over there.'

Eleusia gestured to the plump green velvet upholstery of a chaise lounge that stood in front of the fireplace, and Antauros manoeuvred his way across the room to it, one of the guards preceding him and casting the piles of books that occupied it onto the floor to make room. The gnome looked aghast as Antauros' large, heavy boots scatted the detritus that lay in his path and at the fact that they were about to lay Torben, in his wounded, bloodied state, on what was clearly a very expensive piece of furniture.

'Come on then, we haven't got time for gawking!' Eleusia snapped at the gnome, moving to chivvy him towards the chaise lounge.

'But you don't understand,' he protested, 'I don't think I can do what you're asking. I've never done anything like it before.'

'You haven't?' Eleusia had stopped, a crest-fallen look taking hold of her face.

'No, almost all medical magic was performed by the Imperial Mage himself, as I said I'm only his assistant…most of my experience has been decidedly more domestic, lighting fires, cleaning, parlour tricks and the like…' His voice trailed off as the crest-fallen look on Eleusia's face began to contort into one of anger.

'Have you ever tried to heal someone?' Eleusia hissed.

'Yes, but only minor injuries, cuts and scrapes that kind of thing and mostly on myself.'

'Then that's a good enough basis to give it a try now, don't you think?'

The gnome dithered for a moment, unsure of what to do, and then he hurriedly heaved his heavy book off the floor and tottered over to where Torben lay. He nearly changed his mind as Antauros knelt down by the chaise lounge to speak to him, but the momentum the heavy book gave him continued to drag him forward. The minotaur held out a hand to steady him as he staggered forwards and looked at him with a weary, kindly expression.

'What is your name?' Antauros rumbled gently.

'Egberht,' he replied, a slight quaver in his voice.

'Thank you for your help, regardless of the outcome. The boy here is very dear to us, and we value highly anyone who will attempt to help him.'

'Yes, well, try telling that to her,' Egberht shot Eleusia, who was stalking up behind him a dark look.

'Don't mind Eleusia, she is just worried for our friend, she doesn't mean to be harsh or cruel. Do you wish me to help in any way?'

'Emm, yes, if you could hold this book open for me?'

Egberht heaved the huge book into the open hands of the minotaur, who barely registered its heft, and began furiously flicking through the pages until he found the section that he wanted. Then he began to dash around the room, rooting around amongst the piles until he found what he was looking for, a long, polished wooden box with a tightly fitting lid that he pried open to reveal a collection of quills in a multitude of colours. Selecting one, he stuffed the box into a pocket and set his feet apart, readying himself. Ranulf and the guards in the room drew in close so that they could see what was about to happen.

Egberht began to whisper under his breath in a language that none of them could understand until the end of the quill began to glow as a bead of red light formed on its tip, spreading its light to the rest of the object. Still chanting, he began to glance periodically at the book in Antauros' hands as he sketched out a series of symbols in the air that hung unnaturally in space, created from the same light that had appeared at the quill's tip. Sweat began to bead on his forehead and on his bald pate as his face was twisted in concentration. After several minutes of work, six of the intricate symbols hovered in the air above Torben, bathing him in their crimson glow. As he finished drawing the last one, Egberht drew back his left hand that held the quill and raised his right, index and middle finger raised. Taking a deep breath, he stilled his body and then used the two fingers of his right hand to flick each of the symbols in turn onto Torben's body. As they landed on him, they formed a circle around the puncture wound in his abdomen and began to grow brighter and brighter. Egberht tucked the quill behind his ear, took another huge lungful of air and gulped audibly, the sweat from his head now cascading down his face. He looked once more at the book and then began to resume his hushed chanting. Drawing a small knife from his pocket, he held his right hand over Torben, and it quivered nervously in the air as he brought the knife closer to his palm. Closing his eyes, he slashed a small cut in his own palm and then squeezed his hand, sending several thick droplets of blood falling down towards the symbols. As the blood made contact with Torben's body there was a blinding flash of red light, and Torben cried out in pain.

As the vision of everyone in the room recovered from the burst of light, they craned forward to see what had happened. The symbols had disappeared from Torben's chest and had burned their way through the clothing and armour that lay between them and Torben, though the man's skin beneath was unharmed. Equally, the wound had sealed itself up, and in its place was a large angry bruise.

Torben groaned again and opened his eyes groggily. 'Where am I?'

'Gods be praised, it worked!' Antauros clapped Egberht hard on the back, nearly knocking him flat on the floor, but he was caught by Eleusia, who enveloped the gnome in an enormous hug.

'Thank you, thank you!' she choked, tears thick in her voice and wetting Egberht's cheek.

'Quite alright...' The gnome's voice sounded stunned, 'I didn't think that would work, but it did.'

When released from the embrace, Egberht slumped down against the side of the chaise lounge, clearly exhausted from his work.

'Can we move him, will he be alright now?' Antauros asked.

'I think so. According to the book, he'll be stiff, sore, bruised and weakened for days, but the danger has passed and the wound should be fully healed.'

A low whistle sounded through the room as the guard watching the door and the corridor beyond alerted them of someone coming. Ranulf snapped a quick quiet order, and the guards turned to face the door, weapons levelled and bowstrings creaking. A few seconds later, they all relaxed as the all-clear was called and Roswit and the two guards with her appeared in the doorway. They looked out of breath, their drawn swords had blood on them, and one of the accompanying guards had tied a scrap of cloth around their arm, clearly covering a wound beneath.

'What's the situation?' Ranulf strode forward to greet them.

'The basement passage through the old baths is still useable, but we need to move quickly now. Karpella is under siege, just as when we were trapped in the vault! From what we could tell, hostile forces are already moving through the mainland section and are closing in fast on Mid-Isle, we need to get the Princess out of here as quickly as possible.'

'Run into trouble on your way?'

'Aye,' Roswit said grimly, hefting her bloodstained sword,

'the Imperial Guard here will attack us on sight, but we managed to get the better of the ones that we encountered.'

Ranulf turned back to the room. 'Right, you heard Roswit, let's get ready to move out and back to the vault now, before we're trapped here.

As the guards readied themselves, Antauros lifted Torben carefully into his arms once again. Seeing the movement, Egberht looked around confused.

'Wait, did he say we might be trapped in the castle?'

With that, he seemed to regain some energy as he picked himself up and began dashing round the room once more.

'What are you doing?' Ranulf snarled, his hand on the hilt of his dagger.

'Well, I'm not going to sit here and wait for a horde of angry Sharisians to storm in and kill me, or worse! If you lot are taking a chance on getting out of here, then I'm going with you.'

Before Ranulf could react, Eleusia appeared at his side and whispered in his ear.

'You saw what he did to Torben, he will be very useful to us. Especially if he comes willingly. I'm sure your Princess will value having someone like him as another hostage, and given he's just saved my friend from the brink, I'd advise against doing anything stupid that might hurt him, lest you want to test how handy me and my friend here are in a scrap, even unarmed...' Eleusia inclined her head towards Antauros, who, picking up on the tone of the conversation, tossed his horn menacingly.

Ranulf's hand left the hilt of his dagger. 'Fine, he comes with us. There is a logic to what you're saying.'

'Good.'

As Eleusia withdrew from Ranulf, Egberht was hauling a large, thick leather pack onto his back, the inside of which was completely taken up by the enormous book he had used to heal Torben. Several other book-shaped packages wrapped in oilskin were strapped to the outside of the pack, and he wore a satchel on his front that looked full to bursting.

'Right, lead on!' he said, looking up expectantly at Ranulf and the others.

With a derisive snort, Ranulf began to lead the group out of the room at a jog, the guards falling into place before and behind Eleusia, Antauros and Egberht.

As the gnome scuttled along next to Eleusia, he turned his now crimson face up to her and asked, 'Which unit of the army are this lot from, by the way? They don't look like Imperials as you do, are they from a regiment from outside of the city?'

'You could say that... perhaps it's best if I explain later.'

4

For Gwilym, the wait for Eleusia, Antauros and, hopefully, Torben to return was excruciating. He had returned to his position, perched on the foot of the altar and watched Princess Theodora's troops move to and fro around the antechamber. There was a sense of nervous excitement in the air amongst the soldiers, who occupied themselves checking over their equipment and supplies and talking quietly amongst themselves. Each of them now bore two bulging money pouches secreted about their person, one for themselves and one that was part of the Princess' collective pool of resources for the journey ahead. Gwilym was astounded by the trust the Princess was placing in her troops. Pretty much every other soldier, conscript or man-at-arms he had come across would already be categorically denying ever having been given a second purse in the first place, or would be thinking of how best to lift funds from the common purse without being detected. The cacophonous sound of clinking metal resonated around the antechamber as another group of soldiers, just inside the vault, filled two small strong boxes with coins and jewels that they scooped up from the floor in their helmets.

The dwarf's mind turned to Torben again as he let the

activity around him fade into soft focus. He had no idea what was happening above them; he just had to trust that Eleusia's hunch was right and that the fellow they'd gone off to seek would actually be able to save their friend.

It should have been me that Hrex cursed, Gwilym thought. *If Torben hadn't been woken up when he did, it probably would have been me that bore the brunt of it rather than him...* He pondered for a moment. *First, Torben ends up being stuck in a dead-end halfway up the creek to nowhere, then he gets mixed up with me, then everything that he knows in the world is destroyed, then with Björn, Hrex and all of this bollocks... damned run of bad luck if ever there was one! Then again, if the lad made it through this, then the prognosis going forwards isn't much better. Who knows where we'll be dragged off to by this lot, how long they'll keep us hostage for or what we might be forced into doing. Still, I'd rather that and for us all to be alive...*

His train of thought was broken as one of the Princess' guards dumped four fat purses at his feet and then retired as Theodora and Captain Almar approached him.

'What's all this? Gwilym asked, gesturing at the purses, which were clearly straining at the seams.

'Let's call it compensation for the time that you and your companions will be acting as our guides,' Theodora said.

'Well, at least we'll come out of this with something...' Gwilym muttered darkly.

'As soon as those above ground return with your friend, we will like as not need to move out quickly,' she continued, ignoring Gwilym's interjection.

'If things do not go well up there,' Gwilym responded, 'then will you at least give the three of us some time to pay our respects?'

'Of course, though I'm sure it won't come to that.'

'What makes you so *sure*?' he sneered. 'I'm sure you must have been taught much in your cosy study sessions under the tutelage of a doubtless highly regarded and qualified teacher, but

I'm still sure that you are not qualified to give an accurate outlook on Torben's likelihood of survival!'

As the dwarf glowered up from his seat and spat out his words at Princess Theodora, Captain Almar began to move forward, his hand clenched into a fist, making straight for Gwilym.

'Impudent wretch, how dare you address Her Highness in that manner!'

Before he could take more than a couple of steps, Theodora held up her hand and stopped him.

'It's quite all right, Almar.' She turned and addressed Gwilym again. 'I meant no offence, nor did I wish to imply that I had more knowledge of the situation than you. What I meant was that if Eleusia has managed to track down a member of the court who is able to wield the arcane arts and can convince them to tend to your friend, then you need not worry. I have seen many brought back from the brink by the skilled application of the arcane, including my own father.'

'Yes, well, that sort of thing is much rarer now, and by all accounts less potent...'

Before the words had even left Gwilym's mouth, he was already beginning to doubt the formula that had begun to roll off his tongue. After all that he had seen lately, he was beginning to wonder whether this was even true, or whether there was something else going on beneath the surface.

The low whistle sounded through the antechamber as the guards at the foot of the stairs issued the warning that someone was coming down into the vault. The guards, who had been quietly going about their business, began to scramble to the ready, but they hadn't moved much before a louder whistle came echoing down from the stairs, a response to the initial alarm.

'That's the patrol returning,' Captain Almar said, having turned around to assess the situation.

Immediately, everyone in the room relaxed, but they still moved to congregate in the middle of the space, keen to hear the news that the scouts would bring, along with a morbid curiosity to learn what had happened to Torben. As Princess Theodora turned on her heel to meet the returning party, Captain Almar ahead of her clearing the way through the mass of her guards, Gwilym leapt up and followed. He could hear the guards talking amongst themselves around him as he passed through, but he could not see anything beyond the sea of armoured legs and torsos.

When he emerged from the gaggle behind Princess Theodora, he was directly in front of the entrance to the stairs, and he could see Ranulf, who looked flushed and out of breath reporting to his Princess and Captain Almar. He was only accompanied by two other soldiers, who likewise looked like they had sprinted to get there. The other soldiers gathered behind quietened down as Ranulf snapped to attention and saluted his superiors before reporting the situation.

'Your Highness, the situation is as the dwarf said, much has changed since we came down here.'

Beckoning to one of the two guards that stood behind him, Ranulf took the bundle of items that they had been holding. Unwrapping it, he passed a leather-bound book, an unrolled letter and the bundle itself, which looked as if it was the tattered remains of a flag, one by one to Captain Almar and Princess Theodora for examination.

'There are banners all over the castle and across the city bearing the arms of Dazscor alongside those of the enemy of your noble house, and the soldiers that we encountered all bear the sign as well. Likewise, the Joint Kingdom of Dazscor & Aramore is mentioned in some official documentation that we found,' Ranulf gestured at the letter that the Princess was pouring over, 'and the signatory is named as Emperor Hastel I, alongside his personal seal, which looks as official as anything that was ever issued by your father. The book,' Ranulf indicated the tome that Captain Almar had opened; he was leafing through the pages and pages of numbers, trying to make sense of it, 'is an account book that puts the current date at 553.'

'553?' Theodora's eyes shot up from the page she was scrutinising to stare directly into Ranulf's. 'Then we have been down here for as long as Gwilym told us...'

'That is not all, Your Highness, the situation on the surface is far from peaceful. It would appear that the city is under siege, just as it was when we first came down here all those years ago, though this time the force carries the white horse of Sharisar. There is fierce fighting going on around the bridges to Mid-Isle, and unless we move now, there is a significant risk that we will be trapped here.'

'Have you scouted out the escape passages?' Captain Almar asked, concern evident in his voice.

'Not all of them, sir, we didn't have time, but we do know that the passage to Mid-Isle is still accessible and passable.'

'Hmm,' Almar thought for a second, 'that would bring us out near the East Docks safe house, which would give us ample options for deciding where to move out next...'

'Where is the rest of your contingent, Ranulf? You didn't run into any trouble, did you?' Theodora asked.

'We did, but we were able to resolve the situation quickly, only one minor wound, and my troops ensured that the people they ran into were not able to raise the alarm. I sent the rest of the patrol to wait just inside the tunnel for us to arrive. As the situation demands us to move quickly with as minimal disturbance as possible, I wanted to minimise the risk of us being discovered by the forces now occupying the castle.'

'That's perfectly sensible, Ranulf. What of Gwilym's companions and the boy?'

'They are with the rest of my troops in the tunnel awaiting us.'

Hearing mention of Torben, Gwilym surged forward, elbowing a surprised and angered Captain Almar out of the way so that he could get right in front of Ranulf.

'What does that mean? Is Torben alive?'

'Yes...' Gwilym's sudden appearance and the angry, desperate expression on his face put Ranulf momentarily off his stride. 'Yes, he is alive. The mage that Eleusia took us to was able to save his life. He is still weak, but by all accounts, he will recover well. That's another thing, Your Highness. The mage has agreed to travel with us in exchange for us getting him out of the city...'

Gwilym let the rest of Ranulf's report wash over him as he was overwhelmed by relief. Torben was alive! He was brought out of his reverie by Captain Almar, who jabbed him, slightly harder than necessary, on the shoulder.

'Grab your things, dwarf, we're leaving, now!'

Casting a dirty look in Almar's direction and muttering something less than flattering under his breath, Gwilym padded back to the foot of the altar to gather his things. He scooped up the money pouches and stuffed two into his pack and two into Torben's pack, which had been discarded on the floor nearby. The gold within made them feel much heavier, a sensation which Gwilym would normally have been gleeful at the thought of, but which was lost on him in the whirlwind of the moment.

As he shifted the weight of his pack on his back and tried to find the most convenient way to carry Torben's as well, he saw Almar, who was in conversation with Ranulf and the two guards from his scouting party, gesture towards him, and Ranulf and his two men trotted over to Gwilym and formed around him. Clearly Almar was taking no chances, and they were to be his escort. They ushered him forwards as the mass of men and women in the antechamber readied to move on. After casting a quick, critical eye over the troops, Almar nodded to Princess Theodora and the order was given to move out.

When Torben finally came fully back into consciousness, the air around him felt cold and damp, not like the stuffy atmosphere of the vault, where he last remembered being. He shivered involuntarily as the memory forced itself to the front of his mind of Hrex staring wickedly up at him as she drove her dagger home, the memory of the piercing, agonising pain as it had punched into his belly. That pain had now dulled to an ache that barely troubled his consciousness.

Am I dead? he thought.

Everything was pitch black, but then the realisation occurred to him that his eyes were shut. Indeed, he was slowly becoming aware of the rest of his body, as if his mind had stepped away from his corporeal form for a moment and was only now returning to take stock of his physical vessel. As well as becoming aware of the myriad sensations throughout his body: the regular beating of his heart, the expansion and contraction of his lungs, the flow of blood through his veins; other images began to flit across his consciousness.

He saw the treasure vault again, the sea of coins and jewels stretching out as far as the eye could see; saw Hrex and a tall, pale figure standing at the altar, a swirling mass of green-blue arcane energy swirling around them; a flash of red light, accompanied by strange chanting in a voice he did not recognise; Hrex helping the pale figure into a decrepit looking chair. He didn't know where these images had come from, what they meant, or even if they were real or just figments of his imagination.

He could hear a whispering in his ears that must have been people talking quietly somewhere nearby. He thought he could recognise Antauros' deep rumble, but the words themselves made no sense to him, no matter how hard he tried to focus on them. Then, his whole body was shocked as something cold and wet smacked onto his forehead. He opened his eyes and took in a loud, involuntary breath in reaction to the sensation.

Water dripped from the ceiling of the low, dark tunnel where he had been laid with his back up against one of the curving walls. There was little light save for the flickering of a half-concealed lantern several feet away, whose glow was obstructed by the dark shadows of what seemed like several bodies that were between it and Torben. As he lifted a shaky hand to wipe the large, reviving drop of water from his forehead, the enormous shadow to his right moved, clearly alerted to his consciousness by the movement and his shocked cry, and as it turned, the weak lantern light framed the curving horns of Antauros above the head.

'Torben, you're awake!' The minotaur's voice was hushed, but there was still a clear sense of joy colouring the words.

There was a scrabbling noise from the opposite side of the tunnel. Torben was suddenly aware of another presence now on his left, Eleusia, who took his hand and squeezed it as Antauros' massive hand enveloped his right shoulder.

'How do you feel?' Eleusia's voice was also hushed.

'I've felt better,' Torben said, wincing as he placed a hand on where the knife wound had been.

He couldn't feel a wound there anymore, nor could he feel any bandages or bindings that he had expected to find there, but the broken and bent armour scales and the torn clothing still showed clearly where the wound had been, as did the dried blood that had crusted onto the fabric and metal. Despite there no longer being an open wound there, it still felt incredibly tender when he laid a hand on it.

'Where are we?' he asked, trying to get his bearings. 'Why is it so dark?'

'We're in a tunnel that leads out of Karpella Castle to somewhere on the Mid-Isle,' Eleusia had leaned right in and was whispering close to Torben's ear. 'I won't lie to you, we're in a tight spot. Turns out there were other people who were trapped in the vault with Hrex's master, one of whom is the daughter of Sarper IV no less, and she and her guards are insisting we accompany them for the time being, until when, I don't know…'

'Wait, so we're prisoners then?'

'To all intents and purposes, yes.'

Before Torben could ask another question, the shadows further up the tunnel, which Torben now guessed were some of the guards Eleusia had spoken about, began to stand. He could see more flickering light creeping along the ceiling of the tunnel, adding to that of the solitary lantern.

'Come on now, let's get you up.'

Antauros' huge hands helped Torben to his feet, and the young man winced as his stomach muscles contracted painfully around the wound site. His legs felt weak, and he had to lean on Antauros for support, but as the minotaur moved to lift him into his arms, he waved his hand to stop him.

'It's alright, I can walk, I'll just need a bit of support is all, I don't need to be carried.'

'As you wish,' Antauros replied, 'but let me know if you feel your strength failing.'

Pressing themselves against the wall of the tunnel, Torben, Antauros and Eleusia let the stream of armoured men and women that made up Princess Theodora's retinue hurry past them. When Princess Theodora herself and Captain Almar passed by, Almar looked back and sharply whispered to them over his shoulder.

'Fall in with your friend the dwarf.'

A couple of seconds later, a gap in the line appeared, where Gwilym's smaller figure walked. Ranulf, who was walking ahead of him, ordered the guards following to pause slightly so that they could join the column. As they stepped into the line, the even more diminutive Egberht was thrust into the formation as well from the spot where he had been napping against the wall. He rubbed his bleary eyes confusedly as he was chivvied along by those around him.

Torben didn't remember much of the journey through that tunnel. The blank expanse of slimy walls all around them were practically impossible to tell apart, and the only indication that they weren't just constantly walking through the same section again and again was the fact that the tunnel bowed down deeper underground before bowing back up again as they neared the surface. In what must have been the very middle of the tunnel and the deepest section, the column had to wade through knee-high water that was icy cold. Clearly the passage of the river above was taking its toll on the fabric of the tunnel.

Eventually, natural light began to spill down into the darkness, and a breeze from the outside world drifted down, tousling Torben's hair and helping revive him a little from the exertion of the walk. His wound had become more painful as they traveled, and he felt weak. For the last part of the journey, Antauros had laid a steadying hand on his shoulder, encouraging him on and helping to keep him upright. With the appearance of the light, the column stopped, and they silently awaited further instruction. Ahead, Torben could just about see the side of Gwilym's face as the dwarf, who had yet to actually speak to him because of his place in the column and the relentless pace of the march, as he tried to check whether Torben was alright.

Slowly a whispered order was relayed down the column, 'The column will move at the double, in formation centred on the Princess. We make for the East Docks safe house.'

Another moment of waiting as the order reached the end of the line, and then they surged forwards into the daylight. Torben managed to make the rest of the climb through the tunnel as a shambling jog, but as he reached the top, his weakened legs finally gave way. He would have fallen flat on his face had Antauros not scooped him up and flung him over one of his massive shoulders to be carried along into the city.

They had emerged onto a shabby looking street, whose cobbles were broken and uneven, that was lined with decrepit looking wooden houses sagging under the weight of their roofs. A couple of streets away, the more opulent, stone-built, commercial buildings of the East Docks could be seen towering over the lines of tenements behind, screening them off from the rest of

Mid-Isle. Clearly this was a place where the dockworkers lived, a place that the port authorities and rich merchants who plied their trade there did not want to acknowledge existed. From his position on Antauros' back, Torben saw the last of the guards close the door to the tunnel they had travelled through. The door was lined on the outside with worn bricks, and it blended seamlessly into the wall it was built into and disappeared from sight.

Despite being a heavily residential area, the street was intensely quiet as they jogged along. Many of the buildings looked practically abandoned, their doors swinging in the breeze rolling off the nearby River Arlen, whilst some looked as if their occupants had done everything they could to secure their homes before fleeing, hoping that they would still be intact and habitable when they returned. Clearly, none of the people who lived there expected the City Guard to prioritise the protection of the area against the Sharisians, and they had fled in hopes of finding refuge in a more defensible part of the city.

They made quick headway through the empty streets, with the guards forming into a tight-knit group, with Princess Theodora and Captain Almar at the centre. Not far behind them, but separated from them by a line of soldiers, were Gwilym, Eleusia, Antauros, Torben and Egberht. The street followed the curve of the island until the line of houses on their right disappeared, giving way to a narrow waterfront space that overlooked the river, with the houses that now appeared on their left becoming more refined stone dwellings. Ahead of them, jutting out into the river, was a large warehouse that had been built on a sturdy stone platform, whose foundations were built into the river bed, and which looked as if it would have been able to be used as a large basement for the building on top. As the building came into view, the pace of the formation picked up, eager to reach the building that Torben supposed must be the safe house.

However, as they drew closer, figures started to appear on the waterfront beyond the warehouse, climbing up from the river onto the street. They wore scale mail and hood-like helmets that almost completely enclosed their faces, with upright horse-hair plumes that looked like high ponytails near the crown of their heads. They already had their weapons drawn, and the curved blades of their scimitars glinted in the sun, as did the tips of the arrows that were knocked to the strings of their elaborate re-curved bows. The large, rectangular shields some of them carried were emblazoned with the symbol of a white horse with a golden mane on a crimson backdrop.

Both groups spotted each other at the same time, and as the troops climbing up from the river began to scramble into a semblance of a formation, Princess Theodora turned to her hostages.

'Who are they, can they be reasoned with?'

'Unlikely,' Antauros said quickly. 'They're Sharisian troops, part of the besieging force, and therefore, they'll probably assume we're City Guard...'

Before Antauros could elaborate further, the clattering of arrows skittering across the cobbles along with the thunk of several hitting shields sounded as the Sharisian troops opened fire and began to advance quickly along the street towards them. Princess Theodora's troops instinctively tightened their forma-tion, forming a shield wall that stretched across the street, the guards further back raising their shields above their heads to deflect incoming fire, whilst several others at the back readied their own bows to return fire. From the front of the formation, Captain Almar issued several barked orders, and the soldiers braced themselves for the expected impact, whilst those at the back began to fire over the top of the others, hoping to disrupt and slow the Sharisians bearing down on them.

Inside the shield shell, Torben couldn't see anything of what was going on. Antauros, who still had Torben on his shoulder, had knelt down and bowed his head so that the carapace of shields could extend over the top and protect them from the incoming projectiles. As he looked groggily around, Torben could see the men and women of Theodora's guard standing resolute and firm, each one supporting the soldier in front. Then they were shoved back as the Sharisians attacking them hit the formation and tried to break in. Captain Almar barked another order, and they all began to inch forwards. There were cries of pain and frustration from beyond the first rank of the shield wall as their attackers tried in vain to breach it but were beginning to be driven back. As they trundled forwards, the mass of bodies began to pick up speed as they forced the Sharisians back still further.

'Easy now, wait for it, they're wavering,' Captain Almar's voice sounded out, calm and soothing, then changed to a bellow of rage, 'Now!'

On his order the shield wall broke apart as the Princess' guards charged forwards, scattering the Sharisians in their wake. As the covering of shields disappeared, Antauros straightened up, and Torben could see that they had managed to push their way to the side of the warehouse. Beyond, the Sharisians were in full retreat, with a number of them lying dead on the ground and several others running for their lives, clutching their wounds tightly.

'This way, Your Highness.' Ranulf ushered Theodora down the side of the warehouse, where a thin dirt slope led from the street above along the wall of the basement and down to the river's waters. 'You lot, come along as well!'

Antauros, Torben, Gwilym, Eleusia and Egberht were shepherded down the slope by the guards, who had held themselves back from the onslaught to protect Theodora and mind their hostages. At the bottom of the slope, Ranulf carefully ran his hands along the stonework, counting down the stones until he found the one he needed. He pressed his palm against it, popping the stone half out of the wall, and then used it as a handle to haul open a hidden door in the stonework to the basement beyond.

'Just brilliant, going underground again!' Antauros muttered as they were escorted into the gloom beyond.

5

For a moment, Torben felt as if he were entering a black hole as he was carried into the basement by Antauros. He was blinded by the light streaming through the doorway. As Antauros set him down on his own two feet, the darkness swallowed him, and for a moment, he felt like he was back in the vault under Karpella castle. His heart began pounding, and his head snapped from side to side, expecting to see Hrex bearing down on him, the dagger held in her gnarled, taloned hand. Then, pinpricks of illumination appeared around the space, growing stronger and stronger as the lanterns they belonged to were sparked into life. As the room they were in was slowly revealed, Torben's heart began to slow back down to its regular rhythm, soothed by the light dispelling the demons of his mind.

The basement was an enormous space, tall enough even for Antauros to stand upright in, that completely matched the footprint of the warehouse above, though there was no obvious way to gain direct access to it. Brick pillars supporting the rest of the building above broke up the space at regular intervals, and the room was split over two levels. The higher level where they had entered was rammed full of neatly organised crates and boxes, whilst the lower level had been made into a boathouse, where four large rowing boats were suspended above strips of water. Though the access to the River Arlen beyond was not obvious – it looked to Torben like a solid stone wall lay between the boats and the waterway – he guessed that there must be a set of doors, like the one they had passed through that would allow the boats out.

Torben and his friends were chivvied further into the room as the guard who was keeping watch through the crack in the door threw the portal fully open, and the sound of massed movement could be heard on the street above and the strip of dirt leading down to the basement entrance. As they were pushed back into one of the pillared walkways lined floor to ceiling with packing cases, Torben could hear Gwilym complaining bitterly as he was pressed against the back wall by the mass of bodies trying to fit into the space.

'Stop squirming, will you, this is uncomfortable enough as it is!' Eleusia chided.

'You think you're uncomfortable! My face is going to get a permanent stone effect pattern on it soon if I don't get some more space.'

Fortunately for Torben, he was at the end of the space, with a clear view of what was happening in the rest of the room. He leant against Antauros, who was behind him for support, and he could feel the minotaur's chuckle vibrating through his chest as he listened to Gwilym complain. He stood up straighter as the main body of the Princess' guards returned, filing through the door and spreading out into every corner of the room, as there was not a big enough space for them all to congregate in. The majority of them still looked fresh and alert, but several of them appeared to have picked up injuries in the skirmish and were sat down on some makeshift benches fashioned from boxes to be examined by the medics. Last to enter was Captain Almar, who closed and locked the door to the room behind him, sealing them in the basement. Spotting Theodora, he made his way over to the Princess, who was moving amongst her troops, commending them for their efforts.

'All clear?'

'Yes, Your Highness. We killed most of them and drove the survivors back to their boats. None of them saw us come inside.'

'Excellent, at least one thing seems to have gone our way...'

Theodora sat down heavily on a nearby box and sighed deeply.

'Now comes the hard part, where we have to work out where to go and what to do,' she said despondently.

'Well, if nothing else, we know that Aristotles is alive, even if we don't exactly know where to find him,' Almar answered. 'He was a sworn member of your father's court, and I'm sure that he will honour that commitment to you. After all, it's as much in his interests as it is in ours, given that he is in the same boat as us.'

'Hmm... Bring the dwarf and his companions here, they might be able to give us some more information.'

Captain Almar turned and snapped his fingers at two nearby guards, who made their way to where the friends were corralled in their corner. Gwilym breathed a heavy sigh of relief as they began to edge out of the confined space, and once he was back in the room proper, he spread his arms and stretched widely before trotting after the others who had been escorted into the Princess' presence. Easing his way past Antauros' bulk and the nervously fidgeting Egberht, he took up a position at the front of the group and curtly nodded his head, as much of a formal greeting as Theodora would get out of him. Ignoring the dwarf's aggressive head bob, Princess Theodora looked at Torben, a not unkindly look on her face.

'How are you feeling? Please do feel free to sit down if your strength has not returned.'

'Thank you, but I'm happy to stand for the moment, miss, err, I mean, Your Highness...' As Torben stumbled over the acknowledgement of her station, his face flushed red, banishing the deathly pallor that the wound had brought to his cheeks.

'As you wish.' Theodora turned her gaze to encompass all five of them. 'I would like to thank you all for being cooperative so far…'

'Cooperative?' Gwilym butted in. 'I didn't realise that being dragged around the city by our collars was our own decision. As far as we're concerned, it was either be *cooperative* or be dead!'

'Well, I wasn't going to put too fine a point on it, but that is essentially correct, yes.' Theodora regarded Gwilym with a thin smile. 'As I intimated in the vault, we do not know which of our enemies may still exist, or who might wish to profit from discovering the news that the daughter of Sarper IV still lives. Until we are satisfied that we are safe from immediate danger, I politely request that the five of you accompany us for the time being. As I mentioned, you will be amply rewarded for your services once they are no longer required, as your initial payment should indicate.'

'Initial payment?' Eleusia queried.

'Oh, yes, I'll distribute it later,' Gwilym muttered sheepishly.

'Now,' Theodora continued, 'the faster we get somewhere safe, the faster you will be released from servitude, and a far as I am concerned, the only safe place for us at the moment is with the Royal Mage to the Court of Sarper IV, Aristotles, Hrex's master, so will you kindly go over the details of the agreement you had with her to access the vault?'

'I wouldn't exactly call it an agreement!' Torben spat. 'If we hadn't done what she wanted, she would have killed me, and even when we did follow her orders, she tried to kill me.'

Antauros put a hand on Torben's shoulder to try and calm him down. Princess Theodora stayed silent for a moment to allow Torben's temper to cool before continuing.

'Did she ever mention where she was intending to take Aristotles once you gained access to the vault?'

'No,' Gwilym said, 'she was very careful not to tell us what her intentions were afterwards, partly I imagine because she knew that in order to open the cursed thing, she would have to kill one of us and that the rest of us would likely be after her blood afterwards.'

'Damn right,' Eleusia growled from behind Gwilym.

'Wherever she's gone, we haven't the foggiest,' the dwarf continued. 'As I said before, she used her foul sorcery to just vanish with him, she could be anywhere.'

'Well, that's not strictly true...'

Egberht shuffled awkwardly forwards and looked up at the others as he continued to nervously worry the sleeve of his robe. He had divested himself of his overly large pack and tightly stuffed satchel, which made him look even more diminutive in size. Though clearly still confused about what exactly was going on around him, the ingrained years of living and working in a royal court still held sway over him, and he bowed to Princess Theodora much more respectfully than Gwilym had and then cleared his throat before speaking.

'I believe that it is only possible to use teleportation spells to travel to a location that you have already been to, and in general, those who can will really only ever teleport to a place that they can visualise very well, as the risk of being injured when appearing at the destination is quite high. As it is a highly complex spell to cast, especially under pressure, only a handful of High Mages would attempt to cast it without weeks of preparation.'

'Well, in that case, Your Highness, I would suggest that there is one obvious place that Hrex would take Aristotles, his country residence outside of the village of Haltwic.' Almar had leaned in to speak more discretely in Theodora's ear; nonetheless, his voice carried loud enough for the others to hear. 'Hrex will know the location well, or well enough to take a gamble on travelling there, I'd warrant, even if it has changed over the years. Even if they aren't there right now, it wouldn't surprise me if they attempt to travel there, so I think it would be wise to set our sights on travelling there too. If nothing else, it gives us a concrete destination to aim for and gets us out of Karpella. What little I've seen of the current defensive situation here, I haven't liked, we're at too much risk of being caught in the crossfire, and we can't stay down here forever. The faster we can find Aristotles and Hrex and get their advice, the better!'

'After what Hrex has done, you're just going to let bygones be bygones and pal up with her?' Torben's eyes flashed dangerously as he spoke, and he took an unsteady step forwards. 'If you ask me, she doesn't give a toss about you lot; otherwise, she would have stuck around to make sure you were all all right, wouldn't she?'

'Hrex will answer for her actions at the appropriate time, but for now, that is not our primary concern.' Princess Theodora said forcefully. 'My apologies Torben for what you have been through, but you will be adequately reimbursed when the time is right. Now I suggest you rest before we get underway, we will have a long journey ahead of us.' Turning to Captain Almar, she continued, 'I want an assessment of the condition of the wounded, an overview of our supplies along with the salvaging of as much material as we can get and carry from what is in here. We should be ready to leave at nightfall.'

'That's seriously your last word on the matter?' Torben had taken another step closer to Princess Theodora and Captain Almar, and he jabbed his finger viciously at her as he spoke, flecks of spittle flying from his mouth as he barely contained his anger. 'I nearly died so you could be free, died for someone I'd never heard of, who is apparently willing to take my life for granted, and all you want to do is throw money at the situation. All you care about is preserving your own hide! I thought as a *princess*, you were supposed to be duty-bound to think of those around you rather than just yourself. But it looks as if you'd make just as shit a ruler as your father…'

'As I said, you should all get some rest, you especially so Torben.' The Princess spoke with a cold, steely edge to her voice as she barely turned her head to look at Torben. 'Almar, find them a place where they will not get in the way.'

Almar advanced on Torben, several of the Princess' other guards drifting into step behind him. He looked Torben squarely in the eyes and prodded him in the chest.

'You heard Her Highness, get moving, whelp.'

For a second, Torben stood, squared up to Almar and met the shorter man's gaze. The look in the Captain's eyes held an evil glint, as if wordlessly challenging Torben to resist. The room around them had become deathly quiet, and all of the guards on both levels had their eyes trained on the group. Torben clenched his fist tightly, and then relaxed. He knew better than to start a fight they couldn't win. Almar grinned as Torben turned on his heel and was escorted back to a space on the lower level that had been prepared for them to sit in. A wall of boxes had been set up in the corner formed by the outer wall and wall where the room dropped down to the lower level. It had the unmistakable air of a makeshift prison. They didn't complain, however, as they were ushered in; it was far roomier than the tight space they had been squeezed into before. On Captain Almar's orders, two guards took up their stations at the open entrance to the corral, whilst the Captain himself moved off to begin executing the rest of the Princess' orders.

Torben winced as he began to ease himself down to the floor. Eleusia appeared at his side to help him down.

'Easy now, Torben,' she said. 'You need to take it slow. You're out of the woods, but they're still on the horizon.'

'Eergh, well, I've certainly felt better.' He turned to look at Egberht, who deposited his heavy bag on the floor and was using his rucksack as a seat. 'Thank you for your help. By the sounds of it, I wouldn't be here if it wasn't for you.'

'That's quite alright,' the gnome smiled, 'the manner of asking was a bit more brusque than I am used to, though I'm glad to have been of assistance, nonetheless. I will admit, though, this is not quite what I imagined when I decided to accompany you out of the castle.'

'Don't worry,' Antauros chipped in, 'it's not what we imagined either!'

There was a moment of silence as they enjoyed being still, even if it meant sitting on a cold, slightly damp stone floor, and internally took stock of their situation.

'So, what's the plan then?' Gwilym had sat up and leaned towards the others, lowering his voice so that the nearby guards wouldn't be able to hear.

'You heard her,' Torben muttered bitterly, 'we go with them to find a murderous loon and her potentially even more insane master, which we do either of our own volition or trussed like hogs, or they kill us and dump our bodies in the river, weighed down no doubt with the hush money they intended to pay us when we're no longer needed.'

'You know what I mean, Torben! Get your head back in the game, it's not over yet. We could try our luck and make a break for it now, but without weapons and with so many of them around, we'd need every single deity there is on our side and pushing down on our end of the scale, or we could try and make our escape once we're on the river...'

'Or we could just wait until we land wherever it is they're taking us to and re-assess the situation there,' Antauros chipped in. 'I'm not going to lie, but the outlook of making an escape now or in the middle of the Arlen does not bode overly favourable with me.'

'Or better yet, we could just go along for the ride? I don't know about you,' Eleusia looked from one to other as she spoke, 'but I'd be quite keen to know what's going on here. Why did Hrex just leave a member of the family she was supposed to serve down in the vault? And, after all, what's so important about this Aristotles that means she was willing to wait for hundreds of years to rescue him? What does she think she's going to get out of it, and what is he actually up to that she didn't just write him off as dead when he was sealed in the vault in the first place?'

71

'Well, I don't know about you lot,' Torben said, shifting his position against the wall, 'but I'm far too tired and sore to try doing anything more than sitting on my arse, either here or in a boat, for the time-being.'

He hooked his foot into one of the straps of his pack and dragged it towards him. He extricated his leather overcoat, which had been rolled up tightly and strapped to the top flap, draping it over himself to keep out the chill that hung in the room. He let his head fall gently back against the wall, his eyes half closing as he acknowledged how exhausted he truly was.

'I'm fascinated to hear more about the enchantment on the vault...' Egberht had clearly not been paying attention to the conversation but had been lost in his own little world. 'Tell me, what exactly did this Hrex need to open the vault?'

Antauros, Gwilym and Eleusia looked at one another and then at the gnome, surprised that he seemed rather unconcerned with their current predicament. Torben's eyes were now pretty much closed. Clearly, he wasn't going to contribute an answer to the question.

'She needed an object called the Keystone and...' Gwilym paused, 'she needed blood, a fair amount of it, which is why our friend there was brought to you like a stuck pig.'

'Hmm, interesting... And what was this Keystone like?'

'A round flat metal disc made of silver, about yay big,' Gwilym cupped his hands to indicate the size, 'covered in symbols and squiggles, not of any tongue that we recognised, and around the edge was a serpent.'

'Could you describe any of the symbols? What about the serpent, how was it depicted?'

'The serpent was eating its own tail, but as for the gibberish written all over it, I couldn't even begin to describe any of that to you.'

'Why does any of this matter?' Eleusia butted in.

'The way in which people cast spells and the manner of materials that they need can tell you a lot about the nature of the magic being summoned, it's strength, longevity, type, and the possible effects it will cause. For instance, the fact that this magic that Hrex cast needed a stabilising object, in this case the Keystone, and a significant amount of sacrificial matter to remove it, indicates that this was meant to be an incredibly powerful spell that was intended to last a long time.'

'Tell us something we don't know.' Gwilym half-rolled his eyes as he spoke.

'My point,' Egberht cast a withering glance towards the dwarf, 'is that a spell that needed all of these components and that was powerful enough to not only seal the vault, but to suspend anyone caught inside so that they can be essentially reanimated, with no perceivable ill effects when they are released, must have had additional support from something other than the caster.' Egberht waved his hands vaguely in the air above his head as he finished speaking.

'What, you mean help from the gods?' Antauros almost whispered the words, as if he was afraid of being struck down.

'Potentially, though without having seen the spell for myself, it's had to say. The amount of raw power that would have been required to cast something of that magnitude might indicate that additional help was provided by otherworldly beings.'

'Who do you think that being could have been?' Antauros' voice was still hushed.

'Hard to say without knowing what the symbols and writing on the associated items was. A snake is a fairly common symbol, but one devouring its own tail, that rings a bell...'

Despite his eyes being closed, Torben had roused himself from his drowsiness and had clearly been listening to the conversation as he raised his head from the wall and looked at the others.

'What I don't understand is whether or not I should be looking over my shoulder constantly for fear of being jumped by another witch, mage or whatever. First, I hear that magic users are all but extinct, then that there are some in hiding and then that there's at least one in every court and affluent household! So what is the truth, Egberht?'

'Well...' Egberht looked around nervously, even going so far as to try and peek over the boxes at his back. 'I'm not really supposed to say.'

'What are you worried about?' Eleusia asked. 'Let's face it, Egberht, we may not get out of this situation alive as it is, so you telling us something you're supposed to keep under wraps is very unlikely to get you in trouble.'

'Yes, but...'

'What exactly are you afraid of?'

'The Collective have spies everywhere!'

'Who?'

'Oh, fine!'

Egberht stood up from his makeshift chair and crept into the centre of the corral so that he could talk to the other four with as low a voice as possible.

'There never was a loss of magic, or however you might have heard it referred to, but there was a consolidation. Originally anyone who was deemed to be magically sensitive could be trained in the arcane arts provided that their potential was discovered and that a teacher could be found for them. That all began to change in the year 327. The government of Zhisbon was overthrown by a large group of powerful sorcerers, who took control over the country and began to govern it themselves. These sorcerers were the Elders' Council of the Academy of Arcanology in the city of Harbotha, right on the border between Zhisbon and the Sultanate of Fashaddon and a group of more powerful magic users you would be hard-pressed to assemble. This group formed themselves into the Collective of Arcanologists, and members of the Collective have ruled the nation ever since.

'Zhisbon has always been a rich training ground of magic users. The Sahal who first settled the area are naturally some of the most magically sensitive creatures in the whole of Ulskandar, and it is the only place in the world where there is a well-established, and crucially legal, place to educate people in the arcane arts, Harbotha's Academy of Arcanology. Mages, wizards, sorcerers and what have you that were educated in Zhisbon were always much more highly in demand from those who could afford their services, and the Collective began to use that to their advantage.

'After seizing control of Zhisbon, they began to exert pressure on other nations, not just on this continent of Turoza, but across Ulskandar. Their demand was that only magic users who were members of the Collective of Arcanologists should be recognised as legitimate and that anyone who practiced the arcane arts who was not trained in Harbotha, or who did not agree to join the Collective and be "re-educated," should be cast out and branded as a criminal. In addition, they also demanded the right to send groups of agents, known as Inquisitors, wherever they so choose to root out non-complying magic users, and either force them to conform or kill them.

'As you can imagine, this didn't go down too well with any other nation at first, but the Collective managed to find ways to persuade them. I do not know for certain, as all of the Collective's activities during their ascendance are shrouded in deep secrecy, but I have heard that they stopped at nothing in order to get what they wanted. Rumour has it that a whole raft of assassinations of high-ranking officials and nobility, spanning nearly every single country and kingdom, were carried out on their orders, as well as disruptions to trade routes and guild activities. It would seem that the final straws that broke the camel's back were the death of the elected ruler of the Republic of Castar and the almost complete and sudden annihilation of the Ducal capital of Eisenbrook through some kind of arcane explosion, shattering thousands of lives. The Collective never admitted complete responsibility for these catastrophes, but they implied very strongly that things would continue to happen and escalate unless their demands were met. So, the majority of nations capitulated, not wanting to suffer at the hands of the Collective's espionage, let alone an all-out war with them. Since then, magic has been heavily restricted, save in the few remote or unstable places who didn't give in to their demands but who are deemed by the Collective to be too insignificant to be of trouble.

'As the new regulations and orders began to be implemented far and wide, the sudden contraction in the number of magic users, compounded with the sudden drop off in the availability of their services to the wider populations of the world meant that the vast majority of people began to believe that magic itself had disappeared, a rumour that the Collective were more than happy to propagate in order to subdue common awareness of their activities.'

'If they have done such unspeakable things, why did you join them?' Gwilym asked.

'In my defence, I had no idea about all of this until I became a member of the Collective, and in any case, I wouldn't necessarily say that I *joined*, more that I was drafted in. The Collective's Inquisitors travel far and wide, seeking out the most magically sensitive people they can find, children mostly as they can be trained more effectively, though occasional exceptions are made. The Inquisitors that took me from my home payed my parents more money than they could have hoped to earn in three years for me. My family was large and poor, and the Inquisitors threatened more than certain destitution on them if they refused. None of us had a choice in the matter. I was then taken directly to Harbotha to train at the Academy of Arcanology, and I didn't leave Zhisbon until my training was completed, and I should point out that none of what I have just said was directly communicated to us. I pieced together the information from a huge amount of disparate sources and rumours over many years, only those in the higher echelons of the Collective are actually told the truth on these matters, and they are sworn to secrecy.'

'But since you know all of this now, why still go on working for them? Surely the right thing to do would be to spread the truth so everyone knows what they're up to?'

'Because…' a quaver entered Egberht's voice, 'because I'm scared! The Inquisitors have eyes and ears everywhere. They look for any sign of dissent from members of the Collective who are working away from Zhisbon, and frankly, I've told you too much already. In any case, the governing classes of most places know exactly what the relationship is, and they would denounce me as a madman were I to come forward with anything. Don't take my acceptance of the situation I'm in as me condoning the Collective's activities, though I admit through silence I am just as guilty.'

Egberht slumped back down on top of his pack and hung his head; the others awkwardly shuffled in their spaces as silence descended on the corral, broken only by the noises of preparation going on in the room beyond. Despite his interest in what Egberht had been saying, Torben had been struggling to keep his eyes open since the gnome had started speaking. He blinked sluggishly once, twice and then slipped into sleep.

6

E ven though he knew instinctively that he was still asleep, Torben felt alert and wide awake. In his dreamlike state, he opened his eyes and saw nothing but blackness all around, but even though he couldn't see anything, he could hear a single whispered word drifting towards him across the ethereal space of unconsciousness.

'Ashak.'

He sat up and looked about, trying to pierce the suffocating darkness with his gaze, trying to locate where Hrex's voice was coming from, but he could see nothing.

'Ashak'

Her voice sounded as if it was coming from behind him, and he got warily to his feet, his head flicking back and forth, trying to spot the Lupine sorceress. His heart beat faster and faster as the nervous energy started to get the better of him, concerned as he was that Hrex was about to sneak up on him and ensnare him with her magic again. As his eyes scanned the featureless surroundings, the smallest pinprick of light caught his attention.

As he willed himself to bring his breathing under control, he focused all of his attention on the speck of light. Then he heard

Hrex's voice again echoing from the point, trying to draw him closer.

'Ashak...'

Slowly, Torben began to tiptoe forward towards the light, but as time passed and he felt surer that Hrex wasn't going to leap towards him from out of the darkness, his strides became longer and less cautious until he was striding purposefully towards the light, which grew larger and brighter the closer he got to it. Eventually, the light was so bright that it filled the entirety of Torben's vision to the point that his eyes began to water, and he threw his hands in front of his face to shield himself from its intensity. Despite this, he was still drawn forwards, the periodic sound of Hrex's voice tempting him on until he stepped fully into the light. As the light engulfed him, Torben screwed his eyes shut, trying to keep the oppressive, searing brightness at bay.

Then, its intensity eased, and around him, the noises changed from Hrex's repetitious taunting to the calming sound of wind blowing through trees, the chirping of birds and far in the distance the sound of a large group of people. Slowly he opened his eyes and found himself in a forest, the dappled light playing amongst the leaves. Ahead of him the noises of the still invisible people swelled as a hunting horn sounded, and Torben began to move through the trees towards it.

Through the vegetation, he could see the shapes of tents emerging nearby, which were momentarily blocked out as a group of riders cantered past. Torben staggered back, alarmed that he was about to be trampled, but then one of the horsemen passed straight through him as if he were a ghost. Seeing that he wasn't going to be hurt, Torben let the riders pass by and through him and then started to jog after them towards the encampment beyond.

He didn't really feel as if he was making the conscious decision to follow them, more that he was being drawn in that direction without him really having a say in what was happening. But then, it felt as if he wasn't really part of the world that he was in, more an onlooker spectating a series of events that had either long passed, or had never come to pass at all.

Not long after encountering them, he trailed the riders into the middle of a large clearing where a number of bright, expansive tents had been pitched around an open space that was full of large wooden tables and benches that were full of people drinking and feasting. The far end of the clearing had been turned into a field kitchen, with numerous fire pits belching smoke in columns towards the sky as the sound and smell of roasting meat wafted towards him. Stout-looking scaffolds had been erected all around, with a host of beheaded animal carcasses, boar and deer mostly, hanging upside down, blood pooling and congealing beneath them. Their heads, mounted on spears, liberally decorated the area, their lifeless eyes staring down at their wanton slaughterers beneath them. In front of the largest tent, flying above everything, was a large banner depicting a single, sumptuous red rose on a green backdrop.

The riders that Torben had been tailing had clearly caused quite the commotion as they had entered the clearing, with people standing up from the tables round about and moving towards them, sneering and jeering at the group, who Torben could now see had been dragging along a small group of hunched, scared figures, Lupines. As the riders dismounted, they cut loose the adult Lupines who had been tethered to the horses and been made to run alongside. As these individuals slumped to the ground, it became obvious that some of them had been unable to keep up, as their clothes were tattered and their bodies bloodied from where they had been dragged along the rough forest tracks. One of them didn't get up or even move as their bonds were cut and they were allowed to thud to the ground. Some of the riders lifted down smaller Lupines, who must be children, Torben thought as he drifted closer, who had been trussed like hogs and carelessly flung over the backs of the riders' mounts.

Most of the people in the clearing had formed a small crowd

around the large tent now, and Torben passed through them to get to the front, his ghostly presence allowing him to physically waft through, as opposed to smaller onlookers, dwarves mostly, who were pushing their way through the taller Humans in the crowd to view the spectacle. As the riders' horses were taken away by a small flock of stable hands who had appeared to tend to them, some members of the crowd began to throw scraps of food at the ragged band of Lupines, who had drawn together for protection. Some of the adults scrambled to unbind and draw close the children whose eyes were wide with fright. One female Lupine had dragged the body of the adult who wasn't moving to the group and was cradling its head in her lap, tears staining the fur around her muzzle.

A cheer went up from the crowd as the flaps of the great tent were drawn back and a group of heavily armoured warriors emerged and fanned out around the Lupines, their swords drawn and pointed directly at them. From behind, a large, rotund human man emerged wearing a fine pair of riding trousers and an elegant green velvet tunic, decorated with needlework roses, picked out in golden thread, that was warped and misshapen by being stretched over the man's massive gut. He wore a band of gold around his head that pinned his long greasy auburn hair back behind his ears. His bloated face was split into an ecstatic grin. As he moved forwards, he ushered a boy along by his side with a hand that looked weighed down by the amount of fat gold rings that had been forced onto the podgy fingers.

The boy looked like he must be the man's son, Torben thought as he moved freely around the scene, drinking in all of the details. The lad had the same auburn-coloured hair as his father, but his hair hung round his face and down his back in a mass of curls. His face was much thinner and sallower in build than that of his father, and his narrow eyes surveyed the world with a cruel edge. Lagging a little behind them both was a tall willowy man Torben thought must be an Elf, thanks to the tips of the long, pointed ears that protruded from his long white-blonde hair. As he left the dimmer light of the tent, the sunlight gave his pale grey skin a deathly pallor.

'Well now, what have you brought me, Byrnstan?' the man asked, surveying one of the riders who had approached and stepped into a deep bow before him.

'We found these Lupine scum three miles or near enough from the camp, my lord.' Byrnstan rose out of his bow and surveyed his prisoners with a hungry look. 'We picked up the trail of handsome stag and were tracking it when we came across them. What's more, not only were they trespassing within your royal forest, they had been so bold as to kill one of your deer for their supper. Unlucky for them that we found them...' He spat in the direction of the Lupines and cracked his knuckles threateningly.

'So why bring them to me? If they are common criminals, then I would have trusted you to carry out justice in my name and not interrupt my lunch.'

'Well, my lord, there were those Lupine raids that took place in the north that we received news of yesterday. I didn't think that it would be wise to leave them be, or to dispense your royal justice without first ascertaining what they might know about that.'

'You always were one for the details, Byrnstan.' The man's smile grew wider and more vicious as he took a good look at the Lupine prisoners. 'Have you questioned them yet?'

'Only briefly, my lord, and I'm sure that they are not telling the truth.'

'Please, you must know that we had nothing to do with the raids, we've been travelling south for weeks and we wouldn't risk the lives of our children by drawing your ire!'

One of the Lupines, a woman with ginger fur, had stood, the ginger furred child clutching the hem of her rough dress trying to hide behind her legs. Byrnstan gave the woman a long hard look and then strode over to her and struck her a savage blow across the face with the back of his hand, sending her sprawling onto the ground.

'How dare you address his Royal Highness Rassal II directly, filth! Utter another word without leave, and I'll cut that tongue from your snout.'

'Father, why do you think they were involved in the raiding?'

The boy was looking up at his father, King Rassal, his curly hair tumbling back from his face as he looked up at the taller man.

'Sarper, my boy,' the King crooned, placing a hand on the boy's head, 'here's a lesson in governance for you. Never take what these savages say for granted. Everything they say is twisted to save their own skins and get them another step closer to taking yours. We need to be absolutely sure that they were not involved in the raids, and even if that should turn out to be true, they still need to be punished for trespass on our royal lands, as well as the killing of one of my deer, our deer. And notwithstanding all of that, there is only one way to get a point across to Lupines, and that is to be as savage to them as they are to we more civilised folk. If you don't teach them to fear you, then they will all the more readily stream into our lands looking for plunder and spoils.' Rassal turned to Byrnstan. 'I believe it would be educational for you to teach the Crown Prince a thing or two about how one extracts information from these animals, and how we should make them an example to any of their feral kin that dare to pass this way again.'

'As you say, my lord,' Byrnstan said with a grim smirk. 'Come on, boys, get them to their feet, they've got dancing and squawking to do.'

The guards began to move in, and they dragged the Lupines to their feet and started to drive them off into the woods. King Rassal pushed his son in the direction Byrnstan was taking the prisoners, a pair of the heavily armed soldiers moving to escort him. Torben half-turned his face in disgust as the Lupines cried out in fear as they were forced away and as parents were separated from children. As he shifted his gaze, he saw the grey-skinned elf staring intently at the Lupines, his eyes fixed on the ginger-furred child who was cowering at her mother's feet. The mother was stood defiantly, teeth bared, claws raised ready to strike.

As a pair of soldiers approached her, the crowd nearby began to shout and bay, hoping to see some sport. King Rassal turned to watch the spectacle as one of the soldiers lunged forwards and was swatted back by a powerful blow from the Lupine's paw. A jeer went up from the onlookers as the other soldier was beaten back, followed by a cheer as the first soldier recovered and dealt a wicked blow to the Lupine, their sword slicing across her back and side, matting her fur with blood. She fell to all fours on the ground, and Torben watched as her arms trembled, her strength failing. She looked her daughter in the eye and mouthed a single word:

'Run!'

The child knelt transfixed by her side as the soldier's finishing blow punched through her mother's rib cage, then she ran, only to be plucked into the air by the scruff of her neck by the other soldier, who raised his sword to strike, the crowd hooting with laughter.

'Stop!'

The soldier's arm faltered as he drew it back, his hand stayed by the cold drawl of the elf echoing around the clearing as he strode forwards, his pale blue robes rippling through the air around him.

'Let her go,' he ordered. 'Do as I say, you impudent wretch!'

The soldier flashed a look in the direction of King Rassal, who was observing the interruption curiously and who nodded curtly, indicating the man should do as he was told. The soldier dumped the Lupine child on the ground, and she cried in pain as she landed awkwardly at the feet of the elf.

'What do you want with the child, Aristotles, have you not

eaten your fill already?' Rassal's laughter was echoed by the flock of retainers who guffawed at their King's joke.

Ignoring them, Aristotles knelt down in front of the child, who looked up at him through tear-stained eyes. The Shadow Elf stared back at her, clearly studying something that was invisible to everyone else.

'What is your name?' he said softly.

'Hrex, sir.'

'Come with me, Hrex, stay close, and these people won't hurt you.'

Aristotles straightened up and walked back towards King Rassal and the great tent, firmly but gently guiding the young Lupine with him. Hrex tried to hang back, staring at the body of her mother which was being unceremoniously dragged away.

'Come, Hrex, do not linger lest you wish to suffer the same fate,' Aristotles' voice was frigid and harsh.

Drawing level with King Rassal, he spoke quietly into his ear, so quietly that Torben almost didn't hear what was being said.

'My lord, there is something about this girl...I can sense great magical sensitivity in her, and I wish to explore how well she could be trained. It is unlike anything I have ever come across.'

'Aristotles, do as you wish, you know that you have my support, but on your head be it if she causes any trouble...'

Torben moved closer as the sound of the voices grew more and more muffled, but the sound continued to recede even when he moved to stand right next to Aristotles and King Rassal. Around him, the light was beginning to fade rapidly, and the trees, tents and surrounding crowds began to melt away, giving way to the blackness he had first found himself in. Then he was alone again in the darkness.

For a second, he stood in complete silence until he became aware of shapes looming out of the black, rows and rows of stone and wooden grave markers. Then in front of him, he saw a familiar shape sitting cross-legged on the ground, her back propped up against a stone, her eyes shut and breathing heavy: Hrex.

As the rest of the scene came into sharp focus around him, Torben took a hurried step back. Three bodies, the blood still gleaming fresh and wet around the jagged slashes at their throats, were lying before Hrex's concentrating form, their arms and legs neatly arranged, as if in a grim parody of lying in state. As he staggered back, he tripped and fell to the ground. Though he didn't make any sound as he fell and his flailing arm passed right through a nearby grave marker, Hrex's eyes snapped open. Her eyes darted back and forth, clearly looking for whatever had broken her concentration. Frozen to the spot by fear, Torben couldn't move, but as Hrex looked straight at him, or rather through him, he let out a sigh of relief. She couldn't see him, though he guessed that she could sense that something wasn't right.

Slowly she stood and took a more thorough look around the graveyard. Satisfied that she was alone, Hrex drew her battered quill from the sleeve of her tattered robe and muttering to herself as she approached the first of the corpses. As she bent over the first, Torben recognised the red light that had begun to form at the end of her quill, and he closed his eyes tight as she began to carve the arcane symbol into the man's foot that would bring his body back in a grim mockery of life. For as long as he could hear Hrex's voice muttering the spell, he kept his eyes screwed shut, trying to quell the increasingly louder sound of her voice in his head:

'Ashak, Ashak, Ashak...'

After what seemed like years, the Lupine's voice in Torben's head faded almost to nothing, and he could hear the Hrex before him giving orders to the thralls that she had summoned.

'Go and help the others, gather the bones as quickly as possible.'

As the thrall's shuffling footsteps began to sound, Torben called up the courage to open his eyes and saw the three thralls lurching further into the graveyard, Hrex following them slowly, warily scanning the area where Torben's incorporeal form stood. Eventually, she turned her back on him and stalked after her undead servants.

Only then did Torben begin to follow her. As he moved, he maintained the distance between them, and he flitted from grave marker to grave marker. Even though he was sure that she couldn't see him, he didn't want to take any chances. He followed her further into the graveyard, which lay on a lone hill in the landscape. The moon was shining full and bright, and as they climbed higher, Torben could see a group of houses, a small town or village, about half a mile away from the graveyard. Beyond that was the shining surface of a large river, forest flanking its sides, that curled off in both directions out of sight. As they reached the top of the incline, Torben could see a land-scape of grassland stretching out to the horizon, with what looked like a dilapidated manor house, surrounded by over-grown ornamental gardens roughly a mile from his vantage point. He saw the top of Hrex's head disappear below the slope that led down in the direction of the house, and he quickened his pace to catch up to her.

As he started to descend the slope himself, he could hear scraping and clattering, and Hrex came back into view, watching over a nightmarish scene. Ten shuffling, clearly recently deceased thralls were digging up the graves in that area and were dumping the bones and body parts into large wicker baskets. Several of the thralls were already making their drunken way further down the slope, a basket clutched tight in each set of magically animated arms, in the direction of the manor house.

'Move now, quickly! The night is waning, and we need to get back to the Master!'

Hrex chivvied the remaining thralls, who were pulling them-selves out of graves and dumping the last of the scattered, broken bones and chunks of flesh into the baskets before picking up their macabre load and making their own way out of the graveyard. They moved slowly across the landscape towards the manor house, Hrex constantly checking behind them, Torben tailing the group. As they neared the dwelling, Torben could see that it had clearly been abandoned for some time.

The manor house had been fortified to some extent, judging by the battlements that crowned its roof and the moat full of stagnant, brackish water, but its primary purpose had clearly been as a residence rather than as a defensive structure. There were many windows that looked out over the rows of wild-looking hedges and weed-choked flower beds that lay between the structure and the moat that marked the perimeter of the property. Almost all of these windows looked as if they had long lost any glass that they might have had, and the shutters had rotted away from their exteriors. A pile of rubble lay strewn across the knee-high lawn where part of the building had collapsed, revealing empty, damp rooms within.

Hrex and the thralls followed the gravel path, speckled with little clumps of grass and moss, which led to a single large entrance gate, whose wood was stained with damp. Small slivers of light could be seen peeking through the places where the wood had rotted away entirely. Though the gate was closed before Torben reached it, he continued walking straight at it and stepped through into the space beyond. In what would have been a large, grand entrance hall, the thralls were depositing the contents of their baskets onto an enormous pile of dismembered body parts and bones. Here and there amongst the various components that had once made up living, breathing men and women was the odd complete body, some of which looked decidedly fresh, much like the three thralls Hrex had raised before Torben, who had joined the queue of their fellows waiting to unload their sickening cargo. Hrex herself was clearly leaving the thralls to their task as she was already stalking through the room and onwards into a corridor leading off it. Torben broke into a jog to catch up to her, and he followed her deeper into the manor.

After several minutes of stalking her through dark corridors and up staircases slippery with damp and mould, Hrex opened the door to an upper room and was illuminated by the warm light that spilled out of it. As she closed the door behind, throwing the corridor and Torben back into darkness, he took a deep breath and stepped through the wall into the room.

The space beyond was surprisingly large and cosy. There was a large fireplace set into one of the long walls, with a roaring, comforting blaze within. The rest of the wall space was covered in makeshift bookshelves that groaned under the weight of the heavy volumes alongside glass jars, vials and pieces of arcane-looking equipment that Torben couldn't identify. A rug had been laid before the fire, a large, slightly worn winged armchair set on it. Hrex was standing to one side, slightly behind the chair, as if waiting for instructions from the seated figure that occupied it, who Torben couldn't see. His view of them was obstructed by a dishevelled looking man stood before them, who cowered in fear, wringing his hands.

'Tell me, how many people live in your village?' The voice that oozed from the chair was a cold drawl that Torben vaguely recognised.

'No more than two hundred, my lord, so we shan't be any trouble to you, nor would we wish any upon you! And there are enough of us to work to provide for you and ourselves should you wish it.' The man's voice quavered, with fear and Torben could see him bodily trembling before the unseen figure.

'What do you know of the war between this kingdom and Sharisar? Have you seen any troop movements here?'

'No, my lord. We've heard that Sharisar's soldiers all made their way straight for the capital and that they didn't even send a force to engage the Eastern Army or to cause trouble in this part of the country. Even if they had, we're too small to bother with, I'd imagine.'

'And what of the Eastern Army? Have they passed through this way?'

'We've seen neither hide nor hair of them, my lord.'

Torben slowly and carefully manoeuvred himself to one side of the room so that he could get a better look at the figure in the chair. As his line of vision was cleared, he saw that it was Aristotles, the grey elf that Torben had seen in the woods with King Rassal not long before. He looked almost exactly the same as in the vision, despite the fact that the events Torben had just witnessed took place hundreds of years ago. His white-blonde hair shimmered in the light just as it had before, the gaze of his ice-blue eyes seemed just as piercing as they bore into the terrified man before him, and even the robes that he wore looked almost identical. Hrex looked decidedly older than the elf. At times she looked as if there must be something else at work, helping her to cling onto life, whereas Aristotles looked to Torben as if he could survive unchanged forever.

The only discernible difference Torben could spot between the Aristotles that had stood in the woodland clearing all those years ago and the one sat before him now was the much more palatable sense of discomfort his presence filled Torben with. More than that, it was a sense of dread, fear even, that seemed to emanate from him, and Torben found his eyes being drawn to the spot on Aristotles' body where the source of this energy was. Hanging from a gold chain around the elf's neck was a pendant, about the same size as his hand, of a mask. It depicted the face of a gaunt man, his mouth open in a shout of pain and anguish. It was made of gold, the details of the face, the eyes and the void of the open mouth picked out in black obsidian. Something about it felt deeply, dangerously magical, and Torben had to will himself to look away. He could see it was filling the other man with just as much terror as it had him.

'I think that we've gotten any useful information out of the head of this worm that we're going to get. Don't you, Hrex?'

'Yes, Master.' There was a wicked look in Hrex's eyes as she sneered at the man from over the wing of the armchair.

'Please, your lordship, I won't tell a soul that you're here, or what you're doing.'

'You're right, you won't.'

'No, no, please, don't do anything rash. I can, I will serve you if that is what you wish!' the man said, taking a panicked step forwards.

With his left hand, Aristotles swiftly and deftly drew a symbol that hung momentarily in the air picked out in black fire and then thrust his right hand towards the man. A dagger made of the same black flames flew from his palm and sank up to its blazing hilt in his chest. For a moment, the man looked in horror from Aristotles to the dagger. Then his legs gave way, and he collapsed to the floor, the dagger disappearing from his chest in a puff of acrid smoke as he died.

As the remnants of Aristotles' magic dissipated, Torben saw a different kind of smoke-like substance emerging from the man's mouth and his still open eyes. It glowed with a soft, purple light and looked as if it was being dragged by an invisible hand towards Aristotles. The corpse gave one final convulsion as the substance was pulled from it, and it drifted across the room towards the Elf and the mask he wore around his neck. To Torben, it looked as if it was fighting against the inevitable pull of the thing around Aristotles' neck, until it was dragged right into the obsidian maw of the mask and disappeared, sending a ripple of dark purple light across its golden surface.

Whilst Torben had been watching the substance, Aristotles had been sketching symbols and chanting the same incantation that Hrex had used in the graveyard, and he sent the symbols flying across the room into the man's dead body, which began to twitch and writhe as the Elf dragged it back to life as a thrall. As the still-warm body of the undead man staggered to its feet, Aristotles dismissed it with a curt wave of his hand.

'Go, join the others downstairs and await further instruction.'

As the thrall clumsily lurched across the room and

fumblingly let itself through the door, Hrex moved round so that she was in her master's line of sight.

'How did the collection go in the village, Hrex? Have we enough bones to raise a force to immediately discourage people from poking their noses in our business?'

'Yes, Master, by my reckoning we have enough parts for up to a hundred thralls.'

'Good, good. It will be more time-consuming raising thralls from just bones, fresh bodies are always better, but needs must. Make sure you pay careful attention when I demonstrate the procedure so that you can carry it out yourself in future.'

'As you wish, Master.'

Aristotles stood and smoothed out his robes. He turned fully so that he could look directly at the more diminutive figure of Hrex.

'There is another task that I have for you, Hrex. Thralls make good blunt instruments, but we are also in need of more cunning servants who are more capable of thinking on their own. Find some of your kin, any will do, I care not which tribe they claim to belong to, and recruit them to our cause.'

'Of course, Master.'

'Good, you can set out at first light. For now though, let us begin with the thralls downstairs. We should have enough time to raise a fair number before we must conduct the reinvigoration ritual.'

Aristotles began to stride towards the door, and Torben shuffled back slightly to allow him past, not wanting either the Elf or the mask that he was wearing to pass through him. Though his feet moved silently across the floor, it was as if Aristotles had heard the noise of them scuffing. His head snapped around and his icy eyes stared directly at Torben. His face contorted with rage as his right hand hurriedly drew magic in the air that he hurled straight at the young man.

'Spy!'

7

A s Torben's gaze locked with the icy eyes of Aristotles, he felt his stomach lurch with fear. He began to move, to pitch his still incorporeal being back through the wall behind him, to escape. Before he could move more than a few feet, however, the Shadow Elf's hands whipped precisely and quickly before him, and Torben felt his limbs cease up as a dreaded, familiar word roared within his mind, though this time with Aristotles' sneering tone, rather than Hrex's harsh growl.

Ashak.

Sensing that whatever was before him was now going nowhere, Aristotles visibly relaxed, though his face was still creased with a concerned frown. It seemed to the immobile Torben that though their eyes had momentarily met one another, Aristotles couldn't actually see him, as his gaze flicked left and right, up and down in the general area where Torben was fixed to the spot.

Hrex's Lupine face appeared at her master's elbow as she, too, tried to spot the thing he was seeking.

'What is it, Master?'

'I don't know…' Aristotles took a step forward, sniffing the air, the tip of his nose nearly brushing through Torben's phantasmal cheek as he did so. 'There is a presence here, it has been watching and listening to what we have been doing.'

'What shall we do?' Hrex leaned forwards, her eyes mere slits as she squinted into what looked to her like thin air.

'From what I can sense, it doesn't appear overly dangerous, though that is no crumb of comfort to us. Let us play it safe and send it to be judged by our patron.'

Drawing back slightly, Aristotles took a hold of the golden mask around his neck and held it out before him as far as the chain it was suspended by would allow and directed its maw in Torben's direction. He closed his eyes and began to chant incomprehensibly under his breath. Thin lines of purple energy played over the golden surface of the object, and the disc of obsidian that filled the mouth cavity seemed to grow darker. From Torben's point of view, it looked as if it was warping into a tunnel leading to unknown blackness. As the chanting intensified, Torben felt as if his ghost-like form was being drawn towards the mask, slowly at first but then stronger and stronger until his whole body began to drift across the room towards Aristotles and the mask. Whatever the magic was that the sorcerer was imbuing into the mask, it dispelled the enchantment that was holding Torben in place, for his body suddenly felt free and under his control once more.

He tried to turn, tried to run, his arms reaching out towards the stone wall behind him, his fingers scrabbling through the surface, trying to find purchase, but to no avail. Then, without warning, Torben was completely swept off his feet and flew through the air. One moment he was in the room, and the next he was surrounded by darkness illuminated periodically by flashes of purple arcane energy and the tiny, rapidly receding window of light high above him, the view from the maw of the mask onto the room he had just been in.

He fell for what seemed like an eternity, or at least he thought he was falling. At times his body felt as if it should be travelling upwards or sideways instead of down, but his sense of direction was completely lost in purple-tinged darkness that swirled around him like a billowing column of cloud.

Eventually, the cloud disappeared to be replaced by the domed ceiling of an obsidian cave, the floor of which Torben's form drifted gently down to. The semi-translucent walls of the space glowed with the same purple light that had streaked the clouds and rippled across the surface of Aristotles' hideous golden mask.

Torben had to wait for several seconds, his eyes screwed shut, breathing heavily, trying to quell the sick feeling that had been caused by his transition, that threatened to rise up out of the pit of stomach. Eventually, he opened his eyes to take in his surroundings properly. The cave, whose ceiling stood well over three times Torben's height, was enormous, stretching out for what seemed an endless number of miles on three sides. The fourth side, the last Torben looked at, was dominated by the curving obsidian wall that stretched up to join the ceiling. This cave was clearly part of a much larger system, as a large tunnel, which Torben guessed must have been half a mile away, joined the space on the fourth side. It was then he realised that he was not alone.

As his eyes adjusted to the weird, glowing purple light that throbbed and pulsed at varying levels of brightness, he saw that the space was full of half-transparent ghostly beings that listlessly drifted to and fro. They all appeared humanoid in form, and as Torben climbed warily to his feet, he could see creatures he recognised as humans, dwarves, gnomes, elves and even the occasional Lupine, as well as other creatures he had never seen before. He could hear the figures that glided within arm's reach of him whispering to themselves. Each of them appeared to be saying something different, but all of them repeated their chosen phrase incessantly under their breath. As he listened, Torben heard curses, pleas for mercy and prayers amongst the garbled nonsense.

Sensing movement immediately to his right, he turned just

in time to see the form of a woman whose arms hung limply by her sides, head slumped forward onto her chest, headed straight for him.

'I love you, I love you, I love you...' was the mournful, wistful mantra that she repeated.

Before the thought of moving out of the way had crossed Torben's mind, she had floated right up to him and then straight through his form. He shivered as a horrible icy sensation rippled through his body as the spectre passed straight through him. He wheeled about instinctively and saw the form continuing on its melancholic way, having payed no heed to Torben at all, perhaps completely unaware they had collided.

He side-stepped another apparition that glided towards him with the same lack of intent as the other, and Torben began to edge his way through the floating masses towards the mouth of the tunnel. As he had no idea where he was, or what he should do, the entrance to the tunnel, as the only discernible landmark in this strange place, seemed like the only viable location where he might find some answers. To begin with, Torben made halting, juddering progress through the cavern as he attempted to dodge the strange apparitions, but after nearly an hour of travelling virtually nowhere, he took a deep breath, gritted his teeth and began to walk in a straight, direct line towards the mouth of the tunnel. His gasps echoed off the glassy walls and ceiling as his body was repeatedly racked by icy blasts when the apparitions glided through him. He was shivering so hard by the time he reached the tunnel entrance he could hardly walk. He slumped against the smooth obsidian wall and pulled his legs in tightly to his chest, trying to regain control over his shocked body.

As his breathing grew less ragged and his body began to feel less and less like a block of ice, Torben's senses started to sharpen again. It was then that he heard the sound of footsteps reverberating around the smooth walls of the tunnel to his left, rising above the faint background noise of the spectres closest to him. As they grew closer and closer, he edged along the wall away from the entrance, pressing himself as close to the wall as possible, watching the tunnel with bated breath.

He saw two figures emerge, both of whom were shrouded in long black hooded robes that completely concealed their features and would have made them appear as animated columns of fabric were it not for the toes of their black booted feet poking out from beneath the folds. Their forms looked far more solid than either Torben or the flock of floating spirits, as if they were a true physical presence. Each of them held long silver canes in black-gloved hands, and they moved into the stream of spectres, using the canes to usher the apparitions out of the way. The spectres moved far more energetically than Torben had seen them do so before as they tried to skitter out of reach of the canes.

After a minute of moving through the ghostly crowd, both figures lashed out almost simultaneously with their implements, striking two spectres on their heads, the silver of the canes not passing through the ephemeral bodies. Both victims suddenly halted, and their forms, though still upright, slumped as if they had been knocked senseless. The robed assailants then began to head back to the tunnel entrance, now using their canes to push the prone forms before them, and they disappeared into the passage beyond.

As he listened to their receding footsteps, Torben began to edge his way along the wall until he reached the opening himself. Carefully, he poked his head round to peep down the tunnel and, seeing no sign of the figures, he slinked into the passage. The tunnel twisted and turned this way and that as it wormed its way onward. Occasionally, he would get a glimpse of the two figures, still leading their captive spectres, but he kept his distance and listened to the sound of their footsteps, hoping that the echo prone nature of the tunnel's walls would alert him to any additional movement.

After rounding a corner for what felt like the hundredth time, Torben found himself in a round antechamber with three further passages leading off it. The two side passages were almost identical in construction to the one he had travelled down, whilst the middle passage was sealed off by an enormous pair of double doors made out of solid gold that had been burnished to a mirror sheen. He jumped as his own warm, golden reflection startled him, and he leapt against one of the walls that separated the middle passage from the one to the right. As he calmed his nerves, his ears picked up the sound of footsteps again, coming from the right-hand passageway. He peered around the corner and saw just one of the robed figures reaching the end of the straight section and rounding a corner; the second figure and their charge were gone. Torben was pulling himself back against the wall, wondering where the other figure had gone, when a chink of flickering purple light caught his eye. It was coming from the golden doors, which were ajar.

Inching forward, Torben approached the crack in the doors and looked through. There was a large room beyond, with huge pillars reaching up to support a ceiling that was far higher than the one in the first cavern. The pillars obscured his view of the room, but it looked as if the space was unoccupied. He drew back as he heard the sound of footsteps reverberating around the walls of one of the other tunnels, moving towards him quickly. By the sounds of it, he neither had enough time to inspect each of the other tunnels to identify which one the unseen entity was travelling down, nor could he just stay where he was. After a moment of dithering, he carefully put a hand on one of the massive doors, the metal of which was cool to the touch, and eased it open enough to allow him to slip through into the room.

As soon as he passed over the threshold, Torben, crouching low to the ground, made a dash for the nearest pillar, and pressed his back against it. During the brief amount of time that he had been in the open, he had discovered that he was wrong; there were people inside the room. He edged around the thick base of the column, over five feet in width, and took in the extent of the space and the creatures within it.

He could now see that embedded into all four sides of each column was a golden emblem of a snake devouring its own tail, the eyes picked out by amethysts. Interspersed between the two regimented lines of obsidian columns that marched down either side of the hall were huge, black marble braziers filled with the fiercely burning purple flames that illuminated the room. The floor, made of what seemed like a single piece of highly polished black marble, mirrored the faint glow of the obsidian ceiling high above and the flickering magical flames of the braziers. Interspersed along the channel between the rows of columns, the same symbol of the snake was embedded into the marble of the floor. At the far end of the room, a set of shallow stone steps led up to a huge golden throne, on which sat an enormous, humanoid figure. The creature wore the same garb as the two people Torben had followed, but on a much larger scale. The large hood that crowned where its head should be completely obscured the face and features Torben assumed must be within, the space within the hood covered in a veil of darkness. Before the creature was one of the spectres Torben had watched being led away from the cavern.

As he observed the scene, Torben felt the same sense of dread grow in him that he had felt when he looked at the mask that hung around Aristotles' neck, but he also felt a growing sense of curiosity as to what was going on. He tried to suppress the feeling, knowing that he should trust his gut, that whatever the thing was on the throne was to be avoided, but he could feel himself being drawn forwards. Barely aware of what he was doing, he began to move from pillar to pillar along the back wall, staying out of sight of the throne. As he reached the last column, he crept into the shadow of one of the braziers that stood directly before the throne. Even though he was now so close to the flames, he couldn't feel any heat being given off by them;

indeed, the purple fire felt as if it was drawing the heat out of the air instead.

From behind the brazier, he watched as the creature on the throne, which had, up until then sat stock still, began to stir. It slowly stood, its robe swinging open to reveal the bare flesh of its torso and legs that Torben could now see was horribly decayed, the odd bone protruding here and there and a gaping, fresh-looking wound in the centre of its chest. As it began to move, a miasma of horrific stench rolled across the room, a smell of long rotting meat, and Torben clapped his hand to his mouth, both to try and block out the awful stink and to stifle the gasp of horror and surprise that sounded involuntarily.

The creature walked calmly, regally down the steps until it stood right before the spectre, who floated in space, eyes averted from the horrific form before it. One of the horror's long-fingered hands caressed the spectre's face apparently not passing through the incorporeal substance, and lifted up its chin so the figure's eyes looked directly into the black pit of the hood. Slowly the creature turned the head from side to side, inspecting the spectre carefully. As the head was turned in Torben's direction, he saw the face for the first time, and a flash of recognition struck him. It was the farmer he had seen pleading before Aristotles for his life and for his community. The man Aristotles had killed and raised from the dead as a thrall. Torben's eyes snapped back to the thing that was manipulating the man by the sound of a rattling, raspy voice emanating from the hood, which sent a shiver down his spine.

'Weak, feeble. Hardly the sort of nourishment that befits me.'

As it spoke, its hand slipped swiftly from the man's chin to its neck. With one swift movement, it picked him up and fed him into the pitch-black chasm of its hood. As the man's feet disappeared into the unseen maw, there was a bone-chilling scream, quickly stifled, that bounced around the pillared hall.

'Yes, a miserly portion', the creature hissed, 'but I sense someone with a stronger spirit.'

The faceless hood turned towards the brazier behind which Torben was hiding and began to move slowly towards it.

'What has Aristotles sent me this time? Something more fitting, I think, a taste perhaps of what is to come, proof that my investment in him has not been worthless...'

As the creature continued to stalk forward, clearly aware of exactly where the young man was hiding, Torben began to scrabble backwards as fast as he could until his back connected with the solid obsidian wall behind him. As the creature's shadow began to loom over him, he could smell the odour of decay even more strongly. He looked left and right, desperately looking for an escape route, but then he began to rise from the floor and drift slowly towards the horror's outstretched arm.

Torben struggled, his arms and legs flailing wildly in the air, but it did nothing to stop him from drifting closer and closer to the rotting fingers with their jagged, broken nails extended, ready to clasp around his throat.

'No!' he shouted, summoning all of his will power to try and resist the spell.

All that came in response was a rasping laugh that rolled out of the hood, mocking him. By now, he had been drawn so close to the creature that one of his flailing legs connected with its torso, and he winced as he recoiled his foot back; it had been like kicking a brick wall. The creature hadn't even moved an inch, just continued laughing. Torben's eyes stared, panic-stricken at his impending doom, the void of the hood ready to devour him.

Then, his vision flickered, and for a split second, where the creature had been, there had been a view of a river, trees lining the banks and sunlight, true, pure sunlight. As the scene before him reverted back to his current predicament, he realised that the creature had stopped laughing.

'No,' it growled, lunging forward to grab him.

Torben's view changed back to the river again for longer, several seconds at least. When he reverted back to the obsidian hall, the creature was now behind him, as if he had vanished from before it as it had been trying to capture him and had moved through the space where he had been. It wheeled around, robes billowing about it, revealing more of the horror that was its bloodied, corpse-like body. It cried out an incomprehensible scream of anger before charging towards Torben again, but Torben was gone.

This time, as his vision changed, Torben felt like he was falling and then his whole form spasmed as his incorporeal form returned to his body.

All he had time to register was that he was now, truly, physically in a boat on the river with the shapes of people around him. Then he coughed, spluttered and then lunged forward to throw up over the side. As he stared down at the water, the slick of vomit was rapidly washed away by the flow of the river. He felt water droplets, thrown off from the oars ploughing against the stream further up the boat, playing across his face, a true sensation again! Then, his eyes darkened as he passed out.

Torben awoke with a start, his eyes snapping open as he drew in a huge, strangled breath. He couldn't place where we was; his surroundings were dimly lit, and the light itself was tinted with pink and purple. He sat up, heart pounding, expecting to see the obsidian walls, black marble floor and the horrifying figure, readying to feast on his very soul.

'Whoa there, Torben, easy now.'

A familiar, deep, rumbling voice and the comfortable feeling of a large, heavy hand being pressed gently onto his shoulder, stopping him from rising any further. Antauros.

'You've been asleep for quite a long time now. We thought we might lose you again,' the Minotaur continued.

As Torben relaxed and allowed himself to be guided back

down to a sitting position by Antauros, he realised that he was sat in one of the large rowing boats that had been stashed in the safe-house. The craft was large enough to accommodate himself, Antauros and Egberht, who sat watching Torben warily nearby, along with eight of Theodora's guards. Four of the guards were rowing sluggishly, pushing the boat up against the current of the river whilst two kept watch, one at the stern and one at the bow. The final two slumbered fitfully nearby. It must be nearly night, as the low dusk sunlight threw out its pink, purple and rose-tinted rays, which had tricked Torben into thinking that he was still in the other place. The lines of trees on either side of the riverbank, as well as the acidic tang lingering on his tongue, seemed vaguely familiar, and he remembered the sickening sensation of landing back in his own body and the unpleasant results that had followed.

'Where are we?'

'Three days upstream from Karpella. The wind has been kind to us so far, so we made good progress at first, though now, this lot are having to put in a bit more effort.'

Antauros gestured to the four sweating soldiers heaving at their oars, along with the small mast and its furled-up sail that stood proudly, if uselessly, in the middle of the vessel.

'And the others? Did everyone get out?'

'Yes, we're all alright,' Antauros said, pointing ahead of them to where three more boats were labouring up the course of the River Arlen. 'Our gallant crew here seem to think that we're trailing the others because of a, humph, heavier load… I did offer to row, but they were insistent that their orders meant we were not to interfere with the course of the journey. Their loss.'

The minotaur's black eyes flicked smugly across the oarsmen, who kept their heads low and avoided his gaze as they toiled away. Egberht shuffled closer to Torben, drawing Antauros' attention away from Theodora's soldiers, and the gnome leaned in close to the young man, pushing his small round spectacles up the bridge of his nose to allow for a proper inspection.

'How are you feeling, Torben?' he asked quietly.

'Groggy and still sore from the stab wound, but otherwise I feel fine, I think...'

Egberht and Antauros exchanged a glance, and Torben looked from one to the other of them, trying to interpret what they were thinking. Turning back to meet his gaze, the diminutive mage began to stroke the strands of his wispy beard.

'Do you remember anything since you fell asleep in Karpella? Thoughts, feelings, dreams perhaps?'

'Yeah, I do, dreams. Well, they weren't dreams, it was more like I was actually there as a ghost or something. It felt more real than any other dream I've ever had.'

'The reason that whatever you saw felt so vivid to you is, I think, precisely because it was real.'

'What do you mean?' Notes of panic had begun to creep into Torben's voice. 'What happened to me?'

'Don't worry, it's alright,' Egberht said reassuringly. 'I have an idea of what might have happened, but I think it would be best if you told us what you saw, if you feel you're up to it right now. I don't want to jump to conclusions.'

'Ok, it might do me good to get it off my chest.'

———

By the time Torben finished speaking, it was several hours after nightfall. The only light was from a small lamp that had been fixed to the prow of the boat to show the boats in front where they were, which must have looked like a mirror image of the stern light of the boat ahead of them. In the intervening time, the soldiers had rotated duties, giving some of them a well-earned rest, but rather than sleep, they had stared at Torben's silhouette, drinking in his words as avidly as Antauros and Egberht.

'So what do you think?' Torben rasped, his voice tired and hoarse from talking for so long.

He drank deeply from a water skin that Antauros passed him and looked at the spot where Egberht was sitting in the boat. He was almost completely hidden in the darkness, save for when the odd strand of moonlight made it through a gap in the clouds above and reflected off the crown of his bald head. They sat in silent expectation for several minutes before the gnome finally stirred, sighing deeply.

'Well, I'm afraid my initial thoughts were right. What you saw and experienced was indeed real, I'd bet all of the worldly belongings I've ever had on that. You are suffering from something known as shadowed mind. It's a phenomenon that has been reported to appear in people who have had their minds or bodies either completely dominated or influenced through magical means. If the caster of the spell in question is not prepared enough, or does not cast the spell competently enough, then a bond is created between the two parties, which allows the victim to see into the mind of the caster once the spell has been dismissed. The more powerful the magic used, the more vivid and intrusive the effect of shadowed mind is likely to be and the harder it is to bring back the afflicted when their spirit begins to wander as yours did. It took a fair amount of effort; I've been trying incantations and formulas for days now, as soon as the symptoms first exhibited themselves to try and bring you back to yourself. Clearly, we were successful just in the nick of time...

'When Hrex magically linked herself to you, I think she made a mistake, or at least underestimated the longevity of the connection between the two of you, or perhaps could not conceive of a situation in her plan that would mean you would still be alive and that the potential of shadowed mind occurring would be a concern.'

'Would Hrex know that there is a link between the two of them?' Antauros asked quietly.

'Unless one is specifically looking for it, shadowed mind is incredibly hard to detect, though from what you said Torben, if her master, Aristotles, was able to sense you, then I would guess that he would come to the same realisation as us pretty quickly.'

'So you mean everything I saw in that place he sent me was real as well?' Torben asked with a quaver in his voice.

'I'm afraid so, yes.'

'What was that thing?'

'I think, and bear with me on this, I think that the creature you encountered is a god no less, Kulittu, otherwise known as the Dead God.'

There was a murmur of concerned voices around their boat as the soldiers revealed that they had been listening in. Those who weren't rowing touched their hearts and then looked up to the sky, invoking a sign of protection. Though he couldn't see him, Torben heard Antauros draw in his breath sharply in response.

'You're joking, aren't you?' Torben asked. 'Are you seriously telling me that a deity tried to eat my spirit?'

'I'm deadly serious, Torben. All of the clues add up, your description of the being, his actions, the symbol of the ouroboros, the snake devouring its own tail. Not to mention the fact that before the Aramorians took and joined the two nations, the Kingdom of Dazscor worshipped the gods and goddesses of the pantheon to which Kulittu belongs. Though information about him, beyond the myths and legends that were circulated as part of the religion's doctrine, was highly restricted, Aristotles would have been ideally placed to get what he needed to communicate directly with the Dead God, and the power to both interest him and survive the experience.'

'Why would he make a bargain with such a being, though?'

'For power, plain and simple. What he wants that power for, though, is a different question, one that is much harder to answer, and is likely to be impossible without more information. In any case, the fact that Aristotles has made a deal with Kulittu should be enough warning for us to not trust him.'

Their conversation was interrupted by the guard at the bow of the boat who, spotting the signal from the craft in front of them, turned to relay the order.

'We're turning in for the night, make for the shore on my command!'

As the activity within the boat intensified, Egberht leant forward, beckoning Antauros and Torben towards him.

'Though we don't have all of the facts at our disposal, we should warn the Princess not to maintain her current objective of finding Aristotles. He may well be the only person still alive that she thinks she can trust, but by my reckoning, what you observed, Torben, may tip the scales in the other direction. She, her family and the majority of the people they governed would have been, are, adherents to the pantheon Kulittu belongs to. She should understand the significance of this and will act with far more caution.'

'What do you suggest?' Antauros rumbled.

'When we get off this boat, we need to request to see her at once. I don't think we can afford to beat around the bush on this one. I, for one, don't want to end up being another soul's worth of tribute from Aristotles to the Dead God!'

Just as he finished speaking, Egberht was thrown rather unceremoniously forward as the boat was heaved up onto a large sandy hollow in the riverbank by the oarsmen, who then started to jump out into the water to help drag the craft firmly onto land. To their left, the three other boats were already beached, and Princess Theodora's troops were already busying themselves around the hollow, screened from the rest of the land by the thick tree-line that loomed down around them. Small fires sprang up in several places already, and as the dim light of their carefully controlled flames crept out, Torben could see that there was already a picket line of guards within the trees. He began to rise to his feet but was quickly stopped by one of the guards who had remained with the craft.

'Remain where you are. We will give you leave to exit the boat!'

'That was friendly...' Torben muttered.

'They've all been rather on edge since we left Karpella,' Antauros murmured into Torben's ear, 'and I imagine what they just overheard is liable to make them even more nervous.'

As if echoing his words, there was the sound of sand and gravel crunching under Captain Almar's heavy footfall as the officer approached them with one of the guards who had been crewing their boat, who looked outright scared behind him.

'What's all this nonsense I hear the three of you have been concocting to scare my soldiers?' he spat, barely keeping his voice low enough so that it didn't spread.

'It's not *nonsense*, it's the truth!' Egberht retorted, careful to keep his voice loud enough so that the soldiers busying themselves nearby could hear.

'Keep your voice down! This is the last warning I'm going to give you. Keep your grubby ink-stained fingers and your cock and bull stories to yourselves! If I hear that the men and women under my command are being fed any more stories to make them look over their shoulders or become less attentive to making you lot toe the line, then I will not hesitate to remind Her Highness of my original advice to gut you all. That would be far easier and more preferable to dragging you lot around as meddlesome tour guides.'

'How can you not understand the severity of...'

Egberht had begun to rise to his feet, his face flushed red with anger, but his voice was cut off as Almar smacked him in the throat with the back of his hand, making the gnome cough, splutter and fall back down into the boat. The craft rocked dangerously as both Antauros and Torben leapt to their feet, making the guards nearby leap back, hands flying towards weapons.

'Go on, do it, make my day!' Almar snarled. His sword was

half drawn from its scabbard, the first few inches of the blade glinting in the firelight.

Around them, the other guards had stopped what they were doing and were focused on the group. Many of them were slowly gravitating to back their Captain up, but it was the regal voice of Theodora that broke the silence.

'What's going on here? Almar?'

'Well, what is going on here?' Almar said quietly to Antauros and Torben. 'Just give me the excuse to give the order, go on!'

Slowly Antauros sank back into the boat, Torben, taking his lead from the minotaur, doing likewise.

'I thought as much.' Almar's face was now split with a grin. He turned to face the approaching figure of Theodora. 'Nothing to worry about, Your Highness. Just reminding our guests to mind their manners around your guards.'

As Almar moved towards his Princess to lead her back the way she had come, the soldiers in the hollow began to get on with their business, though many still eyed the three prisoners cautiously. After a few minutes, two of Theodora's guards, Ranulf and Roswit, marched over, ready to escort them to the spot in the camp that had been set up for them. Torben reached down and helped a still unsteady Egberht rise to his feet, and they followed the soldiers and Antauros to a campfire, around which Gwilym and Eleusia were already sat, several additional guards stood on watch nearby. Their two friends rose to meet them as they approached.

'You're awake and about time too!' Gwilym laughed jovially, clapping Torben on the back and ruffling his hair as he sat down next to him in the sand.

'What was all that about just now?' Eleusia said, the concerned look not entirely leaving her eyes as they settled down around the campfire.

'Well,' Torben said, exchanging a glance with the still wheezing Egberht. 'Where do we begin?'

8

Torben awoke slowly and groggily from yet another night of disturbed sleep. For the last three days, his dreams had been haunted by snapshots of Hrex and Aristotles, none of which had been as long or as vivid as his out of body experience, but they had all filled him with a sense of dread. He had watched them swelling the ranks of undead thralls that stood about limply in the ruined manor house, and he had seen flashes of them bargaining with an enormous Lupine, whose dark grey fur was slashed with a multitude of pink scars, and who glowered out at the world with his single, evil-looking amber eye, the other milky and lifeless. He had seen that Lupine and his fellows raiding, slaughtering indiscriminately, under the direction of Hrex, and bringing the bodies back to the manor, piling them up in the entrance hall, where they were resurrected to serve by Aristotles.

Wearily, he sat up and shuffled closer to the small fire that Gwilym was prodding with a stick. Eleusia and Antauros were silently eating whilst Egberht was reading the massive tome that he had rescued from Karpella castle. Seeing him rise, Eleusia handed him a dirty cloth wrapping with a portion of dried meat and barracks biscuit, which was what sufficed as breakfast.

Nearby, dispersed around campfires set at intervals amongst the surrounding trees, the soldiers that made up Princess Theodora's guard were readying themselves to move off for the day.

There was a refreshing breeze that played amongst the green leaves above them, which helped to liven Torben up as he cautiously chewed the tough meat and rock-hard biscuit.

'Did you sleep any better?' Eleusia asked him quietly.

'A little,' he said thickly through his mouthful of food. 'Hard to tell what was going on last night, but there was less screaming, so hopefully that means they weren't out raiding for more corpses.'

'Let's hope you're right,' Antauros muttered, 'not just for the sake of innocent lives, but for our own as well. The more thralls Aristotles is able to raise before we reach him, the more we're likely to have to cut through to make our escape.'

'From what I can tell from the rumours going round the camp,' Gwilym chipped in, 'we're close, should arrive at our destination today in fact.'

Silence descended on the group as they all ruminated on what that might mean.

They had been travelling on foot for three days now, all of which had been spent traversing the immense stretch of woodland they were now in. At first, Torben had been very nervous, their experience of being in the Bar-Dendra Forest weighing heavily on his mind, but it soon became clear that this woodland was an entirely different beast. The trees here were spread much more widely apart, with the undergrowth not being nearly as thick, making the whole area feel much lighter and less intimidating than the tight, dark expanse of the Bar-Dendra. Had they not been held at the pleasure of Princess Theodora, Torben thought the whole experience would have been rather pleasant.

The morning after their confrontation with Almar on the river bank, the campsite had been alive with activity well before the sun was up and not long after dawn, they had moved out. From the moment they had been roused from slumber, it had become apparent that they would not be continuing their journey down the River Arlen. The four boats had been dragged to the edge of the hollow, where the sandy riverbank rose up to meet the woodland above them and had been partially buried, partially disguised with leaves and branches to hide them from prying eyes.

Though Captain Almar had made quite the show the night before of brushing off their concerns, as testified by the angry bruise that was still visible around Egberht's throat, Princess Theodora's soldiers had obviously been discussing what had been overheard of their prisoner's conversations, over the past few days. Although they avoided interacting with them for the most part, unless they were ordered to, all five of them had overheard the worried and discontented murmurings coming from groups of guards who huddled together when not on duty. Many of these conversations had been punctuated or had ended with the participants touching their hearts and glancing skywards, which Egberht had informed Torben was a sign of protection, invoking a goddess called Walanni. Over the course of the endless hours of walking, Egberht, with a surprising amount of input from Gwilym, had informed Torben, Antauros and Eleusia about the pantheon to which Kulittu and Walanni belonged, to which Theodora and her soldiers adhered.

As he tried to pick the string-like strands of meat from out of his teeth, Torben's mind ticked over some of the facts that he had been told. Walanni was the head deity in the faith that was named after her, whose small pantheon only included three other deities, Annella, Labarnas, and, of course, Kulittu. Kulittu and Walanni had once been husband and wife and were the parents of Annella and Labarnas, but while the other three deities had concerned themselves with more peaceable and noble pursuits and concerns, Kulittu had been more and more drawn to pain and cruelty, revelling in suffering and war.

Eventually, desperate to curb the evil that Kulittu wished to inflict on the world, Walanni and her children murdered him and threw his corpse out of their divine domain, where it disappeared, who knows where. Ever since, Kulittu was known as the Dead God. Despite his dubious title, everyone knew that he was not dead, that one couldn't simply kill a deity. Even today amongst the adherents of Walanniism, which was widespread amongst the southern kingdoms of the continent and further afield as well, his name was whispered and feared.

Torben was brought back from his thoughts by a gentle nudge to the shoulder from Antauros, who inclined his head in the direction of Princess Theodora, followed closely by Captain Almar, Ranulf, Roswit and two other guards. Unlike Theodora, Almar and all of the other soldiers round the encampment, Torben noticed that the four soldiers accompanying the Princess were not wearing their armour, nor were they carrying their shields. They were instead dressed in the kind of clothes that a wealthy but restrained merchant might wear, though they all still had swords hung on their belts. The delegation stopped a few feet away from the campfire the friends were sat around, and there was a moment's silence as both sides waited for the other to greet the other first. Eventually, Princess Theodora cleared her throat and took another step forwards.

'I hope this morning finds you all well.' She paused momentarily, waiting for a break in the stony silence that didn't occur. 'Ahem, well, it may please you to know that we are near the village of Haltwic, which is part of, or rather should I say *was once* part of the estate that was granted to Aristotles by my ancestors. His manor house, where we believe he might be, is no more than two hours' walk from the village. This means that for the moment the majority of us will remain here, whilst Lieutenant Ranulf and Trooper Roswit go to investigate the village, and Troopers Osforth and Haldin will go and investigate the manor house. All being well, they'll deliver my regards to Aristotles and request that he shelter and aid us. Gwilym, I want you to go with Ranulf and Roswit as their guide to help them gather information on the area and recent events.'

'And what if I don't want to go?' Gwilym said, scowling up defiantly.

'Careful, dwarf, Her Highness was not making a request but was giving an order,' Captain Almar growled.

He had moved forward so that he stood shoulder to shoulder with Princess Theodora, and he glowered down at Gwilym. The dwarf half-opened his mouth to speak, but sensing the rapidly rising tension and the fact that all of the other soldiers were now staring at them, expecting trouble, he decided against retaliating. He laboriously rose to his feet and nodded a curt farewell to Torben and the others.

'Well, if that's the way it is, lead on, Ranulf.'

The four soldiers bowed to Theodora and made their way off into the trees away from the encampment, Gwilym in tow. As Torben watched them disappear slowly from view, he noticed that Ranulf and Roswit altered the length of their stride so that they drifted back to walk on either side of the dwarf. Before they disappeared entirely from view, Torben saw Gwilym take one last look back and raise his hand in farewell.

After less than an hour of walking, Gwilym and his escort found themselves approaching the edge of the woodland. In the near distance, Gwilym could see the squat shapes of the village, Haltwic, the land in between broken and partitioned into fields and pasture land. Further away towards the horizon was a large hill, whose surface was speckled with brown and grey dots that Gwilym couldn't quite make out.

They paused at the edge of tree-line as Osforth and Haldin parted company with them and began to skirt along the edge of the wood, following its natural curve towards the distant hill and the manor house they had said lay beyond it. As the sound of their jogging footsteps receded, Roswit looked expectantly towards Ranulf, who was scouring the landscape in front of them intently, before clearing her throat to attract his attention.

'What's the plan, sir?'

'We'll need to move quickly, staying low. Getting over this pasture land is going to be the trickiest part, it's far too open for my liking. Once we're into the fields, though, the going will be much easier, a lot more cover which should enable us to get to the village pretty much unseen and...'

'And then what?' Gwilym interrupted. 'Are you going to make us lurk in a back alley hoping that we overhear something useful, or are you going to abduct someone and force whatever information you want out of them?'

'Well, errm, yes, that's what I was leaning towards,' Ranulf said, taken aback by the dwarf's assertive interjection.

'You're mad! I thought the Princess wanted you to gather information?'

'She does.'

'And presumably she wants you to do that as discreetly as possible?'

'Yes.'

'Then stop thinking with your helmet and use your head! If you just go in there and lift people off the street, you'll only get an assemblage of garbled information, half of which will like as not just be a lie made up on the spot in the hope that you'll let them go. That is unless you kill them in cold blood, and I'll tell you straight off that I won't be letting you kill random innocent folk without kicking up a fuss!

'In any case, this community is going to be small, which means that either people will notice someone is missing fairly quickly, or the word will get around as fast as lightning that two lugheads, waving swords around with a captive dwarf in tow, are beating people up and asking weird questions. I highly doubt that the Princess will look on you two very kindly if you lead a hue and cry straight to her. And all of this goes without mentioning that those two shepherd boys have been watching us for the past ten minutes.'

Gwilym pointed surreptitiously across the pasture land, where two small boys, barely taller than the beasts they were keeping an eye on, were watching them intently. They both had their shepherd's slings in their hands, just in case they had to defend themselves or their flock. Ranulf swore and looked angrily down at Gwilym.

'What would you suggest then?'

'That we act like normal people as opposed to some kind of hit squad. We walk calmly through the fields, into the village as one would expect a group of travellers that mean no harm to do, and once we're there, we find a place to inconspicuously eavesdrop and perhaps engage the locals naturally in conversation. I'm sure there'll be a tavern or pub of some description, even if it's just the downstairs room of somebody's house, where we will find an ample number of people to extract information from.'

Ranulf didn't respond but angrily huffed and nodded aggressively towards the village, stepping out into the pasture without a backwards glance.

'I take it this means he agrees with my suggestion?'

'Almost certainly,' Roswit said with a smile, 'though watch your step, he doesn't like being told that he's wrong.'

'Hmm, an unfortunate affliction for a man that's clearly an idiot,' Gwilym said, flashing a cheeky grin to Roswit.

They both stepped out of the trees after Ranulf, Gwilym raising a hand in greeting to the shepherd boys, who cautiously waved back but kept their distance.

As Gwilym had hoped, the walk from the edge of the forest to the village of Haltwic was rather uneventful. They passed a fair number of people tending to the crops and animals in the fields that lay along their route, but scant attention was paid to them, save being scanned by a wary eye, and that was nothing that Gwilym wasn't used to. Eventually, the muddy tracks that they were travelling along meandered through the patchwork of fields and joined up with a much larger, more official-looking strip of compact dirt, which was what passed as the road in this area. Looking back along its length, Gwilym guessed that the road must pass through another area of the woodland that the rest of Princess Theodora's retinue and prisoners were camped in, though he wasn't surprised that they had avoided it. Nothing announced one's presence in the wildness like travelling by road…

Haltwic itself was a reasonably large community that, in Gwilym's mind, stretched the definition of village quite considerably. The mass of one and two-story wooden buildings looked as if they had sprung up higgledy-piggledy to form the community, bulging out to form a hollow ring around a much larger building, which dominated its surroundings. This building, at least another story high again, looked as if it had been designed by someone who had once seen a castle, but who didn't have the means to construct an exact replica.

The rectangular structure was constructed out of ill-fitting tree trunks driven into the ground and bound together to create a palisade blockhouse. There were even ramparts of some description at the top, where the logs had been sharpened into blunt points. As they approached the blockhouse along the road, Gwilym could see a pair of men walking around the top of the building, their bodies half obscured by the makeshift battlements.

As the surrounding buildings stood at a respectful distance from the blockhouse, the area around it had developed into the heart of the community, with many of the buildings supporting businesses on their ground floors, mostly stalls selling goods and sundries of use to a farming community, but there was a baker's shop and a large hybrid workshop where a team of people looked as if they were plying their trades as coopers, blacksmiths and carpenters as the need required. As they drew closer to the centre of Haltwic, it became apparent that the blockhouse, as well as acting as the defensive structure for the village, also doubled as a meeting hall and tavern. The smell of stale beer and cooking odours wafted out of the open, overly large double doors.

It also became apparent that Haltwic was playing host to far more people than normally resided there. The area around the blockhouse was full of handcarts and piles of belongings, with makeshift tents thrown up against the sides of the blockhouse and the building that surrounded it. A line of weary, bedraggled and frankly scared-looking men, women and children snaked into the blockhouse, with individuals emerging with wooden bowls of soup or stew. Gwilym, Ranulf and Roswit stopped at the edge of the area and surveyed the activity.

'Refugees from Karpella?' Roswit asked the others quietly under her breath.

'No, the Sharisian blockade is too strong to let this many people out, and besides, I imagine the people in the surrounding communities wouldn't have made it nearly this far before they were ridden down.' Gwilym muttered darkly. 'My guess is that something else is at play here, and I'd bet that it's linked to your friend Aristotles...'

'Enough of that,' Ranulf snapped. 'We've got a job to do, gathering actual information rather than extrapolating nonsense from the dreams of that crackpot friend of yours.'

The dwarf shot an angry look at the back of Ranulf's head before stomping after him towards the blockhouse, Roswit following behind.

Weaving their way through the makeshift encampment, the three entered the blockhouse. The entirety of the interior was a single large room, the back quarter of which had been set up as a bar with an open plan kitchen and storage space behind, whilst the rest of the space was occupied by long, shabby wooden tables and benches. The interior was actually very well lit, as the numerous and sometimes sizeable cracks between the logs that made up the building allowed a good deal of light to filter in, complimented by the shaft of sunlight that poured down into the space from the open trap door in the ceiling, which provided access to the roof and the battlements via a very rickety looking scaffold. The line of refugees went all the way to the left-hand side of the bar, where a soup kitchen service was being provided by the inhabitants of Haltwic. A good number of the refugees were sitting eating their meals at the tables, and as they passed, Gwilym eyed the weak-looking bowls of cabbage soup with an un-envying eye.

It may look unappetising, he thought, *but I warrant that they're all grateful for it. I would be too if I was in their situation...*

Ranulf led the way through the building to the other side of the bar tended by a rotund, balding male human who was talking to a couple of men, another human and a dwarf. As they approached, the barkeep looked up and eyed them casually, quickly establishing that they were not locals.

'If you want feeding, then you'll have to join the queue over there with the other poor folk seeking sanctuary,' he drawled, barely giving them a second glance.

Despite having led the way to the bar, Ranulf was struggling to come up with a quick response, as he stood motionless, staring at the bar keep, his brain whirring so hard Gwilym was sure he could hear it. Sighing heavily, the dwarf pushed past and fixed his most heart-warming smile on the publican.

'We were actually after a drink, though the offer of hospitality your community is providing for the displaced is most generous.'

'You'll have to pay for it, we're not giving away everything we've got for nowt.'

'Not to worry, my mute friend here can see to that for you, can't you?'

Gwilym elbowed Ranulf slightly too hard in the midriff, making him wince and buckle slightly. The man managed to hold his tongue as he straightened up, staring daggers at Gwilym. His face had flushed bright red, partly from the pain and partly because of the muffled giggling coming from Roswit behind him. Ranulf produced a purse from within the folds of his clothes and brandished it before returning it to the pocket of his tunic. The pleasant chinking was music to the barkeep's ears.

'Very good,' the barman said, smirking at Ranulf. 'What'll be, we have better food to offer paying customers as well if that interests you?'

'We're good for food,' Gwilym interjected quickly before Ranulf regained his breath enough to speak, 'but we'll take an ale each.'

The barkeep nodded and went about his business whilst the two patrons he had been talking to turned inwards to continue their conversation with one another. Gwilym, sensing his chance, sidled over to them.

'Well met, stranger,' Gwilym said jovially, addressing his remark directly to the dwarf. 'What clan do you stand for?'

The dwarf, who had closely cropped brown hair and who was sporting an elaborate set of sideburns that linked directly into the brown tuft of his moustache, held out his arm to grasp the forearm that Gwilym had proffered to him.

'I stand for Clan Saldan, what of you?'

'I stand for Clan Pasmal,' Gwilym replied without a moment's hesitation.

'Ah,' the dwarf's face cracked into a smile, 'then just as our Clans are friends, so shall we be! I am Ioan, first of my name in the house of Balthur, son of Beorn.'

'I am Gwilym, adopted clansman in the house of Ragnar, son of Eofor. What brings you to these parts?'

'Haltwic is my adoptive home. There was good money to be made here trading goods between the different villages. They always have a glut of one thing and lack of another, and an enterprising soul can make a tidy profit connecting the right communities with one another and facilitating the trade. That is until recently, now the populations of over half the villages I did business in are outside this building or in line over there; well, the ones that made it out anyway...'

'What's occurring then? Are the Sharisians beginning to move troops this way from the capital?'

'No, we've neither heard nor seen nothing of the Sharisians, nor come to think of it our own Army of the North. No, the whole of this area is being plagued by Lupine raiders. I'd guessed you'd heard tell of this and brought your lackeys with you, they both look handy with a sword.'

Ioan gestured to Roswit, who was walking over to them, a tankard of ale in her hand for Gwilym along with one for herself, and then on to Ranulf, who was settling up with the barkeep. Gwilym nodded to her in thanks as he took the drink and then turned back to his fellow dwarf.

'No, hadn't heard anything about that at all. I just like to make sure I've got my back protected when I'm travelling.'

'Wise move if you can afford it. Where are you headed?'

'Visiting kin in Anselwic. I figured they were long overdue a visit, and considering that the Army of the North is stationed there, it seemed like an appealing time to pay my respects and take advantage of my open invitation of hospitality. How long have these raids been happening for?'

'Nearly a week now, but the regularity of them is quite like anything we've ever seen around here. Whereas you'd expect a Lupine raiding party to attack somewhere and then lie low for several days at least to stash their ill-gotten gains and let the heat die down before moving on to their next target, these Lupines have been launching attacks every single day, sometimes more than one in a day!'

'How do you know it's the same party of Lupines?' Roswit asked.

'Because they're led by a huge beast, covered in scars and with an eye missing, and a smaller, much older-looking female Lupine with ginger fur, who survivors claim has otherworldly powers. What's more, people who have returned to the raided villages say that when they got back, the corpses of the fallen had all vanished; taken away by the Lupines for one foul purpose or another, I imagine, and that they'd hardly turned the places over for hidden caches of valuables at all. As if they were only after the villagers themselves. Errgh, send a shiver down my spine, it does! Not to mention that people in the village having been saying that the Lupines have been stealing corpses from the graveyard, though I suspect that might be superstitious nonsense, a product of mass hysteria.'

By now, Ranulf had joined them and stood with his arms crossed behind Gwilym and Roswit.

'How far away was the last attack?' he asked.

'Not far from here. This morning we had people coming in from Lassenwic, which is only ten miles away from here on the road to Anselwic, saying they'd been raided during the night. If I was you, I'd stop here for a spell where at least we've got the shelter of this place.' Ioan gestured at the walls of the building. 'It ain't much, but I'd still rather be in here than out there if they come for us.'

As Ioan finished speaking, Gwilym tugged at the end of his beard, deep in thought. He was interrupted by Ranulf, who leaned down to whisper in his ear:

'We've tarried here for too long. We should get back to the edge of the woods to meet up with Osforth and Haldin and head back to report to the Princess.'

Gwilym nodded absentmindedly as Ranulf spoke to him, and then remembering that he was still supposed to be playing a part, nodded more vigorously before turning to slap the man roughly on the back.

'Yes, you're right, Ranulf, we should go and see to our horses.'

Turning back to Ioan and his human companion, who had listened in stony silence throughout the whole interaction, Gwilym pulled a couple of fat gold coins out of the purse he had lifted from Ranulf's tunic, having used the slap on the back to cover his movements, and handed them to the dwarf.

'Here, friend, take these and enjoy a drink on us. Drink to our health on the road to Anselwic!'

'Aye, that we will. Thank you, friend of Clan Saldan, luck go with you!'

Gwilym downed the rest of his drink, putting the tankard on the bar before leading the way out of the blockhouse. He tossed Ranulf's purse casually back to the man over his shoulder, causing a renewed bout of stifled giggling from Roswit, who was watching her superior's face turn from red to purple with anger. Once outside, the three of them began to retrace their steps along the road out of Haltwic, Gwilym deep in thought once more, and Ranulf, breathing heavily, trying to calm himself down.

They were both brought back to reality by Roswit, who held out her hands to stop them and pointed slowly up to the sky where a huge block of low-lying black clouds was moving in fast from the west. As the clouds grew closer, they cast thick shadows over the village and surrounding countryside, as if night was suddenly falling about them.

'I don't like the look of those clouds,' Roswit said. 'I hope it doesn't rain on us before we get back to the camp.'

'That would be the least of my worries,' Gwilym answered, worry creeping into his voice.

'Why?'

'Because there's not a gust of wind around strong enough to knock over a feather right now, but it's as if no one's told those clouds that…'

Then echoing from the wide border of the woodland came a long piercing howl that was joined and amplified by hundreds more Lupines joining in.

'Run, back to the village!' Gwilym shouted.

9

_____

The day had passed by sluggishly in the woodland camp as Princess Theodora and her retinue awaited the return of Gwilym and the scouts that had been sent out ahead of them. Many of the soldiers fidgeted nervously around the dying embers of their campfires, whilst those on guard shuffled restlessly, their eyes darting to and fro. Theodora herself was sat off to one side, a worried look on her face as she held a quiet conversation with Captain Almar. They were all uneasy about staying put in the wilderness for so long.

For Torben, Eleusia, Antauros and Egberht, however, the hiatus in the relentless routine of travelling that had dominated the last few days was welcome, and they lounged by their own small campfire, making a show of not caring about the pause in the journey, but in reality holding their own discreet conference concerned with how best to make their escape. Unfortunately, the past few hours of discussion had brought them little closer to forming even the scaffolding of a plan, the risks it seemed were too great, and the amount of unknown information about where they were going and what would happen to them there was too much.

'Perhaps Gwilym will be able to shed some light on the situation when he returns,' Antauros said softly, tossing some broken bits of stick into the fire.

'Are we sure we're not overthinking all of this?' Torben rubbed his temples meditatively as he spoke. 'Maybe Theodora will be true to her word and let us go once she's happy that she and her followers are in a more secure position? She seems decent enough, our present situation notwithstanding. To me, she just comes across as being genuinely concerned for the welfare of her people, rather than being particularly manipulative.'

'I'm sure we'd all love to believe that, Torben,' Eleusia responded, 'but I'll believe that she'll just let us go when I see it. In my experience, one should never trust anyone, ruler, politician, official, whatever, who holds a significant amount of power. They'll tell the stooges who toil for them in their castles whatever they want to hear to keep them on side, but won't hesitate to chuck them off the ramparts to save their own skin if they have to. My gut makes me doubt that Theodora will be cut from a different cloth...'

'What do you think, Egberht?' Torben asked. 'Does she strike you as being different to King Hastel and his lot? Egberht?'

The gnome didn't respond but was looking up towards the tree canopy and the sky beyond with a thoughtful look on his face. He sniffed the air and licked his lips slowly, the thoughtful expression transitioning slowly to one of concern.

'Egberht?' Torben repeated.

'Someone or something is performing some powerful magic nearby, far too close for comfort,' the gnome said. 'I can feel it in the air...'

'What, what is it?'

'There!'

Egberht pointed to a huge bank of thick, black cloud that was surging towards them, so low that it obscured the tops of the trees and threw everything beneath into a murky twilight. The foursome rose slowly to their feet, as did many of the soldiers around them, watching the unnatural looking edifice cruise towards them at startling speed. That slow movement turned into a scramble throughout the camp as a Lupine howl, which was quickly joined by many more, rang out through the trees.

'Gods spare us! They're very close!' Antauros growled

All around them, the soldiers were hefting shields, drawing weapons and nocking arrows to bowstrings. Eleusia's hand had instinctively reached for where her sword would have been, only to meet empty air. She swore and began to sprint towards Princess Theodora, who was becoming obscured by the mass of guards flocking to her. Torben, Antauros and Egberht hurriedly gathered up their things and followed.

'Your Highness!' Eleusia shouted as she tried to push her way through the soldiers. 'Your Highness, let us help you. Give us back our weapons. You'll need everyone to pull their weight, you can't afford to have us defenceless.'

The guards parted ranks, after a curt order from Captain Almar, to let Eleusia and her companions through to the centre of the defensive ring. Several of the guards in the rear rank turned to keep an eye on proceedings as they were admitted, and Captain Almar drew closer to Theodora, his sword already drawn.

'Please, Your Highness, let us defend ourselves and help keep you safe in the process.'

'I would advise against allowing this,' Captain Almar interjected before Theodora could speak. 'Remember they are prisoners and we cannot fully trust them.'

'The Lupines won't see us as prisoners, they'll see us as easy prey!'

Another wave of howling, which sounded much closer than the first, rattled around them. The defensive formation drew in tighter, readying itself for the onslaught. The look of hesitation on Princess Theodora's face was cast into deep shadow as the black cloud passed over them, snuffing out most of the daylight.

'You're right, keeping you defenceless would be tantamount to a death sentence in such a situation. Almar, don't!' Theodora snapped, hearing the cry of protest from her Captain. 'I've made my decision, and perhaps we should do them the courtesy of giving them a little trust.'

Theodora snapped her fingers, and a couple of guards peeled off from the formation and dumped the friends' weapons in a heap on the ground and allowed them to collect their things. Torben felt immediately more at ease as he gathered his gear, and he could see Antauros felt the same way as he hefted his shield onto his arm and tucked Gwilym's seax and sling into his belt for safekeeping. The minotaur looked down at the diminutive figure of Egberht, who was looking around with a scared, almost panicked look on his face.

'Stay close to me,' Antauros said quietly and soothingly to him. 'You'll be alright, we'll make sure you don't get hurt, won't we, Torben?'

Torben nodded and shuffled closer to Antauros, so close that their shields overlapped slightly, thrusting Egberht, who was now stood at the minotaur's feet, even deeper into shadow. Glancing down, he could see the gnome whispering to himself, hands held slightly apart just in front of his body. Egberht's face became illuminated by a ball of runes that appeared in the space, casting out an increasing strong silver light.

From the trees all around them, the howling started once again, dragging Torben's attention back to their surroundings. By now, the Princess' guard had formed into a tight defensive circle, their shields locked together and spears down. In the centre of the circle, several guards with bows had half drawn their weapons, ready to fully draw and loose when they spotted a target. Eleusia already had her crossbow to her shoulder and was scanning the murky gloom beyond through the gaps between the heads of the soldiers in the shield wall.

The heads of everyone in the formation began to flick back and forth nervously as shapes flitted in the shadows. The howling all around them crescendoed to an even higher level than before, ringing in their ears and making Torben wince as the sound assaulted his senses. Then, abruptly, everything around them fell into silence. Straining his ears for any sound of life beyond their formation, Torben hoped for a second that the Lupines had left to go off in search of softer targets. His hopes were shattered as an almost imperceptible noise tickled his ears, as if something small and swift was cutting through the air towards them.

The arrow landed less than an inch away from Princess Theodora's foot, the shaft trembling as it drove itself halfway up its length into the ground. The sound of more arrows whizzing through the air could be heard more clearly now, and as the cry went up from Captain Almar, and the soldiers in the formation began to raise their shields over their heads, Egberht dashed out from the cover of Antauros' bulk and hurled his silver ball of arcane energy into the air. When the spell rose clear of their heads, he blurted out a command word, and the ball parted swiftly into a silver dome that encompassed them all. As the walls of the magical dome reached the ground and fully enclosed them, sparks flashed across its surface as the Lupine arrows bounced off and spun away. For thirty seconds, the protection held, Egberht's face twisted and red in concentration. Eventually, he staggered, gasping for breath, and leaned against Antauros' leg for support. A final arrow pinged off the barrier, which vanished along with the silver glow it emitted.

The guards instinctively began to raise their shields again, ready to receive more arrows, but Eleusia's voice snapped out above the sound of their movements.

'Don't! They're closing in!'

As the ceiling of shields began to descend, Torben's view outwards became clear again, and he could see shapes moving quickly out of the arcane darkness towards them, solidifying into Lupine shapes charging through the trees, weapons drawn. The sound of flying arrows and the twang of bowstrings came this time from Theodora's soldiers as they let fly at the oncoming attackers, and the sounds of their bows were joined by the crack and thunk of Eleusia's crossbow. Several of the Lupines fell, churning up the dirt and smashing through the undergrowth as they crashed to the ground, but the rest fell upon the shield wall, trying to force their way inside.

The Lupines' savage snarling mingled with the shouts of rage and defiance from the defenders, but after a few seconds, sounds of crying and whimpering began to join the cacophony on both sides, the cries of the wounded and dying. One of the soldiers staggered back into the middle of the formation, clutching at his throat, which was now a torrent of blood. As he fell back, a Lupine barrelled through the weakened section of the defences and leaped at the first figure that stood in their way, Princess Theodora. Theodora, who had her back turned to her assailant, was completely bowled over as the savage creature smashed into her, pinning her to the ground, a wicked-looking, rusty dagger held aloft in its taloned fist.

In the nick of time, Torben realised what was going on. He turned and punched his shield forward, knocking the Lupine back, its arms flailing, and then he followed up with a forceful thrust of his spear, sending it sprawling into the dirt. Kneeling down to help the dazed Princess to her feet, he looked to the point where the Lupine had managed to enter the formation, once again a solid body of soldiers, and then around looking for other potential weaknesses. As he scanned the circle, he realised that no one else had noticed what had happened, Captain Almar, Antauros, and Eleusia were all shoring up the defences in other parts of the formation, whilst Egberht was bent over one of the injured guards, weaving a spell to try and save their life.

Princess Theodora had clearly noticed the same thing, for she grasped his forearm tightly as he helped her back to her feet and nodded to him gravely.

'Thank you, Torben,' she uttered grimly.

Before Torben could respond, another chorus of howling

erupted around them, making the ears of the attacking Lupines prick up and then withdraw quickly back into the concealing darkness. As the last one disappeared from view, the men and women of Theodora's retinue cheered and clashed their weapons together, throwing insults and jeers into the darkness. Antauros, Eleusia and Captain Almar, however, drew back to the centre of the formation, looking just as grim-faced as Theodora did.

'They'll be back and soon.' Eleusia wiped sweat and blood from her forehead with a sleeve as she spoke. 'That was just a probing attack, testing our resolve. There are far more of them out there than we can handle.'

'She's right, Your Highness,' Captain Almar agreed. 'We can't stay here. If we do we'll be picked off one by one or be slaughtered when our resolve finally breaks.'

'Could we make it to the manor house? If we're right in our hunch that Aristotles is there, we'll find aid and a more defensible position there.'

'No, Your Highness, it's too far away. The Lupines would overrun us long before we reached it. We might be able to reach the village, though. That would still be better than being out here.'

'You'd better make your choice quickly,' Antauros rumbled. 'I doubt they'll give us much longer to chat…'

'We'll take our chances,' Theodora said decisively. 'Captain Almar, organise an orderly, defensive withdrawal.'

'Yes, Your Highness. What of the casualties?'

'All who can stand come with us.'

Theodora's voice caught in her throat as she spoke, and Captain Almar nodded brusquely in acknowledgement before wheeling about and issuing orders at a lightning pace. Antauros stooped down to help the soldier Egberht had been tending to onto their feet, and several other casualties were brought into the centre of the ring. Torben rushed over to help prop up another soldier, who was using her spear as a crutch, trying to keep her bloodied right leg off the ground. Three other bodies were dragged into the centre of the ring to join the one that still lay in the centre. Quickly and quietly, their weapons were taken off them, and then Princess Theodora moved between the four bodies, closing their eyes and whispering over the corpses as she did so. Straightening up, she nodded to Captain Almar, who gave the order to move out.

The formation loosened slightly to allow for greater freedom of movement, but still close enough that they could tessellate back together if set upon again by the Lupines, who were clearly following them, some so bold as to jog ahead of the concealing shroud of magic. They travelled as fast as they were able through the woods and then eventually out into the fields that lay in the hinterland of Haltwic. Occasionally an arrow would zip its way towards them, but they were fired randomly and carelessly, as if the Lupine archers were not really trying to hit their mark but were simply goading them onwards towards the village. Indeed, the Lupines that followed kept their distance, though there was a great deal of snarling and boasting from them.

Not long after breaking out from the cover of the trees, another chorus of howling erupted from the Lupines as four of them paraded triumphantly across their front ranks, waving aloft their spears, each of which now bore one of the heads of the slain soldiers that had been left in the woods. Several of the soldiers visibly bristled at the sight, with a couple even stopping and looking as if they intended to charge forwards, until Almar dragged them back into formation.

'Remember your orders!' he barked. 'You'll die too if you go charging in there, and how would that help to spare their honour? The best thing you can do is hold fast to the cause that they kept until their dying breaths!'

Torben, who had been looking back at the disgusting sight and completely oblivious to where he was going, pitched forward as he tripped over something, nearly sending himself and the soldier he was helping to walk crashing to the ground. Managing to recover his balance in the nick of time, and apologising profusely to the soldier, who had cried out in agony at the sudden, jolting movement, he looked down to see what he had stumbled over and saw a small boy, his chest a bloodied, mangled mess, who still clutched a shepherd's sling in one of his cold hands.

It did not take much convincing to get Ranulf and Roswit to follow Gwilym back into the centre of Haltwic. As soon as the howling had started and the shadow of the unnatural black cloud had started to bear down on the community, distinctively Lupine shapes had been seen emerging from the trees before being concealed by the arcane shadows. They had joined an increasingly panicked stream of people running in from the fields, hoping to find protection within the village.

Haltwic's centre was a scene of pandemonium as the villagers and refugees jostled impatiently with one another to get inside the blockhouse. Shouts and screams of panic sounded all around them as the three joined the crush of people and began to push their way inside. Within the blockhouse, the benches and tables were being hurriedly piled to one side to create more room for the mass of people trying to gain access by harried-looking villagers who had turned up with a rag-tag selection of weapons, mostly knives and hunting bows, to defend their community.

When they finally gained access, Gwilym spotted Ioan standing on a barrel in the centre of the room, trying to bring some sense of direction to the chaos, but with little success. He hailed Gwilym as the three of them entered, shouting at the top of his voice to be heard above the frenetic activity.

'Am I glad to see you three again. We could do with a hand clearing the space and shoring up the doors, not to mention the assistance of your guards' swords.'

'Consider it done!'

Ioan looked relieved as Gwilym, Ranulf and Roswit began to throw themselves into the activity. Soon the blockhouse was a seething mass of people waiting nervously and praying for the storm to pass them by. The volume in the room decreased dramatically to a nervous hush as the large wooden doors were finally shut, a thick wooden bar dropped across, and several tables were stacked against them for extra support. Many of Haltwic's flung-together militia were climbing the scaffolding to gain access to the roof and its battlement, and Gwilym nudged Roswit and Ranulf to get their attention as he watched the people ascend.

'We should get up there as well, it'll give us the best point to view how deep the cesspit we're in is. We might be able to get some indication of whether the others have been caught up in this as well…'

'Good idea,' Ranulf replied. 'The two of you go up and check out what's going on; I'll stay here and see if there's an alternative way for us to get out of here if we need to bolt.'

Gwilym nodded in agreement and set off with Roswit on his heels to reach the roof. The scaffolding felt very unstable as they started to climb, and the worryingly thin wooden poles that had been lashed together to form the structure groaned and creaked unsettlingly as it begrudgingly accepted their weight. They both breathed a sigh of relief as they hauled themselves up onto the slightly sloped roof and scrambled across it to a thin straight walkway that ran around behind and abutted the palisade parapet.

The village militia were nervously peering out across the village and what little of the landscape beyond they could see, and they largely ignored Gwilym and Roswit, who did a quick circuit of the blockhouse, looking out in all directions. There was little to be seen to the south where the woodland bordered the pastureland and fields, but to the north and west, Lupines could be seen making their way quickly towards the settlement. Some of the militia had seen this as well, for they all thundered around the roof and crowded that section of battlement, readying their bows and their dull-pointed hunting arrows. After a few more tense seconds, the first twang of bowstrings was heard and peaking over the top of the rampart, Gwilym could see Lupine shapes skulking in the shadows of the nearby buildings.

'Somethings not right,' he said quietly to Roswit. 'Why aren't they attacking? They're not even looting the houses by the looks of it...'

'It's as if they're waiting for something,' Roswit replied.

'Hmm, I wonder...'

Gwilym edged his way awkwardly past the militiaman who was trying to fire his bow over the top of the dwarf's head and returned to the now-abandoned southern section of rampart, which should have provided an overlook of the distant trees. At first he couldn't see anything, but then he thought he saw a blob of movement coming from the tree-line and heading their way. As the shape emerged from the trees, another clamour of howling surged from the woods.'

'Roswit, can you see that, the movement over there?'

'Yes, just about, what is it?'

Before Gwilym could answer, shouts of jubilation came from the other side of the rampart, where the militia had been trying to pick off the Lupines in the village.

'They're drawing off!'

'Thank the gods, they've had enough!'

Moving quickly back to the band of ebullient temporary soldiers, Gwilym muscled his way back to his viewing spot. The ground around the blockhouse, along with the walls of the neighbouring buildings, were littered with arrows, wasted shots all, but the Lupines that had been moving in had vanished back deeper into the darkness. Here and there, Gwilym was sure he saw flashes of weapons and hulking shapes briefly materialising from the arcane cover. He wheeled around and snapped at the militia, who were making for the scaffolding, looking to toast their victory.

'Stay where you are, this isn't over yet!'

'What are you talking about? They've scarpered, can't you see?' one man with a gap-toothed grin scoffed, his companions echoing his sentiment.

'They won't have been scared off by whatever the hell you call that shoddy display of martial prowess. They've withdrawn where we can't see them, and I swear to you if you go back down there and leave these ramparts undefended, they'll be up those walls like a shot and tear everyone down in there to shreds.'

Before Gwilym could say anything else, Roswit's voice called out for him from the other side of the blockhouse, and he padded around to see what she was calling about, several of the militia following him.

'Look there, that movement is the Princess, but look how many Lupines are following them!'

Roswit pointed as she spoke to just beyond the first of the village's buildings, where the unmistakable shapes of Theodora's armoured retinue, the obvious silhouette of Antauros among them, could be seen making their way quickly in loose formation into Haltwic. Behind them was a seething mass of fur and metal, hundreds of Lupines loping casually after them as if they were letting them withdraw into the village.

'We need to get the doors open; otherwise, they'll be stuck outside, and I don't want to start guessing how long those Lupines will hold back for. Roswit, stay here and keep an eye on things, try to attract their attention if you can. It'll be better for all of us if we can get them in here to help defend this rotting pile of twigs.'

Roswit nodded as Gwilym finished his instructions and began to head up the slope of the roof to the access hatch and the scaffolding. As he scrambled up the rough wooden boards, the dwarf barked orders at one of the knots of militia, who were still milling around the parapet, not sure of what to do with themselves.

'You four, come with me. The rest of you, spread out, keep your eye peeled and be ready to fire at any Lupines that come close.'

The militia complied, glad that someone else was shouldering the responsibility of leadership. Gwilym felt the scaffolding vibrate under the strain of his new command's heavy footfalls as he made his way back down to the ground, far faster than he would have liked. Once back on the solid, compacted earth floor of the blockhouse, he pushed his way through masses crowded round to hear any news of what was going on outside. With some difficulty, Gwilym managed to force his way through to the double doors, the four militia behind him. Turning round to issue further orders, Gwilym saw that Ioan had made his way through the crowd as well, eager to hear what was happening.

'Right, you two, keep that lot back and out of our way as best you can. You two, start shifting the barricade,' he snapped at the militiamen, who warily began to comply. 'Ioan, don't worry!' he said, seeing the dwarf begin to sprint forward with a concerned look on his face. Then raising his voice so that as many people in the room could hear, 'There is a force of troops pushing their way through the Lupine savages to help defend our position. I need as many strong backs as possible to help clear the barricade and be ready to throw it back into place once they're inside. Everyone else, get back as much as possible!'

After a moment's hesitation, Ioan, who had been staring intently at Gwilym, weighing up the truth of what his fellow dwarf had said, turned and began to shout his own orders into the crowd, summoning people forwards and telling the others to get back, much to Gwilym's relief. That expression of relief faded from his face, however, as he saw Ranulf pushing his way through the mass of people.

'Gwilym, what the hell is going on? Where is Roswit?'

Seeing that the soldier's hand was on his sword hilt and the blade was partially drawn, Gwilym raised his hands slowly in front of him to show he meant no harm as he began to speak.

'Ranulf, there's nothing to be alarmed about. We spotted Princess Theodora and your comrades making their way here. They're being pursued, but I reckon they'll make it. Roswit is still up top, trying to get their attention so they know they can seek shelter here. There, do you hear that?'

From above them, the sound of a poorly made, weathered bell being struck could be heard, beckoning the troops outside to their location. Growling something incomprehensible, Ranulf pushed his blade back into its sheath and moved to help clear the barricade, barging past Gwilym as he did so. It took a worryingly short amount of time to clear the detritus that had been hurriedly thrown against the blockhouse, most of which, Gwilym noticed, were too light to have added any additional defensive weight to the portal.

With the entrance clear, Gwilym pressed his face to one of the ample cracks between the ill-fitting planks and squinted out into the space beyond. The bell was still sounding overhead, and beneath its discordant clanging, he could just about hear the sound of massed footsteps tramping along the dirt road. After several more seconds of waiting, the bell's ringing was abruptly silenced, and the noise replaced by Roswit's voice shouting down into the room, and Gwilym saw the first of Theodora's troops racing into view.

'Open the gate. Now!'

Gwilym leapt back from the doors just as Ranulf, his sword drawn, pushed several of the militiamen forwards to remove the crossbar and then heave the door open. As they swung open, the sounds of massed activity erupted outside, Theodora and her soldiers sprinting to safety, the sound of a new Lupine assault and the whistle of arrows being let loose from above. Then

Theodora's retinue spilled into the blockhouse, and the activity reached an all-new level.

Even before he was completely through the threshold, Captain Almar was barking orders left, right and centre. Soldiers started climbing the scaffolding to the roof, others began searching the room, pushing the civilians aside in their quest to make sure the building was secure, whilst the last few men and women through the doors wheeled about and slammed them shut, throwing their weight against them to stop the tide of Lupines from breaking through and buying enough time for the crossbar to be placed and furniture dragged across to shore up the barricade.

'You made it then!' Gwilym hailed his friends as he focused in on Antauros' bulk sticking out above the crowd.

'Yes, but if those Lupines hadn't held back, I doubt we would have.'

Having helped the soldier he had been supporting up onto a table, Antauros turned and grasped Gwilym's forearm in greeting before pulling the dwarf's belongings out of his belt and handing them over.

'Here, these adverse conditions have made our captors see some sense at last.'

'What is our position like here?' Eleusia asked Gwilym, who was now fiddling with his belt and seax.

'Only one official way in and out, but I'm sure you've noticed that this place is hardly watertight, and a lot of that wood between the holes looks like it's seen far too much damp to weather much of a storm. There are ramparts up top though we can shoot down from, and if that damned weird cloud wasn't hanging around, you'd get a pretty good view up there too.'

'Right, come on then, let's make sure you haven't forgotten how to use that sling.' Eleusia led the way towards the scaffolding. She turned to talk over her shoulder as she walked, 'Torben, with us, I want you watching our backs in case the Lupines start scaling the walls; Antauros, stay here, make sure nothing gets through that gate!'

'Sounds good to me,' Antauros snorted, eying up the ceiling, which looked as if it was bowing under the weight of the defenders already up there. 'I wouldn't want to test the strength of the floorboards...'

Eleusia had already begun the climb to the roof before she'd finished speaking, and Torben was just starting to make his way up, spear and shield clutched in one hand to give him a free one to manoeuvre. Gwilym finished reattaching his gear and sighed heavily as he eyed the scaffold. As he tramped towards the swaying, flexing wooden edifice, he slapped Egberht on the back in greeting, the gnome turning his head from the patient he was ministering to nod in acknowledgement.

The roof and ramparts of the blockhouse were a hive of activity. Captain Almar stood on the slope of the roof, ordering anyone in the vicinity around, his own soldiers and the increasing nervous-looking militia, who kept throwing worried glances in his direction. Theodora was standing nearby, taking in the scene, her face a blank mask. Hauling himself up onto the roof, Torben made a beeline for where Eleusia had established her position and hovered behind her, close enough to peer over the ramparts but not close enough to get in the way of her loading her crossbow.

Torben had expected to see the Lupines swarming all around the base of the blockhouse, attacking the doors and trying to climb up to assault the defenders up above. Instead, the area around their haven was clear, save for the arrow peppered bodies of a few Lupines who had tried to rush in when the doors had been opened.

'They've retreated back to the cover of the buildings.' Roswit, who had stationed herself next to Eleusia, a scavenged bow in her hand, guessed what Torben had been thinking. 'I don't understand what's going on...'

The dark cloud had centred itself directly over them now,

completely restricting their vision to the dirt around the block-house and the façades of the surrounding buildings.

'Can't see a bloody thing!' Gwilym had finished his climb and puffed his way towards them. 'You could hide a whole bloody army in there.'

'They have,' Eleusia curtly responded.

'Movement near the gates!'

One of the soldiers close to them issued the warning, and they all turned their attention to a street directly opposite their position, where shambling shapes could be seen materialising out of the gloom.

'Hold your fire! They're civilians, open the...'

'No!' Eleusia snapped, drowning out the soldier's report. 'They're not civilians, they were, but they're not now. Look at them.'

Everyone who had a line of sight on the figures peered down as the arcane darkness finally relinquished its hold on them and they were fully revealed. There were at least twenty individuals before the blockhouse now, with more indistinct shapes moving through the cloaking cloud. Although they were dressed in the garments one might expect village folk of that area to wear, albeit heavily bedraggled, they all walked in a halting manner, as if willing their limbs to move, and they all bore horrific injuries, injuries which should have killed them, which had originally killed them.

'What in the Mother's name is going on?'

Princess Theodora had pushed her way up to the ramparts so she could see what was going on, and an ashen-faced Captain Almar craned his neck behind her.

'They're thralls, Your Highness.' Torben spoke grimly. 'They're undead puppets dragged back from their rest to serve a twisted living master.'

Silence descended on Haltwic, broken only by the shuffling feet of the thralls as they formed into ranks before the entrance to the block-house, a mocking parody of an army. After nearly fifty thralls had entered the space, they awkwardly parted ranks to allow a group of Lupines to drag forward two bloodied figures, their heads bowed. Their Lupine captors threw them to the ground and stationed themselves on either side, waiting. One of the prisoners pushed themselves unsteadily onto their knees, though their head remained downcast, concealing their face. The other, however, lay motionless in a crumpled heap on the ground.

'That's Osforth and Haldin,' Roswit whispered.

'So, it is indeed true. I must admit, Princess Theodora, I did not think it likely that you and so many of your minions would have survived the siege, let alone so many years held in limbo between life and death. My congratulations to you all for surviving for so long.'

The cold, clear drawl of Aristotles rang around the centre of Haltwic, magically projected so that it rang loud and clear in all of their ears as if coming from every direction at once. Then the Shadow Elf stepped from out from the area of his concealing spell and began to walk nonchalantly down the channel between the serried ranks of the dead. He was followed closely by two Lupines, one, an enormous creature with black fur streaked with grey, body pitted and slashed with scars, who cocked its head at an awkward angle so that it could survey the world out of its one remaining eye, and a smaller, skulking Lupine with ginger fur. Torben gritted his teeth as he saw Hrex scuttling in the shadow of her master, and he heard Gwilym curse behind him.

'I have already ascertained from your messenger boys here as to why you are seeking me out, but I'm afraid that I cannot help you.'

'You are a subject of Sarper IV, by rights you should honour your pledge to him by paying homage and fealty to his daughter!' Almar barked, his anger causing spittle to fly from his mouth and over the parapet.

'Ha! Unlike you, I do not confine the philosophy of my existence to a man who was unable to keep a hold of what little power he had. Be a good Captain and run along now, go find someone with a dirty helmet to shout at.'

Aristotles flicked his hand up, a small flash of light blinking at his fingertips, and Captain Almar was hurled back from the parapet and crashed into the sloped roof of the blockhouse behind him. The wood of the ceiling cracked and groaned under his sudden impact but did not give way, leaving him lying stunned and speechless on his back.

'As I said, Princess Theodora,' Aristotles smoothed a rogue lock of hair back into place as he spoke. 'I am not in the position to help you, but perhaps you might wish to help me?'

'You, who have abandoned the teachings of Walanni and who now meddle with the sacrosanct affairs of the dead, wish for me to help you?' Theodora's voice was calm and steely, expressing the seething of her internal anger far more effectively and sharply than Almar's rage.

'It is a sad thing to have someone match the low expectations one puts upon them. You were always a literal one, Theodora, only taking what you can see or what you are told into account, never looking deeper at the bigger picture, never thinking how one move might affect the rest. Yes, I have accessed beings and levels of power far greater than your Walanni, and through that, my prospects and the likelihood of me reaching my goals are increased a hundredfold. Whereas you, where is your hope, my dear Theodora? A princess without a kingdom; stranded in a land now owned by the people who killed her father; surrounded by a dwindling band of followers, who I'm sure are all looking for a way to save their own skins rather than yours; who stands now in a place she has no hope of leaving... Your house is dead, your power gone and forgotten in the mists of time. Join me, and when I am successful, I will ensure some of the spoils are scattered in your direction.'

'You would abandon your people without a second thought?'

'You have never been my people, merely a populace I could

blend in with to achieve my aims. Nevertheless, I am grateful for the help your father and grandfather gave me; without the access they granted me to the resources I need, I would not be here today. Because of that I am happy to extend my offer to you. I need living servants of a more socially acceptable ilk than Lupines, but my offer is short-lived, so make your decision quickly.'

'I will never submit to a traitor who uses the blessed dead as their playthings!'

Aristotles laughed as he took several paces forward, closing the distance between himself and the prisoners.

'A pity. I did wonder if, in your currently dire situation, you would remain embedded to your principles. It doesn't matter though; I still have need of other servants, you will serve me willingly in life, or willingly in death.'

He nodded to the Lupine guards who drew their weapons and stabbed down at the bodies of their prisoners. The man who was on his knees cried out in pain, whilst the other remained motionless, clearly already dead. As the kneeling man collapsed to the ground, a smear of purple light was drawn out of his body and sucked into the mask that hung around the elf's neck. Aristotles raised his hands up, one over each of the corpses, his eyes closed, lips moving wordlessly. Within seconds, both dead men began to haul themselves unnaturally to their feet.

As the two thralls stood, Aristotles turned to Hrex, and the large Lupine stood behind him.

'Attack at your pleasure, bring Theodora to me alive if you can, kill the others so that they can swell our ranks.'

The scarred Lupine tossed his head back and howled, and the Lupines hidden from view joined in. Then the ranks of the dead surged forwards to attack the gate as the Lupines sprinted out of side streets and began to claw their way up the side of the blockhouse.

10

The whole fabric of the blockhouse shook as the mass of thralls ploughed into the gate and the tide of Lupines began clawing their way up the sides of the wooden structure. All around the ramparts Theodora's retinue and the Haltwic militia began to loose their arrows. Soon the whimpers of dead and dying Lupines mingled with the savage battle cries. Still they came.

Torben lunged forward and thrust his spear into the chest of one beast whose head and upper body had crested the parapet and was close to climbing over the wooden barricade. It tried to maintain its hold on the woodwork, its claws scrabbling desperately, sending up splinters of wood and sawdust, but then it tumbled down the ground and out of sight. Torben tightened the grip on his spear as he saw the clawed hands of another Lupine, immediately replacing its comrade he had just driven off the side of the building. He took a step back and gritted his teeth, ready to receive the foe as it vaulted over the parapet. Its feet had barely touched the wooden boards before it was thrown back, its throat a bloodied mess, ruined by one of Eleusia's crossbow bolts.

'We need to keep them off the roof, Torben!' Eleusia shouted, moving forward to tip the Lupine's body off the roof. 'The only advantage we have over them is that they're vulnerable whilst they're climbing.'

Torben nodded and dashed over to another section of the defences, where one of the militiamen was desperately trying to beat back two Lupines that had nearly climbed up the wall and were threatening to pull him off. Stabbing down at the nearest, Torben managed to divert it enough that it let go of the man's tunic, but wasn't able to stop the other from heaving the helpless defender from his position. Torben shivered as he heard the man's screams turn into a crunching thud as he hit the ground, and the distraction was long enough to allow the first Lupine to spring onto the roof. His thoughts snapping back to the task at hand, Torben punched his shield forwards, the boss smashing into the beast's face, making it recoil. He dropped his spear – he was too close to his adversary for it to be useful – and drew his shortsword and closed the distance. Using his shield to pin the creature against the parapet's stakes, he stabbed upwards several times. He could feel the creature's hot blood flowing over his hand and felt its weight slump fully onto his shield as its life ebbed away.

Before he had time to think, another wolfish face appeared in his peripheral vision, arm raised to strike at him. He just about managed to raise his sword to meet the blow, but the strength of his opponents strike blasted his arm out of the way. Fortunately, his parry had deflected the blow enough that the rusty, chipped blade skittered off his chainmail. He winced from the force of the blow, knowing he was badly bruised, and grunted in pain as he dragged his arm back to guard position. The Lupine was already moving in for another attack, but as it thrust forward, its head snapped suddenly and unnaturally to the side, the skull caved in by a slingshot bullet. Torben stepped out of the way of its dying thrust and looked in the direction the bullet had come from. Gwilym was standing astride the pinnacle of the sloped roof, his eyes already on another target, the sling in his hand making the air around it buzz.

Gwilym flicked his wrist skilfully, sending the sling bullet zipping through the air and smashing into a Lupine's chest, not enough to lay it low, but enough to make it stagger back, giving the soldier before it time to drive his sword into its belly. As he readied his sling to fire again, Gwilym surveyed the area before him. His location gave him an ideal point of observation on the whole roof, allowing him to pick his targets much more strategically, but it also meant that he could see clearly how fragile their situation was.

Torben had recovered his spear and was stabbing down at unseen foes ascending to join the fray. Nearby, Captain Almar faced off against a Lupine, whose claws and muzzle were still wet with the blood of the soldier it had killed. Drawing the axe from its belt, it traded blows with Almar, each matching the other in their ferocity. Princess Theodora was also in the thick of the action. Her sabre, already slick with blood, sliced through the air towards the head of a Lupine who had grabbed the shield of one of her guards. It gouged a wicked red line down the creature's face and back, sending it reeling away in pain. Spotting his next target, Gwilym whirled the sling and let fly, the bullet finding its mark and sending another Lupine crashing to the ground, clutching the wound on its shoulder.

He pivoted around his position again. He heard the snap of Eleusia's crossbow as she fired down into the hostile mass below. She stepped back, letting one of the soldiers, bow-half drawn, take her position so that she could reload. Her hand scrabbled around the empty leather bolt pouch, and she cursed, threw the crossbow onto the slope of the roof and, drawing her sword, moved to support a soldier trying to stop three Lupines gaining access to the roof. Gwilym sifted his remaining sling bullets through his fingers, counting them. Only seven shots left... They were struggling to hold back the tide. Almost all of the lightly armed and armoured militia were wounded, dead or dying.

Theodora's troops were holding up better, but a worrying number were lying still on the wooden roof boards, and it looked as if there wasn't a single one of them that was not carrying an injury.

Plucking one of the bullets from its pouch, Gwilym swiftly loosed his shot at a Lupine that had just vaulted over the wall and had been bearing down on Roswit, who had her back turned to the parapet as she helped another soldier towards the scaffolding down to the interior of the building. The projectile whipped over Roswit's head and downed the Lupine, their body splaying out onto the ground.

Six shots left.

Roswit was oblivious to what had happened behind her; all of her attention was focused on getting the man next to her down into the building, out of harm's way, where Egberht and the soldiers trained in battlefield medicine might be able to tend to him. Gingerly, she and her charge began to descend the rickety scaffold, the injured soldier wincing as he was forced to exert himself far more than he would like.

The atmosphere was tense inside the blockhouse. The air was full of sounds, the incessant thudding of the thralls against the door, the scrabbling of the Lupines crawling up the side of the building, the chopping of wood as others tried to break through the wall, the whimpering of the men, women and children sheltering there, and rising above it all, the screams and groans of the injured. Roswit had a perfect view of the scene as she slowly descended the scaffolding, easing her comrade down the structure. The civilians had, for the most part, tried to squeeze themselves behind the bar and into the storage area beyond, to keep themselves as far away as possible from danger, though groups of them still huddled in the middle of the room, looking around nervously. Almost all of the long tables that had filled the room had been sequestered to shore up the barricade of the main doors, with another having been claimed by Antauros, who was holding it up against a hole that had been hacked through the wall, just about stopping the Lupines from gaining entry. The remaining tables, which had been dragged into the middle of the room, had become the field hospital, with Theodora's two soldiers with medical training tending to the wounded and dying, alongside Egberht.

As Roswit's feet finally touched the floor and she helped her grateful charge down onto solid ground, she could hear Ranulf, who had taken charge of matters at the gate shouting encouragement to his troops, his voice rising over the splintering of wood and the groaning of the doors as they began to buckle under the assault. Spotting Roswit relinquish her comrade into Egberht's care, Ranulf hailed her from the other side of the room.

'Roswit, get back up top and request more troops for the gate. We can't hold out much longer!'

'They can't spare anyone, they're as close to being over-whelmed as you are.'

'Well, at the very least, you stay down here, that's an order!'

Roswit was about to reply in a less than cordial manner when there was a crash and grunt from the other side of the room as Antauros was momentarily forced back from his position, his table barricade slipping enough to allow two Lupines through the gap. Only one managed to slip fully into the room, however; the other was caught between the wall and Antauros' make-shift barricade as he heaved the table back into position. The creature yelped pitifully as its torso was crushed, its head and one exposed arm writhing in agony. The refugees and villagers screamed as the second Lupine charged towards the medics, but it didn't get far before it was flung back against the wall by a torrent of arcane energy. Egberht had turned, his hand outstretched, quill in hand, the last vestiges of the symbols he had hurriedly sketched fading in the air before him.

Seeing her chance, Roswit, drew her sword and sprinted forwards. Her opponent, though dazed, was certainly not out of the fight. It managed to collect itself enough to parry her incoming blow and then drive her several paces back with a wild swipe of its longsword. The two squared up to one another, Roswit stepping carefully to the side, sword held in both hands before her. The Lupine matched her movements, saliva dripping from its jaws as it snarled. Its attack came quickly and wildly as it suddenly lunged towards her, sword sweeping down to attack her leg. Roswit stepped back and then around, slashing the creature's arm as its sword skidded across the ground where her foot had just been. Angered by the blow, the Lupine leapt forward again, but this time, Roswit held her ground until the last moment, then took a step back, used her sword to deflect the creature's blade away and then followed up with a brutal strike to its shoulder and neck. The Lupine's momentum dragged it forward for two more unsteady steps before it dropped to one knee and then collapsed on the floor.

Roswit, along with everyone else in the blockhouse, was only allowed a second's respite before warning shouts rang out desperately from the doors as their upper sections finally buckled and collapsed. Bloated grey hands and faces began to appear where the parts of the doors had been, and the dead thralls began to claw and slither their way over the benches and tables in the barricade towards the defenders. As the first of the undead came within striking distance, Ranulf roared a shout of defiance and charged forwards, his soldiers pressing in behind. Seeing that the area around the main barricade was too crowded for her to be of much use at that moment, Roswit ran over to where Antauros was still pressing his table against the breach in the wall with all of this might.

'Watch my back, will you?' he grunted, muscles and sinews straining all over his body with the effort. 'I can't hold them off on both sides.'

'Aye, will do.'

Roswit turned her back on the minotaur and readied herself to meet any attackers that might slip past the defenders. Her heart sank as she focused her gaze back on the entrance and could already see that Ranulf and his soldiers had already been pushed back several paces into the room, with more and more thralls hauling themselves into the space with every passing second. None of the first wave of shambling figures looked to have fallen at all, though they all looked as if they had sustained new injuries, some of which would have been terminal had they not already been deceased. Several of them had lost limbs, which writhed and wriggled on the floor, disembodied from their owners. They made no effort to defend themselves from the slashes and jabs of the defenders' weapons but continued to shuffle forwards relentlessly, their hands outstretched, grasping towards their victims.

Frustrated at their lack of impact on the horde, one of Roswit's comrades summoned up a burst of energy and barged forwards, knocking several thralls to the ground and hacking from side to side as he forced his way back within touching distance of the barricade. His war cry, however, soon turned to one of terror as the thralls ignored his blows and surrounded him, their jagged nails tearing, teeth sinking into any unexposed flesh. Some of those knocked to the ground didn't even bother to climb back to their feet, but simply crawled along the ground to attack the man's legs. A renewed surge of energy raced through the other defenders as they desperately tried to reach the man and drag him back to relative safety. By the time Ranulf and several others had forced their way forwards, the soldier had buckled under the sheer weight of the dead, who continued to tear and scratch at the now immobile form.

'Get back, defensive formation on the double!' Ranulf yelled.

As they drew back, the tide of thralls refocused their attention and began to lurch forward once again as Ranulf and his troops locked their shields together, forming a wall over which they could jab out with their spears and swords. Unconcerned by this, the thralls continued to plough forwards, beating at the covered wood of the shields, trying to tear them out of the way and reaching over the top, attempting to claw at eyes and faces. Soon the defenders began to groan and curse under the strain of so many bodies piling into them, and feet began to slip back along the floor involuntarily, dangerously warping the defensive barrier.

'Roswit, get upstairs and call for reinforcements!' Ranulf bellowed over his shoulder. 'We can't hold them on our own.'

Roswit stood, looking from her comrades in the shield wall, to Antauros and back again. Both looked like they were being strained to breaking point, and she didn't know what to do. Even another order shouted across the room from Ranulf was unable to bring her mind into sharp enough focus to make a snap decision. Fortunately, however, it did bring aid from elsewhere in the room, Egberht.

Roused from his bubble of concentration, the gnome's head snapped up, surveyed the scene and then he began to sprint as fast as his legs would carry him across the room, leaving his current patient still clutching their wounds. As he ran he pulled the quill from out of the sleeve of his robe and began sketching symbols in the air, which joined together into a mass of arcane energy that practically trailed behind him as he careered towards the shield wall. Skidding to a halt behind Ranulf, he continued to work, eyes tightly closed in concentration for a few seconds more, until the ball of energy above him was almost as large as he was.

'Roswit!' he cried out, finally bringing her back out of her dithering panic. 'Give me a boost.'

'What?' she said as she ran over to help.

'A boost, lift me up. I need to get this spell as far in as possible so that it affects as many of those thralls as it can, which I can't do if I can't see where I'm aiming.'

Ducking to avoid touching the crackling ball of arcane energy, Roswit gripped the gnome around the middle.

'On my mark, 3, 2, 1, go!'

Roswit heaved Egberht into the air and above her head so that he could get a clear view of the chaos beyond the ever more fragile barrier of the shield wall. Once clear of the obstruction to his vision, he chose his spot and flicked the quill towards it, sending the spell arching over his head and the heads of the soldiers to land right in the centre of the area that had been conceded to the thralls. As it landed on the ground, the arcane sphere collapsed, crumpling into itself and creating a shimmering smudge of transparent energy on the floor. The thralls nearby stopped moving, and many took a staggered step backwards towards the sphere. Red runes began to show on their decaying skin and were dragged out of the corpses and into the sphere where they disappeared. Relinquished of the magic that was animating them, the thralls crumpled to the ground, truly dead once again.

Lowering him back to the ground, Roswit could feel that Egberht had expended a lot of energy in casting the spell, and he leaned heavily on her for support as his feet touched the ground. The soldiers in the shield wall were looking around bewildered at what had just happened and the gnome cleared his throat loudly to attract their attention.

'You haven't got long. The spell was only powerful enough to dispel the magic animating the thralls in this room and closest to the gate. They'll be back and quickly, so block up the holes as best as you can. I won't have the strength to cast that again for quite some time.'

Before he had even finished speaking, the scrabbling of more thralls clawed their way up the remaining woodwork of the door towards the blockhouse beyond. As Ranulf directed his troops to shore up the defences and plug the holes, Egberht began to make his way unsteadily back to the tables where the wounded were being treated. Seeing how weak he now looked, Roswit walked with him, leaning down and offering the diminutive figure her arm to hold onto. Taking it, he nodded thanks, his kindly eyes looking large and watery. She helped him to one of the few benches left in the room, and he sat, breathing heavily. His hand shook as he ran it along his forehead, gathering up beads of sweat.

'I've never felt such power holding those thralls together as I did just then,' he muttered, half to Roswit, half to himself. 'I wasn't expecting that spell to take so much energy from me, but had it not, it would have been ineffective. Aristotles will know now though that one able to wield the arcane arts is in here, and I highly doubt he'll let me do that again, even if we survive long enough for me to regain the strength needed to cast it...'

Kneeling beside Egberht and steadying him as he sat collecting himself, her gaze was drawn back to the area around the door, where already the sounds of the dead hammering at the wood could be heard again, making the barricade shudder and rattle. She closed her eyes and breathed slowly and deeply. She had been trained and conditioned to act without thinking, to follow orders and carry them out even if it was likely to lead to her death. Now that she was staring her own demise in the face, however, she realised that she wasn't ready. She would never be ready, and for the first time she could remember since entering the service of the Royal House of Dazscor, she felt truly afraid.

Then, in the distance, she heard a sound that brought hope back into her heart. The sound of a horn.

Those on top of the blockhouse heard the noise too. Gwilym, who had just loosed his final sling bullet, cocked his head as the sounded drifted to him over the wind and spun around to face the direction he thought the sound was coming from. Though he couldn't see much through the arcane darkness beyond the first few houses, he could hear and feel another sound rumbling towards them. Jumping down from his vantage point, he made his way, seax drawn, to the western side of the building, pushing past the defenders to get to the parapet, where he could see the ground around them more clearly. His companions and the soldiers around him were also turning to investigate the sound, as were the Lupines that still swarmed the area around the blockhouse.

Several Lupines emerged from the spaces in between the houses opposite, crying out to their fellows in their snarling guttural language, causing them to turn uneasily towards the west, shuffling nervously. As the last Lupine emerged from an alley, Gwilym could have sworn that it wore a look of fear, panic even on its wolf-like face. The creature's cry of warning was cut off as a spear passed through its upper chest, the horseman wielding the weapon morphing from the blackness let go of the spear shaft and drew a curved sword as they spurred their horse onwards into the centre of Haltwic. Other mounted warriors emerged into sight, both behind the first rider and from the other streets leading onto the open area.

They bore down swiftly on the first Lupines and smashed through them, blood and splinters filling the air as they set about the grim work of clearing the village. Seeing the impact of the charge, most of the Lupines turned tail and fled well before the commanding howl of the scarred Lupine, who stood beside Aristotles, echoed out as it tried and failed to rally them.

Aristotles himself stood watching the oncoming tide of horse and rider with an expression of absolute fury on his face. As the Lupines around him fled, he thrust out his hand towards the nearest group of riders, silver runes spilling from his fingertips, sending both beast and trooper head over heels backwards. He barked an order to the massive, scarred Lupine who had peeled off with some of its fellows that were still obeying orders to attack the riders, and the beast sprang back to his side, several others scurrying after. As he threw both hands into the air, a web of golden symbols blossomed from his fingertips, encompassing himself, Hrex, the scarred Lupine and several of the other beasts. As the dome grew quickly in strength around them, it almost obscured the individuals inside from sight and it clearly protected them as well as several thrown spears bounced and splintered off it. The few remaining Lupines unlucky enough to not be incorporated scrabbled uselessly at its golden surface before being cut down. The arcane shield let out a pulse of blinding golden light, so bright everyone in the area had to shield their eyes.

The light died away as quickly as it had appeared, and as Gwilym blinked rapidly to dispel the spots of light floating across his eyes, he looked down into the village once more and saw that Aristotles and his accomplices, along with the sphere, had vanished. It was then that he noticed that the dark, concealing cloud that had hung over the village like a spectre of death had vanished as well and that Haltwic was bathed in the warm, pink-tinged natural light of late afternoon.

Down on the ground, some of the cavalry kicked their horses into action once more, galloping after the Lupines that had fled the village, whilst others dismounted and carefully began to make their way into the surrounding buildings, clearly looking for any Lupines that might have sought refuge there. Leaning further out over the parapet, Gwilym could see that the mass of thralls now lay motionless on the ground, choking the area before the doors to the blockhouse.

Aristotles must have abandoned the spell to concentrate on making his escape, he thought. *Either that or whatever he just cast was so powerful it destroyed the arcane force animating his creations...*

More movement in the space caught his attention as another retinue of cavalry entered and paused before the building, assessing the scene and allowing the defenders on top of the blockhouse to get a good look at their saviours for the first time. The cavalry troopers wore long chainmail hauberks that reached down to their knees, with their lower legs protected by sturdy leather boots and greaves; their upper bodies were further protected by large disc-shaped breastplates that covered their front and back, whilst their arms up to the sleeves of the chain hauberks were encased in leather gloves surmounted by metal bracers. They wore rounded helmets, with square openings for their faces, where a long metal bar had been attached to cover their noses, and the helmets were surmounted by coloured crests made of stiffened horsehair. Two of the riders held large banners, one of which bore the stag and rose of the Kingdom of Dazscor

& Aramore, whilst the other bore a white-winged horse on a blue background.

'Who are they?' Torben asked, worming his way with Eleusia through the onlookers to Gwilym's side.

'I don't know, but they're friends, at any rate. See, they carry the banner of the Joint Kingdom. Eleusia, do you recognise the other standard?'

'No,' she replied, 'and they don't look like regular soldiers in the Aramorian army either. My guess would be they're a company of mercenaries in Dazscor & Aramore's employ.'

'Hmm.' Gwilym stroked his beard thoughtfully. 'This plays to our advantage in a way, makes it easier for us to come up with a story as to why we're here, but we'll still need to navigate this carefully.'

The deputation below had clearly finished having a similar conversation about the defenders of the blockhouse, for the leader of the group spurred their horse forwards to approach the base of the tower, their companions trotting close behind.

'Greetings,' a male voice emanated up to them from the helmeted figure, 'I am Bandarro, Sergeant in the Pegasus Company and deputy to our leader Shenesra Tador, who is hunting down the Lupine scum around this village. We are in the employ of the Kingdom of Dazscor & Aramore, and those that serve the Joint Kingdom should fear nothing from us. Who are you up there, and who do you fight for? You are far too well equipped to be a mere village militia.'

Captain Almar muscled his way to the front of the parapet, strapping a piece of cloth around a wound on his forehead, trying to stem the trickle of blood from reaching his eyes. He stood next to Gwilym, who was still deep in thought and pulled himself up to his full height. Princess Theodora appeared next to Eleusia and surveyed the cavalry below warily.

Hearing Almar's deep intake of breath next to him, Gwilym acted quickly and decisively. He struck Almar hard in the groin with the pommel of his seax, causing Almar to fold over and slump to the floor, gasping in pain. Manoeuvring himself so that Torben was between him and the stricken Captain, Gwilym looked over to Theodora, whose face wore the ghost of a smile pulling at the corners of her mouth.

'Apologies, Your Highness, but it would be too risky to have the good Captain say anything too stupid. Might I speak on your behalf?'

'I differ to your better judgement and knowledge,' Theodora mumbled, stifling the snigger that threatened to erupt into laughter.

'Greetings, Sergeant Bandarro, I am Gwilym of the Strong Horn company. We, too, serve the Joint Kingdom. You lot couldn't have come at a better time.'

'Well met, mercenary brother,' Bandarro replied. 'Tell me, who is your leader? I have not heard of the Strong Horn Company.'

'Antauros of Rahhail is our leader.'

'Antauros, the minotaur?'

'The very same, he is below in the building helping to shore up the defences down there and sends his apologies that he is not able to come up and speak to you himself.'

A whisper rippled through Bandarro's deputation and into the smaller groups of cavalry that were emerging from the buildings they had been searching or who were returning to the area around the blockhouse from outside of the village.

'We are delighted to have been of assistance to such a... great warrior as Antauros of Rahhail and to his company. Night is fast drawing in, and we will camp the night here in the village. My leader Shenesra would be delighted if we could all break bread together.'

'Of course, it would be our pleasure. Though you will have to give us time to break ourselves out of our defences.'

'Naturally, we look forward to welcoming you shortly.'

Bandarro and his deputation wheeled their horses about and retreated slightly, heading for the side of one of the houses where they could dismount and tether their mounts. Gwilym breathed a sigh of relief, which was quickly stifled by the appearance of Almar's red angry face as he forced his way through the crowd to get to the dwarf.

'You impudent little wretch, when I get my hands on you, I'll fling you off this roof!' Almar growled, spittle flying from his mouth. The surrounding soldiers made way so that they didn't get caught between the two, but Eleusia and Torben raised their weapons, ready to defend their friend.

'Almar, stand down!'

Princess Theodora moved past the trio to stand between Gwilym and her Captain and fixed the man with a hard stare.

'I admit that Gwilym's methods of stopping you from speaking were unorthodox, but I think he spoke wisely for us.'

'Wisely?' Almar straightened as much as the throbbing pain in his groin would allow, his face still apoplectic with rage, though he attempted to lower his voice now that he was addressing Theodora. 'He dishonoured you and us with his ruse that we fight for that beast downstairs. We are proud of the cause we serve, your cause, and should rightly declare it.'

'Almar, we cannot afford to play to courtly niceties here, now. It pains me to hide the name of my house too, to deny my family, but we must, lest our survival should come to nought.'

Almar growled incoherently, his slightly bloodshot eyes staring daggers at Gwilym, who took a step forward, confident enough that the Captain's rage had been stifled for now.

'You're right, Your Highness,' he said. 'If you go around declaring who you rightly are to all and sundry, that will create a lot of awkward questions very quickly. We're lucky that those men and women down there are mercenaries. They are far less likely to ask difficult questions about who our commanding officer is, who gave us our orders and what those orders actually are. By posing as mercenaries ourselves, we can easily fabricate a cover story that we were sent out here to investigate reports of

Lupine raids and say we were caught off guard and had to dig in here.'

'But why claim that Antauros is the leader here?' Almar's voice crackled with barely contained anger.

'Because, in the world of mercenaries, reputation is everything. No offence, Your Highness, but you and your retinue are unknown here, and the appearance of new mercenary companies doesn't go unnoticed. Many a savvy general has tried to infiltrate another's forces by sending in their own troops disguised as a mercenary band looking for work. No, we needed a name, either famous or infamous, to hide behind and Antauros fits the bill perfectly. He's well known amongst the circuit of mercenaries that serve the Guild-houses and well beyond, which means that people know that he has been a mercenary for many years and he has the record to prove it. All we need to do now is complete the ruse by showing our leader to this Shenesra Tador. So dust yourselves off, we've got a good impression to make.'

11

The scaffolding that led to the roof of the blockhouse quivered under the weight of so many bodies as the remaining members of Theodora's retinue and the Haltwic militia climbed back down to ground level. As Torben entered the space and began to make his way down, he could see that the soldiers around the barricaded front doors were still looking tense and on edge and that Antauros was still bracing himself and the large table against the hole in the wall. Swivelling his body round to get a clearer view of his next foothold, he saw Egberht was moving slowly through the soldiers and militia who had descended from the ramparts, pulling aside those that needed medical attention. Muttering filled the room as the assembled refugees and villagers speculated on what was happening beyond the fragile walls of their refuge. Gwilym, who had already reached the floor, was deep in conversation with another dwarf who was looking increasingly more relieved at what Gwilym was telling him. Torben caught the last part of the conversation as he neared the bottom of the scaffold.

'...don't worry, Ioan. I know the people here who have helped defend you and the village; they mean you no harm, nor do I imagine that troops outside do either. Just tell your people to sit tight for a little longer whilst we work out what is going on and whether we think it is safe for you all to go back to your homes.'

'I will do, thank you, friend of Clan Saldan. We will not forget this, and I'll make sure to send word to my kin in Mishtoon to tell them of your valuable help and service.'

'Think nothing of it, I'm just glad that most of us made it out alive.'

The two dwarves grasped forearms, and then Ioan walked off to inform the people of Haltwic what was going on. The villagers crowded around him as he drew near, eager to hear what he had to say, quickly shielding the smaller figure from view. As Torben's feet touched the ground, Gwilym beckoned him, Eleusia, Theodora and Almar to follow him and led them towards Antauros. The minotaur had relaxed somewhat, but he was still holding his barricade up against the wall with the whole of his body weight channelled through the beefy arm he had squarely set against the wooden planks. Roswit, who stood beside him still had her sword unsheathed, Torben noticed.

'You can stand down, Antauros!' Gwilym hailed as he drew near. 'We no longer have that kind of problem to contend with.'

'I sense there's a "but" coming though.' Antauros said, straightening up and beginning to massage the muscles of his arms and shoulders.

Gwilym drew the group close together, and the six of them leaned in so that they could hear the dwarf's lowered voice. Roswit, who had not been admitted into the circle of confidants remained a respectful distance away, but she did lean in to try and listen in to what was being said.

'So the good news, Antauros, is that the Lupines have been scared off, along with their vile puppet master. However, we do now need to make a good impression on our new friends who are currently waiting for us to emerge from our shell and say hello properly.'

'They're not Sharisians, are they? It sounded like a lot of

mounted troops from what we could hear down here.' Worry shadowed Antauros' voice.

'No, thankfully not, they're a mercenary company in the employ of Dazscor & Aramore, so we're lucky on that front, but we do need to think very carefully about what we do and say next.'

'Do you know which company they are, who leads them?'

'Yes, they call themselves the Pegasus Company, fly a banner of white-winged horse on blue. The man we spoke to says they're commanded by a Shenesra Tador.'

'Shenesra Tador, a Vittra woman?'

'No idea, we only spoke to her deputy. Why, do you know of her?'

'I think I've met her before, have a vague recollection of her and her men being brought in as extra muscle to escort a Fisel caravan up through the Free States, bound for the Republic of Castar and its capital Wardeen, but that was many years ago now.'

'Perfect, I'm sure that you'll both be thrilled to catch up as equals.'

'Wait, what? Equals?'

'We needed a cover story for why we're here, and I had to use my improvisational skills to buy us some time.'

Torben's ear twitched as he heard Almar begin to grind his teeth next to him. Inclining his head slightly towards the man, he could see the red flush of anger beginning to move up his neck towards his face.

'What did you say, Gwilym?' The worry had returned to Antauros' voice.

'That we're mercenaries as well, the Strong Horn Company, under your command.'

'Right,' Antauros sighed heavily and turned to Theodora, 'and I assume that you and your men will buy into this ruse?'

'We really have no choice, but in truth, I'm beginning to see the wisdom of taking Gwilym's advice, even if his plan does seem a little...off the cuff.'

'Look, just remember that for better or worse, we're all in this together, aren't we,' Gwilym added pointedly. 'I certainly don't want to be strung up on suspicion of being a Sharisian agent, and I'm sure you don't either. If I may make a suggestion, Princess, perhaps you could order your guard to start disassembling the barricade on the main doors so that we can go out and greet our saviours, whilst the four of us,' he gestured to himself, Torben, Eleusia and Antauros, 'pull together the best cover story that we can.'

'As you wish,' Theodora agreed. 'Almar, help me spread word to the troops of what is about to happen, we need to impress the importance of maintaining this ruse.'

Almar didn't say anything but nodded curtly and stomped off to gather the rest of Theodora's retinue to be briefed and receive their orders. As Theodora turned to follow, she heard Antauros mutter to Gwilym.

'The Strong Horn company, really? That's the best you could come up with?'

'I had to think quickly, and fortunately for you, I didn't pull anything worse out of my arse.'

'What am I supposed to say anyway? Shenesra Tador does not suffer fools lightly, and she is sure to be on high alert given the situation.'

'We'll just have to wing it, but don't worry about it. I'll be right next to you, ready to bail you out if necessary.'

'How comforting...'

By the time the double doors of the blockhouse were ready to be opened again, the atmosphere in the room had become tense again. The jubilation brought by their reprieve that had suffused the residents of Haltwic became substantially muted by the nervous attitude of the soldiers in Princess Theodora's retinue, though Ioan and the other Haltwicians had no idea what the cause of this nervousness was.

When the now heavily cracked and splintered wooden bar that held the doors shut was prized out of its metal brackets, Antauros and his companions were stood before them, waiting to step out into the evening light. All of their eyes narrowed as the doors groaned open, and they were bathed in pink-tinged sunlight. As their eyes adjusted, they could see that a great deal of work had been done by the mercenaries of Pegasus Company, who had moved the corpses of fallen Lupines and thralls away from the centre of the community. As they stepped out of their refuge, Torben glanced down one of the side streets and saw that the bodies of the Lupines had been hauled just beyond the houses and gathered into piles. The macabre mounds were already starting to stink. The odour was dragged into Haltwic by the wind, along with the background hum of the flies that were swarming around them.

The space around the blockhouse was now full of horses, which had been tethered to any available or easily improvised hitching post. The air was full of their earthy smell, which went a good way to cover the more rancid miasma of the dead, and the animals tossed their heads, snorted and whinnied as they too picked up on the scent of the slain. The mercenaries from Pegasus Company were everywhere, tending to their mounts, patching up their wounded, sharpening their weapons and starting to cook over a multitude of campfires that had sprung up in the centre of the village and throughout the surrounding streets.

The mercenaries looked hardened in a way that Princess Theodora's retinue didn't, much more like men and women who lived life roughing it from one army camp to another, ever ready to saddle up and move on, as opposed to standing in gilded hallways guarding doorways. They were a far cry away from the mercenaries of Guild House Fisel Torben and his friends had travelled with from Karpella into the Bar-Dendra Forest; these people looked like professional soldiers, trained killers, rather than caravan guards.

Dragging his head back to the task at hand, Torben quickened his step slightly to catch up with the others, who had drawn ahead of him slightly. Antauros and Gwilym led the group, headed for one of the large workshops whose sliding double doors had been drawn back to reveal an interior that was littered with wood shavings and sawdust. A large table had been set up near the door behind which Bandarro stood, several other mercenaries with him, watching them approach. The table had been laid with plates, cutlery and clay cups, which had been sourced from the houses round about, as had the jugs that were set alongside them. Bandarro raised his hand in greeting as they drew near.

'Well met, Antauros of Rahhail. Commander Tador has still not returned from her hunting beyond the village but has sent word that we should entertain you until her arrival.'

'At whose expense?' Eleusia muttered, gesturing to the furnishings on the table.

'Don't worry, the people of this village will be reimbursed for everything that we use, as is the law for all members of the Kingdom of Dazscor & Aramore's armed forces and their associated auxiliary units.'

Bandarro fixed Eleusia with a thin smile as he spoke, and her face flushed red with embarrassment. Clearly she had not expected him to hear her remark.

'Please do sit down. You must all be tired and thirsty after your ordeal,' Bandarro said to them all.

Antauros sat in the seat that had been set on the middle of their side of the table, Gwilym and Theodora on his right, Torben and Eleusia on his left. There was not enough space, or indeed a chair for Almar to sit in, so he hovered awkwardly in the background for a moment before Gwilym beckoned him over and whispered in his ear. Torben smiled as Almar, a look of malice on his face, moved to stand behind Antauros' bulk, mirroring the stance and bearing of the mercenary that hovered behind Bandarro, clearly acting as a servant.

Bandarro and three other mercenaries took their seats on the opposite side of the table, leaving the central chair on their side unoccupied, reserved for the currently absent Shenesra Tador. Behind Bandarro and his fellow officers, Torben could see other mercenaries busying themselves around forge at the back of the workshop, which had been commandeered to serve as a cooking stove. As soon as they were all sat, one of the mercenaries began to move around the table, pouring a dark-coloured beer into the cups before them. Torben took his and drank greedily, suddenly aware of how long it had been since he had last taken a drink.

As Antauros made small talk with Bandarro, Torben's weary mind began to wander again, as did his eyes, moving from the room they were sitting in to take in the movements around the blockhouse. A small patrol of Theodora's guards were pacing slowly around the ramparts, surveying the land beyond the roofs of the houses, whilst several others had been stationed on guard outside of the main doors. A small but steady stream of Haltwic's inhabitants emerged and making their cautious way back to their homes, nervously eying the newcomers, whilst refugees from other settlements began to pick through the scattered mess of their belongings that were now strewn about the square, searching for their own possessions. A group of solemn-looking residents stood in a group near one of the blockhouse walls, grimly surveying a line of corpses that had been respectfully laid out on the ground, the militiamen who had been slain in the battle. Another larger pile of civilian bodies had been assembled more carelessly nearby, through which several people were picking through, looking for loved ones. Torben tried to tune out the strangled cries and sobs that drifted over to them and pried their way, unbidden into his consciousness.

His mind was brought back to the matter at hand by the sudden thundering of hooves sounding throughout the village once more, which also brought the awkward conversation to a halt. They all turned to look outside as the centre of the village was swamped with mounted troops once more. One rider peeled effortlessly off from the group around them, steering their horse at a canter almost into the building and deftly jumped down out of the saddle, a member of Pegasus Company appearing seemingly from out of nowhere to take the reins of the white stallion. The figure strode purposefully towards them and around the table, fiddling with the strap of their helmet, they stepped into the space created as another mercenary pulled back the vacant chair and then tossed their helmet to the soldier, before turning back to face Antauros and his companions.

Shenesra Tador was unlike anyone Torben had seen before. Her skin was deep blue and her hair, pulled back into a tight ponytail was a lighter blue-grey in colour. Piercing silver eyes, which had no pupils, ran their gaze over all of them and her slightly squashed, crooked nose, which had been broken once upon a time, twitched as she did so. Reaching a blue-skinned hand across the table, she took the much bigger forearm that Antauros offered her, smiling as she greeted the minotaur, several gold teeth gleaming out of her mouth.

'I must admit, Antauros, I was surprised to hear that you of all people was leading the unfortunates trapped in that mockery of a castle.' Shenesra's voice was loud and clear with a definite edge of confidence to it, the voice of one used to giving orders on the battlefield. 'The word being passed around the various companies was that you were still dragging your feet alongside the caravans of Guild House Fisel, not leading your own company into the fray...'

'Well, I'm sure you heard about the trouble that Fisel and several other Guild Houses have had with Sharisian troops or their Lupine allies attacking their caravans? After being on the receiving end of one such attack in the Bar-Dendra Forest, I decided that if working for Fisel was now going to put me in as much danger as serving as a mercenary in an army, I might as well offer my services to the Kingdom of Dazscor & Aramore and get paid more for the risk.'

'A wise choice. Are you attached to the Army of the North?'

'No, to the Army of the South.'

'I thought I hadn't seen your name on the roster of mercenary companies...' a sly smile passed over Shenesra's face as if she was enjoying probing Antauros' story for weaknesses. 'You were not trapped in Karpella then, I take it?'

'No, we were not able to get to the city in time to aid in its defence. We attempted to join up with the remains of the southern army, which had at last report established its base in Malmwic, but the Sharisian army and their roving bands of Lupines stood between us and them, making it impossible to get there. I took the decision that we should head east and try and join up with the Army of the North instead.'

'So you've been doubly lucky then, even if you had attempted and succeeded in re-joining the southern army, you would doubtless have been killed not long after. Northern Command received word last week that all of the Kingdom's forces in the south, not trapped in Karpella, were destroyed by the Sharisians a couple of days after the siege began.'

Shenesra, sensing a flurry of movement behind her, waved her hand carelessly above her head, beckoning forward the mercenaries who laid food before them on the table. Antauros was clearly in need of the respite provided by the activity, for he sat back in his chair, which creaked loudly in protest, and breathed out heavily. He straightened up and tried to bring the nervous expression on his face back under control as the soldiers-cum-servants receded and Shenesra fixed her silver eyes once more upon him.

'There's no need to stand on ceremony. Please help yourself.' Shenesra spread her hands over the food and pulled one of the dishes towards her, prompting the others to dig in too. 'So how did you end up here in Haltwic?'

'During our journey to link up with the northern army, we picked up the trail of a band of Lupines and decided to track them. Given the Sharisian's unique relationship with them, it seemed prudent to check if they were operating on Sharisian business or going about their own devices. We passed through several raided communities before ending up here in the nick of time to help defend the blockhouse.'

'Lucky for them that you were nearby. Did you manage to make an assessment as to whether you believe this Lupine pack are working for the Sharisians?'

Antauros' eyes flicked briefly down to Gwilym, who did not meet his gaze but continued staring at the food on his plate. Leaning forward ever so slightly, Torben saw the dwarf quickly indicate downwards with his thumb beneath the table.

'Unfortunately, until today we have not been able to actually observe these particular Lupines, so it is hard to say either way,' Antauros responded.

'I see. Did the Lupines chase residents from other settlements into Haltwic before their arrival?'

'Yes, there were a number of refugees sheltering inside the blockhouse with us.'

'There were also a large number of them piled up before the entrance to your sanctuary, not to mention scattered amongst the bodies of the Lupines. Were you not able to get them into the building in time?'

Antauros' mouth opened and closed several times as his brain scrabbled around for an answer. Neither he, nor Torben for that matter, had considered that they would have to explain the presence of the thralls, whose mangled bodies held no hint of Aristotles' magic that had animated them. To the mercenaries of Pegasus Company, they must have looked just like any other civilian once the magic binding them had disappeared, which must have happened when Aristotles and Hrex fled. Thankfully for Antauros and the rest of his companions, Gwilym stepped in smoothly with a response.

'By your leave commander; we were unable to save the people outside the walls. They were driven into Haltwic just ahead of the Lupines, an old trick I've seen used by the beasts to devastating effect before. The ruse is based on the defenders opening their gates to admit those fleeing, at which point the Lupine war band will rush from their hiding places and overwhelm all inside before the gates can be shut. I saw the raiders skulking about the buildings and recommended that the gates not be opened, lest the lives of all inside were lost.' Gwilym's voice was cold and matter of fact, a far cry from the way he normally spoke, as if he had put on a mask.

'You're lucky to have such experienced troops in your company,' Shenesra said, looking from Gwilym back to Antauros. 'I'd have done the same thing in your position, better a small tragedy than a large one...'

There was a moment's silence as Shenesra finished picking over the remains of the chicken carcass on her plate, drained her cup and refilled it. She pushed the jug across the table towards Antauros and leaned back in her chair, silver eyes surveying the minotaur once again.

'The attack on the caravan you mentioned, I have it on good authority from a contact in Guild House Fisel that happened only around a week before the Sharisians besieged Karpella. No offence, but it seems unlikely, even for a man of your talents, that you were able to train these men and women up to the standard they appear to exhibit, let alone equip them as you have, in just a week...'

'No, well, errm...'

As Antauros began to flounder again, he nudged Gwilym as hard as he thought he could get away with. His elbow connected with the dwarf's shoulder. Gwilym coughed slightly too loudly to cover his surprise and surreptitiously swapped the hand he was holding his cup in, the other moving under the table to wipe the beer that had been slopped from it, thanks to Antauros' shove, on his trousers.

'Our company had been camped on the edge of the Bar-Dendra a few days after the attack the commander here was involved in,' Gwilym said, throwing a dirty look to the minotaur out of the corner of his eye. 'We were recovering from an attack by Sharisian cavalry that we only just managed to escape, though at the expense of our then commander's life. Fortunately for us, Antauros stumbled across us, and given his reputation and the fact he knew the local landscape, we were happy to let him guide us back to safe territory. Knowing that we would need a strong leader to keep things ship-shape until we reached the remains of the southern army, we voted to elect him as our new commander.'

'Quite the adventure it seems you've all been on then.'

'Indeed, and what about your own orders, Commander Tador?'

'We have been ordered to cover the northern army's advance towards Karpella, where the powers at be thoroughly intend to break the siege and send the Sharisians scurrying back to their sea of grassland. Whether they will be successful in this or not is another question, but they don't keep me and my riders on their books to provide advice, just brute force.' Shenesra leaned in closer across the table and lowered her voice. 'Unfortunately for the poor souls of Haltwic and the surrounding villages, we're not here to specifically eliminate threats we come across, just assess the danger they pose to the column and neutralise or drive them away if necessary. That means we'll be heading back to the column tomorrow, not sticking around to become a local defence force.'

'But what about the Lupines that were here?' Torben blurted out. 'Won't they just come back to finish the job once you're gone?'

'Orders are orders, young man, a good lesson for you to learn,' Shenesra snapped sharply. 'In any case, from what I can see, the Lupines are fleeing back west with their tails between their legs. If they are in the employ of Sharisar, they'll be headed the way we and the people here want, back to their army outside Karpella.'

'Is the Army of the North not concerned about their movements being reported or tracked?' Eleusia chipped in.

'You would have thought they would be, but no. As far as they're concerned, the Sharisians know we're coming and they don't want to lose precious days trying to cover our movements, days where the city could be lost. No, they want to get there as quickly as possible.'

Shenesra pushed back her chair suddenly and stood, Bandarro and the other officers on her side of the table scrambling to their feet in reaction.

'We'll be leaving at first light. I hope that you and your company will join us, Antauros. Extra swords and spears will be welcomed by General Guthlaf, the Marshall of the North, not to mention you've got a better chance of being paid if you're on the books of an army that still exists... I hope to see you in the morning.'

With that, Shenesra strode out of the room, her officers following her, several of them looking wistfully back at the remaining food on the table, clearly disappointed that their meal had been so abruptly ended. Antauros sat back heavily in his chair and let out a groan of relief.

'Thank the gods that's over!'

'You did well, though you need to learn to be more subtle about asking for help,' Gwilym chuckled.

'Do you think she believes what you said?' Theodora leaned forward to look down the length of the table at them all.

'Let's hope so,' Gwilym replied. 'She believed us enough not to immediately kill us where we sit at any rate.'

'What are we going to do?' Torben stood, the better to see everyone around the table.

'Do what she says, march out at dawn and join the Army of

the North. It will look suspicious if we do anything else, especially given that's what we said we were trying to do.'

They all nodded mutely, half too stumped for any alternative suggestions, half too tired after their ordeal to think straight.

'I'll go inform the guard, Your Highness,' Almar muttered and then plodded off back towards the blockhouse.

Slowly the others rose and began to follow. Torben dragged his feet, letting Antauros, Gwilym, Eleusia and Theodora draw ahead of him. By the time he entered the building, they were all bustling around relaying orders to Theodora's retinue, who were enjoying a welcome meal courtesy of the grateful villagers of Haltwic and gathering their possessions. Slinking across the room, Torben made for the scaffolding and quickly and quietly made his way to the roof. After the horror of the day, he just needed to be alone for a bit.

Reaching the exterior and the cool, refreshing breeze of the ramparts, he sat down next to his pack, shield and spear that he had left there and leaned his back against the slope of the roof. He took a deep breath and tried to forget what had happened over the past few hours.

12

When Torben opened his eyes, he knew he was dreaming. Neither the roof of the blockhouse where he had dozed off nor the village of Haltwic were visible anymore. Instead, he stood on a rocky, jagged slope that was carpeted by squat, hardy looking trees. Through the spaces in the foliage, he could see another slope ascending upwards, he guessed less than a mile across from where he stood. Below Torben, the two slopes met, forming a steep-sided valley, which stretched down as far as Torben could see in the dark towards a blanket of treetops further down.

As he tracked his vision back up the valley, straining his eyes to pick out any concrete landmarks in the area, he noticed the faintest glimmer amongst the trees on the valley floor. There was a yellow glow that flickered, almost disappearing at points, only to reappear again, a campfire. Slowly, cautiously, he began to make his way towards it. Though he knew that in this ephemeral state he was unlikely to be harmed physically – his ghostly form passed through trees, rocks and undergrowth with ease – he was intensely aware of what had happened last time, of what Aristotles could do to him, where he could send him.

The closer he got to the valley floor, the more noises crept up to meet him. At first, they were only slight, incidental sounds, the odd snapping of a twig or scatter of stones being kicked across the ground, but when he reached the ground level where the campfire was situated, he started to pick up the sound of hushed voices that snarled and snapped gutturally at one another. He nearly leapt out of his skin as a Lupine sentry suddenly appeared from out of the gloom and passed straight through him as it stalked along its allotted patrol route. Torben let the creature go on its way, primarily to allow his heartbeat to settle down again rather than a fear of being discovered, then he crept forwards once more.

The fire that Torben had glimpsed from further up the slope was not the only one; muted glows were dotted all around the area, the campfires that created them skilfully hidden by the Lupines that crouched around them. They all looked tired and many of them were tending to wounds or patching up holes in the ragged assortment of armour that they wore. Nearby, one individual whimpered pitifully as they were held down so that another Lupine with a rusty set of blacksmiths pliers could remove an arrowhead from their back. Though Torben couldn't understand the conversations that were happening around him, he noticed that many of those drawn together in surreptitious conversation kept throwing glances further up the valley, to where a group of individuals sat slightly apart from the rest. Taking his cue from the grumbling of the Lupines, Torben made his way towards the group. As he got closer, he slipped into the undergrowth that surrounded the more sparsely vegetated area where the Lupines had set up camp, hoping that he might be able to more convincingly mask his ghostly presence from Aristotles if he was out of his direct line of sight.

Moving close enough so that the outlines of the figures in the group solidified and their faces were illuminated by the subdued glow of the campfire, Torben instantly recognised two of the figures. The imperious elven profile of Aristotles was hard to mistake amongst all of the surrounding Lupines, whilst Hrex's features were illegibly burned onto his memory. The third figure, a Lupine that was much larger than the others, threw Torben for a moment, though he knew that he had seen them before. Then realisation dawned on him as the creature moved its head, illuminating the side of its face in the firelight and revealing the empty, heavily scarred space where its other eye should have been, the Lupine who led the tribe that had sworn loyalty to Aristotles. It was speaking to the others in a harsh voice, one that was clearly more used to talking in its native tongue than the common speech.

'Another group of survivors re-joined us less than ten minutes ago; they don't believe there are any more behind them.'

'What does that take our full strength to, Zarrax?' Aristotles asked the Lupine. He didn't look at the creature but stared into the fire, the light dancing and glinting in his ice-blue eyes.

'Just shy of three hundred. At least fifty must have been killed in the village or between there and the woods by the horsemen. There may be others looking to link up with us, but by now they won't be travelling in numbers large enough to make a difference.'

'Curse whichever foul deity allowed that mercenary scum to intervene in my plans!'

As Aristotles spat out the words, the fire before him swelled as if in reaction to his anger. Both Hrex and Zarrax eyed the flames nervously and waited for the Shadow Elf to continue talking. After several long, uncomfortable moments of silence, Zarrax summoned up the courage to break it.

'What are your orders, my lord?'

Silence still. Neither Hrex nor Zarrax, nor indeed Torben, could actually say for certain if Aristotles had heard the Lupine's question, so intently was he staring into the fire, lost in a web of his thoughts. This time, with no answer apparently forthcoming, Hrex shattered the silence.

'Perhaps we should continue our raiding of the surrounding villages, continuing harvesting souls from this area whilst the armies of the mortal kingdoms move against each other and leave this part of the country undefended? There are at least another five or six communities within striking distance that we haven't touched, not to mention the fact that the towns hereabouts will only be defended by a skeleton garrison, making them ripe for...'

'No!' Aristotles had been roused from his rumination and glowered across at Hrex, who visibly shrunk down into her robes. 'We cannot afford to lose any more time flitting about these parochial hamlets, reaping a few here and a few there. By the time we have either enough Lupines or thralls under my command to surround and slaughter even one of the smaller towns in this area, either Dazscor or Sharisar will have prevailed against one another and will send a force to neutralise us. As demonstrated so well by our adversaries today, thralls have their limitations, and without overwhelming numbers, they can be easily outmanoeuvred, whilst Lupines will fight like demons only for as long as they retain their courage. I have waited too long to wage a war of attrition, and my master's demand for souls as payment for our bargain will only grow stronger with each passing day. He, too, has waited far longer than he expected, and his patience is now paper-thin.

'No, we need a situation that will allow us to gather as many souls as possible in the shortest amount of time, without us being the centre of attention. Despite the annoyance of it, I believe that our current predicament has given us that. Those mercenaries were covering the advance of an army headed towards Karpella; there is no other logical destination for them to aim for. That means they intend to confront the Sharisians head-on and hope to break the siege and rescue not only their capital and its people, but their pride as well. I highly doubt that the Sharisians will simply withdraw; they will have just a much riding on such a culmination of events.

'We need to be there when the battle rages. That way I can harvest as many souls as we need as quickly as possible, and by the time anyone realises something is amiss, it will be too late. I had hoped for a similar opportunity when the forces of Aramore besieged Karpella all those years ago. Had our containment spell not been so powerful and unstable, the final battle for the city would have certainly provided enough souls to meet the quota.'

'But how will we infiltrate the battlefield without being drawn immediately into the fighting?' Zarrax queried. 'Though the Sharisians have my kin amongst their ranks, they will not be deploying them in the heart of the fighting. Despite their willingness to strike a bargain with us, they still view my Lupine brothers and sisters as little more than animals, and trust them less than they would a pet dog. Most likely they will be ordered to occupy themselves trying to turn the Aramorian flanks or attack their baggage trains. Our appearance in the middle of the fighting would doubtless draw a swift response from both sides.'

'We will infiltrate the Sharisian army, and from there we can wait for the battle to come to us. That way, we will either be present when the Sharisians make their final assault on the city, or when they are intercepted. We're already ahead of the Dazscorian Army of the North. There is no risk that they will arrive and engage the Sharisians before us. You're right, though, Zarrax, your Lupines will be ordered to attack the flanks and rear of the Dazscorian formation, whereas I need to be in the heart of the maelstrom for the best results. Thankfully though, I know at least one way that we can be placed within their formation without attracting too much untoward attention.'

Aristotles read the puzzled expression that crossed Zarrax's muzzle before the Lupine voiced his question. He held up a hand towards the creature and sketched symbols with the index and middle finger of his right hand in the air, blue tendrils of arcane flame trailing behind, leaving the marks hovering in the air. He flicked them across the campfire, and they settled on the fur of Zarrax's arm and sank into him with a faint hiss. Zarrax flinched slightly as the runes disappeared. Torben could see a faint singe mark on his arm, a ghostly impression of the writing.

As they all stared at Zarrax's arm, the outline of his body began to grow fuzzy, a fuzziness that spread across his whole being, obscuring his distinctly Lupine features in an opaque film of faint blue fire. Then the cocoon of energy dissipated, and Zarrax's form solidified and sharpened again but was revealed not as a Lupine, but as a Human, large, wild-looking, perhaps a tad overly hairy, with a missing eye. Zarrax held his hand up in front of his face, inspecting the squatter, human fingers and bare pinkish skin, mesmerised.

'The army that sits before Karpella will be wary,' Aristotles said, unfazed by the transformation that had come over Zarrax. 'They know that if they fail, then not only will they lose all the ground they have gained in this campaign, but that their defeat may well result in an Aramorian attack on their own lands, not to mention that their lives will be forfeit to Queen Alliona. This means that the Sharisians will happily accept all of the help they can get, and the arrival of a band of mercenaries, even rough warriors from the wilds of Kjörnsholm only trusted with being held in reserve as a last resort, will be more than welcome at the eleventh hour. As you said, Zarrax, they wouldn't be comfortable letting their Lupines completely off the leash, but a group of humans, that is a different story.'

He snapped his fingers, and suddenly Zarrax the Lupine sat once more by the fireside. He shook himself like a dog, sharply drawing in breath. The transformation was clearly an uncomfortable process at best.

'What of Princess Theodora and her companions?' Hrex asked. 'Though they don't know our aims, they do know what you are capable of and who serves you. If they get wind of what is going on, they could scupper our plans.'

'Ha, I am not concerned by them. She is an outcast in this time with no plan and no one to fall back on for advice but that offish Captain of her Guard and the rag-tag individuals that you so rightly judged to be prime for manipulation. Even if she pursues us, what can she do?'

Hrex didn't answer but shuffled nervously in her place.

In the camp behind them, the noise level rose excitedly, making Aristotles, Hrex, Zarrax and Torben turn to see what the commotion was about. Four Lupines, their fur streaked and matted with mud, were jogging through the camp, their fellows resting around them rising to their feet and asking them questions. The four ignored everything and made straight for Zarrax, falling to one knee before him and beginning to speak in the harsh, guttural Lupine tongue. Aristotles looked on expectantly.

'Well, what is it, Zarrax?'

'Returning scouts, my lord. They say that the Army of the North is making a forced march through the night, taking the royal road towards Karpella. They march with enough strength to trap the Sharisians against the walls of Karpella'

'Good, then the pieces are in motion as I suspected. All being well, we will easily be able to intercept the Sharisians. Assemble your beasts, Zarrax, we have much work to do.'

Zarrax leapt to his feet and began barking out orders that echoed around the walls of the valley. There was a scramble of activity as the Lupines below gathered their things, excitement rising in the air. Aristotles slowly got up and made his way regally into the mass of savagery before him, Hrex trailing on his heels. As she passed where Torben was lurking, her ears pricked up, and then her head whipped round in his direction. For a long second the two of them stared into each other's eyes, a snarl of anger and disbelief spreading across Hrex's face. Then, Torben felt a tug at the back of his neck, as if an immensely strong being was pulling him back. The scene around him went black as he fell back and awoke with a start in his own body, lying on the roof of the blockhouse.

He breathed out heavily, an immense wave of relief washing over him. It was only as he stared up at the stars winking high above that he realised how scared he had been. His body still felt on edge, the adrenaline continued to pump through his veins, though his mind was starting to relax again. He could have ended up back in that hellish place with that thing.

As the pounding of his heart in his ears subsided, he heard voices whispering animatedly to one another: Princess Theodora and Captain Almar. Looking around and seeing that there was no one else nearby, he slowly wormed his way up the sloping pitch of the roof so that he could hear better what they were arguing about, for despite the low volume of their voices, they were certainly disagreeing over something.

'Your Highness, I cannot stand here and mutely agree that going off with these mercenaries to join a war is in your best interests.'

'What else would you have me do? Stay here in this back-water village and start growing cabbages?'

'Of course not. I would recommend that we set our own course, seek out the old allies of your father who might be willing to take us in and hear your petition. In my opinion, that would be the safer and more logical option than going off to cavort in a war-zone with people we don't know if we can trust.'

'They are going to defend my people, Almar. I cannot just stand aside and do nothing.'

'With all due respect, Your Highness, they are not your people. They may live in the same places and do the same things, but no one of the short-lived races residing in this kingdom was alive when the House of Dazscor ruled here. I warrant that the few individuals of the long-lived races still here-abouts would feel overly sympathetic to you either. That is why we need to reach out to those that might still honour the agreements made with your father, honour the old alliances.'

'And who exactly would you suggest, Almar? The Kingdom of Reinhart? Unless you've forgotten, Gwilym has already told us that my father's most steadfast ally has disintegrated into a bunch of squabbling minor houses. Would you still recommend that we go there, that I become a pawn in a petty scrap for a throne in a ruined city? Or Rahhail, perhaps, where the

Merchant Prince is as mercantile with his friends as his name suggests? Or perhaps we should look further afield, beyond the Ocean of Memaran, to places that might have dispatched a single embassy to my father's court?'

Though he couldn't see him, Torben heard Almar shuffle uncomfortably, clearly not voicing whatever else he was thinking.

'In any case, Almar,' Theodora continued, 'what good has seeking out old allies done for us so far? All that policy has led us to is a near-death experience in this tower.'

'What do you think we should do about Aristotles?'

'I have no idea. He could have bolted anywhere. Though it pains me to say, I suspect he is a problem for us to think about once we have managed to secure our own place slightly more.

'So we march with Shenesra and the minotaur tomorrow?'

'Yes.'

Almar excused himself, and Torben felt the vibration of his heavy footfalls through the wooden boards of the blockhouse roof and parapet as he headed for the access point to the building below. His footsteps stalled as Theodora called out to him:

'You're right, though, Almar. These aren't my people anymore, but I can still fight to preserve a place I swore to defend so many years ago. With nothing else left to cling onto, I can still hold on to that, even if it does lead to my own death.'

'Your Highness,' Almar muttered and then began his descent to the ground.

Hearing Almar go, Torben slid quietly back down so that he sat once again on the parapet, with his back on the slope of the roof. Pondering over what he had heard, he didn't notice that Princess Theodora had walked over to his part of the parapet and was staring out over the moonlit village of Haltwic and the surrounding countryside. As his subconscious became aware of her presence, he instinctively flinched, his boots scuffing over the wooden planks, giving him away.

'Torben?'

'Err, yes, Your Highness.'

'I suppose you heard all of that, between myself and Almar?' Theodora's gaze, which had snapped round to focus on Torben, drifted back to its vigil over the village. Her voice had a faraway edge to it rather than the more severe one Torben had been expecting.

'Yes, I did. My apologies, I didn't mean to eavesdrop, I just didn't want to disturb you.'

'That's quite alright. You've learned nothing more of my predicament that you couldn't have guessed already... What would you do?'

'Pardon?' Torben, who was thinking more about extricating himself from the conversation so he could update his friends below on his dream, was taken aback by the question.

'If you were in my situation, what would you do?'

'Well, I would carry on as you are until you find another road that you know for certain you want to take. If I may, Your Highness, I know how you feel. I know what it's like to lose everything you know and love and be cast adrift by life. It's hard, there's no denying it, but the currents of fate are kinder than we think. Sometimes we just have to be willing to let them carry us down stream for a bit until we work out what to do next.'

'Thank you for your candour, Torben, I appreciate it.' She paused and fidgeted with the end of her plaited hair. 'I em... I owe you an apology, Torben, your friends as well, but you especially. You warned me of what to expect in coming here to seek out Aristotles, what he had turned to. Had I heeded what you saw in your dreams, the choices before me might be more favourable.'

'But, if we hadn't come here, then like as not all of Haltwic's people would have been killed and forced to work for him as thralls, so some good has come out of our being here.'

'You're right, thank you.'

She smiled at Torben and nodded her head as if about to excuse herself from the conversation. She stepped back, half turning away from him, and Torben dithered about whether or not he should reveal what he knew of Aristotles' next move. Theodora took another step, and Torben made up his mind.

'Your Highness…'

Theodora stopped and turned back to him.

'Yes, Torben?'

'The dream I had before, which let me see what Aristotles and Hrex were doing, I've had another.'

Gwilym snorted loudly as Torben shook him awake where he was sleeping in the corner of the blockhouse.

'What's going on? What time is it? The sun isn't even up yet!' he complained before Torben clapped a hand over his mouth and held a finger up to his lips.

Looking around, Gwilym saw that Antauros, Eleusia and Egberht were already huddled around the glowing embers of a brazier in the far corner of the room, Princess Theodora and Captain Almar with them.

'Come on, and keep your voice down,' Torben whispered.

Torben and Gwilym skulked across the room to join the others, and as they were admitted into the circle of confidants, Theodora began to speak.

'I'm sorry to wake you all before the dawn, but Torben has had another vision, and I wanted you all to hear the details before we have to get moving again. Torben.'

All eyes in the circle turned to Torben, and he took in a deep breath and began to retell what he had seen in his dream again in a low voice.

By the time he had finished speaking, the faintest fingers of dawn were playing on the horizon. The wood in the brazier had been reduced to little more than black soot, speckled with the odd orange glow.

'So,' Gwilym said, turning to survey the dark outline of Theodora, 'what do you wish to do with this information?'

'I intend to carry on as we had agreed with Shenesra Tador, to travel with them and join up with the Army of the North. Once we're established in their camp, we'll travel with them and start searching for any signs of Aristotles and his vile brood of followers and hopefully intercept and unmask them for what they are. If that fails, then I and my soldiers will seek him out on the battlefield and disrupt whatever foul ritual he will attempt to enact. Either way, as the last living member of my father's house and heir to the throne of Dazscor, I intend to take that traitor's head and put an end to this act of heresy against life and divinity he has sold his soul to!'

'And what makes you think that we'll help you with that?' the dwarf scoffed.

'Because I said we would,' Torben's voice was hoarse from having spoken for so long, but he still managed to project enough confidence into it to keep Gwilym silent. 'We all want revenge against Hrex for what she did to us, and by my reckoning, this is by far the best way to get it.'

Murmurs of approval rose from where Antauros, Eleusia and Egberht were stood in the darkness.

'Well, in that case, we'd best get cracking then!'

Torben couldn't see Gwilym's face, but he could imagine the rakish grin that he was sure was splitting his friend's face.

13

Torben and Gwilym panted as they mounted the crest of one of the many rolling hills that littered the landscape. Around them, the men and women of Princess Theodora's guard slogged onwards. Torben was gratified to think that even these professional soldiers were beginning to wilt under the efforts of the prolonged forced march they were undergoing. The mounted warriors of Shenesra Tador's Pegasus Company were littered amongst them, but many more were gathered on the flanks and rear of the formation or flitted back and forth scouting ahead and behind them. Ahead of them and already at the bottom of the slope of the hill he stood on, Torben could see Shenesra Tador herself, sitting regally in her saddle, holding a conversation with Antauros, who looked as tireless as ever. His stature meant that even though Shenesra was mounted, the two were close enough in size that they were pretty much at eye level with one another, giving their conversation a vaguely comical look.

As Torben and Gwilym caught their breath, Egberht's flushed face appeared between them, and the gnome doubled over, hands on his knees as he huffed and puffed.

'How much longer do they intend for us to ruin ourselves

like this?' he wheezed. 'I'd be surprised if anyone will have the strength to fight once we reach the Army of the North, if we ever even get that far.'

'Chin up, Egberht.' Gwilym slapped the smaller figure on the back, nearly sending the gnome head over heels. 'If you want my opinion, then you're doing very well for someone who's more used to reading about places than actually being in them. Speaking of which...' Gwilym rapped his knuckles on the sturdy, leather cover of the enormous book that Egberht had strapped to his back. 'Was it really necessary for you to bring that with you? You'll fair better on the move without it weighing you down.'

'I shall do no such thing! For your information that book is worth a whole library of arcane volumes. Even the Librarian of the Harbotha Academy of Arcanology would give his right arm to get his hands on another copy of this book. Melchizedek's Memoranda is an incredibly rare volume, only three others are thought to be in existence, and the amount of potential knowledge it holds for any spell caster makes it an invaluable tool for the field. For instance, if it were not for this book, I would neither have been able to bring good Torben here back from the brink of death, nor back from banishment to the realm of Kulittu.'

'Right,' Gwilym said uncertainly, still casting his eyes over the other oilskin wrapped books that were lashed to the sides of the harness Egberht used to carry the tome, as well as the bulging satchel that dangled over his front and dragging him forward into a stop. 'And the rest of it is equally as invaluable?'

'Exactly,' Egberht replied, pushing himself back upright and beginning to totter down the slope.

After exchanging a glance and a shrug, Torben and Gwilym followed him down the hill. They had left Haltwic two days ago and had spent the entire time since then marching from dawn until dusk. When they had arisen that morning, they had confidently been told by the scouts Shenesra constantly had patrolling around them that they should catch up with the Army of the North by sundown, but that was a long way away. Torben's feet had begun protesting almost as soon as they had set off again.

The hours crawled by, barely faster than their walking pace, or so it seemed to Torben. Most of the monotony of the trudge was only broken by the sounds of the soldiers around them complaining under their breaths, and the occasional chivvying remark from Captain Almar. Many of the troopers in Shenesra's company, who were not out scouting their surroundings, had dismounted to allow their horses a rest and keep them as fresh as possible.

Around noon, a relay of shouts went up from the scouts on the perimeter and then from within the loose formation; the advanced party was returning. They all slowed to a halt to see what news was being brought back about the situation before them. At first, Torben couldn't see anything, but then the figures of riders appeared on the crest of a distant hill and began to weave their way towards them, their horses cantering in and out of the hills and tussocks that lay in between. Shenesra's second, Sergeant Bandarro, led the group, and Eleusia rode nearby him, looking comfortable in the saddle of the spare horse she had borrowed to accompany the deputation.

As the riders drew near to Shenesra and Antauros, Torben saw the Minotaur nod his head to Eleusia and then jerk his horns backwards towards where they were standing. Nodding back in mute understanding, Eleusia peeled away from the other riders and trotted her horse towards Torben, Gwilym and Egberht.

'They're back then?' Almar's gruff voice sounded close at hand as the man appeared behind them.

'Well observed, Captain,' Gwilym's voice had a mocking edge to it, 'Your Highness.' The tone dropped from his voice as he acknowledged the presence of Princess Theodora.

Torben turned his head and smiled a greeting to Theodora, who smiled back and moved to stand next to him. Almar grumbled under his breath at Gwilym's insolence, following her at a distance. Eleusia's horse snorted heavily as she guided it right up to them and dismounted. She ran her hands over the sweat-streaked flanks of the beast and patted its thick neck in thanks.

'Glad to see you,' Torben said. 'I hope you've brought us good news.'

'Yes,' she replied, passing a hand over her eyes which were shadowed with weariness. 'The Army of the North is moving ahead of us, but so slowly that we'll easily reach them before dark. My estimate would be that it will take us another three days at least to reach Karpella and the Sharisians at their pace, that is, unless they move to meet us.'

'Do you think they will do that?' Theodora asked.

'Hard to say. Shenesra had given orders to Bandarro to take the detachment as close to the walls of the city as we could once we'd established the location of the Army of the North; that's why we were away for so long. From what we saw, it doesn't look as if they intend to move any time soon; if anything, it looked like they were readying another assault of the walls...'

'Hoping to take the city before the relief force arrives,' Gwilym chipped in. 'Be a hell of a lot easier to repel the Aramorians if they held the city and could use its defences against us.'

'That would be my guess as well. We couldn't hang around to see if they were successful or not. We were chased away by their skirmishers not long after arriving.'

'Hardly surprising, can't imagine they looked kindly on you snooping around.'

Their conversation was interrupted by a barking shout from Shenesra ahead of them, chivvying them all into moving again. Sergeant Bandarro and his retinue of scouts guided their weary mounts forward once more as man, woman and beast around them grumbled quietly as the trudge began once more. It did not take long for silence to descend on them all again, their weary legs sapping all of the additional energy from their bodies.

Spirits and conversation briefly picked up again around mid-afternoon as a dark smudge hove into view on the horizon, the Kingdom of Dazscor & Aramore's Army of the North. They heard the enormous column long before they saw it, the breeze wafting over the noise of thousands of troops all moving together, the sound of their armour and weapons clanking, the clamour of voices punctuated by the whinnies and grunts of mounts and pack animals and, beneath it all, the rumble of countless wagon wheels. The army was snaking its way through the landscape far more slowly than they were and, just as dusk started to tinge the sky with its pink and purple hues, their formation was approached by scouts riding out from the main mass.

'Welcome, Pegasus Company.' One of the riders hailed Shenesra as he cantered up to her. 'Commander, the order has been given to make camp for the night. I'll lead you to the billets that have been set aside for you and then I can escort you onto the General's headquarters.'

'Very good, lead on,' Shenesra replied before falling back into conversation with Antauros.

Another fifteen minutes later, Torben and his friends, along with Theodora, her retinue and the cavalry troopers from Pegasus Company, were settling down in their 'billet', which was in reality just another patch of bare grass amongst the countless others that made up the encampment. The majority of the soldiers in the army, Torben had noticed, simply lay on the ground, wrapped in their travelling blankets, around the multitude of campfires that were springing up across the landscape, but here and there, a few tents popped up. There was a large concentration of canvas in the direction that Antauros and Shenesra had been led by the rider, which Torben assumed marked where the General and his staff had set up shop.

Torben, Gwilym, Eleusia, Egberht and Theodora had nearly

finished their weary meal when Antauros and Shenesra finally returned to their part of the camp. Antauros looked dog tired, and he clutched a thick roll of parchment. At the edge of their allowed area, Shenesra excused herself and strode across to where Sergeant Bandarro and a couple of her other troopers were sat eating round another fire. Antauros trudged over to his companions, and as he did so, Torben noticed Almar's angry, narrowed eyes following the minotaur from where he had chosen to rest with some of guards, noticeably apart from Princess Theodora.

'Well, we're bonafide now, and we're on the payroll, so at least we'll get something out of all of this, even if it is only a meagre mercenary's wage each,' Antauros said as he slumped down next to Torben, and graciously accepted a portion of rations.

'How is Shenesra reacting to all of this?' Gwilym asked, leaning in closer. 'Is she still buying our cover?'

'As far as I can tell... but it's hard to say, really. I feel like she's been giving me the third degree ever since we met her in Haltwic. I'm losing track of all of the lies and near-truths I've had to tell her. I don't know how you do it, Gwilym.'

Gwilym's face split into a smirk. 'Lying is a very under-appreciated art. At least now we're where we need to be, we can split off from Pegasus Company and lose ourselves in the mass. The longer we're around the same people, the higher the risk that they begin to realise that our story doesn't quite smell right.'

'Almar has heavily impressed on my guards what they should say and do, and has ordered them all to abstain from strong drink, lest they let slip anything when their inhibitions are lowered,' Theodora said, the edge to her voice giving away her suspicion that Gwilym's comment was aimed towards her.

'I don't doubt that, but all it takes is for one person to let their guard down and the jig's up, which is why tomorrow we need to discreetly separate ourselves from Shenesra Tador and her company.'

'That's going to be easier said than done,' Antauros rumbled uneasily. 'We've already got orders to act under Shenesra's command; she's calling the shots here, not us.'

'But that's preposterous. I thought you said we'd been recognised as a separate mercenary company?' Theodora blurted out, slightly too loudly.

'No, we've been recognised on the payroll, but high command think that as a group we're too small to operate effectively on our own, so they've lumped us in with Pegasus Company for the time being. I'm sorry, there's nothing we can do about it without drawing more unwanted attention our way.'

Conversation dried up after that, partly because they were all too tired to carry on, and partly because they began to dwell on what the next few days might bring. Princess Theodora retired to a separate campfire and sat alone for a while, staring into the flames until Eleusia got up and sat with her, and the two of them wiled away another hour or so with whispers until they too lay down to rest.

The next morning they awoke with the dawn, its tendrils of light easily finding enough purchase on their closed eyes to drag them from sleep. Even if they had been sleeping in a tent, it would have been impossible to slumber for much longer as the army camp was awash with the noise of so many bodies rousing themselves and getting ready to move out.

When Shenesra approached the smouldering remains of the campfire where Torben, Gwilym, Egberht and Antauros had spent the night, she already looked alert and ready, as if she had been up for several hours already.

'Good morning Antauros!' she said, slightly too loudly for Torben's liking, the words pounding through his head like a mallet.

'Morning,' the minotaur said groggily, hauling himself to his feet and swaying slightly before Shenesra as his body got used to being vertical once more.

'Apologies if I dispense with any additional pleasantries, but we've had some orders cascaded down to us, and we need to get a move on now.' Not waiting for Antauros to respond, Shenesra continued talking briskly. 'There's a village up ahead, not on the main road to Karpella, but close enough for any Sharisians hiding there to cause trouble. We've been ordered to send out a patrol, and I thought as we are now brothers and sisters in arms, it would be good for some of your lot to ride out with me. We've got enough spare horses for you to select ten of your best riders, and we'll be off as soon as you're ready.'

With that, Shenesra wheeled around and began snapping out orders to the contingent of Pegasus Company who she had earmarked to ride out with her, leaving Antauros standing, mouth slightly ajar, after the brusque exchange.

'If I may make a suggestion?' Gwilym asked, sidling forwards to look up at the towering figure, 'I would suggest sending as few of the Princess' guards as we could possibly get away with, and enough people we can trust to ensure none of them are left alone with her lot. Ask Almar to pull together six of his best riders, and then the good Captain, Theodora, Eleusia and Torben should go with them.'

'Me?' Torben blurted out. 'I can't ride a horse.'

'You grew up on a farm, though, didn't you?'

'Yes, but we had no horses, Oxen yes, but they were draft animals.'

'Well, that's good enough. As long as you've spent a lot of time around animals, you'll pick it up quickly enough,' Gwilym responded with a grin pulling at the corners of his mouth.

'Why don't you go, or Antauros?'

'Don't be silly, those horses are far too big for me to control on my own, and conversely, none of them would be big enough for Antauros. We'd have to find a cart horse for him to ride, and a large one at that, but such a beast would be far too slow to keep up with the beasts of Pegasus Company. Have no fear, Torben, you'll be fine. Eleusia will be right there with you making sure nothing untoward happens.'

Torben squatted back down next to the remains of the fire, unconvinced by what Gwilym had said. He remained unconvinced as he finished his hurried breakfast and became even more so again when he hauled himself uncertainly onto the back of a bay mare, held in place by a still grinning Gwilym. The other members of Theodora's guard eyed him with an air of amusement too as he tentatively eased the horse forward towards the rest of the scouting detachment. Beneath him, the horse fidgeted and pawed the ground with a hoof, feeding off and reflecting the nervousness of her rider.

Surreptitiously, Eleusia skilfully guided her horse in front of Torben, blocking the head of his mare from view. She reached down and quickly tied a piece of rope to the bridle of her horse and then attached it to the bridle of Torben's, linking the two beasts together.

'It'll save you from having to do anything but hang on,' Eleusia responded to Torben's quizzical look.

Before he had time to respond, Shenesra Tador strode into view and vaulted over the back of her own horse and into the saddle, giving the order to move out as she did so. As the group of twenty riders began to canter off, Eleusia gently spurred her own horse onwards, Torben's jolting into movement a second later as it was coaxed forward by the tension on the lead. Torben gripped the pommel of the saddle with both hands, his whole mind simply concentrating on staying on the back of the beast. He heard Almar scoff at him as he trotted past, making Torben turn his face away to hide the flush of embarrassment that had flooded his cheeks.

It did not take them long to canter through the ranks and ranks of soldiers, who barely took notice of them as they packed away their things and readied themselves for another day of marching. After a few minutes they had managed to negotiate their way around the people and wagons that were already recommencing their crawl towards Karpella and were riding out along the open road, the military mass behind them rapidly dwindling into the distance.

In addition to the ten volunteers that Antauros had put forward for the excursion, Shenesra had brought along ten of her cavalry troopers, all of whom looked far more comfortable in the saddle than Theodora's guards were, let alone Torben. Even Almar, despite his snide remark to Torben when they had set off, looked as if he was struggling to keep up with the quick pace that Shenesra and her riders were setting. Theodora, however, looked comfortable astride her mount, as did Eleusia, even though her steed was leading Torben's. Torben's eyes couldn't help being drawn to Theodora, her auburn hair flowing out behind her and sparkling in the sunlight, an expression of happiness that he had not seen her wear before illuminating her face.

They rode along the main roadway for nearly an hour before abruptly turning off onto a much more rugged dirt sidetrack that snaked away towards an outcrop of woodland several miles distant. The land swiftly changed from the unkempt heather and gorse of Dazscor's plains to the type of scrubby farmland that reminded Torben of the fields that surrounded Bywater Village. After they had ridden a little way into the fields, Shenesra raised her hand from the front of the formation, causing those behind her to rein in their horses and eventually come to a halt. Ahead of them, a flock of sheep had slipped through an open gate and were busy feasting on the crop of cabbages and carrots that lay within.

Now that they were stationary, Torben was emboldened to stand up in his stirrups to get a better view of the surrounding fields and the village beyond, and he sank back into his saddle wearing a concerned expression.

'Something's not right,' he muttered to Eleusia and Theodora, who had trotted up beside him. 'If I owned either this field or those sheep, you can bet I'd be here within a heartbeat to get the little buggers out of there and keep them from destroying the crop. There's no one about working either. This is prime daylight that being wasted here. It's too quiet...'

Shenesra, was clearly similarly minded, quietly relayed the order to dismount, tying the reins of her horse around a fence, everyone else following suit.

'Jazar, Mellina, stay here and guard the horses; the rest of you, with me. We'll approach quietly, no discussion unless absolutely necessary. Weapons at the ready, I don't want us getting caught in their unawares.'

As the two troopers moved to check that the horses were secure, the rest of the detachment followed Shenesra as she moved into an adjacent field for cover, all of them drawing their weapons as quietly as possible.

The closer they got to the village, the more they noticed the obvious lack of life signs coming from the community. As they stalked through the fields, they didn't see or hear anyone, and it was not until they had begun to move in-between the first few houses that they found what was left of the community's inhabitants.

The village was an irregular sprawl of twenty main buildings, with numerous smaller structures, outhouses, sheds and storerooms scattered around the larger dwellings. The place could only have been home to just under a hundred people, almost all of whom must have eked out an existence as subsistence farmers. The houses had been roughly grouped around an open grassy space, which would have served as a communal space for the villagers to gather in industry or celebration, and perhaps also an area to corral the livestock at night or during the winter months. Now, however, the village green had become the sight of a massacre.

The grass was stained with blood, in some areas so thickly that it made whole patches appear deep red rather than green. The centre of the green was now a hideous mound of bodies, men, women and children. Most of them were humans, but there were a fair number of dwarves and even a few gnomes scattered amongst the dead. Torben tried not to look too closely, but even with an averted gaze, he could tell that they were civilians all. There were no soldiers here, no one that would have been a threat.

'Spread out, search the houses.' Shenesra's face had a hardened, almost impassive look as she turned to relay her orders and directed smaller groups to different buildings. 'You two, with me,' she said to Torben and Eleusia before heading over to the nearest building.

Theodora flashed a grim smile to Torben as she and Almar turned to check out the house they had been assigned. Eleusia fell in step beside Torben, pulling down the scarf wrapped around her neck, which she had used to cover her nose and mouth as she had inspected the corpses more closely.

'All of them have had their throats cut,' she whispered.

Torben wasn't able to respond before they entered the house after Shenesra, but he could tell from her tone that Eleusia had a strong suspicion of what had befallen the place.

Inside, Shenesra was already roughly sorting through possessions in the large downstairs room, pushing toppled furniture aside and looking for anything that might give any indication of what had happened.

'All their stuff is still here by the looks of it,' she said, straightening up to face them. 'Whatever brought ruin and death here, it wasn't looking for plunder. Eleusia, check upstairs; you boy, help me move this table so we can look under the stairs.'

Eleusia and Torben had barely managed to take a single step towards their allotted charges before the table in question was shoved sharply back, revealing a man who charged out of the space under the stairs and pounded towards Shenesra, trying to take her off her feet. In his hand he was brandishing a tarnished, dulled butcher's cleaver. He got more than he bargained for as Shenesra deftly side-stepped his clumsy advance and followed up with a savage kick to the back of his knees, sending him crashing to the floor. Before he could rise to renew his attack, the cleaver had been kicked out of his reach, and Shenesra lifted him onto his knees by his hair and held the blade of her long sword to his throat. As Shenesra incapacitated the man, Theodora and Captain Almar barrelled through the door to the house, weapons raised and ready, having heard the commotion from outside.

'No, stop, please!' a voice sounded from beneath the stairs, where a woman's face, streaked with blood and dirt, had appeared. 'Please, my husband meant you no harm. Please, don't hurt us.'

Shenesra regarded the man struggling against her grip and then the woman for a moment before releasing the man's hair and withdrawing her blade, allowing him to fall to the compacted earth floor of the house. She nodded to the others, all four of whom lowered their weapons.

'Thank you, thank you...' the woman's voice trailed off as it became choked with tears.

'It's alright. We serve the Dazscor's Army of the North; we mean you no harm,' Shenesra said quietly. 'What happened here?'

'They came yesterday afternoon,' the man said hoarsely, avoiding making eye contact. 'Lupine scum swept through here like wildfire. I was feeding the pigs across the way when it happened. One minute all was quiet, the next you couldn't see for the ravaging savages. I ran round the back of the house to get the weens indoors, and I found...'

The man choked back a sob and pointed with a shaky hand to his wife. A wide-eyed, frightened little girl was staring out from the hiding place, half-hidden by her mother's torso and the object that Torben noticed clutched in her arms. A boy, no older than six or seven years, deathly pale with an arrow lodged deep in his chest, surrounded by a blossom of blood staining his dirty tunic. He wasn't breathing.

'I scooped them both up,' the man continued, 'and got into the house. My wife had already cleared the space under the stairs for us to hide in. We barely got in and covered before the beasts burst into the house. They didn't take anything, though; they weren't interested in carrying off anything. It felt like once they thought no one was inside, they lost interest. We managed to avoid detection. Even though Wilf must have been in awful pain, he lay there silent as you like.

'We could hear all manner of noises coming from outside, screaming, shouting and wailing. I managed to look through a crack in the wall and could see pretty much everyone else in the village herded up on the grass outside, looking like lambs to the slaughter, as indeed they were.

'Those Lupines were being bossed around by an enormous creature, bigger than any other I've had the misfortune to see before, with black fur and only one mean looking eye. He was taking orders from this other man, though, who chilled me right through to the bone. Tall, lean elf with grey skin and white hair, one of them shadow dwellers I reckon. He wore this strange pendant around his neck about a handspan across, like a hideous mask it was.

'He ordered the Lupines to start cutting the throats of my neighbours, my kin. As the breath left them, these wisps of purple light were pulled out of their bodies and straight into the maw of that mask. I watched one come out of our son as he breathed his last, saw it go straight through the wall towards that horror. They killed everyone they found, dumped them like sacks and then walked away.'

The man hung his head as he finished speaking, tears starting to speckle the sides of his cheeks.

'It was his soul,' the woman chimed in, still in her position under the stairs, 'my boy's soul, that evil bastard has taken it! You were all so close, and you did nothing, nothing!'

Cradling her dead son in her arms, she began to rock backwards and forwards, letting loose the pent-up grief she had kept hidden during their breathless, silent hiding. The man, too, wept openly, careless as to the presence of the strangers within his house.

Shenesra indicated to the rest that they should leave, and she produced a small purse from a pouch that hung off her belt and dropped it softly before the man, whose great racking sobs made him oblivious to the gesture.

'Head east, towards Anselwic. That will take you far away from the fighting. I hope you find some peace,' Shenesra said, shuffling past the prostrate figure and pushing through the others to leave the house.

Almar followed her out swiftly, without a backwards glance, but Torben, Theodora and Eleusia lingered slightly longer, shamed but also transfixed by the display of raw suffering. Torben couldn't help but watch. He knew exactly how they felt, people who had lost everything and now had to navigate an unknown and dangerous world. He wished that he had had the strength to voice his own emotions of grief at having seen everything he once knew and cared about vanish before his eyes. Instead, ever since he had left Bywater, he had forced those emotions as far down as he could, hoping a fool's hope that they would get lost in dark recesses of his soul and never bother him again.

He felt a tug at his elbow as Eleusia began to guide him wordlessly towards the door. He reluctantly followed, wishing he could leave them with words of comfort, anything that might let them know that there was a way through, that they could survive. As words clumsily swam together in his head and he turned back to speak, his eyes met those of the little girl. She had left her mother and the hiding place and was standing next to her father, her little hand resting gently on his shoulder. Her eyes looked hollow and were ringed with deep dark circles, testament to the fearful, sleepless waiting for death they had endured. Her look made Torben mute again, his mouth opening and closing like a fish, so he turned and left the house.

He blinked as he stepped outside into the light again and

joined the sober group waiting there. Shenesra was pacing back and forth, deep in thought, ignoring the looks of her troopers who were beginning to gather back around her, having finished their reconnaissance. Eleusia looked equally grim-faced, though Almar next to her looked cold, apparently unaffected by what he had just witnessed. Torben stood beside Theodora and saw her wipe away tears from her eyes. Instinctively he put a reassuring hand on her back, and she looked up and smiled wanly at him. The look was broken as the gravelly voice of one of Shenesra's troopers cut the silence.

'All clear in the other buildings, Commander. What are your orders?'

Shenesra didn't respond but continued to pace, her face lined in deep concentration.

'Commander?'

'Here's what I can't get my head around,' she snapped, ignoring her man and rounding on Torben, Eleusia, Theodora and Almar. 'I can't get past the fact that what happened here is so similar to what was going on at Haltwic when we found you.'

'What do you mean?' Eleusia's voice was calm and level.

'Lupines sweep down out of nowhere and attack that community, leaving any goods of value, and focus on rounding up the poor bastards who live there instead, cut their throats and leave them, without even butchering some of the carcasses for meat. Very out of character for such creatures, to do so once would be highly unusual, but to do so twice within days – now that is downright unheard of.'

'Perhaps it was two different groups?' Eleusia replied. 'Lupines are known to do unspeakable things in service to their savage gods. Who knows what truly happened here.'

'Well, that's what I was thinking, but what would be the chances of two groups of zealous Lupines led by a monstrous specimen with a single eye and a Shadow Elf with a mask necklace around his neck?'

'What are you talking about?' An ever so slight quiver crept into Eleusia's voice that she wasn't able to mask quick enough.

'My forward scouts saw this Shadow Elf when they approached the village to see what was going on before we charged in. They saw him talking to you, my dear, in not unfamiliar terms,' Shenesra indicated Theodora with the point of her still drawn sword, 'as well as the gobby dwarf, who seems all too keen to speak for your commander, who appears to have a much better idea of your business than Antauros does.

'What's more, no one I've spoken to neither amongst the other mercenary commanders nor the pencil pushers at command has ever heard of Antauros and his *Strong Horn Company*, not a good sign in my line of work... Most believe that the minotaur still serves Guild House Fisel, but some even go so far as to say that he was killed along with all hands on the attack on that Fisel caravan in the Bar-Dendra. But, low and behold, he appears with you all, fit and well with no compunction to go back to his former masters, a slight he knows will result in severe retribution once the Guild catches wind of it.

'Part of me wants to think that none of you are involved in all of this, but things keep sticking to you that are too hard to dismiss. I think that you've all got some explaining to do, and I hope to great Walanni herself that Antauros and the rest of you are just damned unlucky and that there isn't something more sinister going on. Perhaps it's time you tell me who you really are...'

14

The silence that hung over the village was deafening and full of barely contained tension. Shenesra continued to stare pointedly into Eleusia's eyes, waiting for her to respond. Eleusia's eyes, in contrast, were already beginning to flick from side to side, assessing potential escape routes. Despite her complaints, she was really missing the fact that Gwilym and his silver tongue was not with them.

'Well? I would hasten your response if I were you, lest your silence condemn you,' Shenesra said, taking another step forward, both her hands firmly gripped around her sword hilt.

Seeing the Vittra step forward, Captain Almar took a decisive forward pace himself, half drawing his sword so that the blade glinted in the sunlight.

'I wouldn't do that if I was you. There's no need to do anything rash, back down!'

Torben looked on, nervous and confused. Whatever Almar had been hoping would happen, Torben guessed that it certainly wasn't what his action provoked. In response to the movement, Shenesra took a step back, her longsword flying up into a guard position, her troopers at her back drawing their own weapons as well. This prompted an echoing scrape of weapons being unsheathed from Almar and Theodora's guards, with both sides beginning to square up to one another, waiting for the next to make the first decisive move.

Then, before the tension reached critical mass, Princess Theodora stepped forwards between the two groups, her empty hands raised before her.

'Stop, there's no need for further bloodshed here.' Turning to her guards, she said, 'Lower your weapons.'

'But, Your Highness,' Almar responded, 'that is not a wise decision to...'

'Now, all of you!'

The tone of command was unmistakable in the Princess' voice, and her guards, including the concerned-looking captain, lowered their weapons reluctantly. The troopers on Shenesra's side relaxed slightly in response, but their commander did not drop her guard.

'Speak your piece,' Shenesra growled through gritted teeth.

'You're right, we are not what we seem, but neither are we your enemy. My name is Theodora, daughter of Sarper IV, Princess of the Kingdom of Dazscor. The Shadow Elf that was here and that you saw in Haltwic is named Aristotles, and he was once the Royal Mage to my father's court. He imprisoned himself, me and my personal guard deep beneath Karpella Castle, but before doing that, he sold his soul to Kulittu, the Dead God, for power.

'Since breaking free, he has been seeking a way to draw upon this power that was granted to him, which involves the slaughter of innocent lives for his own gain. With the help of Antauros, Eleusia, Torben, Gwilym and Egberht, I am looking to bring an end to Aristotles' treachery to the Royal House of Dazscor and the affront that he is causing to life itself. We cannot afford to stand by and let him work his dark magic to reach whatever twisted goal he is striving for. I'm not asking you to join us, or even to help us, I'm just asking you to stand aside so that we can continue to track him and hopefully bring him to justice. If not for our sakes, then for the sake of these innocent people who have had their lives cut short.'

As Theodora finished, she gestured to the pile of bodies beginning to stink in the midday sun with one hand. The other slipped behind her back, and Torben could see her cross her fingers as she waited nervously for Shenesra to respond.

Though her posture had relaxed and she had lowered her sword from its guard position, the Vittra's silver eyes bored into Theodora, scrutinising her.

'That's a hell of a tale, but how the hell do you expect me to believe that?'

'If you don't believe who we are, that's fine, but our intentions are true. You've seen with your own eyes and heard with your own ears what evil has taken place in this village, Haltwic, and who knows how many others, and this evil will continue as long as Aristotles is allowed the freedom to roam the world. Even if you doubt our identity, if our goal is to stop a massacre like this from happening again, then how can your conscience let you stand in our way?'

'Even if I did believe even a part of what you've said, how in the name of all the Gods do you expect to be able to do such a thing? Firstly, the Army of the North now has a record of you and your followers signing up as mercenaries; they'll sure as hell not let you leave before battle is joined. They need everyone they can get to drive the Sharisians out, and anyone they suspect of desertion will be crushed under General Guthlaf's mailed fist to dissuade anyone from thinking they can make their escape.

'Secondly, how in all damnation do you think that you with less than forty soldiers will be able to make it on your own, on foot, from here to wherever this Aristotles is going, with Gods knows how many Sharisian patrols between here and Karpella spoiling for a fight, let alone the ravening pack of Lupines your man has at his beck and call?

'As far as I can see it, you're just kidding your own conscience into leading the men and women following you to their deaths without guilt. If everyone had the ideals of a trumped-up highborn, then no-one would suffer at the hands of their own conscience. We could all kid ourselves into thinking that what we did had a noble purpose behind it, from the highest of lords to the ones shovelling muck from the latrines, but just believing it doesn't make it so. The *noble* ambitions and ideals of monarchs and the gentry are nothing but a curtain they can pull over things that they do not wish to see, over realities they would rather ignore, lest it tarnish their wondrous goals.

'You go after this Aristotles and his wild beasts if you want, but at least have the decency to ask those that blindly follow you if they are willing to die for your revenge. You have no idea of the evil that the Dead God is able to bring to bear on our mortal realm. If you did, you'd be getting as far away from him as you could, not naively blundering after him spouting nonsense with every breath.'

Shenesra turned from Theodora and barked at her troopers, 'Move out! We're leaving.'

Turning on her heel, Shenesra stormed off back towards the road that led out of the village and where their horses had been hobbled. Her troopers parted to let her pass, clearly not wanting to get in her way, and then fell in step behind her, several of them looking warily over their shoulders as they left.

As the detachment of Pegasus Company disappeared out of sight behind a building, Theodora breathed a sigh of relief and leaned forwards, her hands on her thighs.

'Well, that could have gone better.'

Taking a step towards her, Torben laid a hand on her shoulder.

'You saved our lives, Your Highness. All in all, I'd call that a success.'

Theodora didn't reply but straightened up and looked at Torben, her eyes communicating both the thanks for Torben's words, but also that deep down, she wasn't sure she believed what he'd said.

'We'd best get moving,' Eleusia said. 'We can't really afford to let them get too much of a head start.'

'Aye, who knows what surprises they'll try and organise for us back at the column,' Almar muttered darkly.

They began to move out of the beleaguered village, and as they began to round one of the houses towards the road, they could see that Shenesra and her cavalry troopers were already mounting up and spurring their horses on, kicking up a cloud of dust.

Something tugged at the back of Torben's mind. He felt he was being watched, and he turned to look back. The little girl was standing in the doorway of the house, staring after them, as if asking why they were just leaving them in this place of death. He shook his head, trying to dispel the feeling of guilt and turned his back to the girl, her parents and the dead village.

They rode hard to rejoin the Army of the North as quickly as possible, but despite their unrelenting pace, they were unable to catch up with Shenesra and her more experienced riders, who remained little more than a speck on the horizon. Torben could do little but hang on for dear life as his horse struggled to keep up with Eleusia's mount it was tethered to.

Eventually, the sluggish mass of metal and beast that was the army column hove into sight, and they slowed so that their approach looked less panicked, hoping that it would draw less attention. The decrease in their speed gave Torben the confidence to do more than cower as low as possible in his saddle. As he watched the soldiers marching on their weary way grow closer, he wondered what kind of reception they would receive when they returned.

To be frank, he wasn't even sure that they should have all returned, lest Shenesra had set some sort of trap for them. Surely it would have been better to send in a single rider to try and warn the others more discreetly than all ten of them to barrel back into the midst of the army... But then, how long would they have, even if they were able to warn the others and get them out, before their absence was noted and the hue and cry to track down the deserters began?

They all bunched together and collectively held their breaths as they passed through the cordon of scouts leading the advance, only pausing to state who they were to the bored-looking officer who approached them and waved them on without a second thought. Making their way through the mass of troops and wagons, they were pretty much ignored as they tried to seek out the rest of their group, all save the grumbling comments of the footmen, who bemoaned the fact they were able to ride a horse.

Eventually, they spotted the Pegasus banner of Shenesra's company and headed warily towards it. From his position near the back of the group, Torben could see that Almar already had his hand on his sword hilt, and his body was tensed, ready for the fight he expected to break out once they reached their destination.

They were all thankful to find the rest of Theodora's guards, along with Antauros, Gwilym and Egberht trudging onwards alongside the cavalry of Pegasus Company, who guided their horses on at an easy pace and chatted in a relaxed manner amongst themselves. As they drew to a halt and began to dismount, Torben noticed that Shenesra was not amongst her troops, but that her riderless white horse was being led by one of her troopers. Sergeant Bandarro looked to be absent too.

As Torben's feet finally met solid ground again, he looked to the sky and thanked whichever deity might be listening that he had survived the hellish journey in one piece, and he resolved never to travel on the back of a beast again as long as he could help it. His relief was quashed somewhat by Gwilym, who bustled over to him, Eleusia, Theodora and Almar, with Antauros and Egberht in his wake.

'What the blazes happened out there?' the Dwarf whispered

harshly. 'We thought all sorts of things might be afoot when Shenesra and her riders returned without you. She wouldn't even stop to tell us what was occurring, but took off straight for the general's retinue without a backward glance.'

'Our cover's been blown,' Eleusia snapped back.

'What, how?'

'Aristotles and the Lupines had been through that village, and Shenesra started putting two and two together and came up with Haltwic. She started getting twitchy and began asking difficult questions. Our gracious employer here took it upon herself to tell Shenesra the truth, near enough all of it.'

'What? Why in the name of all the devils and demons of hell would you do that? Why didn't you come up with something less incriminating?' Gwilym turned to look at Theodora, whose cheeks had grown red with anger and embarrassment.

'I did what I thought best to stop the situation from descending into bloodshed,' Theodora responded.

'Of course, but you may only have stalled the inevitable. She might be right before the general now dobbing us all in!'

Gwilym began to pace back and forth, rubbing his temples with one hand and worrying his beard with the other.

'We don't know that,' Theodora insisted. 'I asked her to do the right thing and let us get on with our job of hunting Aristotles down.'

'You asked her to do the right thing? Perhaps you've forgotten that she's a mercenary whose sword and conscience belong to the highest bidder, who at this very moment happens to be this massive hoard of armed and angry soldiers surrounding us!'

Gwilym had stopped his pacing and had squared right up to Theodora, who, holding her ground, stared down imperiously at the angry dwarf. Almar had drawn in closer too, clearly concerned or perhaps hopeful that Gwilym would escalate the situation. Egberht, too, had noticed Gwilym's anger beginning to get the better of him. The gnome squeezed between the two of them and leant his weight against the heavier dwarf, forcing him back a few steps.

'Now, now, let's not lose our heads over this!' he grunted with the effort of shunting Gwilym. 'Regardless of which of you is right, it would surely be wiser to at least extricate ourselves from Pegasus Company and work our way to the edge of the column. Then if we deem it necessary to make a break for it, we're in a much better position than we are bickering amongst ourselves without a care in the world.'

'Some sense at last,' Theodora said, not taking her eyes of Gwilym.

'Fine,' Gwilym huffed, 'let's do that. Better to wait for the inevitable somewhere that gives us false hope of escape; tends to put everyone in a better mood.'

'Almar, round up the Guard, tell them we're going to push for the south side of the column and to be ready to make a break for it if it comes down to it.'

The captain immediately peeled off from the group and began approaching the knots of Theodora's guards, who were looking on with concerned expressions, to surreptitiously spread the order. Within minutes, the guard had formed up into a group around Theodora and the others, and Almar returned and affirmed that they were ready to move out.

Slowly at first, the group began to ease its way towards the southern edge of the column, drifting away from Shenesra's troopers, who appeared to not notice the increasing distance that grew between them. However, Torben could see that Eleusia was constantly looking back to where Pegasus Company marched. He knew that Eleusia suspected they were being tracked. He couldn't help glancing back as well, and his heart leapt into his throat whenever he saw a lone rider, thinking them to be a scout sent by Shenesra.

For hours they marched in step with the other troops in the Army of the North, and as they wormed their way through the press, Torben inspected all that they passed. The grim silence of the veteran soldiers, whose scarred faces and bodies looked like they knew the harsh realities of their lives; the nervous-looking recruits, who looked even more out of place that Torben himself did, their agitated conversations giving everything an anxious edge. There were archers, pikemen, swordsmen, cavalry, every manner of armoured man and woman that Torben could think to muster from stories and his imagination. He began to wonder how many of them would survive what was coming and how many of them would be able to live with what they were about to do.

Eventually, the sun began to retreat, casting long shadows over the formation, and the order was relayed up the column to halt for the night. There was a collective groan as the weary warriors slumped down to the ground and began to muster the last of their strength to get themselves fed and watered. By now the group was within sight of the edge of the formation, only a regiment of surly engineers and sappers, with their wagons of stakes and disassembled war machines stood between them and the open expanse of scrubland that stretched off to the south.

Like those around them, they sat in solemn silence, breaking their fast and waiting for the order to move out. Torben, Gwilym, Antauros, Egberht and Eleusia sat around a small campfire and said little to one another. Both Antauros and Eleusia were checking their weapons, the minotaur tightening the strapping around the handle of his war-hammer, Eleusia checking the tension in the string of her crossbow. They were clearly both expecting a fight, and Torben surreptitiously unsheathed the blade of his shortsword to check its sharpness, hoping that he wouldn't need it.

It wasn't until night fell fully over the camp, leaving only the myriad small campfires and the light of the moon and stars to illuminate them, that Theodora came over to their fire with Almar and whispered that it was time to leave. One by one the companions and Theodora's guards began to peel off from where they were sitting and slip into the mass of wagons that the engineers had parked next to them.

Eleusia went first from around their fire, then Antauros, Theodora, Almar until it was finally Torben's turn. As he picked up his things as quietly as possible, he nodded to Gwilym and Egberht, who were still awaiting their turns. Just before he stood up, Gwilym leaned in close to him and whispered:

'Torben, if things go south, we run, do you understand? We don't hang about for Theodora and her lot, right. We make for the hills and don't look back. We don't owe them anything, do you understand me?'

Torben didn't say anything but grimaced in response and slipped away from the flickering light. He made sure to avoid the light that pooled from campfires around other groups and passed quickly and quietly through the rapidly diminishing number of Theodora's guards until he reached the cover of the wagons. Once amongst them, he took a straight line and began to count the rows of wagons, as they'd been instructed to do. At the sixth row, he turned sharply left to crouch behind one of them and nearly collided with Eleusia, who was crouching just within the deep shadows, keeping watch.

Suppressing the startled cry that rose involuntarily to his lips, he slipped past her and into the comforting bulk of Antauros' shadow. He looked further down the row and could just about see similar groups crouching behind their own cover, Theodora's dispersed guards. Theodora and Almar were with them too, and they were swiftly joined behind the cart by Egberht and then finally Gwilym.

'All clear!' he whispered sharply.

In response, Almar stepped forward out of the covering shadows and raised his arm in the air. He brought it sweeping back down again to point towards the open countryside beyond them, the signal for them all to move out. Silently the groups began to slink through what remained of the parked wagon train.

Torben was keenly aware of the noises that he was making, from the minuscule sound of his feet rustling the grass to the occasional dull thud of his shield bouncing against his legs and torso. They crouched low as they moved, even though there were no groups of engineers camped nearby. Eleusia was leading their group forward, and she stopped at the edge of each row of wagons to check that the coast was clear. However, after clearing three such rows, she threw up her hand to signal the halt. As Torben leaned out from behind Antauros' bulk, he could see that there was torchlight playing on the grass in the open space before them. Torchlight that was moving towards them.

Faint scuffling came from the back of the group, and Torben's head snapped to look back. There was light advancing down the row behind them as well, and then Gwilym whispered sharply.

'We're being surrounded!'

'Quiet!' Almar snapped hoarsely back. 'Stick to the shadows and let them pass.'

The light continued to advance on both sides. Torben screwed his eyes shut and held his breath, hoping that Almar would be right. He wasn't. Instead, a familiar voice spoke to them.

'Theodora, Antauros, I know you're there.'

Opening his eyes, Torben flicked his head back and forth, taking in the torchlit silhouettes of a group of soldiers behind them, wearing the armour of Pegasus Company, another group before them, with Shenesra's blue-skinned face barely perceptible in the gloom.

The others all leapt to their feet, beginning to draw their weapons, but the creak and groan of bows being drawn back in response made them all pause.

'Calm down now. There's no need to do anything hasty. I didn't come seeking a fight.'

'Lay down your arms,' Antauros said, letting his warhammer slide back into its belt loop. 'We're fish in a barrel here.'

As they all relaxed and returned their weapons reluctantly to their sheaths, Shenesra took another step forward, one of the torch bearers following behind her to properly illuminate her face.

'Well said, Antauros. It's a shame that you're not actually in charge of this outfit. By all accounts, you were always a steady and level-headed hand on the tiller.'

'What do you want, Shenesra?' Antauros growled warily.

'Well, I'm sure you've guessed that I'm not here to simply comment on this being a strange time for a stroll, but I'm sure you'll be relieved to know that I'm not here to turn you in to General Guthlaf for attempted desertion. No, I'm here to help you.'

'You could help us by getting out of the damned road and letting us be on our way,' Gwilym snapped.

'True, but you know as well as I do that what you were about to do is tantamount to suicide. Getting out of the camp is just the easy part, and I would bet all of the gold that the Kingdom of Dazscor & Aramore are paying me for this venture that you wouldn't get more than a hundred feet before the scouts in the picket line spotted you and raised the alarm. How long do you think you could outrun the battalion of light cavalry sent to hunt you down? Not long, I reckon, especially if they sent me.' Shenesra's couldn't stop the wickedly edged grin from spreading across her face. 'But I'm not here to teach you how to suck eggs. I'm here to offer you an alternative. I can get you out of here, including all of your troops, Theodora, in a perfectly legitimate way. All you have to do is return to my Company's section of the camp so we can all make ready.'

'And why exactly should we trust you?' Gwilym moved from his place in the line and approached Shenesra, his face entering the orb of light thrown out by the torch. 'I saw you head straight for the general's staff as soon as you got back this morning. How do we know that you haven't got a whole lot more troops waiting back there to arrest us as soon as we arrive?'

'You'll have to take my word for it, Gwilym, along with the

fact that I'm not trying to arrest or otherwise incapacitate you right at this moment. You're right though, I did head straight to make my report when I returned, and in truth, I thought strongly about letting the general's staff know that you were planning to desert. Instead, I thought about what you said, Princess, and although I still don't believe everything you told me yet, my conscience cannot let me deny your overall goal. So instead, the report I made to the Commander of Cavalries heavily emphasised that we be allowed to track and hunt down the band of Lupines who perpetrated the crime as my assessment was they pose a significant threat to the army's supply lines. The good commander agreed with me and ordered me to set out as soon as possible in pursuit with all the troops under my command, which, lest you have forgotten, includes all of you.'

Princess Theodora stepped into the torchlight as well and held out her hand to Shenesra.

'We will take you at your word then.'

The Vittra took Theodora's hand and shook it vigorously. Gwilym blew out a loud sigh of relief and let his frame relax, echoing the sentiments of the others.

'Just tell me one thing,' Theodora continued. 'Why are you helping us? Why now?'

'You said that this Aristotles served the Dead God and that he carries a symbol of the deity, a mask with a gaping maw? That is not mere ornament or talisman; it *is* a Mask of Kulittu, a foul and potent item given to only the most promising of his servants, to capture the souls of the dead and dying for the god's fell purposes. Many years ago, another who bore such a mask killed my brother when zealous adherents of Kulittu attacked my home town, looking for souls to harvest.

'After that day, I tried to get as far away from the influence of the Dead God and his sordid followers as I could, even turned my back on my faith to Walanni and her children who stand against him. Yet, sometimes, life has a way of forcing you to confront that which you tried to escape. The appearance of Aristotles in this place, so far from my homeland, where the Walannite Pantheon and Kulittu are little more than a distant memory, is an omen. An omen of great strife and hardship to come. But I also think that your appearance at the same time is an omen of hope, and by my faith and the memory of my brother, I am dutybound to help you. Come, we must make ready to move out.'

With that, Shenesra began to stride off back into the camp, whistling through her teeth for her troops to follow. As Pegasus Company disappeared from sight, Theodora's guards drew in from their hiding place around her, waiting for orders.

'You heard Commander Tador, let's move out.'

As they all sprung to action and began to backtrack through the camp, Torben felt a spot of rain on his head and looked up into the inky blackness. He cursed as more flecks of drizzle spattered his face, and he shivered at the thought of the coming rain.

15

Soon the rain was lashing down across the Kingdom of Dazscor & Aramore. The same rain that fell on the Army of the North was also drumming on the roofs of the houses inside Karpella's tired walls and on the myriad tents that made up the besiegers' camp. The downpour turned the tracks that snaked through the Sharisian positions into muddy streams, which made the journey from the front line back to command head-quarters even tougher for the messenger boy, whose legs were already wearied from a day of running back and forth.

He slogged gamely on, peering out at the murky world from beneath the brow of the helmet that he wore, two sizes too big for him, that was constantly threatening to slip down over his face and blind him. His clothes were saturated with water, which further weighed him down, and he wished that he could get away with casting aside the short sword that rubbed and chaffed against his left leg.

He soldiered on through the camp, and his pace picked up as he saw the large, embroidered mass of the command tent loom out of the gloom before him. He splashed his way at a jog round the side of the edifice to a small opening with an awning set up outside it. Other messenger boys were crowded around a lit brazier, and the newly returned messenger had to shoulder his way through the press to be nearer to the light and warmth of the flames.

As life slowly began to creep back into his hands, he turned his head to peer through the side entrance into the interior, his attention caught by the raised voices inside, which rolled out of the tent in a confusing hubbub of formless noise.

Within, around a large round table strewn with maps, charts, reports and supply lists, ten men were stood having a heated exchange whilst an eleventh sat calmly in a high-backed chair watching the proceedings.

'We need to send out a force to stop the advance of the Army of the North!' declared a man with an enormous grey handlebar moustache that dominated his face and matched his equally prodigious eyebrows.

'If we do that, Kaspar, we'll take too many troops away from the fight that are needed to storm the walls,' said bald man, whose stubbled face was slashed by a deep scar that ran across his left cheek down to the corner of his mouth. He gesticulated at Kaspar across the table with a hand that only had two fingers left on it.

'We'll only need those men if your engineers have actually done their job and made more workable breaches in the walls, Jakkar,' Kaspar spat back.

'Why don't we consider pulling back?' piped up another, a cavalier whose long black hair hung around his face and matched the horsehair plume of the helmet he had clutched under his arm. 'Why not give ourselves more manoeuvrability and the choice of ground for this fight?'

'Pull back, are you mad? After all, we've worked for to get to our current advanced stage of proceedings?' Jakkar bellowed.

'Advanced? I would call having our troops in command of the city waiting for the defenders in Karpella Castle to sweat out their last *advanced*, not still squatting where we pitched up in the first place,' the cavalier said slyly.

'My men have died doing all that they can to make this city as accessible as possible. It's hardly our fault that Kaspar's footmen and your preening cavaliers haven't got the guts to push through and make any headway.'

As the noise level once again erupted around the table, the man sat in his chair sighed a deep exasperated sigh and stood, holding up his hand for silence. He was wearing a fine set of scale mail, embellished with gilded scales in decorative lines, the skirt of which came down to just below his knees. Over the tops of the mail, he wore a breastplate decorated with two gilded horses facing each other and rearing. At his sides he wore a finely crafted curved sword and dagger, both of which rested in bejewelled sheaths. His face was now more starkly illuminated by the candles strewn at irregular intervals across the table, revealing his bright blue eyes, sleek pale face, neatly trimmed blonde moustache and the golden nest of his hair which had been pulled up into a bun.

'Gentlemen, calm yourselves. I did not summon you here to bicker like a bunch of boorish fishwives. I want calm, level facts, not chaos. Jakkar, would you be so kind as to take us through the current results of the siege works and bombardment?'

'Yes, of course, Your Highness,' Jakkar said sheepishly, wiping beads of sweat from his bald head and then rifling through the mass of papers on the desk and pulling out a map of Karpella's walls, which was covered in additional lines and circles drawn in red ink. 'So far, we have four breaches in the walls, here, here, here and here.' He pointed out the respective circles on the map. 'My engineers reckon that within another day or two, we will have an additional two breaches here and here, and that within another four days or so, we should have landed enough hits on the gate and gatehouse to make assaulting it with a battering-ram a feasible option.'

Prince Lanmar peered carefully down at the map, drinking in every detail, before turning his piercing eyes to Kaspar, who was looking just as nervous as Jakkar.

'How many troops do you think we would have to redeploy away from the city to check the Dazscorian advance?'

'By my estimates, sire, a force of four thousand could harry them enough to slow their advance to little more than a crawl, but they are so numerous that committing even half our force to engaging them would still run the risk that they might break through.'

'And what would be your prognosis for us taking the city before they arrive?'

'If Jakkar's engineers cannot provide us with additional entry points by tomorrow, then no better than our previous attempt to storm the city. Though Karpella's defenders are outnumbered, they have managed to fortify the breaches to make them small fortresses in their own right. I fear that we would just be throwing more troops to their deaths for no significant gains.'

'Hmm.' Lanmar paused for a thoughtful moment and then turned his attention to the cavalier. 'I agree with your assessment, Melchan, we are being outmanoeuvred here, and soon we will be at a distinct disadvantage. Committing enough men as you say, Kaspar, to stand a chance of defeating the Army of the North risks exposing ourselves to a counterattack from Karpella's garrison, whilst remaining in our current position will inevitably lead to us fighting on two fronts. I will not allow us to be caught between this hammer and anvil; we will withdraw to the south. If I remember rightly, Melchan, your scouts identified a good dance floor for us to engage the Aramorians at should we end up fighting them in the field?'

'Yes, my prince, two days journey south there is an ideal location with a crescent ridge in the south that loops up on both sides towards the north. It would provide a good defensive position for our infantry up on the ridge where they wouldn't get overwhelmed and provides plenty of places for our superior cavalry to launch an ambush. There is even a village, Cookridge, that could be converted into your command headquarters and a field hospital.'

'Good, start relaying the orders. But let me stress that this is not a defeat, far from it. This is merely a tactical withdraw that will, all being well, convince our adversaries to send the Army of the North and most of the city garrison after us, in the naive hope of crushing us on the march. In any case, our horses grow restless, and we all know how much more efficiently we will be able to slay these dullards from the saddle. At Cookridge, we can outmanoeuvre, surprise and crush them, leaving them with no-one but a skeleton garrison to defend their capital. When we next return, all we shall have to do is walk through the gates.'

The commanders surrounding the table roared their approval, and Melchan snapped his fingers to summon an ink-stained scribe, who was promptly dispatched to a table near the side entrance where he and three others began scribbling down copy after copy of the order to break camp. Less than a minute after the decision was reached, the runners were pushed into the tent one by one, given a copy of the orders and a destination and all but thrown out into the rain again.

The boy with the ill-fitting helmet grumbled under his breath at having to get back to work so soon, and his unguarded comments earned him a cuff from one of the guards standing watch over the tent. As the boy turned to give the man an angry stare, he could see Prince Lanmar and his commanders raising a toast to the success of their plan. The boy wished he could have just a sip of the blood-red wine they were drinking to warm him up, but he knew none would be forthcoming. He snatched the dispatch from a scribe's hand, barely staying long enough to hear where he had to go before stomping back out into the pouring rain.

Unlike his recent journey back to command headquarters, the going was much slower, not solely because of the rain, but now also because there were people everywhere running back and forth starting to get themselves ready to move out. The boy weaved and wormed his way through the crowds, one hand clasping the dispatch to his chest to try and keep it dry, the other keeping his helmet out of his line of vision.

Eventually, he reached the mercenary muster station where he was meant to deliver the orders, and he began to look amongst the more hotchpotch assemblage of soldiers, who all wore and bore a variety of arms and armour, rather than the standard scale mail and scimitars of the true Sharisian troops.

He flitted between tents, sticking his head far enough inside each to see if the Mercenary Quartermaster was within, but not far enough to be within range to catch a cuff from the occupants. Eventually, though pursued by the cries of outraged angry mercenaries bemoaning his disruption of their privacy, the boy spotted his target stood beneath the canopy of a large tent which was open on two sides and dominated by the man's desk, which groaned under the weight of the thick accounting and recording volumes piled on top of it.

Despite the recipient of his message being so close now, the boy's feet began to drag across the ground, and his pace slowed to a sluggish walk as he became aware of the group that the Mercenary Quartermaster was speaking to. Before the man was a large group of wild-looking humans whose tattered clothes were stained with mud and what looked like blood. Many of them had no shoes or boots and were walking barefoot. Their weapons and armour were a motley assortment of different styles and conditions and looked to the boy as if they had been taken from whoever had been unfortunate enough to get in their way. All of the men and women who made up the company had masses of unkempt hair and teeth that looked just slightly too pointed for the boy's liking, but it was their eyes, which stared out of their faces and had a savage, feral glint to them, that scared him the most. Slowly, he crept nearer the tent, doing his best to avoid the gaze of the strange people, but he could feel himself wilting with fear whenever one threw a look in his direction, a look that smacked of something like hunger.

As he slipped under the shelter of the tent and stood in the shadows behind the Mercenary Quartermaster, he could hear the officer conversing with a thin clean-shaven man with greyish skin and silver hair. He did not look as savage as the others, but there was something about him that made the boy warier of him than of any of the others. The Mercenary Quartermaster seemed quite perturbed by the people in front of him, but the paperwork that the strange man provided looked official enough for him to nervously turn his back so that he could stamp the documents. He jumped as he turned to the desk and saw the runner trying to hide from the mercenaries in the shadows.

'Gods! Bral, what are you doing here? You nearly scared me half to death.'

Wordlessly Bral handed over the dispatch to the Mercenary Quartermaster, who took it eagerly, clearly grateful for a distraction from the strange company of mercenaries who were still waiting for the return of their papers.

'Great, this is just what I need right now,' he muttered over the paper and then turning to Bral. 'Stay here, lad, I'm going to need you here to run orders round. How they expect me to be able to break camp at such short notice when I have to administer all manner of ill-organised and ill-disciplined odds and sods I have no idea.' He turned back to the strange mercenaries and passed the now crumpled papers they had given him back into the grey-skinned man's hand. 'This looks just about in order. Make yourselves useful and start spreading word to the other mercenary companies to pack up their gear. We're moving out.'

'Why are we retreating?' The silver-haired mercenary asked in a voice that was far more refined than his appearance.

'We're not retreating, we're redeploying. Moving so that we aren't caught between the city and the Army of the North, and so we can take them both on with the advantage. Don't fret, you and your kin will see plenty of bloodshed soon enough.'

'Excellent,' the man drawled, a wicked smile spreading across his face. He turned and issued some barely audible orders to his retinue, and they moved off into the camp.

The officer breathed a sigh of relief as he watched them go and then began scribbling out dispatches to give to Bral. The departure of the mercenaries also encouraged Bral to emerge from the shadows of the tent. He watched them disappear into the seething mass of the camp and shivered.

'I don't like them, sir, give me the creeps they do. Who are they anyway? They certainly don't look like Sharisians.'

'That's because they aren't, Bral. Who knows where they hail from, but the same could be said for most of the mercenaries I'm supposed to keep an eye on here. Our Commander, in all his wisdom, is more than happy to take on mercenaries of all sorts, be they mounted knights or mountain savages. As I've heard him and the other commanders say many a time, "I'd rather put idiots who fight only for coin in harm's way than a good Sharisian soldier. After all, we can always reclaim our investment from their corpses...". Now then, take these to as many of the mercenary captains as you can find and be quick about it!'

The quartermaster handed the thick wodge of dispatch slips with a kindly but wearied smile and watched the boy dash off into the rain again, noting that he decided to go the opposite direction to that which the strange mercenaries had gone. Turning back to his desk, he began shifting the massive piles of books and papers, trying to get them into a more organised state, and wondered how on earth he'd be able to get the mess ready for transport.

Whilst the Sharisian army camp became a hive of activity in the failing daylight, in Karpella itself, the city's guards and inhabitants were waiting warily. From their positions behind the walls and the hastily thrown up barricades, the soldiers on duty peered through the growing dark, trying to make head or tail of the renewed vigour amongst the Sharisians. They muttered amongst themselves that another attack was imminent, and they began steeling themselves for another night of panic and slaughter.

Across the mainland part of the city, people were trying to get on with their lives as best they could, picking their way through the debris of destroyed buildings back to their homes or to their favourite night haunts. Many combed through the rubble around the breaches in the walls or where stray catapult shots had flown or bounced wildly into the city, trying to find their lost friends and relatives. The streets that lay in the immediate shadow of the walls had become makeshift mortuaries, where the Aramorian dead were laid out so that people could come and identify them. Many, however, remained there day and night, growing more and more putrid by the day, those that once knew them too afraid to approach the walls, or perhaps amongst the dead themselves.

Even the grandeur of Medallion Square had not been spared from the carnage. Many of the ornate Guild House buildings had taken stray shots that had overshot the wall, and the recruiting tents had been packed up and stored for the reappearance of happier times, when the Guild Houses' caravans could once again come and go as they pleased. The open area in the square around the statue of Hastel I had been turned into a makeshift mess area and hospital, the cries of the wounded and dying ringing in the ears of the defenders who had been given leave from the walls to fill their bellies. The waters of the fountain that surrounded the feet of the imperial statue's white marble horse had become stained red with blood, as the surgeons' assistants cleaned their master's gruesome implements there at the end of each day.

On Karpella's middle island, whose homes and businesses were well out of range of the besiegers' artillery, life was able to continue much more normally. The only major change was that there were more guard patrols that stomped through the streets, especially those that skirted the shoreline, and that the great melting pot of commerce that was Spicer's Square lay all but silent now day or night. Whichever of the merchants that had come to ply their wares in the city when the siege arrived had long since sold up their stock and gone to find places to spend their coin and try to forget about their current predicament.

Many of the richer merchants had taken to darkening the doors of Ivy House in their confinement to Karpella, rubbing shoulders with the officers of the city garrison and the more affluent soldiers and commanders of the Imperial Guard. Since the Sharisians had tipped up on their doorstep, business for Ivy House and Madame Fleurese had been booming, but despite knowing how much extra gold was streaming into her coffers every night, the Madame could only bring herself to put on a thin, weary smile as she moved through her perfumed parlours and courtyard.

The increased business meant that there was even more work for her to do than normal, ensuring that her guests were well fed and entertained and that her girls remained safe and well. But it was not the additional pressures of the hostess that weighed heavily on her mind, it was knowledge that she hadn't heard from Eleusia and her companions since the morning they had stepped through her doors and gone with the witch Hrex to Karpella Castle. She had no idea if they had been successful or not, no idea if they were alive or dead.

Every night since then, as she made her rounds, greeting regulars, welcoming newcomers and ensuring that all was right and proper, she had kept her ears open for any news, even the merest scrap of what might have happened to them within the opulent walls of the Emperor's halls. Whenever an officer of the Imperial Guard came to Ivy House, Madame Fleurese would spend hours gently trying to coax information from them, aided by a steady stream of wine and food on the house. Here, diligence meant that she had learned many things.

She now knew that Hastel himself had fled the city many weeks ago, taking most of the court with him. Though the vast majority of the Imperial Guard had been left behind to guard

Karpella Castle and the treasures within, none of them apparently knew where the Emperor had gone. Some thought that he had gone north to the town of Anselwic to mastermind the war effort from a position of safety, whilst some muttered darkly that he had fled to the Republic of Castar to seek refuge there and had totally abandoned them.

The Madame had learned much from Captain Sudthorpe, who oversaw the Emperor's dungeon as well, and had exploited his love of brandy so much that she now knew the names of nearly all of the prisoners being held at Hastel's pleasure, along with the charges levelled against them all. But what she did not know, however, was what fate had befallen her foster daughter and her friends.

By the time that night had fully fallen, Madame Fleurese had already ascertained that there was no one of a high enough rank within the courtyard or common rooms of her establishment who could hope to give her any information that she didn't already know. As she passed through the main taproom, crowded with fat merchants and the bulky forms of men and women in their armour, she avoided the call of greeting that Captain Sudthorpe, clearly hoping to avail himself of more free brandy, hailed her with, and averted her eyes from the corner of the room he sat in, hoping to make it seem like she hadn't seen him. She weaved her way swiftly and expertly through the massed throngs of her patrons and into the safety of the kitchens.

As she entered, her head chef, Kamlar, was barking orders left, right, and centre as he always did, the slight dwarf bustling amongst his small army of cooks and hands, his clean-shaven face constantly aglow with a ruddy hue. His constant flow of instructions paused for only a second to nod a greeting to his employer before starting again. Madame Fleurese leaned against the wall in a place where she wouldn't disrupt the workings of the industrial scale operation Kamlar had running for her and sighed deeply.

Her attention refocused on the room before her when

Kamlar's high-pitched bark of a voice intruded on her consciousness as he relayed instructions to one of the serving girls.

'Take this to the guests in the Silent Room. Remember, do not hang around, just drop off the order, re-fill any empty glasses and be on your way. For your own good, you'll forget anything that you hear in there, understand?'

Madame Fleurese lifted her head off the wall to look at who Kamlar was addressing. She didn't recognise the nervous-looking girl, who must be one of the new recruits she had been told about that morning, brought in to help meet the increased demand in these troubled times. Before the girl had a chance to pick up the tray, heavily laden with pitchers of wine and plates of food, the Madame had strode across the room and gently laid a hand on her shoulder and regarded the girl with a kindly smile.

'Let me, my dear, things one hears in the Silent Room can become an unintentional burden for we innocent providers of refreshments, and I wouldn't want you being weighed down with secrets too soon after starting in my employ.'

The girl bowed her head respectfully and stepped back to be redeployed by Kamlar, who gave Fleurese a sly look out of the corner of his eye. He knew what she was up to. Even though the Silent Room was still part of her establishment, even Madame Fleurese did not enter it once there were clients within unless there was a specific reason for her to do so. She had not had an opportunity to enter it all night, nor did she know who was within, but it would seem that she had entered the kitchen at exactly the right time.

She scooped up the tray and walked purposely, heeled boots clipping on the flagstones down the corridor to the first of the room's thick, iron-banded doors. Expertly moving the tray so that its weight was supported by one hand, she pulled the golden cord by the door to sound the bell within. Though she couldn't hear the tinkling chimes, she did hear the scrape of the inner door being opened, followed by the shifting of the locks within the door before her. It was opened by a large, battle-scarred human dressed in the livery of the Imperial Guard, who immediately relaxed at the sight of her.

'Good evening, Madame,' he intoned, allowing her to pass through.

'Good evening, Aethal, so good to see you again!'

This was no mere pleasantry, Madame Fleurese was very happy to see the man because she knew that he was the body-guard of the City Marshall, Beoric Stornson, a key advisor to the Emperor and, since Hastel's disappearance, the highest authority in the city, and overall commander of the garrison. Her smile grew wider and more genuine as she passed through the inner door to the room and began to float around the table and the men and women within, whispering words of welcome and greeting in their ears as she generously refilled cups. All of the people within were known to her, though she knew one better than any of the others, a thin, sallow man named Thran, a Captain in the Imperial Guard. Normally, she would avoid Thran like the plague, thinking him cruel and overbearing, but seeing that the wine he had taken so far was already flushing his cheeks, she moved over to engage him in conversation, and thereby increase the time she would be tolerated in the room.

'Well met, Madame, we are very lucky indeed for you to grace us with your company,' Thran said with a smirk across his face, a slight slur creeping into his speech.

'It is my pleasure, Captain. I am always glad to see my estab-lishment blessed with such patrons as yourself. Tell me, how is life treating you? I'm sure there is much weighing on your mind in these troubled times.'

As Thran launched into a monologue, Madame Fleurese fixed him with the most attentive smile she could muster and refilled the glass before him, which was greedily snatched up and depleted in the frequent breaks that disrupted the flow of his words. The expression on her face and her body language belied the fact that she was not listening to a single thing he was saying. She had heard this same drivel from Thran three times before and knew which moments to make appreciative or sympathetic noises. Instead, she focused on what the larger man with a balding head and pencil moustache on the other side of the table was saying.

'I am still resisting sending down contingents of Imperial Guards to man the main defences as you have requested, but I cannot guarantee how much longer I can do so for, before the commanders of the City Guard crack,' City Marshall Stornson droned, twiddling with the end of his moustache. 'By my estimates the defences as they currently stand will survive another wave, but after that I fear that we shall have to consider abandoning the mainland portion of the city and concentrate our forces on this and the Castle Island. When that time comes, I will need all Imperial Guards at the disposal of the general defence; otherwise, the common populace will start to say that we are only interested in protecting the Emperor's and our own possessions, and we can't throw such a volatile thing as civil unrest into this situation. But, for the meantime, I see no reason to give that fool General Lenwic more troops to throw at the situation. He's already lost more than enough of his own City Guard launching his foolish counterattacks. I do not want him to believe that I am extending his leash in any way whatsoever.'

Madame Fleurese's heart sank as she listened to what he was saying. She had heard similar conversations hundreds of times before since the siege had started and knew that there was little else she could learn here. Besides, as Thran was running out of things to gloat about, it was time for her to leave. As she made her excuses to Thran and straightened up, one of the other officers around the table piped up to ask the City Marshall a question.

'What of the Army of the North? When will they arrive to relieve us?'

'Who knows. No word has reached us from them directly,

and we've had varying reports from the Sharisian prisoners we've been able to capture. Some say they are weeks away, some say days, and some say that they aren't coming at all. We are better off assuming that we are on our own for the moment...'

As Madame Fleurese made her way back round the table towards the inner door, the bell that hung above it jingled wildly, as if whoever was ringing it beyond was in a terrible hurry. Aethal motioned for her to stay put and moved through the door, closing it behind him. Everyone in the room could hear the faint echoing of a frantic voice beyond negotiating with the Imperial Guardsman. Then Aethal's great bulk filled the doorway once more.

'Beg pardon, my lord,' he said to the City Marshall, 'there's a messenger outside, says it's urgent.'

'Fine, fine, let him in.'

Aethal beckoned the figure in, stopping them only to pull their sword out of their scabbard before they were admitted, and allowed a man dressed in Imperial Guard armour who was thoroughly drenched through into the room. His blonde hair was plastered to his face, and droplets of water were already pooling around his feet. He was breathing hard and was clearly struggling to stand upright as if he had sprinted full pelt to his destination.

'My lord, permission to speak,' he spluttered, sending water droplets that had nestled in his beard spraying across the table, much to the chagrin of the City Marshall, who delicately wiped them off the sleeve of his velvet jacket with a handkerchief.

'Yes, yes, get on with it!'

'My lord, I bring news from the wall. The Sharisians are withdrawing!'

'What?' the City Marshall blurted, nearly ejecting his mouthful of wine over himself.

'They're withdrawing, my lord. They've nearly broken camp, and some of their troops have already started leaving. All officers and soldiers of the City Guard are being recalled to their posts in case this is some new ruse, though General Lenwic is preparing to sally forth and attack the rear of their column.'

'Arrgh, trust that hotheaded cretin to try and throw away the luck just handed to us.' The City Marshall hauled his large frame out of his seat, and everyone else stood as well with a scraping of chairs. He steadied himself with a podgy hand on the back of his chair and turned to face the messenger fully. 'Go at once as fast as you can and tell General Lenwic that he is to hold his position, do you understand me? Hold his position! If anyone under his command moves even an inch to attack the Sharisians, it will be treated as treason. Well, don't just stand there, go!' The messenger scrambled out of the room, barely stopping for long enough to collect his sword from Aethal. 'Thran, Guthkeld, Gertrude, with me, we're heading for the defences to ensure that Lenwic does as he is told. Everyone else, recall every Imperial Guardsman and woman to the castle and place everyone on high alert. I will not have this city be saved from assault only to fall victim to idiocy.'

With that they all began to leave the room, one of the City Marshall's retinue pausing to deposit a fat coin purse on the table to settle their tab. Madame Fleurese stood, stunned for a moment, then swept up the purse and followed them out of the Silent Room.

The news of the Sharisian retreat had already spread like wildfire through Ivy House, and most of the soldiers and officers that had been occupying the courtyard and common rooms left in a hurry to return to their stations and await further orders. Only a few stragglers from the military contingent remained, most of whom were dashing down from the upstairs rooms trying to dress themselves as they went. There were a few though who were too inebriated to move particularly swiftly and who progressed towards the large double doors out of the courtyard as if they were traversing the pitching deck of a ship in a storm.

That was not to say that Ivy House had suddenly become

deserted. News of the breaking of the siege had spread far and wide throughout the city before it had reached the ears of the City Marshall, and the courtyard was already thronged with a new mass of people come to celebrate their salvation. Many of them were pressing through into the common rooms and the tap room, desperate to get something to toast in the joyous news.

Gaining the courtyard, Madame Fleurese watched the influx of revellers. As if echoing the celebratory mood, the rain had finally ceased, leaving puddles that reflected the coloured lamps suspended all around. She didn't feel like joining in the festivities; the sudden shift in mood could not dispel the worry in her gut for Eleusia. If anything, it made it worse. She picked a richly embroidered blanket up from the back of a nearby chair and wrapped it around herself. She needed a walk to take the air and try to clear her head. Pushing her way gently through the crowds, she exited onto the street beyond and let her feet take her where they will.

She walked aimlessly through the streets, deep in thought. Without realising, she passed through Spicer's Square, crossed one of the bridges to the mainland and soon found herself walking down the now much more dilapidated thoroughfare towards Medallion Square. It was the cries of the wounded that finally brought her back to reality. Knowing that she didn't want to pass through the macabre plaza, she veered off to the right, taking a side street that she knew led to one of the sets of access stairs to the wall. As she was here, she might as well confirm what she had overheard for herself.

The broad stone steps that snaked their way up the wall were surprisingly busy with civilians coming and going, who, like her, were keen to confirm the rumours they had heard. When she reached the landing, she had to push her way to the battlements through the onlookers who had crowded onto the walkway alongside the annoyed soldiers, who were trying to maintain some semblance of martial order. Slipping through, Madame Fleurese leaned against the crenelations, staring out into the darkness, which had only the night before been a sea of campfires and torches. Now the only lights that could be seen were the stars, the moon and the faintest winking of torch light in the distance, marking the end of the Sharisians' retreating column.

As she looked out, she heard behind her that the other onlookers were moving away from this section of the wall and the hairs on the back of her neck prickled uncomfortably, picking up on something that the rest of her senses had not. She turned in reaction to the sound of a soldier who stood at his post nearby, edging away from her, his armour clinking softly, eyes nervously flicking to something behind her.

Turning to follow the line of his gaze, Madame Fleurese's face fell into the immense shadow of a large, muscular creature, with a single yellow eye staring out menacingly from the centre of his forehead, Gord. The cyclops was stood with his arms folded, surveying her with a sly smile, and around him, several of Björn's other henchmen drifted around, insuring that civilian and soldier alike moved out of the immediate vicinity.

'Taking in the sights, are we, Fleurese? It's a lovely night for a stroll.' Björn's voice proceeded the dwarf as he stepped out of Gord's shadow and came to stand next to her, leaning against the parapet nonchalantly.

'What do you want?' she responded coldly.

'Me? Oh, nothing. Just like you, I just came to see if the gossip I've been hearing is true.'

'Well, I've seen enough to satisfy me, so I'll be on my way. Good day.'

Madame Fleurese moved to take her leave, but Gord shifted his position and shook his head as he leered down at her.

'It's strange, Madame,' Björn said, turning so that he still faced Fleurese and idly stroked his large silver beard, 'I've always been led to believe that you were always so welcoming and willing to chat, but here you are not even deigning to exchange more than a few words with me.'

'I only talk to those whose conversation I enjoy, or who stand a chance of telling me something I want to know.'

'Hmm, interesting, and you think that I don't have anything to say that you would want to hear? That's not what I've been led to believe from the things you've been trying to extract from people in your establishment.'

Madame Fleurese turned to face the dwarf once again, the colour draining from her face, betraying the steady tone that she managed to project into her voice despite her nervousness.

'I don't know what you mean.'

'Really? It saddens me to think that you've become sloppy of late. Perhaps your worry for Eleusia is clouding your judgement.'

'You know nothing of what I'm going through,' she spat in response. 'Perhaps if you opened your heart up to anything but profit, you would know, but that's impossible for you.'

'I'm quite sure, but with that in mind, I know that if I was in your position, I would be willing to work with anyone who stood a chance of helping her.'

'Don't play games with me. What do you know?'

'At the moment I can't give you more than you already know. My men have been watching the castle day and night, and so far neither hide nor hair of Eleusia and her companions has been seen, but neither have we heard any whispers about them from the Imperial Guard or my contacts within the castle…'

'Then this is a pointless conversation, isn't it!'

'Not when I have the resources, the men and the means to retrace their steps within the castle and give you more information than decades of your whisper hunting could get you. All I need from you is to tell me what their plan was and what they intended to do.'

'I don't know anything about that. They kept it to themselves.'

'I'm sure that's not true. Eleusia is strong, one of the strongest people I've ever had the pleasure of having work for me, but her one major weakness was you. Who knows how many details and snippets she told you in your motherly heart-to-hearts. But play it your way. The night grows deeper, and my belly grows hungry. You know where to find me, Madame. If you want to stand a chance of seeing your foster daughter again, though, I wouldn't leave it too long. We have no idea about how much time she has left...'

Björn whistled softly, and his men gathered back around him, Gord bringing up the rear, leaving Madame Fleurese alone on the rampart. The dwarf's words had cut her deep, and tears started welling in the corners of her eyes. She knew exactly why Björn had offered his assistance, and it wasn't because of any tenderness he might harbour for Eleusia. Like as not, he was still angling to get his revenge on Gwilym and Eleusia for turning on him, as well as looking to get his hands on the gold they had been seeking in the bowels of the castle. But what choice did she have?

She wavered for a few more seconds and then took off at a run down the stairs, following the path Björn had taken into the darkness.

16

As dawn began to break over the Kingdom of Dazscor & Aramore, the rain finally trailed off, leaving behind it a landscape splattered with puddles and small rivulets that reflected the growing strength of the sun, giving the whole expanse of the Dazscorian Plains the look of a giant mirror from the air. Though the storm had passed, the conditions on the ground had by no means improved. The hammering rain had turned the grassland into a sucking pool of mud that clung to the hooves of Pegasus Company's horses, slowing their pace considerably.

It had been two days since they had parted from the advancing column of the Army of the North, and they had barely stopped to rest since then. Though Shenesra Tador had been able to rustle up enough horses so that Princess Theodora and all of her retinue could ride as well, the arrival of the rain had forced them all to dismount to spare the horses and stop them from becoming stuck or slipping in the increasingly boggy conditions. Torben laboured onward, dragging his unwilling horse behind him, and he cursed under his breath as the cloying mud latched onto his boot with an iron grip and tugged it from his foot with ease. Hopping around on his remaining booted foot, he managed to haul his other boot free of the mud, and he leaned against the neck and left foreleg of his horse to balance himself as he tugged the article back on. The beast, unsympathetic to its new master's plight, shuffled to one side, sending Torben falling back with a wet thud to the ground, throwing up splashes of water and mud.

A wave of muddy water splashed over his face, caking him in grime, the shock of the sudden dousing in the frigid water causing him to open his mouth in shock and swallow a large mouthful of the muck. He coughed and spluttered so strongly that he barely registered the enormous hand plucking him from the ground and placing him back on his feet. He doubled over to help heave up the last of the dirt from his lungs and looked up through his sopping hair to nod thanks to Antauros, who was stood next to him. The minotaur was patting him gently but forcefully on the back with one hand to help expel the last of the water from his lungs. His other hand was holding the reins of an enormous carthorse, the only beast judged to be capable of carrying him that could be located at such short notice. Gwilym and Egberht were sat on the creature's back so as to avoid the mire below. Both of them looked as if they were trying to stop themselves from falling into fits of laughter.

As he straightened, Torben made sure to avoid looking directly at their amused expressions and focused his gaze in the direction they were travelling in, pulling his horse forward into a reluctant walk slightly more forcefully than he had intended, eliciting a snort of warning from the beast. They had been travelling cross country ever since they had left the main column, following the tracks of Aristotles and his company of Lupines, which had taken them on a winding route away from the roads, but thankfully not towards anymore isolated villages along the way. Torben squinted into the distance and the copse of trees that were clinging to a small hill. Eleusia and Shenesra were about halfway between them and the hill, both of them ranging out ahead to follow the Lupine tracks before they were churned up and lost by movements of the others and their horses. The two of them had been inseparable ever since they had left the Army of the North, roving up and down together ahead of the column, clearly revelling in the task of tracking down their quarry.

From what he could see, it looked as if Eleusia and Shenesra were deep in conversation as they were bent over what looked like another unremarkable patch of muddy grass and gesturing up towards the hill and its trees. Eleusia rose from her crouch and, leaving Shenesra with their horses, began to run lightly back towards the rest of the column, nimbly leaping from dry patch to dry patch, deftly avoiding the treacherous mud. She weaved her way through Pegasus Company, making a beeline for Antauros' recognisable figure, and came to a halt before them. As she paused to catch her breath, her eyes slid towards Torben and the corners creased with amusement.

'Took a tumble, did we?'

'Don't, Eleusia,' Torben growled. 'Between this mud and this grumpy old nag, I'll be surprised if I make it through the rest of the day, let alone to Karpella.'

'What news?' Antauros asked, steering the subject away from Torben's bruised pride.

'The tracks lead into those trees at the top of the hill. I think it will be a good idea for a couple of us to go up on foot to scout it out, rather than all of us blundering into what could be a trap. Shenesra agrees with me and asked me to pick those I think would be most suited to the task.'

'So naturally you're picking us, the best and the brightest!' Gwilym said, beginning to lift himself gingerly down from Antauros' massive horse.

'If that's what you want to believe, that's fine,' Eleusia responded with a sly smile.

Seeing Princess Theodora approach with Captain Almar,

Eleusia disengaged from them to report and then flitted off to find Sergeant Bandarro. Torben, Antauros, Gwilym and Egberht shouldered their gear and began to make their way on foot to the front of the formation, a couple of Theodora's guards taking the reins of their horses from them. Torben looked back and saw Theodora making her way towards them, and he waited for her to catch up.

'Are you joining us, Princess?'

'Yes, I want to stretch my legs some and get away from the stink of so many muddy horses. Captain Almar and Sergeant Bandarro are taking joint command of the column whilst Shenesra and I are away.'

As she spoke, she skidded on a particularly slick piece of ground, and Torben instinctively reached out to catch her, dropping his spear in the process but managing to stop her from falling.

'Thank you!' Theodora said as she regained her footing, using Torben's arms to stabilise herself. 'I'll be mighty glad when we're out of this treacherous marsh.'

'Yes, me too,' Torben muttered, his face colouring as he realised how close she was to him.

The Princess smiled at him as she continued on her way, making Torben blush even more fiercely as he stooped down to collect his spear. He used the haft of the weapon as a walking stick to help him navigate his way to where the others were waiting for them, and when he caught up, they moved off, away from Pegasus Company towards Shenesra's waiting form. As they drew closer, the Vittra slapped the rumps of her and Eleusia's horses, sending them trotting back towards the rest of the column.

'The tracks are relatively fresh,' she said as they got within earshot. 'Our guess is they passed this way last night. No sign of anyone in the trees now, but you never can tell with Lupines, best we go in quietly and make sure we're safe.'

'Let's get moving,' Eleusia added. 'Keep low and keep quiet.'

With that, she and Shenesra led them at a jog across the remaining open ground, moving off towards the left-hand side of the trees, scouring the ground as they went, examining the trail. Torben had little idea of what they were following so intently. For the most part, the ground looked unremarkable, save for the occasional isolated Lupine paw print, which meant nothing other than the obvious to him.

As they reached the edge of the trees, Eleusia held up her hand to bring them to a halt, and she began to scan the area through the low hanging branches whilst Shenesra scoured the ground for any additional signs of the Lupine's passing. Apart from Torben, whose spear was already in his hand, the others had drawn their weapons, just in case, not wanting to leave anything to chance. With a slight wave of her hand, Eleusia ordered them forward, and they began to slip as quietly as they could through the trees.

Torben's eyes flitted from trunk to trunk, branch to branch and leaf to leaf, the lightest movement of the wood around them making the adrenaline surge through his body. His mind was thrown back to the flight through the trees that he and Gwilym had made in Burndale as they had fled Bywater and their Lupine pursuers. That felt like a lifetime ago, but this moment felt much worse, if only because, unlike then, he couldn't hear the howls of their pursuers, which had at least told them they were still in danger. His heart began to pound in his ears as Eleusia threw up her hand again to stop them and stared hard into the forest before them.

'What's wrong?' Antauros whispered.

'There are bodies in the clearing up ahead.'

'And Lupines?' Gwilym ventured.

'No, I don't think so. Looks like they're long gone.'

They crept forward to the edge of the clearing, and even though Torben couldn't yet see the carnage up ahead, he could smell the sickening metallic tang of blood and hear the buzzing of swarming flies.

'All clear,' came the cry from Eleusia, and they all straightened and walked warily onwards.

In days gone by, Torben would have turned away from the clearing in disgust, but now he just grimly pressed on, trying not to breathe through his nose, swatting away the flies that rose up to try and settle on his face. The clearing before them was a mass of bodies, both men and horses laid out in the dappled sunlight, the ground swamped with so much blood that it had started to turn into a crimson marsh. Though he tried not to look, he could tell that many of the mounts and their riders bore the characteristic claw and fang wounds of Lupines using their innate weapons against them. A number of the corpses were also lying practically naked, their clothes and armour nowhere in sight.

'Who are they?' Princess Theodora asked, her voice muffled by the hand clamped to her mouth.

'Look like Reavers from Free States,' Gwilym replied, pushing one of the still clothed corpses onto their back with his foot to inspect their garb. 'Must have been drawn across the Eira-Gwyn Mountains to Sharisar with the promise of plunder. He came a long way from home indeed to die...'

'There are others here too,' Shenesra called from the centre of the clearing. 'They look no different to the villagers we've seen from here back to Haltwic, but we haven't seen a settlement anywhere near here. They surely couldn't have outrun a group of cavalry for so long that they ended up out of sight of their homes.'

As the others turned to look at the bodies Shenesra was examining, they heard a spluttering fit of coughing break out from the opposite side of the clearing, and as they whipped around, weapons raised, their gaze focused on a bloodied man slumped with his back against a tree. They all relaxed when they realised he was the cause of the noise. His torso was a bloody mess, and his breathing was so soft his chest didn't move at all.

There was no way he could be a threat to them. Slipping his seax back into its sheath, Gwilym picked his way through the bodies towards the man and knelt down beside him so that their faces were level. The others drew in closer as well. The dwarf's appearance at his side caused the man to open one eye a fraction, the other sealed shut with dried blood that had flown from a wound beneath his gore-matted hair.

'Water...' he whispered faintly.

Gwilym untied a skin he had suspended from his belt and held the neck to the man's dry, cracked lips, letting a soothing trickle slip down the man's throat, enough to slake his thirst, but not enough to start him coughing again.

'What's your name, lad?' Gwilym asked softly.

'Danmorran,' came the response, his eye following the dwarf's gaze down to the grizzly crater in his midriff. 'It's bad, isn't it?'

'I'm afraid so.'

'I thought I'd got away lightly at first, but when I realised I couldn't walk, I knew it was going to do me in.'

'What happened here, Danmorran?'

'We were ordered to patrol the ground between here and Karpella, to cover the retreat and hot-foot it back when we spotted the Dazscorian's approaching,' he began, his voice faint and faraway, his eyes unfocused as he spoke. 'We found their column and began heading back to the formation to report how close they were when we spotted some peasant folk walking near the road, bold as you like. We should have smelt something was off in the air, but we'd been sat on our arses outside of that city for so long, we were all ready to blow off some steam. Commander gave the order, and we set off to ride them down, get a bit of sport out of it, he said. The whole thing didn't sit right with me, but orders is orders, so I went with it, but held back, let the others do the murdering, I thought.

'Well, they led us on a merry old chase, running all funny like they all had two gammy legs, but by the Mother, they could run, but that wasn't the strangest of it. Every time one of our lot got near them and managed to land them a blow, it was like they couldn't even feel it, they just kept going. We should have known then to give it up, that something was wrong, but the Commander had got exactly what he wanted, a chase, a hunt, so he kept pushing us on. They led us all the way up here and stopped stock still in the centre of the clearing, and as we moved in for the kill, they all collapsed like rag dolls and didn't move again.

'Before any of us could say anything, they were on us from all sides, the Lupines. I copped it early on, one of them leapt on me, pulled me from my horse and gave me this gift.' He gestured weakly at his mangled body and laughed wheezily. 'I thought I'd got away with it though and lay still as my mates and their nags toppled around me, hoping they'd think I was dead and leave me be. That's when I saw him, the grey-skinned elf. He was striding through the chaos bold as brass, not bothered at all by what was going on, just taking it all in and laughing. He wore this nasty mask around his neck, and whenever one of my comrades breathed their last, a strange wisp of light was drawn out of their bodies and straight into the gob of that thing…

'When the killing was done, the elf stood amongst the Lupines and ordered them to strip the clothes off us, boots and all. They left me be, as they'd written off my threads when they killed me, but soon each of the beasts had a set of clothes and armour. Then their man started mumbling, chanting and waving his arms in the air, and I swear by all my kin living and dead, those Lupines were turned into humans, ragged and shabby all, but humans, nonetheless. Then they put on the clothes and left without a backward glance, didn't even stop to feed…'

As Danmorran had been speaking, Egberht had come over to him as well and had been inspecting his wound, a half-unwound bandage hanging vainly and unused in his hand. Hearing the hoarseness begin to take hold of the man's voice again, Gwilym poured another mouthful of water into his mouth.

'After they left,' Danmorran continued, 'I thought I'd try and make a break for it, but soon found out that I was going nowhere. I made it as far as this tree before I passed out with the pain. Tell me, is there aught that can be done for me?'

The man's eye refocused on Gwilym as he asked the question. Gwilym didn't say anything at first but looked to Egberht, who withdrew slightly from Danmorran and shook his head grimly.

'I'm afraid the wound is too grievous. Even with all the magic in the world, you'd struggle to heal such an injury as this,' he said quietly.

'What was that, sir?' Danmorran asked.

'I'm afraid not, my lad,' Gwilym said, placing one of his hands on the man's shoulder, the rings on his fingers flashing in the sunlight.

'You won't leave me here, will you?' A note of panic crept into Danmorran's voice for the first time. 'That is, not without sending me on my next journey?'

'No, that much we can do for you.'

'Do it then, and I hope that you will not have the misfortune I had to meet those demons on the road.'

Gwilym didn't respond but drew his seax once more and slit the man's throat in one quick movement. Danmorran gasped and shuddered, and then his head slumped onto his chest, dead at last. They all waited for a moment, their heads bowed.

'Poor bugger,' Gwilym said as he stood up. 'That's no way for someone to die, no matter who they call master.'

'Do we believe what he said?' Theodora asked.

'I see no reason not to,' Antauros answered. 'I don't think he had any idea who we really were and those who have suffered as he has rarely have the guile left to mislead.'

'His story explains why half these troopers are naked, and come and look at this,' Eleusia called, summoning them over to the other edge of the clearing where a mass of confused foot-prints scarred the dirt. 'Look, in this area, only Lupine footprints entered the clearing, but only humanoid ones left it, and I would judge that they're heading back in the same direction as the Sharisian army. They're well ahead of us, and I'd imagine that, by now, they'll have managed to infiltrate their ranks.'

'So not only have we got to find a way to infiltrate an army without being spotted, we've got to search for people who we don't even know what they look like!' Gwilym complained.

'Have you heard of this manner of magic?' Antauros turned to direct his question to Egberht, ignoring Gwilym's frustrated outburst.

'Yes, but it has been many years since I've last seen it enacted, and then only on a single person. I have never heard of it being cast by one person on so many others!'

'Do you think you could break the spell, though?'

'Possibly, though I would need to be within sight of Aristo-tles in order to do it, ideally when he is distracted doing some-thing else.'

'And then what?' Gwilym interjected. 'Once the spell is dropped, we'll know where our mark is true enough, but we've got no hope of taking them on, especially with the limited numbers we'd be able to sneak in there, let alone the fact that the ruckus would draw in all of the soldiers within earshot.'

'Would the appearance of a group of Lupines in their camp not be a cause for concern?' Torben said. 'Surely the Sharisians would move to defend themselves and attack Aristotles and his band.'

'You're forgetting, Torben, that there are Lupine tribes working for the Sharisians as mercenaries,' Gwilym responded forlornly. 'Sure, it might shock a few who are passing by and might see the change, but I doubt it would cause more than a few frayed nerves.'

'That's not true,' Shenesra stepped forward. 'Our intelligence suggests that though the Lupines are in their employ, the

Sharisians do not trust them enough to let them camp with them. From what we've seen, the Lupine auxiliaries range ahead of the main army, miles ahead, and act as a skirmishing force to clear the road and make sure they are the ones who spring any surprises waiting for them. That is if they haven't already been dismissed with their coin and let off the leash to run riot across Dazscor & Aramore. It may not cause panic, but it would certainly raise questions and put them all on edge.'

'So what, we're hoping to have them administrated to death?' Gwilym huffed.

'Don't be stupid! It'll give us enough time to get a clear shot on him,' Eleusia said, swinging her crossbow off her shoulder to emphasise her point.

'And how will you track them down?' Shenesra asked. 'They certainly won't be the only group of rough-looking mercenaries hanging around.'

'I think I would be able to help you there.' Torben stepped forward, a resigned expression on his face.

That night, Torben found himself lying face down in some long grass, not daring to move even to survey what was before him. After leaving the clearing earlier that day, they had rejoined Pegasus Company and galloped as close as they dared to the snaking column of the Sharisian army. When the army had finally stopped for the evening, Torben, Eleusia, Gwilym and Egberht had crawled forward alone to wait for their moment to sneak past the picket line.

Whilst Antauros had resigned himself to not accompanying them, due to his size and his rather obvious appearance, it had been more difficult convincing Shenesra and Theodora to not join them. Though Torben would have been glad of them both being there, Eleusia and Gwilym had been firm in their resolution that as few as possible of them should enter the camp to help avoid detection. So Shenesra had only accompanied them with a few of her troopers to the shelter of a nearby hill, where they waited with horses ready to whisk them away.

Now all Torben could see was the back of Egberht's head as he lay as flat as he could on the ground. He could hear Gwilym's heavier breathing behind him and the occasional rustle of the vegetation as the dwarf tried to see what was going on. Though none of them had said so, all three of them were painfully aware of their nerves. They all jumped when Eleusia suddenly materialised from the shadows in front of them, Gwilym letting out a muffled curse and Egberht a whimper.

'All clear,' Eleusia said, her voice barely louder than the breeze tousling the blades of grass. 'Let's go, now!'

Not stopping to check they were following, Eleusia set off again, heading swiftly in a low run back into the gloom. The others sprang to their feet and did the same, Torben and Gwilym with their hands clamped to their weapons to stop them from clanking. Torben had been compelled to leave his spear and shield behind with Pegasus Company, and though he was glad of not having to bear the extra weight, now that he was trying to move stealthily, he felt exposed without the comforting bulk of his shield to hide behind. He didn't fancy his chances if things escalated with just his shortsword and knife to protect himself.

He nearly tripped over the body of a Sharisian soldier who had had the misfortune to be on guard duty when Eleusia had made her initial foray to the camp. The man's face still bore a look of surprise, which was echoed by the grim mockery of a mouth that had been slashed across his throat. Trying not to look back, Torben stumbled on until a line of tents loomed in front of him, with Eleusia, Gwilym and Egberht crouched in one of the spaces between.

'So far, so good,' Gwilym said softly. 'Torben, over to you.'

The man nodded and then closed his eyes in concentration. Ever since she had hexed him, Torben had been able to sense when Hrex was close, had been able to hear again the faintest murmurings of the maddening words that had coursed through his sleeping and waking thoughts incessantly for days on end. Even though the witch had lifted the spell on him, that link remained, and even when she was not close, he had realised that if he cleared his mind and reached out, he could sense her words again, though no more than a tingle of awareness, but it was still there scarring his mind. As he felt for that place he had tried to seal off from the rest of him, he orientated himself physically like a compass needle until he faced the direction where he sensed Hrex's presence most strongly.

'That way,' he said, pointing off to the northern end of the camp.

'Ok, we'll keep in cover if we can,' Eleusia said, drawing them all closer. 'If we have to pass near or through any groups, act natural.'

As she led them off the way Torben indicated, Egberht tugged at Gwilym's sleeve.

'What does she mean, act natural?'

'It means try not to look like you're about to soil your breeches in fear,' Gwilym smiled through the night at the terrified gnome. 'Don't worry, stick with me and you'll be fine.'

They moved as stealthily through the camp as they were able, pausing periodically to allow Torben to re-evaluate where they should be heading. To keep the courses he set, there were several times where they had to skirt past groups of Sharisian soldiers and mercenaries resting from the day's march, but they moved quickly and quietly, trying to make themselves as unobtrusive as possible. Eventually, they reached a row of hobbled horses, who were whinnying and snorting nervously, and Torben held up his hand to stop them.

'The group on the other side of these horses, I think that's them.'

'You sure?' Eleusia responded.

'Yes, though I don't know which one is Hrex or which Aristotles, but I can hear her in my head, I know she's there.'

Gwilym peered through the legs of the beast in front of him, assessing the mercenaries beyond.

'They certainly look wild enough to be Lupines that have been transfigured into humans. They all look like they've been beaten once or twice by the ugly stick, let alone the fact that their table manners are even more atrocious than I would have suspected.'

'The horses can sense them too,' Eleusia said, trying to calm the beast closest to her by stroking its head. 'They can smell that somethings not right about them. Can you see any that might look like our targets?'

'Maybe...further down the line there are three sat round a campfire, a big brute of a man, a smaller woman and a wraith-like man, seems like as good a fit as I can see to Aristotles, the witch and that bloated Lupine captain of his.'

'Do we need to get any closer?' Torben asked, the worry evident in his voice.

'The closer I am to the source, the easier it will be for me to identify the strength of the magic and what I might need to dispel it,' Egberht chipped in.

'Alright, let's go. Torben, let us know when you're sure one of them is Hrex,' Eleusia said, beginning to lead them forward.

'I don't need to get any closer,' Torben muttered. 'I know it's her.'

As they crept forward, Torben could feel that fell voice in his head getting louder and more intrusive.

'Ashak, ashak, ashak...'

When Eleusia finally halted them as close as she dared come to the group, Torben had to fix his whole attention on drowning out the voice. He was aware of Egberht crouching down next to him, beginning to mutter under his breath, his eyes shut begin-ning to start his analysis, but as another wave of sound assaulted his thoughts, he screwed his eyes tightly shut and clapped his hands ineffectually over his ears. The others were unaware of

Torben's predicament, Egberht was too fixated on his work, whilst both Gwilym and Eleusia were focused on listening into the conversation the group on the other side of the horses was having.

'...in order to get the best results,' the wraith-like man was saying, 'we need to be as close to the centre of the battle as possible. That means you need to keep your pack on a tight leash, Zarrax.'

'Understood, master,' the enormous man said in Zarrax's deep growl, 'but there will be those who will take poorly to watching the battle rage around them without having the opportunity to slake their own bloodlust.'

'Their patience will be rewarded a hundred fold. There will still be enough killing to do once the ritual is complete to satisfy them. Better yet, as the other packs have been dismissed to raid and pillage as they wish, there will be no other Lupines to challenge you for the spoils. When I have all the souls I require, I will no longer need protecting and you and your kin can engage in as much wanton slaughter as you wish.'

Gwilym's attention was drawn away from the conversation by a faint but growing golden-yellow light emanating from Egberht's swiftly moving hands, where a spherical nexus of light, strung with tiny runes, had formed in his hands, into which he was staring intently.

'Any luck? I don't like being this close to them,' Gwilym hissed.

'Nearly,' the gnome replied through gritted teeth. 'Hopefully won't be too much longer.'

Around the campfire the ragged woman shuffled uncomfortably.

'What is wrong, Hrex?' Aristotles asked, his cool, refined voice at odds with his wild appearance. 'Surely you of all people are not getting cold feet before our day of triumph.'

'No, master, not at all, it's just that feel as if the boy is close, and there is something else...'

'I sense it too!' Aristotles snapped, springing to his feet, a look of rage on his face.

He clapped his hands together, sending the faintest hint of arcane energy rippling around him. It caused the true forms of all of the Lupines and Aristotles himself to be revealed for a split second before the illusions reasserted themselves, but the orb of light in Egberht's hands was snuffed out.

'Zarrax, send scouts out into the camp. Theodora's puppets are here. Find them!'

'Time to go!' Gwilym blurted hurriedly, helping a dazed Egberht to his feet and starting to drag him away.

Eleusia, seeing that Torben wasn't moving but had his eyes shut, shook him roughly and slapped him across the face to bring him back to reality. Torben watched her mouth moving but could hear nothing over the torment inside his own head. He let himself be hauled off the ground by her and bundled away. With every step he took, he felt the voice grow weaker and his own thoughts grow clearer until he was able to move freely on his own, without Eleusia's assistance.

They moved much faster through the camp than they had before, drawing a few stares from those they passed, until Gwilym dived into a dead space behind some wagons, and they hid there, catching their breaths and looking to see if the Lupines had picked up their trail.

'All clear,' Eleusia eventually said. 'Torben, are you alright?'

'Yeah, I'm fine. It's just that whenever I get close to her, it's like she's trying to curse me all over again.'

'It's your shadowed mind connection with her,' Egberht wheezed, bent over double trying to calm his breathing.

Gwilym reached over and patted Torben gently on the shoulder, and the young man reached up to grasp the supporting hand in his own.

'Did you get enough information, Egberht?' Gwilym asked.

'Not as much as I would like, but enough to at least work out how to roughly go about things, but Aristotles will need to be far more distracted in order for me to banish his illusion from under his nose.'

'We should get moving.' Eleusia had crept her way to the edge of the wagons. 'We're not home and dry yet.'

The other three followed her as she slipped out of their refuge and began to make their way as carefully as they dared back to the edge of the camp and to their escape.

17

B efore the sun had fully roused itself the next morning, the sounds of battle could already be heard drifting through the pre-dawn gloom. Less than two miles from the village of Cookridge, the sickle-shaped hill it stood upon and the Sharisian army's position, two groups of scouts had blundered into one another, and their quiet morning patrols had escalated into a bitter fight for survival. The sounds of soldiers and horses screaming could be heard in the Sharisian camp to the south and amongst the slowly moving mass of the army of Dazscor & Aramore that trundled onwards to close the gap between itself and its quarry. In the darkness it was hard to tell friend from foe, and several on both sides fell inadvertently at the edge of their comrades' blades.

Somehow though, the commander of the Dazscorian patrol managed to dispatch one of his riders from the confusing maelstrom, and that man galloped as fast as he could from the carnage, hoping against all hope that he was headed in the right direction and not hurtling towards yet more enemies. As his horses' hooves ate up the distance, the man's vision grew dimmer, and he stared in disbelief as the hand he raised to check his forehead, where a throbbing pain could be felt at his ginger hairline, came back wet with blood. His eyes clouded, and he lolled forward onto the neck of his still racing horse, his senses deserting him.

The sudden icy shock that struck him next made him feel as though he had jumped head first into the waters of death. He coughed and spluttered, aware all at once of the sensation of the chill water and the pounding pain in his head. His eyes snapped open, and as his vision swam back into clarity. He started and tried to scrabble away from the figures that loomed into sight, fearful that he had been taken by the enemy. One of them was talking to him though his ears had not quite managed to connect to his brain again.'

'What...name...which...company...'

As the disjointed sounds drifted towards him, his vision finally snapped into focus. His pulse began to slow as he recognised that the dark moustached man and the brown-haired woman kneeling over him were both wearing Aramorian uniforms and armour. His hearing cleared too, and he finally able to make sense of what the man was saying.

'What's you name, son? Which company did you come from?'

'Eofor, sir,' he replied. 'Member of the Upland Scouts, we ran into an enemy patrol, and I was sent back to report.'

'We'd better get him to command so he can tell his tale,' the woman said. Both of them helped to heave Eofor to his feet and helped him walk unsteadily through the vanguard of the formation.

The men and women of Dazscor & Aramore's army parted to make way for the trio, but Eofor was unable to take much in as the blood that had flown from his scalp wound was drying and crusting across his forehead and eyes, half sealing them shut and making his eyes water. Eventually, he heard the distantly familiar, smooth deep voice of General Guthlaf speaking nearby. He had heard the General speak before, but only when addressing massed gatherings of troops. Other than that he had little to do with him. He was the commander of the Army of the North, after all, and Eofor was but a lowly cavalryman. He knew of Guthlaf's strict and harsh reputation, though, and he looked around nervously, trying to distinguish which of the silhouettes in his blood obscured vision was the General. That nervousness turned to fear when his hearing came sharply back into focus, and he realised that General Guthlaf was speaking to him directly.

'I said report, soldier! In case you haven't noticed, we're in the middle of a war. There isn't time to be standing around gawping like landed fish. Speak!'

'Apologies, sir,' Eofor stammered. 'Captain Beorhtric of the Upland Scouts dispatched me back to bring news of the enemy movements.'

'Well... get on with it then!' The General's voice had an impatient, dangerous edge to it.

'S-sir, the Sharisian's have established their infantry in position on the hillside and are using the village as their field command, apart from the cavalry patrol that we had the misfortune to run into, their massed cavalry are nowhere to be found. From what we could tell they've continued to head south, we came upon the signs of their passing before we were jumped.'

'Hmm, Talesin, bring the map.'

General Guthlaf stood deep in thought, pondering Eofor's words as an aide scurried back to gather a map tube from a pannier on his horse. As Talesin rushed back, unfurling the map and holding it before the General, the rest of Command crowded round to see.

'Cookridge is the most easily defensible point on the road between here and the Bar-Dendra,' the General said, using his riding crop to circle the village's location on the map. 'I'll warrant it's a good position to make a last stand, and with their cavalry still heading south, my assessment is that they've decided to launch a holding action, sacrifice their infantry so that the majority of their force can reach the safety of the Bar-

Dendra from which it's a straight and easy road home to Sharisar for them. We've got them grossly outnumbered, and even with them holding the hill, we should be able to smash through them and onwards in pursuit of the rest easily enough.

'Give the order to march on. I want to swat them out of the way as quickly as possible.' Noticing that Eofor was still standing unsteadily nearby with his two helpers, the General barked, 'And get him out of here, it's hard to concentrate with him slowly expiring in front of me.'

'Yes, sir,' the moustached man responded, moving up to Eofor's side with the brown-haired woman. 'Come on, son, let's get your head seen to.'

As Eofor was led away, runners began streaming off in every direction as General Guthlaf got back into his flow and began issuing his battle orders left, right and centre.

Less than fifteen minutes after the messengers had been dispatched from command to relay orders to divisional commanders and then on to company commanders, a red-faced boy, who was so winded he could barely speak, staggered towards where Pegasus Company were camped in the shadow of their blue banner and stuffed a dispatch paper wordlessly into Bandarro's hand before lurching off as fast as he could to his next destination. Seconds later, the dispatch was in Shenesra's hands, and she broke the hurriedly affixed seal where she sat next to a campfire with Theodora, Almar, Gwilym, Eleusia, Antauros, Egberht and Torben.

'Ah,' Gwilym exclaimed, gesturing to Shenesra, a wicked grin on his face, 'fresh news about where they're going to send us to die!'

'Is it really that bad?' Torben asked, not noticing the jocular tone in the dwarf's voice.

'Well, we're certainly not all here to have a tea party, are we?'

'Hush, Gwilym,' Antauros said, lightly punching Gwilym's arm to stop him from laughing to himself and realise that Torben's face had gone grey with worry.

Princess Theodora cast Gwilym a dirty look across the fire and placed her hand supportively on top of Torben's. The young man was roused from his morbid thoughts by the touch and blushed as he saw her hand on top of his. He hurriedly looked at the ground, trying to hide his sheepishness.

'What are our orders?' Eleusia asked.

'We're being deployed to the left flank as part of the cavalry screen,' Shenesra replied, her brow furrowed as she read the hastily scrawled writing. 'The enemy cavalry is thought to have withdrawn from the engagement, so our orders are to harry any Sharisian infantry that try to advance down the left flank and to be prepared to execute flanking and pursuit manoeuvres when ordered.'

'The enemy cavalry is thought to have retreated?' Antauros repeated. 'They think the Sharisians will fight under their rearing horse banner with no cavalry in sight? Something doesn't seem right here at all.'

'Well, it's still better than us being sent in pursuit of them,' Eleusia responded. 'If that had been the case, we would have had to find a reason to be present on the battlefield so we could track down Aristotles. And let's hope they're right. Milling around on the flanks will give us ample time to work out where he and his Lupines are hiding.'

Horns began to sound across the camp. Shenesra stuffed the dispatch into a pouch hanging from her belt and stood, easing the stiffness out of her joints.

'That's the signal to prepare to move out,' she said to them, and then raising her voice so that everyone nearby could hear her, she said, 'Pegasus Company, saddle up, and prepare for battle!'

As the sun crept towards midday, the Kingdom of Dazscor & Aramore's Army of the North came into sight of the village of Cookridge, the curved hill on which it sat and the Sharisian positions around it. From the position that Pegasus Company had taken with a number of other light cavalry units on the left flank, Torben looked on gobsmacked as he took in the view they were riding towards. He had heard stories about the clashes of great armies, the sheer scale of such conflicts, but even travelling amongst the train of the Army of the North hadn't prepared him for seeing the Sharisian army draped across the hillside. It was a beautiful day, the rotten weather of the nights and days before having given way to glorious sunshine that winked and glinted off the weapons and armour of the Sharisian's serried ranks. Above the enemy formations, he could see the familiar banner of the rearing white horse with a golden mane on a field of red.

As Pegasus Company and the other cavalry on their flank drew to a halt, orders were bellowed back and forth behind them and were swiftly swamped by the rumbling noise of the Joint Kingdom's infantry jogging into position, a deafening maelstrom of chainmail and weapons rattling, shields banging and feet stomping. Then silence descended eerily across the battlefield, broken only by the sounds of the men and women on both sides awkwardly shuffling.

'What's going on?' Torben asked of Antauros next to him in a hushed whisper. 'Why is nothing happening?'

'General Guthlaf and his command are sizing up our foe, and they are no doubt doing the same to us,' the minotaur replied. 'It is so at the beginning of every battle, we lesser folk must stand and wait before the precipice of doom whilst those above plan and counter-plan, looking to set traps and trying to spot traps laid against us. Eventually, they'll talk enough confidence into themselves to order us forward. There's no fear of that not happening.'

'Do you think there are traps out there waiting for us?'

'Undoubtedly, but talking won't expose them. I only hope that command are getting a whiff of the same bad smell I am...'

'What do you mean?'

'Sharisar is a nation of nomadic horsemen and women, and whenever they go to war the majority of their armies are composed of mounted warriors. These people before us are likely to be either the poorest of their kind whipped off to war to act as catapult fodder before the walls of Karpella, or are mercenaries like ourselves, most of whom would know well enough when a fight with low odds of survival is approaching and who I wouldn't expect to stick around for long. It may be that Sharisar has decided to abandon those that have no chance of reaching the border, but for them to come all of this way and simply give up...that's the bad smell I'm detecting. If we survive this and their cavalry have truly bolted for the border, I'll eat my warhammer!'

'Careful, Antauros,' Gwilym said from his position on the back of the minotaur's horse. 'I'll hold you to that.'

As Antauros chuckled to himself, Torben looked deep in thought and then cut through the jocularity with another question.

'Well, what can we do?'

'There is nothing we can do except keep our eyes peeled and prey to the gods that we survive.'

Behind them a horn sounded, a long low note that sent a shiver through the ranks of soldiers. Antauros reached over and placed one of his enormous hands on Torben's shoulder.

'Stay close and luck be with you, Torben.'

Torben didn't respond. To their right the lines of infantry had begun to march forward with the relentless beating of drums that started up amongst them urging them on. The riders ahead of them nudged their mounts onwards as well so that the cavalry screen moved up with the infantry. Many of the cavalry troopers were nervously eying up the area of woodland that lay off to their left, and Torben noticed Antauros staring hard at the trees as well, looking for any sign of movement.

Torben watched the blocks of infantry march mutedly before them, not envying them in the slightest for what they were marching towards. Many of the infantry troops appeared to be regarding the lazily moving cavalry with resentment, even hatred in their eyes, and Torben heard some of the less than flattering remarks that were muttered in their general direction, even over the sound of so many troops stomping onwards. Then, for a split second, he thought he heard something else, like a snap or a crack from up ahead.

He turned to face the Sharisian position again and narrowed his eyes as he spotted something moving through the sky, getting closer and closer. It looked like a stone ball about the size of a large pumpkin, he supposed. Others had seen it too, and a scuffle broke out in the nearest block of infantry as they jostled one another to get out of the way, but they were too late. The ball plummeted towards the ground, catching at least two victims with its murderous momentum and sent them crumpling to the ground in a spray of blood and bone. It bounced as it hit the earth and carried on its course, ripping through the ranks behind, heedless of the people in its way. Other similar dramas played out all across the line, and Torben turned his face away, his greening complexion revealed to Antauros, Gwilym and Egberht.

'Must have taken some of the catapults for the siege with them when they retreated.' The playful tone that generally inhabited Gwilym's voice was gone.

The signal horn sounded again, this time two short, sharp blasts, and the infantry formation broke into a jog, looking to close the distance between them and the enemy, as much to get out of the devastating catapult fire as to actually engage the Sharisians. Pegasus Company and the other cavalry on the flanks spurred forward to keep pace, Torben struggling to keep upright on his fractious mount. The Aramorian archers and crossbowmen peeled off from the back of the formation, preparing to fire as the enemy came within range, but no sooner had they begun to draw back their bows and raise their cross-bows to shoulders as a whistling sound filled the air. The Sharisians had got their initial volley in first and people started dropping like flies all around. Torben raised his shield in front of his face as some stray shafts winged over into the cavalry and he felt the impact and scrape of one being deflected off the curve of his shield. When he was finally brave enough to lower his shield again he realised that a member of Pegasus Company who had been riding next to him was dead, though still upright in his saddle, arms limply hanging by his sides and an arrow embedded almost to the fletching in his throat.

As Torben stared dumbstruck at the man's lifeless body, he saw a wisp of purple light, almost imperceptible in the bright sunlight, leaving the body, as if being pulled forcibly out. As the wisp was dragged through the air, Torben followed it with his eyes as it drifted across the battlefield.

'There look!,' he cried, 'Can you see it?'

'See what? What is it?' Gwilym responded, leaning out from behind Antauros but clearly watching the movements of the troops rather than the wisp.

'I see it Torben, a soul,' Egberht replied. 'Aristotles is here alright, somewhere in the centre of the enemy formation, look!'

The gnome pointed his long dexterous index finger across the battlefield. From the bodies of the troops claimed by the exchange of missiles, other strands of purple light were being drawn too and were rising above the heads of the combatants, being drawn towards the Sharisian side. As Torben's eyes strained to track the passage of the souls further, his gaze was drawn by an increase in the speed of the infantry's movement. When both sides got within a few hundred feet of each other, the air was split by a deafening bellow as the Sharisians and the soldiers of the Joint Kingdom charged. The bloodcurdling war cry gave way to the crunch of metal and man as the two sides collided with each other, followed shortly by the ringing of metal on metal and the screams of the dead and dying. As they watched from the cavalry screen, a cloud of purplish wisps formed above the mêlée, so thick and fast that it caught the attention of the other cavalry companies, whose members began to talk in nervous whispers amongst themselves.

However, they did not have time to worry about the spectacle for long. On both of the Army of the North's flanks and to its rear, horns were sounding, not like the deep mellow sound of the Aramorian signals, but a harsher higher pitch that sent all of the cavalry scrambling to draw their weapons.

'I knew it!' Antauros roared, wheeling his horse around so violently that Gwilym and Egberht nearly tumbled from their perches.

Torben didn't need to look to the rear of the army to guess what was happening. The sounds of battle could be heard running rampant through the reserves and the baggage train already. A frantic messenger galloped into view and dragged his horse to a rearing halt at the edge of their formation, bellowing at the top of his voice.

'Commanders Briffax, Meliot, Shenesra, and Pallomedes, the General wants you to move your companies to the rear, now! Sharisian cavalry are attacking the...'

His words were cut off as three arrows buried themselves in his chest, sending him slipping off the back of his restless horse and thudding to the ground. Then the air was thick with arrows coming from the trees to their left, followed shortly by a wave of Sharisian riders. The first Sharisian riders streamed past them, parting seamlessly to move around their still stationary opponents. As he raised his shield to shelter himself, Torben marvelled at them, their skill and grace as they loosed arrows with deadly accuracy from the back of their galloping mounts, many twisting completely round in the saddle to continue the bombardment once they had passed. The horse archers were followed by others wearing heavier armour, plate and scalemail riding stockier warhorses who shimmered under their own protective coats of iron. The ground shook as the Knights of Sharisar ate up the ground between them and the Army of the North's light cavalry, their lances levelled, a bare-headed captain, sword held high above his flowing shock of red hair urging them on.

As the cries of the riders and the terrifying screams of horses fought with the sounds of battle and began to drown out everything around him, Torben heard a voice rising above the pandemonium, Shenesra's voice.

'Pegasus Company, with me!'

Shenesra's troopers and Theodora's guards kicked their horses on, following the Vittra and her flowing banner away from the rapidly approaching heavy cavalry and into the space behind the struggling blocks of infantry, where the horse archers were zipping up and down, firing indiscriminately into the backs of the Aramorian foot soldiers and gleefully running down any whose nerve had broken and were trying to flee. As they hurtled away, Eleusia urged her horse in between Torben's and Antauros' and yelled at them over the muddying swirl of noise.

'This is exactly the distraction we need! We've given orders to move around the battlefield as best we can until we pinpoint Aristotles' location, and then we'll find an opening and charge them. Hopefully that will give us enough surprise and momentum to distract him enough so you can dispel his illusion, Egberht. Hopefully then their true forms will sow enough chaos that we can stop him once and for all and make good our escape.'

'Who's "we"?' Gwilym shouted back.

'Shenesra and I. Theodora has agreed to the plan too, so brace yourselves, we're in for a bumpy ride!'

As Eleusia accelerated past them to relay the orders on to the rest of the company, Gwilym drew a hand across his forehead.

'That's it, she's finally lost it. Antauros, how much of my share of the treasure beneath Karpella will I need to forfeit to get you to turn this horse around and get us the hell out of here?'

'You know I can't do that!' Antauros bellowed back in reply.

'I should have known letting Eleusia and Shenesra get too chummy was a bad idea,' the dwarf grumbled, 'now look what they've gone and done…'

As they thundered along the back of the Army of the North's line, it was clear that they were losing. All along its length Dazscor & Aramore's infantry were being pushed slowly but surely back down the hill, the solid, impenetrable wall of Sharisar creeping closer, the arrows of the horse archers wearing them down from behind. Clumps of soldiers were already starting to peel off and flee, and wherever a rout began, the tide of Sharisar surged forwards. There was one place, however, where the Sharisians weren't trying to advance even though they were clearly winning, and troops of the Joint Kingdom opposing them looked just as shaken as the others. Torben stood unsteadily in his saddle to get a better view as they approached and saw that the Sharisians in that section of the line were mercenaries, ragged men and women who fought like animals whenever an opponent got close, nevertheless holding their ground. The frequent flashes of purple light were coalescing above them and being drawn down to a point within their lines.

'There do you see it?' Torben yelled, pointing with the tip of his spear, though he wasn't sure if anyone had actually heard him over the surrounding din.

Shenesra and Eleusia at the front of their column had clearly seen it too, for she guided the formation sharply left as a mass of Dazscorian soldiers broke and began to flee, their assailants leaping forward in pursuit. They ploughed into the unexpectant

Sharisians, scattering many of them left and right, and trampling many more under their horses' hooves. Their progress stalled as they urged their mounts to wade through the crush of troops, many of whom were turning to face the new threat, and up the slope of the hillside. Instinctively Torben stabbed down again and again with his spear, though he was never sure if he found his mark or not. As the front of Pegasus Company finally made the ground beyond the Sharisian line, their progress accelerated, but not before some of Shenesra's riders and Theodora's guards were pulled from their saddles or skewered on spear points.

Torben couldn't believe his luck when he cleared the mass of infantry unscathed, save for a few scratches. He looked around wildly for his friends and spotted Antauros' and his passengers mounted on his stocky horse with Eleusia and Shenesra not far in front. He turned back to look for the Princess or any of her guard and only just managed to avoid the spear thrust that had been aimed at his back. He twisted around and thrust his own spear down only to find that the point had broken off in the scrummage, and the end was now nothing but a splintered mess. Desperately he struck out with the haft, but the Sharisian soldier confronting him grabbed it and nearly pulled Torben from his saddle. As he flailed his arms to try and regain his balance, he saw the man bearing down on him, spear raised. Not a moment to spare, Torben managed to haul himself back up into the saddle and out of the path of the jabbing point, but before he could draw his sword, another group of riders who had managed to extricate themselves from the infantry flew past, and one brought a glittering sabre down in a sweeping arch that cut across the Sharisian's back, dropping him to the ground.

Princess Theodora, accompanied by the last of her retinue, reigned in her horse to look back at Torben. She looked tired but unhurt, but the blood dripping down her curved blade spoke volumes on how hard she had fought to survive. Next to her, Captain Almar had a pained grimace stitched on his face, and he held his left arm awkwardly in front of his torso, a large blood-stain marring the armour and cloth around the armpit.

'Torben, are you alright?'

'Yes, I'm fine, thanks to you.'

'Good, come on then. The others are a little way ahead.' Theodora flashed him a broad smile and waited for him to draw level with her before setting off.

As they kicked their horses on, Almar leaned over to him, wincing through the pain as his horse jostled him about in the saddle.

'Remember boy,' he rasped, 'in battle, you keep moving, you keep going, you keep pushing to survive. If you stop, you're a dead man, you don't get a second bite of the apple.'

'Do you need help?' Torben asked concerned.

'I'll be alright. It's too risky to stop anyhow. You mind your-self, I'll mind me.'

They raced behind the Sharisian line to reach the tattered remnants of Pegasus Company who were waiting nervously a good distance away from the infantry, which was now more concerned with pursuing the beleaguered Aramorians to take much notice of them. They were drawing more and more fire from the Sharisian archers as they realised that Pegasus Company was not on their side. As Theodora's retinue drew alongside, they all rode on and began to make for where Aristo-tles and his disguised Lupines were still holding the line. The Shadow Elf had picked his position well, where the fighting was fiercest, not because the Army of the North's troops in opposi-tion there were made of sterner stuff than the others, but because the Sharisian formation had been able to curl around them and seal them in, forcing them to fight to the death.

As they rode closer and closer to the churning mass of bodies, with the storm of captured souls above, Torben could see Egberht was deep in concentration as he bounced up and down on the back of Antauros' horse, Gwilym straining every muscle in his body to keep him steady. The web of golden yellow light was growing between his hands once again, its light much stronger than it had been the night before in the Sharisian camp. As they streamed past the wild-looking group, Antauros bellowed at the top of his voice, 'Now, Egberht!'

The gnome's eyes snapped open, and he flung the ball of light high into the air where it hovered for a moment before bursting into a silent wave of light that stretched out in all directions, completely engulfing the nearby combatants, who stopped their life-and-death struggle to marvel at what was happening. Pegasus Company came to a halt and watched as one moment, the wild-looking mercenaries appeared as humans, the next they stood as Lupines again. Both the Sharisians and the Aramorians stepped back instinctively at their sudden appearance. In the midst of the Lupines, Torben could see Hrex wheeling around dumbfounded, eyes staring wildly as she tried to work out what had just happened. Aristotles could be easily spotted too, his tall, thin figure stood rooted to the spot in the centre of his followers, head bowed deep in concentration, lips moving in silent incantation, the Mask of Kulittu clutched in both hands.

Chaos erupted all around then, with some of the Sharisians and Aramorians turning and fleeing at the Lupines' appearance, some moving to attack what they viewed as the new threat and some continuing to attack each other. The Lupines gleefully fell to attacking anyone who came near them, though they still stood their ground, the hulking figure of Zarrax striding amongst them barking orders in their harsh guttural tongue, keeping them in line.

'Something's wrong, Aristotles isn't stopping,' Torben said.

'He must think he's already captured enough souls and is close enough to the end of the ritual to push on rather than escape,' Egberht replied. 'There are not enough troops from either side attacking the Lupines that pose enough of a threat to overwhelm them. We need to do something.'

'You're right,' Theodora said, 'we need to act!'

Before anyone could stop her, she kicked her horse forward and began to charge towards the fight, sabre held out before her.

'What the hell are you doing?' Torben shouted after her.

'She's going to try and end this by killing him herself,' Eleusia said then snapped, 'Come on, let's get a move on. She'll stand no chance without support.'

Freed from their momentary shock, the last of Pegasus Company and Theodora's guards spurred after the Princess, weapons drawn, thundering down the hillside, making straight for the Lupines. Ahead Theodora was already entering the mass of snarling Lupines. Her horse had bowled two over, and another had already met its end at the curve of her blade, but more were turning to meet her lone charge. Their expressions turned from delight to fear as the rest of the riders smashed into them, beating back the Lupines who had turned to react and carving a bloody path towards the centre of the savage formation. With a howl of anger, Zarrax bounded into the fray, knocking a horse to the ground with the speed and strength of his countercharge and then leaping on the unfortunate trooper from Pegasus Company whose leg was trapped beneath their terrified mount.

Though almost all of the Lupines were now piling in, trying to stop them in their tracks, the momentum of their charge brought them closer and closer to Aristotles. Torben was so close now that he could see the sweat beading at the Shadow Elf's temples, as well as the terrified expression on Hrex's face as she dashed to-and-fro around him, unsure of what to do. For a moment, Torben's heart sang as he was sure they would succeed. Theodora was now only feet away from him. All it would take was a few more galloping steps, and Aristotles' head would be in range of her outstretched sword. But that momentary elation was drowned as the Mask of Kulittu began to glow with such a bright purple light that the whole of Aristotles' person seemed to glow with it, and his head snapped up, eyes wide open and alert. His right hand shot above his head, a glowing rune soaring above him, and he spoke a single word that echoed in the ears of everyone in the vicinity.

'Ashak!'

Torben groaned as the familiar leaden feeling seized hold of his limbs, much faster than when Hrex had cast the spell, causing all of them, Sharisian, Aramorian, Lupine and horse alike to stand stock still, frozen in their struggle. From his vantage point on his horse, Torben could see that not everyone on the battlefield had been affected, but many of those on both sides still able to move were cautiously drawing closer to see what was going on. Out of the corner of his eye, he saw Aristotles turning round to survey the scene, laughing. When he turned to face Torben, the young man could see that the Mask of Kulittu still glowed with a fierce light and that the Shadow Elf's being was changing. Deep, dark purple veins appeared across any exposed skin, his nails were growing long and pointed and had turned jet black, as had his teeth. His eyes also were changing into purple pools that emitted the same light as the mask.

Aristotles' gaze settled on Theodora, and he tapped the blade of her sword, which was inches from his face, with one of his warped nails, making the metal ring.

'So close, little Princess, but not close enough. I told you that you would not be able to stop me, but I'm glad that you're here to witness my final triumph, to bring the peace of Kulittu to quell the squabbling in this tired, fractured land. I admire your courage, but it was always a fool's courage. Acting impulsively with no care for the facts and little details was always a failing of your family, but then, without that familial trait, I wouldn't have been given the free rein and resources by your father to do whatever I liked. So I owe you Dazscorians that much I suppose.'

He sauntered calmly away from Theodora to the frozen figure of Hrex and placed a hand on her shoulder.

'I owe you a debt of thanks as well, Hrex, now that we have reached the end of your apprenticeship. It will sadden you, I'm

sure, to know that this is where our journey together ends, but
here is your final lesson from me. No mage, wizard, witch or
sorcerer can become truly powerful without the help of another
who gives them the materials that they require. Had you stumbled across this knowledge in your long years of exile, you
would have been reticent to come back for me. But I'm glad that
your loyalty blinded you to the truth that has ever been bearing
down on you. Take comfort that, even at the end, you helped me
get what I have desired for centuries.'

Aristotles drew back from Hrex and picked up a discarded
sword from the ground, weighing it in his hands. He swiped it
through the air a couple of times and then slashed it across
Hrex's throat. As her blood welled from the wound and flowed
like a black river from her frozen body, Aristotles knelt before
her and bathed the Mask of Kulittu in her blood, muttering once
more under his breath. He angled the mask so that most of the
blood flowed into the mouth and disappeared. When her blood
was spent, the mask pulsed and hummed, and the mage held it
above his head and cried out:

'It is done!'

A shockwave of energy burst from the mask, breaking Aristotles' spell over those around and battering into them. The force
pitched Torben off his horse and nearly brought the animal
down on top of him. The creature just about managed to retain
its balance and bolted away as fast as it could. Torben's vision
swam as he lay on the ground, his ears ringing. He could see
Aristotles was ascending into the air, hovering unnaturally
above the battle, cackling to himself. He jumped as he felt
someone place their hands on his shoulders, and he turned to
see Theodora next to him, one side of her face blooming into a
purplish bruise, a trickle of blood running from her nose. She
was speaking, he could see her mouth moving, but he couldn't
hear what she was saying. She half helped, half hauled him to
his feet and onto the back of a horse that the still mounted
Antauros was stopping from running away. Gwilym and

Egberht were shouting at him too, but their voices were lost to him as well. As his senses began to return, he slung his shield onto his back and put his arms around Theodora just in time as they bolted off away from the battlefield.

Aristotles watched them go and called after her in a voice amplified by magic so that it boomed.

'Run all you like, Theodora. Neither you nor the line of Dazscor hold any sway here now. I am the power in this pathetic mortal kingdom now. Fear not, though; I will have you hunted down and ensure that the your bloodline is extinguished forever!' Turning his attention to the soldiers of Sharisar and Dazscor & Aramore who were cowering around him all across the battlefield, he proclaimed with an unnaturally amplified voice:

'The nations of this continent of Turoza are weak, petty and meaningless. Their rulers send you out to die for no greater cause than the inflation of their own egos. I am offering you a chance to join a truly great power, to serve a truly great master, who will give unto you just rewards for your service. Join me in life and share in the spoils beyond your wildest dreams, or join me in death in an afterlife of eternal servitude.'

Aristotles began to descend back to the ground as all across the bloody field, men and women from both sides sheathed their weapons and looked to join him. His feet touching the ground, he beckoned over Zarrax.

'Take your brood and bring all that submit here to me. Those that do not surrender are yours and your kin's do with as you will.'

Zarrax's face curled into a snarling grin, and he barked out orders as he loped away, drawing the other Lupines behind him, their triumphant howls sounding from their bloodied maws. As they left, Aristotles closed his eyes and held his arms before him, palms facing the ground. As his new followers edged nervously towards him, the dead spread all around like fallen leaves began to twitch and stumble once more to their feet.

18

Dusk was bathing the city of Karpella in a rosy pink glow, and after the deprivations of the siege, the city and its surroundings were mercifully quiet, but Karpella was still under siege. It had been three days since the Sharisian Army had withdrawn, followed by the Joint Kingdom's Army of the North with the majority of the city's garrison going with them as reinforcements. The uncertainty of what was happening beyond the walls to the south had become a menace on the minds of Karpella's multitude of inhabitants far more insidious than the physical soldiers of Sharisar had been. Doubts circled around people's minds, false truths, superstitions and vain guesswork that drove people near mad with worry. It was this worry that drove people from all quarters of the city to continually make the trek to the city's walls to stand watch with the skeleton garrison that had been left to defend them, to fruitlessly observe the third sunrise with no news and what now looked like the third sunset as well.

On the battlements atop the gatehouse, a small crowd of onlookers, mostly citizens with a few soldiers scattered amongst them, stared despondently out towards the swiftly disappearing horizon. The guards knew that the civilians were not supposed to be there, but having more people around gave them a sense of comfort, as if they had a crowd of comrades at their backs rather than onlookers, even if they would prove bootless in a fight.

A young officer dressed in the armour and livery of the Imperial Guard politely negotiated his way through the gathering, worrying a battered notebook in his hands as he weaved his way to the battlements, to where he could see the iron tip of the spear of one of his charges held above the heads of those who had been drawn from all over the city to the watch. As the officer reached his destination, the soldier, an older, stocky man named Freomund, made a nod to standing to attention and wafted a rather lacklustre salute near his forehead. The officer looked exhausted, Freomund thought, his eyes were black-rimmed hollows and his cheeks looked drawn and gaunt. Though he was an Imperial, and Freomund himself was actually one of the City Guard, the old soldier had taken a shine to the officer, who treated all he came across with a respect that had swiftly become abused, which no doubt added to the tired lines and furrows marring his previously youthful and smooth forehead and cheeks.

'Freomund, good evening,' the officer said. 'Anything to report?'

'Not a jot, sir. Almost feels quieter than yesterday.'

'Hmm, I had a feeling you'd say that.'

The crowd on the battlements had quietened down when they realised that the young man was an officer and were angling to eavesdrop for any information that they might not have otherwise known. One of them, a bald man with thick bushy sideburns who did not have the patience of the rest, called over the heads to the officer:

'Any news from the army? What's happening out there?'

The officer turned, looking flustered at the sudden intrusion, and he began to stammer nervously as he realised that the eyes of everyone in the vicinity were drilling into him, looking for even the slightest hint of information that he knew, but they didn't. As he floundered, whispers began to hiss out from all corners as people began to speculate what his silence meant.

'If we've not heard anything by now, they must have lost! We should make our escape before the Sharisians come back,' said one.

'No, it probably means that they've won and are hunting down the last of the invaders,' said another.

The platform above the gatehouse erupted into a confused mass of conversation, and Freomund turned away from the noise and leaned on the crenelations, staring out vacantly into the night. He didn't know which outcome, victory or defeat was most likely. He had learned after many hard years of soldiering to leave the debate to the generals and politicians; engaging with things beyond his control just led to worry and superstition in his experience. He was focusing so hard on blocking out the hubbub behind him that it took several minutes for his eyes to register the pinpricks of flickering orange-yellow light moving towards the city from the horizon. He blinked and rubbed his eyes, straightened up and squinted more intently into the darkness. They were torches, hundreds of them, if not thousands.

'Sir,' Freomund said tentatively, trying to drag the young officer's attention away from the old woman he was having a rather frustrating circular sounding debate with. 'Sir, you should see this…'

Silence fell like a lead weight over the gatehouse as the civilians and other soldiers registered the concern in Freomund's voice and the Officer turned to respond.

'What is it, Freomund?'

'Someone's coming back, sir, see? That many torches heading this way can only mean one thing, we're about to have an army tip up on our doorstep.'

'Njördr's beard! Let's hope it's the right army!'

Freomund shuffled awkwardly in his spot, waiting for

orders from the officer, who just continued to stare, mesmerised by the oncoming torches and the possibility of what they might bring.

'Ahem, what are your orders, sir?'

'Orders? Oh right, yes, orders!' the officer said, shuffling backwards and forwards indecisively for a moment. 'Freomund, sound the alarm bell. I want all of the garrison out just in case. You there!' he shouted to one of the other guards. 'Round up some men and get these civilians off the walls. We can't have them blundering about if it comes to a fight.'

The walls became a hive of activity as the guards leapt to it, leaving the officer still standing above the gatehouse, surveying the lights of the approaching force. He let out a sigh of relief hearing the harsh strains of the old woman who had been grilling him fade away as she was ushered off the battlements with the other city folk.

'A few moments peace at last!' he murmured to himself. 'Hopefully, they won't be my last...'

Half an hour later, the entirety of the meagre garrison left to defend the capital of the Kingdom of Dazscor & Aramore was spread out in a thin line across the curtain wall of the city. The officer was still standing in his spot on the gatehouse, and Freomund had returned to take up his position with a number of other City Guard, who had arrows already nocked to bowstrings and crossbow bolts already loaded in their weapons.

By now the foremost row of the torches had stopped approximately where the officer thought the frontline of the Sharisian siege works had been, though it was hard to tell in the darkness. They could see silhouettes of foot soldiers and riders flickering beneath the torchlight, but they were too far away to tell who they were, and there were no banners in sight.

'Movement over there, sir,' Freomund said, pointing into the gloom where two horsemen could be seen slowly making their way across the land between the walls and the siege camp. The right-hand rider was holding a torch above both their heads, illuminating them in enough detail that once they were almost beneath the walls, the young officer could pick out details of their faces and accoutrements. The rider on the left was a tall, lean elfin figure with grey skin, sliver-blonde hair and unsettling pupilless, purple eyes that seemed to glow faintly in the darkness. The other figure he recognised as the City Marshall.

'It's Beoric Stornson, the City Marshall,' he called back to his soldiers, who responded with excited chatter amongst themselves. 'Greetings, sir,' the young officer called down, 'we are glad to see you!'

'And I am glad to be back,' Beoric replied. 'What is your name, soldier?'

'Asulf, son of Beowulf, Lieutenant in the Imperial Guard.'

'Lieutenant Asulf, I hereby order you to stand your men down and open the gates.'

'Stand them down? Forgive me, sir, but is there a need to do that? They are the City Guard, after all, sworn to protect this city and the Emperor's property within from danger.'

'And therein lies part of your answer, Lieutenant. Emperor Hastel has proven himself of late to be incapable of protecting his people and incapable of acting in the best interests of the Joint Kingdom.'

'So you stand with Sharisar now?' Asulf growled back, his hands clenching the crenelations so hard his knuckles turned white.

'Not at all. On the contrary, the Sharisian Army is no longer a concern either. A new order is stepping up to ensure good governance and provide for the prosperity of all. So I repeat, stand down your men, lay down your arms and open the gates! The people of Karpella have suffered enough.'

Asulf's brow beaded with cold sweat as Beoric's words rung around the surrounding stonework. He didn't know what to do. Was this a clever Sharisian ruse, or a test of his loyalty? Could he really order the City Guard to fire upon the City Marshall? Could he face the burden of deciding that the men and women under his command should have to face their deaths once again and that the people of Karpella should suffer again under a new siege?

Freomund leaned in and whispered in Asulf's ear, 'Sir, what are your orders.'

Asulf didn't respond. His mind was whirring too much with the stress of it all, a thousand and one scenarios whizzing through his brain, things that might happen, decisions that he might be judged by, decisions which could kill people. Before the gates, Aristotles turned to Beoric.

'A pity, I'm growing weary and was hoping that this would be a smooth transition. Ah well...'

The Shadow Elf extended his hand towards the gates, and a bolt of purple energy flew from his fingertips and battered into the heavy, iron-studded wood of the barrier, splitting the cross-bars behind as easily as kindling and flinging the enormous gates open. Beoric Stornson circled his horse around and encouraged the troops still lurking in the darkness onwards, and the army of Lupines, thralls, Sharisian and Aramorian deserters surged forwards. On the walls, most of the skeleton garrison simply dropped their weapons and ran, leaving those that remained to discharge their weapons ineffectually into the horde of troops spilling into the city.

'Sir, what do we do?' Freomund urged, shaking the Lieutenant unceremoniously by the shoulders.

It was enough to bring the young man back to reality, though, and his eyes focused again.

'We need to get back to the castle now and warn the Imperial Guard left there what is happening. There might be a chance to hold them off there at least.'

As Lieutenant Asulf and Freomund sprinted from the walls, Aristotles lazily trotted his horse onwards to enter the city.

Halfway across the city, the area around Rose Street and Ivy House was mercifully quiet, its inhabitants and patrons unaware of what was happening in the mainland part of the city. It had been a slow night for Madame Fleurese and her staff, worryingly slow. Since the breaking of the siege, the rampant hedonism of the city's inhabitants had dropped off dramatically now that they didn't feel like every day might be their last, not to mention the loss of business that the absence of most of the City and Imperial Guards had inflicted on her establishment.

It was so slow that night that the Madame sat on plump cushions with a group of her girls in the courtyard around what should have been one of the most sought-after tables in the house, but which was instead devoid of patrons. They sipped at goblets of warmed, spiced wine, chatting amongst themselves, though their eyes took turns in glancing longingly at the entrance, hoping for an injection of excitement into their evening. All of them turned to face the gate and its archway when they heard a crash echoing from somewhere behind them, but seeing no one striding through the door, they settled back down.

'What was that do you think?' one of the girls with a pile of red hair stacked a top her head, Clarice, asked.

'Probably some drunkard knocking things over,' responded Eadwine, a serious-looking young woman whose black hair contrasted greatly with the milk-white of her skin. 'You know the Rose Hip tavern on the street corner hasn't entered a slump as we have. I took a walk past there a few hours ago, and there were people spilling out of it into the street.'

'Yes, well, the winds of fortune seldom tend to blow on everyone with the same strength,' Madame Fleurese said quietly. 'Doubtless in a few days' time that brutish dwarf of a tavern keep will be sat on his own stoop wondering why he has no customers, and we are quite so busy.'

'It might help if we lowered the prices here a bit,' Eadwine muttered darkly, 'or if we actually sold beer. Only those born with a silver spoon in their mouths think of drinking wine before anything else. And when all of the rich toads have gone off to watch a battle or die in it, there's no one left who wants to drink here.'

'Yes, but we don't just offer beverages now, do we?' Madame Fleurese replied coyly, making Clarice giggle. 'Besides,' she continued, gesturing to the goblet in Eadwine's hands, 'if only rich toads drink wine, what does that make you?'

'You know what I mean,' Eadwine said, a smile tugging at the corners of her mouth.

The three of them turned their heads as the echoes of voices drifted through the courtyard, emanating from somewhere beyond their walls.

'What was that?' Clarice asked.

'I don't know, but it didn't sound like revellers at the Rose Hip to me...' Madame Fleurese stood as she spoke and took a step towards the gates, head cocked to listen more intently.

'Listen, that sounds like horses and armour to me,' Eadwine also rose to her feet as the jingle of harness and weapons began to grow louder as if riders were trotting up the street.

'Great!' Clarice exclaimed, 'perhaps we'll have some excitement at last, not to mention some more coin in our pockets.'

Neither Madame Fleurese nor Eadwine looked as convinced as the three of them moved over to the gate and opened the smaller access door so that they could step out into the street. Rose Street was illuminated by the glow of lights coming from many an unshuttered window as people all around peered out of their windows or from their doorways to see what was happening. There were indeed horsemen coming down the street, a large number of them, the lead riders calling out to people as they passed, causing them to hastily close their windows and doors again against the night. One of them spurred their horse forward, leaving the group behind, hailing Madame Fleurese, Clarice and Eadwine.

'Ladies, for your own safety, you are instructed to remain inside your establishment and to only come out when told to do so. Those found to be away from their residences for the rest of the night will be arrested on suspicion of being disturbers of the peace.'

Now that the rider was directly in front of them, illuminated more clearly by the light spilling out from the Ivy House courtyard, Madame Fleurese noticed that, though he was wearing the armour of Karpella's City Guard, his shield had been covered in black cloth, hiding the city's symbol of the Rose and the Scales, and he wore a band of black fabric around both of his upper arms. Eadwine was already starting to ask questions, demanding to know why this was happening all of a sudden, so Madame Fleurese prodded her sharply in the ribs, ignoring her squeal of protestation and ushered her and Clarice back into Ivy House.

'What did you do that for?' Eadwine demanded, glowering at her mistress as Fleurese closed and bolted the door behind them.

'Hush now! Somethings not right, couldn't you see?'

'What do you mean?'

'Come on, follow me!'

Hitching up her skirts, Madame Fleurese led the other two across the courtyard, through the taproom and up the network of back stairs to the roof and the balcony. As they jogged through the halls, doors opened around them, enquiring faces at each asking what was going on, but the Madame ignored them all. When they reached the balcony, they had picked up a trail of others, more of the House's girls and a few of the serving and kitchen staff as well. Madame Fleurese, Eadwine and Clarice leaned heavily on the balcony rail, catching their breath after their speedy ascent and watching what was happening in the street below.

Beneath them, more cavalry were passing through the street,

some of them carrying Sharisian-style short recurve bows and long curved swords and wearing helmets with distinctive horse-hair plumes flowing behind, whilst others looked more recognisable, soldiers of Dazscor & Aramore in their conical helms, with straight swords and kite shields. There were others, too, moving amongst them, whose presence was clearly making the beasts nervous. They moved with a shambling, unnatural gate and held no weapons or shields even though they wore armour. Some of them looked like they shouldn't be able to move, bearing grievous injuries that should have slain them.

'Oh gods!' Clarice said, turning away from the sight, her face palloring white tinged with green. 'What's wrong with them, they're disgusting. Like dead men!'

'Listen,' Eadwine called from the other end of the balcony. 'It sounds like there's fighting going on at the castle.'

As their heads turned towards the dark outline of the castle in the distance, the sound of snarling and a single piercing howl made them whip back around, some of them screaming with surprise and fear. There were Lupines padding down the street now, many of whom were eying up Madame Fleurese and her staff with hungry eyes. One, a particularly feral-looking creature, with wild staring eyes and whose dark brown fur was streaked with blood tugged at the ivy winding its way up the building and then began to climb towards them, thick stands of drool dripping from its jaws. All on the balcony took a step back, except for Madame Fleurese, who watched defiantly as the Lupine began to scale the side of the building.

It did not get far, however, before an enormous black-furred Lupine leapt up and dragged the other down, cuffing it around the head so hard, the Madame thought it should have been killed. But the other Lupine just wined and scuttled away up the street towards the castle, tail tucked between its legs as the larger brute snarled at it in their guttural language. The black-furred Lupine sensed that Fleurese was watching it, for it flashed a look up at her, briefly revealing its scarred face and single remaining eye before it moved on, barking orders left and right.

'Madame Fleurese, so good to see you again!'

The shout from further down the street made the Madame jump, and her eyes snapped from hideous creature to hideous creature until her gaze lighted on a familiar figure riding towards her, Beoric Stornson, the City Marshall.

'My lord, what's going on?' she replied.

'Nothing for you to worry about. Everything is fine and well under control,' Beoric replied, his voice sounding obviously patronising.

'Beg pardon, but everything doesn't look fine! There are Sharisians, Lupines and who knows what else marching through our streets!'

'It is all for the good of the defence of this city and its people, I assure you. Everything will become clear in time, you just need a little patience, my dear. Besides, I consider you and all within your establishment to be under my personal protection. In fact, Aethal!' he turned to address his bodyguard, 'take ten men and set a guard outside this fine establishment, to put the ladies' minds at ease. You even have my leave to station yourselves within should they desire the comfort of your presence a little closer.'

The City Marshall trotted out of sight, laughing to himself as Aethal gathered some troops, all of whom the Madame was glad to see looked like men who should have belonged to the Imperial Guard, and they detached themselves from the others surging through the street and took up position in front of her doors. Aethal looked up to the balcony and nodded when his eyes met Fleurese's. He had a look of deep concern written all over his face like she had never seen before.

Since re-entering Karpella, a smile had been permanently spread across Beoric Stornson's face. The smirk had been there when he had stood before the gates, when he had ridden through the streets as one of the victorious conquerors of the new order, when he had watched the scraps of the Imperial Guard surrender the castle, and it was still written across his face as he reclined in the deep cushions of one of the sumptuous armchairs that decorated the personal study of Hastel I. He had never been allowed into this hallowed sanctum before, so he revelled in every moment he had his dirty riding boots propped up on the highly polished mahogany desk, savoured every sip of the deliciously fine wine he took from the delicate crystal glass he cupped in one hand. However, he was not there alone. His new master Aristotles was sat in another enormous wing-backed armchair next to the fire roaring in the decorative marble grate, and the Lupine Zarrax was leaning against the opposite wall, clearly uncomfortable with all of the pomp and finery surrounding them.

Before the three of them was a nervous officer, previously of the army of Dazscor & Aramore, who was delivering his report in a tremulous voice, unnerved by Zarrax's savage presence and the otherworldly sense of dread that now emanated from Aristotles, whose purple eyes bore into the man.

'We've transferred all captured troops, both City Guard and Imperial Guard, to the upper holding cells, my lord, and the remainder of the Imperials who are yet to surrender have been pushed back to the south tower, where they have taken refuge in the upper levels. There is no way they can escape from there, so we're holding to see if they surrender.'

'Why have you not pressed your advantage, Captain?' Beoric asked, the wine slackening his voice into a drawl. 'The more time you hold back, the more time they have to rest up for the next bout.'

'Begging your pardon, sir, but they have a very strong position, and my assessment is that we will lose a lot of troops trying to flush them out from there. By giving them some respite, we're also giving them time to cool down and come to the realisation that their situation is hopeless.'

Beoric opened his mouth to respond, but Aristotles held up his hand, silencing him.

'I agree with the assessment of my City Marshall. I will send up a detachment of thralls to help you deal with this situation, Captain. After all, the renegades cannot kill those that are already dead. Speaking of which, have you found a suitable location for the thralls to be based?'

'Yes, my lord,' the Captain replied. 'We've cleared out the lower dungeons for this use. My estimate is that should provide ample space along with scope for an inflation of their numbers.'

'Good, you are proving to be quite the asset, Captain. You may go, bring us news once the last of the renegades have been either captured or destroyed.'

The Captain bowed and shuffled backwards a few steps before turning on his heel and scuttling out of the room, ensuring to give Zarrax a wide berth as he left. Aristotles stood up from his chair and moved to the desk, filling his crystal glass with wine. He glided back to his place by the fire and settled back down, his eyes downcast towards the flames in thought. He took a long, contemplative draught of wine and then spoke to Zarrax and Beoric, eyes still downcast, but now to the Mask of Kulittu which he held up to the light with his free hand.

'We have won a great victory this day for Kulittu, but I must now think carefully about what the next move will be. To fulfil the terms the Dead God set, I must ensure that there is peace in this land so that folk are able to remain, grow, thrive and breed and from thence become either new adherents to bolster the ranks of the faithful or a source of sustenance for our Master to feed upon. Fulfilling this means that I will continue to be able to access powers far beyond those imaginable by any of the mortal races, which means that I will be able to continue providing for both of your wants and desires.

'There are a number of factors that we will have to consider and navigate exceedingly carefully, lest we ruin any sense of stability that we strive to attain. Though Sharisar to the south has been cowed sufficiently that they no longer form a threat, we still have the Kingdom of Kjörnsholm to the north and the Mountain Principalities to the northeast to be mindful of. Both will be watching what happens here with a careful eye.'

'I wouldn't worry about them!' Beoric scoffed. 'Queen Evelina has her own problems to contend with; dissent amongst the Jarls, the remains of her brother's rebellion, not to mention discontent amongst their own slave population. As long as she thinks you will not make a move against her, she will be satisfied with pushing the regime change here to the back of her mind. As for the Mountain Principalities, none of them have been able to see eye to eye since the collapse of the Kingdom of Reinhart. They're too concerned with fighting one another than they are with caring about what happens in the wider world.'

'True, Beoric, true, but there is one variable you are forgetting, one that could prove to very much be a poisoned thorn. Between us and the Mountain Principalities is Heilagur, the holy city that is the heart of the Pantheon of the North, and I cannot see them lightly stepping aside as a power they held religious sway over disappears into the night. If they hold the potential of uniting both the squabbling babes of the Felsspitze Mountains and the warrior houses of the north against us, a problem I would rather not have to deal with for the time being...'

Aristotles' voice trailed off, and his eyes flicked to the door as someone beyond knocked loudly.

'Enter!'

The door opened, and a Lupine sloped into the room and executed a clumsy bow before Aristotles and then turned to look at Zarrax, to whom he began to speak in the Lupine language.

After a few seconds, Zarrax began to translate in his guttural, growling voice.

'He says, my lord, that they accessed the vault beneath the great hall as you requested and that the treasure held within is still there and work has already begun assessing the value of what is at your disposal.' Zarrax paused and cocked his head in confusion at the Lupine's next statement. 'He also reports that they found and captured a group of thieves inside the vault, that they have brought up directly to receive justice at your pleasure.'

'Bring them in,' Aristotles said in the Lupine language, the guttural words feeling even more unnatural as they left his elven lips.

Beoric took his feet off the mahogany desk and leaned forward with interest as the Lupine opened the door and ushered in none other than Björn, Gord and three other men, followed by several other Lupines who forced them to their knees before Aristotles. The Shadow Elf was clearly quite intrigued by them as well, for he stood up and began to walk around them, looking each of them carefully up and down.

'How curious. The treasure that lies beneath this castle has lain undisturbed for centuries, nearly two hundred years, and yet in the last month not one, but two groups of would-be thieves have tried to lay their grubby hands on it. Well, as the first band of reprobates have so far managed to evade my ire, perhaps I can take out some of my frustrations on you unfortunates instead…'

As his voice trailed off, Aristotles transferred his wine glass to his left hand and held his right palm up, conjuring a crackling ball of purple fire there.

'My lord, if I may interrupt,' Beoric Stornson said, carefully choosing his words. 'I believe that you might find some of these unfortunates to be of much greater value than you are currently aware.'

'Really, how so? Do you know these vagabonds?' There was a dangerous edge to Aristotles' voice the City Marshall had not heard aimed directly at him thus far, and it made him exceedingly uncomfortable.

'Yes, my lord. The dwarf is called Björn, and he is widely known to be head of the most influential crime syndicate in the city and well beyond.'

'Truly? And yet in your previous office, you never thought to use this *widely known* information to rid Karpella and your Emperor of such a scourge?'

'I recognised that Björn had innumerable uses and contacts that far outweighed any problems that he might make for the Joint Kingdom. Uses and contacts that will still be very useful to you. He knows Karpella better than any other I can think of, knows which pockets to fill with coin so that people do what you want, and which throats to have cut so that you have as few surprises as possible...'

'Interesting, and you will vouch for this dwarf, Beoric?' Aristotles asked, coming to a halt directly before the kneeling Björn and looking down at the top of his bald head.

'I will, my lord.'

'And you're prepared to put your life on the line for that assertion?'

'Yes, yes, I am,' Beoric gulped nervously.

'Well then, I'm in need of a good spymaster and propagandist. Rise, Björn.'

Gingerly, Björn rose to his feet, grimacing as he became aware of the pain in his knees. He still looked wary, but from his spot near the desk, Beoric could see the familiar fire and sly cunning growing stronger in the dwarf's eyes again as he realised his hour was not yet up.

'Björn,' Aristotles continued, 'will you swear loyalty to me and to mighty Kulittu, to do whatever is asked of you and protect the institution that I am creating here?'

'I will, my lord, I swear it,' Björn replied.

Aristotles smiled as he extended his hand, shimmers of purple energy running over the smooth surface of his black nails, and Björn took the proffered hand in his own and planted a fleeting kiss upon it.

'Good,' Aristotles said, sweeping back to his chair again. 'I will have work for you to begin very shortly. What of these folk with you, Björn, how much use are these four to you?'

Björn turned to look at the hulking figure of Gord, who still looked menacing even when on his knees, and the three other men in his shadow.

'I would ask clemency for my bodyguard, Gord. He has many uses other than his size and strength. The others you may dispose of as you wish, my lord. As your new spymaster, I advise that it is best not to risk word of anything that is said within these walls getting out into the wider world.'

'Well said, Björn. Beoric, I'm glad to see that your recommendation is already bearing fruit!'

The three men kneeling beside Gord began to shuffle back, looking nervous as Aristotles stood and began to stalk towards them. One, a freckled man with mousy hair sprang to his feet, drawing a knife from the sleeve of his coat and charged at Aristotles. Though Zarrax and the City Marshall instinctively leapt to their feet as they saw the man's intention, the Shadow Elf didn't move but watched the man charge towards him and plunge the blade into his chest. Something was not right, though. The expression on the man's face turned from desperation to confusion as he looked down and saw that the blade of his knife had crumpled against his target's skin, as if Aristotles were wearing a steel breastplate instead of loose robes. The elf smiled and flicked his hand casually towards the man, who rose up into the air, a nexus of runes written in purple fire surrounding him.

'A brave fool, but a fool nonetheless. I am the anointed of Kulittu, empowered by him to bring about his conquest of this sorrowful land. No normal blade of iron can slay me,' Aristotles hissed, eyes narrowing as he regarded his would-be assassin.

He muttered under his breath, hand extended towards the floating figure, whose flesh began to dry and wither as if all of the moisture was being drained from his body. He writhed in agony and opened his mouth to scream, but no sound came out, only a plume of flesh-coloured dust. The wispy purple light of the man's soul was pulled from the body and into the maw of the Mask of Kulittu, and as life left him, Aristotles dismissed his spell, sending the husk of parchment skin and bones clattering to the floor. He swiped his hand across the air before the other two prisoners, who became wreathed in purple flame that scorched their skin to the bone, their cries of pain and anguish echoing around the chamber. When they too fell dead to the floor, Aristotles turned and leaned heavily on the mahogany desk and poured himself another glass of wine. Without turning, he clicked his fingers. There was a scuffling noise as both Björn and Gord tried to shuffle away from the corpses, whose bones were clicking back into alignment and animation as the skeletal thralls rose once more.

Aristotles rang a small handbell that was on the desk, summoning an impassive-looking butler, who barely flickered an eyelid at the scene before him, but who stood awaiting orders. Aristotles turned back towards the room and dismissed the thralls who made their shambling way out of the open door and fixed his eyes on the butler.

'Find our chief spymaster here rooms befitting his new station, and ensure that quarters are made ready for any staff he deems necessary to have in his employ.'

'As you wish, my lord,' the butler said, escorting Björn and Gord from the room.

As Aristotles returned once more to his chair, he surveyed Beoric and Zarrax again.

'There is only one more order of business tonight: I want you both to find your best hunters and track down Princess Theodora and her accomplices. I want them brought back to me alive, understand?'

'Yes, my lord,' they both chorused.

'Good, then leave me be, I am weary and need to rest.'

Zarrax left the room without looking back, but Beoric paused a moment to drain his glass before moving to leave. As he reached the door and looked back, Aristotles was staring into the fire once more. The flames now appeared to flicker purple, and a hooded face stared out from them at the Shadow Elf. The City Marshall passed a hand over his eyes and closed the door.

'Must be the wine,' he whispered to himself.

He shivered and made his way as quickly down the corridor as he could, trying to put as much distance between his new master and whatever he was doing as fast as possible.

O nly weeks ago, the small farmstead nestled in its valley, with the softly flowing stream running down alongside, it would have been quite idyllic, but war and hardship had taken their toll, and the farmer and his family had been forced to abandon their homestead to become refugees. Now the roofless, fire-scorched farmhouse and its outbuildings were playing host to a new group of refugees, refugees who bore the banner of Pegasus Company.

Since their flight from the Cookridge battlefield, the remains of Shenesra's mercenaries and Princess Theodora's retinue had galloped and then cantered and then finally walked their horses for as long as they could keep them going before both rider and beast were in desperate need of rest. Eleusia reckoned that they had managed to cover nearly fifty miles in the day and a half since their flight had begun, which should give them a good head start depending on the speed and skill with which they were being pursued. For Theodora's guards and Shenesra's cavaliers, however, the distance mattered not as long as they could rest.

Most of them had lain down to grab what precious minutes of sleep they could, but some of them were filling their bellies with whatever rations they could eat without a campfire and its tell-tale smoke, whilst some saw to the horses or their injuries picked up from the day before. More than one of those who were still awake had downcast heads or tear-stained cheeks as they mourned their comrades who hadn't been as lucky on the day of the battle. Almost all of them ignored the sound of voices that drifted from within the ruined farmhouse, where their command retinue discussed what to do next. They knew that they didn't need to chase for orders; they would come and interrupt their respite soon enough.

Within the makeshift headquarters, Shenesra, Theodora, Captain Almar, Eleusia, Gwilym, Antauros, Egberht and Torben sat around a warped and battered table, some on chairs, some on whatever piece of detritus found within would serve well enough as a seat. Shenesra was reading off from a scrap of paper she had jotted down some numbers on, the others listening on gloomily.

'We lost a lot of good folk yesterday. Current headcount not including ourselves is twenty-nine of my riders and thirteen of your guards left, all of whom picked up some injury or another yesterday. We've got fifty-three horses, enough to saddle some of the spares up as packhorses to lighten the load on the others, but obviously nowhere near enough to provide any form of rotation system to keep our mounts fresh. All in, we've got enough rations and water to get a couple of days additional distance between us and Cookridge, which will hopefully buy us enough time to do some proper foraging. I'm sure we'll agree that we've all had better odds…'

'Well, this seems as good a time as any to work out our next moves,' Gwilym said, leaning back as far as he dared on the wobbly chair he was perched upon. 'At the moment we're sailing blind, and that's bad business when we're likely to have a pack of seasoned cavalry and Lupines nipping at our heels.'

'You're right, Gwilym, we need to address the issue of how we are going to stop Aristotles!' Theodora declared, her eyes flashing defiantly out of sockets rimmed with tiredness. She prodded the table aggressively with a forefinger as she spoke, making it rock back and forth.

'Err, beg pardon, Your Highness, but I was actually referring to our more immediate concern of simply staying alive.'

'As far as I am concerned, Gwilym, working out how we should approach Aristotles addresses exactly that. Can't you see? This isn't something that we can just hide from! He has been given untold reserves of power by a creature known to be the anathema of all that is good in the world. The Dead God won't be content with what Aristotles has already achieved for him. Kulittu will push and push for him to kill more people, to enslave thousands of others and spread his vile influence over as much of Turoza and the rest of the world as he can, all the while dangling the carrot of additional strength and power before him. 'Aristotles won't stop, he cannot stop, and that means that wherever we go, we will still find ourselves at risk in the end. Either we can work towards stopping him now, or we flee, tails between our legs and live out a few uneasy years far to the south, all the while glancing to the north expecting to see the hordes of undead and corrupted living bearing down on us. No, I am of the bloodline of the royal house of Dazscor, I cannot stand by and let the lands that my father ruled over and the descendants of his subjects be put to the lash and forced to do all manner of unspeakable things in service to the Dead God!'

Theodora slumped back in her chair, breathing heavily and staring daggers across the table at Gwilym, who was sheepishly inspecting the toes of his boots. Antauros tentatively broke the silence by clearing his throat and leaned forward, elbows on the table, causing the wood to pitch up towards him slightly on its unstable legs.

'I think it's safe to say that no one here disagrees with you, Your Highness. We all know the gravity of what we saw and that we, with our intimate knowledge of the entire situation, are best placed to combat Aristotles and his fell lord. What we need, though, are facts. We have no idea what he is now capable of, or what would be our best chance of stopping him. Egberht, you alone of us have the best knowledge of the arcane. Can you, or the tomes you saved from the castle, shed any light on what has happened to Aristotles?'

The gnome sighed and rubbed his temples with one hand, the other fiddling subconsciously with the straps of the enormous book he carried strapped to his back.

'In truth I'm afraid I can't,' he replied slowly. 'What happened on that field of war is far beyond any knowledge I have of arcanology or its associated disciplines. To better understand what has happened, we need the advice and knowledge of someone much wiser and more powerful than myself.'

'If you're suggesting travelling to the Academy of Arcanology at Harbotha for answers, we might as well give up now,' Gwilym muttered gloomily. 'It would take months to get there, and many months more to convince them to help us, if we made it across the Sonsuz Desert to Zhisbon at all, that is.'

'Don't write off everything just yet, Gwilym,' Egberht replied, raising a long, bony finger. 'My master, the Imperial Mage to the Court of Hastel I, fled Karpella on the royal barge, bound for the shelter of the Joint Kingdom's friends in the Republic of Castar. If we make for Castar, then I'd bet that I will be able to make contact with my master if he made it there too. If not, there is another powerful mage resident there, who serves the Republican Assembly in a similar capacity, who may be convinced to help us.'

'I don't think it would be wise for all of us to make for Castar,' Eleusia said, looking from Egberht to Theodora. 'You least of all, Your Highness.'

'And why is that?' Theodora responded.

'Though Aristotles swore to hunt you down and kill you, you will by no means be the only person on his list of loose ends. He will dispatch people loyal to him to track down and either bring back or kill Hastel, his family and anyone in their retinue who escaped with them. It would serve our purpose and your safety well to not combine all of his targets in one place. Let us not forget that the government of Castar relies on a majority of the Republican Assembly agreeing that a thing should be so. There is always the risk that Aristotles need only find the right people to turn the Assembly against Dazscor & Aramore's royal exiles and force them to move on. One of our priorities should be your safety, ideally somewhere we know that you are among allies, and where we can take stock of our information and the situation properly.'

'I concur,' growled Almar, his voice sounding pained. He was still clutching the wound beneath his left arm, and his face was pale, 'but the problem is that any allies of the Royal House of Dazscor will either be dead by now or long turned their allegiance from Sarper IV and his line. You're right, though, Eleusia, it would be folly for all to head for Castar – we'd be too easy to track – the question is where?'

'What about Sharisar,' Torben asked.

All round the table turned to stare at him, their looks ranging from confused to horrified. Gwilym leaned forward and spoke in a low, slightly slower voice, as if he felt as though he needed to ensure that Torben fully comprehended what he was saying.

'Torben, are you mad? The Sharisians invaded Dazscor & Aramore; they hold no love for this land nor its people.'

'Yes, I understand that,' Torben scowled in response to being treated like a child. 'I would point out that none of us knows the true reason why Sharisar invaded in the first place, and given everything that's gone on, doesn't that surprise you? There's something else going on beneath the surface that needs rooting out there too. Regardless though, that reason, whatever it is, is highly likely to be linked to Hastel I, not yourself, Princess. Let's not forget either that Sharisar's army has just been defeated by Aristotles, and many of its troops have thrown in their lot with him. He is both our enemy and the enemy of Sharisar, so I'd warrant that the Sharisians would throw in their lot with Princess Theodora if it meant getting revenge.'

'I take it back, Torben,' Gwilym said, a smile spreading out over his face, 'You're not mad, you're brilliant, still a touch insane, mind you, but that idea is just the right amounts of both to have a shot at working! The only snag that I can think of is the nature of the Sharisians themselves. As nomads, we'd have no idea of where to find the Royal Caravan. We could lose weeks trekking across the grasslands trying to find them.'

'What date is it?' Antauros asked thoughtfully.

'About twenty days before midsummer,' Egberht replied. 'Why?'

'Because every midsummer the Royal Caravan returns to the Sharisian capital, Uighurtai, for the annual midsummer celebrations there. As long as you can get to the city by then, you are guaranteed to find Queen Evelina there, and perhaps also in a more positive state of mind than if you simply tracked her down in the wilds of the Övsnii Sea. With twenty days until the celebration, I'd warrant whoever sets out for there has more than enough time to reach Uighurtai with days to spare.'

The clattering of hooves sounded in the farmyard beyond, followed shortly by the scrambling of the troops outside springing to their feet in alarm. Chairs scraped along the floor as all of them around the table stood, hastily drawing their swords. A sharp rap sounded on the planks of the cracked door to the room, followed barely seconds later by a member of Pegasus Company, whose armour was caked in dust.

'Commander, they're on our trail.'

'What did you see?' Shenesra asked, sheathing her sword, the others following her lead as they all relaxed a little.

'A detachment of cavalry, their arms and armour look like a mix of both Dazscorian and Sharisian, accompanied by Lupines. They're all carrying black shields and wear black armbands. They're a fair ways off yet, but it looks like they've picked up our trail.'

'How long do you think we have?'

'No more than an hour until they track us here. They're moving very quickly.'

'Tell the Company to make ready to ride, we'll be with you shortly.'

The cavalier touched his forelock in salute and wheeled around, leaving the room. The sound of his voice snapping out orders could be heard before he had even closed the door behind him. Shenesra sank back slowly in her chair, regarding the others in the room grimly.

'The time for debate is over,' she said. 'Where shall we head for, Castar or Sharisar?'

'The situation is too pressing for us to go to one then the other; there simply isn't the time,' Antauros rumbled. 'To fulfil both parts, we need to split, Princess Theodora and one group going to Sharisar and Egberht and the other heading for the coast and onto Castar. Not only does that facilitate both ideas simultaneously, it will also add additional confusion to our pursuers.'

'But how will we find one another again?' Torben asked, worry and nervousness in his voice.

'Good point, well made,' Gwilym answered. 'There is a town at the foot of the Carreg Pass, Troedcawr in the Union of Mishtoon. It lies near the border with Sharisar, and those that travel to Castar will be able to travel up the Solenz Pass to get into the mountains and then down to the town from there. As Troedcawr is a busy trading hub, we'll be able to blend in there easily enough. There is a tavern in the south of the town called the Leaping Goat. I know the barkeep well; she's a good lady and will help us. If we plan to rendezvous there in five weeks, that should give both parties enough time to reach their destinations, complete their business and travel to Troedcawr, provided there are no delays on the road. If there are any delays, then one or the other should send a trusted messenger on ahead to touch base.'

'And what happens if one group never turns up at all?" Torben asked.

'Well, then we re-evaluate our options...'

There were solemn nods all around the table, and no one spoke up against Gwilym's suggestion. Finally, Antauros stood and regarded them all seriously.

'That's settled then. As far as I can see, there is only one question that remains. Princess Theodora, Captain Almar, I would guess that the loyalty of your guard is beyond question and that they would follow their lady wherever you commanded?'

'Of course,' Almar said through teeth gritted with pain, 'they have all sworn their lives to protecting her. I have no reason to doubt them.'

'Good, but, Shenesra,' the minotaur turned his dark eyes to the Vittra, 'the same cannot be said for your company. I do not doubt their courage, but their engagement with you is based on contract, not, to be blunt, loyalty. It would be unfair and potentially dangerous to ask them to undertake something that they did not sign up to do. After all, Pegasus Company is not about to take up another mercenary contract, and this path we're about to embark upon offers little chance of getting paid.'

'You're right,' Shenesra said resignedly. 'I'll raise it with them now and let those that want to make their own way do so.'

As Shenesra left the room, there was silence for a moment as they all pondered what had to be done and the imminent parting.

'So, who goes which way?' Torben ventured.

'Egberht obviously must head to Sharisar and Theodora to Sharisar,' Gwilym said. 'I would suggest that Shenesra and what remains of her company heads to Castar. You may have need of more troops when you reach the coast. Who knows how long it will take you to charter a craft, but it might give any pursuers time to catch you up. Your Highness' guard will naturally accompany you, and I suggest myself, Torben and Antauros as well. Eleusia, you still have contacts in Castar if I remember rightly?'

'I do,' she replied.

'Then you should head there with Pegasus Company, no doubt you and Shenesra will be able to keep Egberht safe.

Eleusia didn't reply but placed a hand on the gnome's shoulder and squeezed it gently in encouragement. Nothing further was said in the room. They all stood and made their way out into the farmyard, where Pegasus Company and Theodora's guards were gathered around Shenesra. A group of cavaliers were riding out of the farmstead, headed northeast at speed. Shenesra turned as the other exited the house.

'Ten decided to part company with us,' she said, 'but they have agreed to head off in a different direction and hopefully provide another distraction to those hunting us. Are we ready?'

Princess Theodora nodded, and Shenesra barked orders to the riders waiting before her. Both Pegasus company and Theodora's guards mounted, and they drifted to different sides of the farmyard, expecting to ride off in different directions. As they parted, the men and women from both companies shook hands and embraced, the looks on their faces clearly indicating that they had become fond of one another during their journey.

Eleusia and Egberht were bidding farewell too, and tears began to well in the corner of Torben's eyes as Eleusia approached him, and he embraced her in a huge hug that took her by surprise.

'Stay safe,' Torben choked through his tears.

'You too,' Eleusia replied, and as she was released from the bearhug, she put a hand on his shoulder. 'And make sure you keep Gwilym safe too, you hear? That dwarf is still worth a lot of money to me if this all goes south.'

Torben laughed through his tears and withdrew to allow Eleusia to mount her horse. Theodora's mounted guard took off their helmets in respect, and Torben, Antauros, Gwilym and Theodora watched before them on foot as Pegasus Company spurred away, heading west. Theodora took Torben's hand and squeezed it as they watched them go, and he squeezed it gently back.

'Your Highness, we need to go too,' Almar said quietly from his horse.

Princess Theodora nodded, and those left on foot mounted and began to ride south. As they left the place of parting, Torben looked back and saw Eleusia looking back too, now on the crest of the valley's west side. She turned her horse, making it rear onto its hind legs, and raised her hand in farewell. Then she was gone.

END

Dear reader,

We hope you enjoyed reading *Heresy*. Please take a moment to leave a review, even if it's a short one. Your opinion is important to us.

Discover more books by C.J. Pyrah at https://www.nextchapter.pub/authors/cj-pyrah

Want to know when one of our books is free or discounted? Join the newsletter at http://eepurl.com/bqqB3H

Best regards,

C.J. Pyrah and the Next Chapter Team

ABOUT THE AUTHOR

Born and raised in the Newcastle Upon Tyne in the northeast of England, C.J. Pyrah moved south to Oxford, where he studied Classical Archaeology and Ancient History and now resides in the shadow of the *Red Castle* in south Wales. Since graduating, he has spent most of his spare waking moments writing and tinkering with the minutia of the many fantasy worlds that he has created.

Heresy
ISBN: 978-4-86747-745-8

Published by
Next Chapter
1-60-20 Minami-Otsuka
170-0005 Toshima-Ku, Tokyo
+818035793528

24th May 2021

Lightning Source UK Ltd.
Milton Keynes UK
UKHW010733090822
407056UK00001B/304